"Lynn Mullican's debut novel **Bad Elements: Crystal Dragon** delivers with its believable characters and serves up a solid one-two punch with its distinct and often bleak atmosphere in underground fighting." - Dale L. Murphy, Owner of Graveside Tales

**"Bad Elements: Crystal Dragon** is an edgy, well-written novel. Character development is very good, with believable personalities that develop at a nice pace over the course of the story. It is dark and at times quite intense with elements of erotica that work well within the story, as opposed to being gratuitous.

Crystal is like a tank on steroids when she's in the ring; she is strong, determined and a survivor. She is wary and watchful during her captivity but ever hopeful that she'll escape. Crystal and other characters in Bad Elements deal with issues of loneliness and trust and each deal with those issues in their own way. The end was a bit predictable but also has some surprises. The only complaint I have with the novel is that at times it gets too close to Paranormal Romance for my taste, which is something I'm just not into.

Overall, Bad Elements: Crystal Dragon is an entertaining read. I give it three chainsaws out of five." - Colleen Wanglund, Reviewer at MoreHorror.com

"**Bad Elements: Crystal Dragon** by Lynn Mullican throws in the Fight Club formula and mixes it with an unexpected added recipe: werewolves and vampires.  What's not to like?

It has all the right ingredients of a fun, exciting and riveting good read. Throw in popular genres to make an entertaining story. This could be one of those books that if it gets the right attention it could very well make a cult novel and perhaps one day, a fine cult movie, deservingly so." - P.M. Thomas, Author of "Humanity Lost"

# DEDICATION

I'd like to thank my family, who endured the disappearance of their wife, mother, and daughter. I spent many hours locked up and hidden away so I could write my novel. Thank you for your support, your love, and your frustration during this time!

To my husband, Patrick, thank you for taking care of the family while I was busy on my book. You're a fantastic husband, father, and cook! Thank you for being there when I needed you!

To my children, Cassandra, Bridget, and Joeseph, thank you for allowing dad to take care of all of your needs and wants while I was consumed with my book. Thank you for your encouragement and your understanding!

To my mother and my stepfather, Martha and Rich, thank you for your encouragement and for being there when I needed you.

You have all been an inspiration to this novel!

Also by Lynn Mullican


SACRIFICIAL BLOOD

# Bad Elements: Crystal Dragon

Lynn Mullican

This is a work of fiction. The characters, names, incidents, places, and plot are products of the author's imagination or are used fictitiously. Any resemblance to actual persons, companies, or events is purely coincidental.

BAD ELEMENTS: CRYSTAL DRAGON

ISBN: 0985547103
ISBN-13: 978-0-9855471-0-3
Published by
Cryptic Bones Publishing
Phoenix, AZ 85046

PRINTED IN THE UNITED STATES OF AMERICA

# IMPRISONED

My head was woozy, my body tired and drained. The pain in my eyes when I tried to open them was nearly unbearable so I let them close. Curling up into the fetal position, I wrapped my arms around my legs, the cold air overwhelming me. Chills ran down my spine, goose bumps swelling over my skin when I realized I was lying on a cold floor, possibly concrete. Debris fell from my skin. I pulled my hands back and my eyes shot open, pain tearing through my eyelids. I bolted into a sitting position and batted at my skin, afraid of what was on me.

What the hell was on me and better yet, where was I? Worried about that and who was nearby, I struggled with the urge to cry out for assistance. Should I or should I not yell out? Darkness surrounded me and there was no telling who stood within it.

Instead, I bolted to my feet. My legs gave way and threw me right back down to the ground, knees first. Pain tore through my kneecaps and expanded into my thighs and calves. A moan escaped my lips. I sat back on my heels, tears forming in my eyes. I rolled onto my side and rubbed my knees, whimpering. I resisted the urge to cry, but it was too painful and tears dripped down my face. Agony coursed through me.

I tried to keep my cheek from touching the cold ground but pain shot through my right shoulder. I groped at the other side of my neck and shoulder, massaging it when I found something odd. I pulled my hand away and held it out in front of my face, trying to see it in the darkness. There was liquid on it—cold, thick, and pasty. I put my hand in front of my face but was unable to see it. I trembled, unsure of where I was.

The strain of my neck muscles gave way. Tears flowed down my cheeks. My face hit the concrete, and pain shot through the side of it. I struggled against the tears welling up in my eyes again. Touching my cheek, I realized it was the size of a baseball. I gasped in horror and rubbed the other one. The right cheek was huge in comparison to the other. More tears erupted from my eyes. As I continued to evaluate my injuries, I realized my eyes were bruised and swollen too.

I decided it was best to measure up my injuries since I couldn't remember where I had been last, what had I done, or who I was with. Carefully, I studied the details of my body beginning with my feet. They were bare. No shoes, no socks, nothing. My feet and heels were bruised, and my ankles swollen. The muscle along the bone on my calves were inflamed and bruised, mostly on my right leg. My knees hurt and my thighs ached, along with my hips and stomach. A couple of my ribs felt out of place.

My left breast was bruised and more painful than the right, along with my left arm and neck. I inched my hand down past my shoulder along the right side of my back. One of my fingers caught within a fold of skin. I gasped in pain. I had stuck my finger into a large gash. I tensed up and pulled my finger out, blood now stuck to it. The gash was thin and about two or three inches long. Possibly a knife wound. Parts of my back were sore. A headache lingered behind my eyes.

Once I completed my checkup, I leaned forward on to my hands. My fingers crept across the cold concrete. I touched something small and hard. It took a moment to realize it was the debris that had fallen off of me. I plucked some up. They weren't alive, so I sniffed them. Pine. I was covered in woodchips. With that done, I decided it was time to figure out where I was.

Because my knees still hurt from the hard fall I took, I searched the darkness for something to support myself with as I carefully transitioned from my knees to my feet but with no such luck. My head felt faint. My stomach grumbled and lurched. Bile rose up in my throat. I turned my head and threw up. I leaned over while my body convulsed with the pain violating my body. After a minute, I straightened up and wiped my mouth with the back of my hand.

I took a step forward, and then halted. I cocked my head and listened. Silence. Not even the ticking of a clock.

I took another step forward, defying the pain still reverberating through my legs. I groaned and took another step, and another. Then I stubbed my toe on something hard. I drew in a hard breath and whimpered. I stuck my arms out in front of me, trying to discern what was in my path. My fingers struck several steel rods that were spaced apart. I froze in place, recognizing the objects before me. They were circular, slick, and cold. I wrapped my hands around them and leaned my face into the bars that imprisoned me. Fear surged through my body. Was I in jail? What happened to me? Why couldn't I remember that put me here?

I turned my back to the bars, slid down to the floor, and brought my knees to my chest, wrapping my arms around them. I gave in to the weaker side of me and cried myself to sleep.

My dreams were brutal, even the ones where I was with friends. The faces looked familiar, but I couldn't fit the names. I woke up several times throughout the night, pain throbbing inside my body. Each time, I cried myself back to sleep.

§

I awakened to my body being dragged across the floor. A strong arm was wrapped around my chest from behind. My head lolled forward and then to the side. I tried to control it, but found I could not.

A male voice bellowed from outside of my prison cell, "I'd be careful if I were you. She might wake up."

"Yeah, I know," replied the man who held me.

A couple of laughs echoed throughout the room and then he tossed me onto a cot. I struggled to open my eyes so I could get a good look at him afraid he was going to try to have his way with me, but he pulled a blanket over me. When I opened my eyes, his eyes met mine and then he was gone.

§

I awoke in a fright to somebody turning me over onto my stomach. I turned my head to get a glimpse of him when he pushed my face back down into the cot. I couldn't breathe, couldn't get my face out of the surface of the bed. I thrashed around to free myself. Something hard struck me in the middle of my lower back. A sharp pain traveled up the muscles next to my spine. My back arched in pain as I pushed myself up. A large pair of hands slammed down in the upper middle of my back and pushed me back into the cot. I was barely able to turn my head. Just as I did, cold water splashed onto my upper right shoulder, my face, and mouth. I drew in a deep breath and choked on the water.

Two men in my prison cell argued with each other.

"Stop her, she's moving too much," replied the irritable man.

"She's got water in her mouth," said the one pinning me down.

"No she doesn't, she's just trying to get loose."

"No, she's choking," said the guy who held me down by my shoulders. "Don't start yet."

He relaxed his hold a little.

I pushed up onto all fours. My body trembled as I continued to cough. I spit water and blood up onto the cot. With a lighter pressure, he continued to hold me down. My vision was blurry. I didn't know who he was or what he wanted, but I did know exactly where he was.

I shot to a kneeling position and turned as I delivered a right back fist to his face. He grabbed my chin. Before I knew it, he threw me backwards onto the cot, the weight of his body on mine.

"Don't you ever do that again," he whispered in my ear. "You don't know the damage I could do to you."

I glared back at him.

He moved in closer to me and whispered, "Be thankful I'm the one handling you and not them."

I tried to make out his face but could not. Instead, my eyes focused on his. I'd seen those eyes somewhere before.

He held my chin and pressed my head back.

He lowered his mouth to my ear. "Now, you turn over and be a good girl. We don't want you to get hurt."

With that, he released my chin, grabbed my shoulder, and forced me onto my stomach. I managed to turn my head to the side. Unaware of what their intentions were, I tried to focus on something, anything. With that, I stared at the dirty concrete back wall. His weight straddled my lower back while he continued to hold me down.

I closed my eyes and cried. As he poured water over my shoulder and brushed a cloth over it, I realized he was cleaning the upper right part of my back.

"Shut up and stop moving around," said the man standing next to me.

"Stupid woman. Hey, didn't somebody say she was a tough bitch? Obviously not."

His hand found the wound on my shoulder and pressed down hard. I winced in pain.

"She doesn't know what's going on," the man straddling my back said.

"What the hell?" The man standing next to me sounded angry.

"Are you getting soft on me?"

"No, I'm not, but you need to back off a little. We want this wound to heal properly and not get infected, alright asshole? Now, get the job done." He lowered his mouth to my ear. "You need to stay as still as possible so that we can get this wound cleaned and stitched. Okay?"

I stared back at him through the corner of my eye.

"Yes," I muttered into the mattress.

"Good." He turned his head to the other man. "Let's get this started."

I clenched up, closed my eyes, and tried to avoid moving as much as possible when a series of sharp pricks stuck me in the back. I came to the realization that the man standing next to me was stitching up my upper back and that he was a doctor, only an obnoxious one.

After taping up the gauze he placed over the wound, he asked, "Can you sit her up please?"

The man on my back complied. He climbed off of me, stood up and helped to prop me back up against the wall behind me. I shivered against the cold concrete. The doctor grabbed my hand and poured some pills into it. Then he removed a water bottle from a pocket in his doctor's coat and handed it to me.

"Take those for the pain. They'll help you feel better. We'll bring you some food in a little bit, too."

When the men turned to leave my prison, I looked down at the pills. Were they really for the pain? Or were they to sedate me? I debated. Should I or should I not take them? Granted, my entire body hurt and I could probably use them, but I was wary of the men's true intention.

Once the men left my cell, I threw them at the bars behind them. Some flew out and others fell within my prison. I opened the water bottle in haste, spilling some of it. I was thirsty as fuck. I couldn't remember the last time I had some water. As I chugged it down, the doctor rushed back into my cell and struck the bottle. The bottle shot up out of my hand. Water splashed all over me and him. I glanced up at him. He sneered down at me.

"You ungrateful bitch," he said. Then he slapped me.

That was when I snapped. I leapt to my feet. I punched him at the same time my legs wavered beneath me. Some of the men yelled for him to stop and a couple of the others screamed, "Fight!" When he attempted to backhand me again, I threw my left arm out and blocked him. I threw an uppercut with my middle knuckle extended into his solar plexus. His head jerked forward, the air rushing out of his body. With the same fist, I threw another uppercut into his Adams apple. He staggered backwards into the bars. The other man who had held me down rushed into the cell. The color of his blue eyes shifted from an aqua blue to a deeper blue hue. I would later identify this man as Blue Eyes.

Blue Eyes glared at me. "Maybe he deserved that, but you need to stop now."

"Why! What the hell am I here for!" I glared back at Blue Eyes and then at the doctor, who staggered toward the cell door.

I took a step toward the doctor while he tried to regain his breath. Then Blue Eyes stepped in front of me, blocking my path to confront the doctor again. "Not now."

Dammit, I wish I could see his face, could see all of their faces. Due to the swelling around my eyes, I was barely to see through the slits of them. Even then, I was scarcely able to differentiate Mr. Blue Eyes and that was only because of the exquisite hue of them. I stood my ground, but my legs threatened to give. In the room surrounding my prison, I was barely able to distinguish approximately five to six male figures in the room, all of whom were now silent. My jaw clenched. I feared what I was here for. I tried to look around the room but found it difficult through the haze of my vision. Even though I was fueled with anger and heated from the fight, chills ran up my spine and along my neck. I swallowed hard.

"Now come here," said Blue Eyes.

I looked at him.

"Don't try anything stupid. Understand?"

I stared at him.

"Do you understand, or do I need to lock you up?"

The others grumbled amongst themselves.

My gaze shifted back to Blue Eyes.

I muttered, "Yeah, I understand."

I approached him and allowed him to take my arm. Gripping onto it, he led me past a hallway and then through the room to the left of my cell.

He walked me through the room which looked like some sort of training facility. Then he led me to the restroom on the right. It looked like a prison shower for there were multiple shower heads in multiple stalls. The lighting was minimal. When he spun me towards him, our faces were inches from each other.

"I want you to clean up, use the bathroom, and then we'll get some food in you. Okay?"

"Okay," I replied, complying. Though I was hesitant, I decided it was in my best interest to do as they said. This of course, was a temporary decision which was subject to change later, depending on my circumstances.

"This is the only door, so don't try to run." His eyes glared into mine. The last four words came out of his mouth slow and precise: "Don't piss me off."

I took him for his word.

He gripped my upper arm and led me to a bathroom stall. Once I was inside, he turned me around to face him.

"I'm sure you can figure everything out from here." He shut the stall door.

Once I was done, I opened the door and saw the dirty mirror across from me. I walked to it, as if mesmerized. I had to know. His gaze lingered on me, to the point of resisting the urge to squirm. To avoid doing just that, I turned to the mirror and focused in on it. I tried to wipe the dirt off the mirror but it only smeared instead. I turned the faucet on and splashed the mirror with water, still afraid of what I might see. The dirt rinsed away and revealed what looked like a Halloween mask. I stared in horror at my reflection. I wanted to cry.

He moved up behind me, his mouth almost in my ear. "Don't worry. It'll heal."

I paid no attention to his reflection, but only to my own horrendous twin in the mirror. Even though I couldn't see all the details of my wounds, somebody had beaten me up pretty bad. My face looked worse than I had imagined. It was distorted. My eyes were black and blue, along with other areas of my face. My cheek was almost two times its size. Tears welled up and slowly, painfully, trickled down my face.

Studying my face, I asked, "What happened to me?" Carefully, I touched it, tracing some of the distinguishable marks on it, including the fine lines around my eyes. The small wrinkles reminded that I was a middle-aged woman. I didn't even glance at him when he answered.

"You were in a bad fight," he replied, emotionless and cold. There was no reassurance in his voice whatsoever.

"What is happening to me?"

He turned me towards him.

My mind drifted back to how I had woken up confined, hurt and the reckless way I had been treated from that moment on. That combined with the way my face looked convinced me I was literally in hell.

"Listen to me," he said. "I'm not going to be here all the time, so you need to do what they say. I know you don't know what's going on, and that's probably for the better, but you need to strengthen the survivor in you. Do you understand?"

His eyes almost bore into my skull.

Uh, no, that wasn't for the better. I needed answers, something, anything to give me some light as to why I was here. Just who the hell were they, anyway? What gave them the right to keep me prisoner here in this piece of shit hell hole?

"Who are you? And, who the fuck are they?" The more time I spent thinking about my situation, the more I became irritable and angry.

He straightened up, dropped his hands from my shoulders, and sighed.

"The less you know, the better." He walked me towards the showers and then turned on the one at the end. "You need to clean up."

I glanced at him. "And you're going to watch?"

"Trust me, I don't like this any more than you do."

"I highly doubt that," I said.

He smirked, and then as he moved around behind me, he grabbed the lower part of my shirt.

I jerked my arms down.

"You're not going to be able to get this off without some help."

"And what gives you that idea?"

He replied, "Because you're sore, bruised, and that shoulder of yours is not going to be nice to you. Now let me help you. This isn't a sexual thing. It's strictly medical. You need to clean up. You have cuts and wounds that need to heal. Otherwise they'll get infected and you'll get sick."

As hesitant as I was, I let him remove my clothes. Not only was I embarrassed about being seen naked by a stranger, I also was not the fittest woman in the world. I'm twenty-five pounds overweight and five foot three inches. Just because I'm slightly overweight, I'm still proud of my body. I have a little extra weight around my waist and hips. My legs are stout and muscular. The same with my shoulders and arms. My hips are curvy.

Though my vision was still blurry, I tried to make out the details on his face. Should I have the opportunity to escape, I not only wanted, but needed to know what my abductors looked like. If I could identify them then maybe I could put them behind bars from what they had done to me. But when I realized his attention wasn't completely focused on my face, I looked away.

He removed my hair tie, allowing my dark hair to fall in waves below my shoulder blades. I stepped under the warm water. The water relaxed my muscles, but stung my wounds at the same time. I tried not to think about the man who watched me.

Instead, I enjoyed the water cascading down my skin. I reached up to run my fingers through my hair. My muscles cramped and locked at ear level. I winced from the pain.

I tried to force my arms up higher but they remained locked. The pain was just as bad when I lowered them. Christ, all I wanted to do was wash my hair. The urge to curl up in a ball and cry was overwhelming. Again, I tried to force my arms higher, but now they were tired and resistant despite my effort.

I tilted my head back to get the dirt and grime out of my hair, but even that hurt. A grimace escaped my lips when his hands touched me.

Alarmed he would approach me when I was at my weakest, I opened my eyes. But why should I be shocked? He was just like the others. I turned to face him and threw my arm up, blowing his hands off of me. Boy, was that a mistake. A sharp pain shot through my shoulder. I doubled over, gasping and cringing. When I tried to move my arm again, I realized it was useless.

Annoyed, he said, "Would you relax? I'm not going to hurt you." After a slight hesitation, he sighed and asked, "Are you alright?"

He bent toward me, a look of concern on his face.

"No, I'm not," I said, my voice shaky. "I think I threw my shoulder out."

The pain settled deeper into my bones causing my shoulder to ache more. I fought the urge to cry. Straightening up, I realized he had walked fully clothed into the spray of the water, only his feet bare. He held his hands up as if surrendering.

"I have toiletries for you."

I stood silent, staring at the shampoo bottle in his hand.

"You look like you need some help."

I continued to stand there, leery of his intent. Embarrassed, I tried to cover my female assets. I wanted to hide my vulnerability, but couldn't. He walked further into the water, toward me.

A look of embarrassment encompassed his face when he realized that his attention had shifted elsewhere. Focusing on my face, he added, "Look, this is just as awkward for me, too. Let me help you."

He took another step, his wet shirt clinging to his body. I glanced around the room. It was darker than the one that housed my prison.

I stared up into his face, which was still not clear to me. It frustrated me that I had no clues to use to identify my captors. I could only blame the darkness for so much though. My wounds obstructed most of my view. He reached out to me, holding the shampoo bottle in his other hand, and flicked it open with his thumb.

I was worried that his hands might wander over my flesh.

"You're not going to do anything funny, are you?" I asked.

"No, I'm just going to wash your hair for you," he said.  "I know how you women are."

"How do I know I can trust you?"

"You don't.  But you can rest assured that I could have easily done something to you already if I'd wanted.  Have I?  No, I have not."

For a brief moment, his pupils seemed to darken, a hint of evil hiding behind them.  I closed my eyes and then opened them again.  The blueness of his pupils stared into mine.  For some odd reason, I trusted him.

He was smooth in his steps and in the way he handled my hair.  Still, he was a little too close for comfort, but he could not wash my hair from afar either.

I wanted to know who he was.  Even though I told myself he was like the others, he was not.  Yes, he threatened me and yes, I detected something evil inside of him, but he handled me like I was a diamond, or an exquisite crystal.  Something that could be broken if not handled right.  His hands were kind, gentle, almost compassionate, unlike earlier.

Even though I was in danger, I still felt reassured around him.  It put a different kind of fear inside of me, something I couldn't identify.  I closed my eyes and relinquished myself to him, his hands becoming one with my hair and then my head.  His fingers massaged my scalp.  The touch of his fingers relaxed me.

He moved ever so slightly nearer to me, his breath in my ear.  Goosebumps broke out along my neck.  A wave of shock trembled through my body and almost sent me to the ground.  Instead, he caught me with his arms just below the breasts and pulled me to him.  His body temperature was too cold for any normal man, but I was still compelled to remain in his arms as if a hypnotic trance kept me under his spell.

*The moon shone brilliantly in the sky, illuminating the large pine trees.  Just then, the outline of a man moved above me in the night, his face unidentifiable.  His tongue lapped over my lips, his hands caressing the curvature of my bare breasts.  We lay in the midst of the forest, the sweat from his leather jacket against my back.*

*His hands rounded my hips.  His hardened manhood stood defiant against my body.  I wanted him inside me, wanted him to take me here and now.  I wrapped my legs around his waist.  The thrust of his groin sent me into a momentary wave of pleasure.  I moaned and arched my neck when his lips found the soft spot on my neck. I gave up any and all free will to him.*

*"Yes," I moaned.*

*"Take me now."*

His hand moved away for a second as the water moved ever so elegantly over my face. I savored this time, allowing myself to let this vision take full reign over me even though I knew something was not right.

*I turned my head slightly to the side when ecstasy took hold.*

*He pulled back. Then he was on me again, his mouth on my neck. A gasp escaped my lips when the penetration of his fangs sunk into my skin. A mixture of pleasure and pain filled the void in my body. My breath caught in my throat, followed by the taste of blood which engulfed my mouth.*

As fast as the vision had come, it left. A taste of copper lingered in my mouth. I was now alone under the water. Though he stood by and watched, I avoided glancing in his direction. I washed up the best I could despite my soreness.

Once I was done, I stepped out of the shower onto the floor. He moved forward to help me dry off and dress. I had a little more trust in him since he had not attempted anything sexual in the shower. I was more embarrassed of my vision.

Once I was ready, he led me back to my cell. Only two men remained in the main room now. When he tried to take me through the cell door, I halted. I thought I would catch him off guard. Instead, he stopped quicker than I'd expected and turned me to face him.

"Don't..." he began.

I pressed my body into his and whispered, "I'll do anything. Just get me out of here. You're not the same as them. Please, I'll do anything."

I begged for mercy. His eyes were piercing.

I pressed him against the cell door, my face inches from his. "They trust you with me. I trust you. I don't know why, but I do. Please."

He stood silent, his eyes darkening. Underneath, there was something evil yet compassionate. Afraid to push him too far, I backed into my cell. The door shut in my face. Exhausted from what little physical activities I had done, I laid down and fell back asleep.

# CRYSTAL

When I awoke the next morning, I remembered Blue Eyes had told me he wouldn't be here the entire time. That disappointed me. If I had an ally, it might have been in him. He was different...much different. I would rather have dealt with him than the others.

I was facing the wall, my body buried under the covers, when I rolled onto my back and stretched. Muscle spasms shot through my neck, shoulders, and back, but nothing like the pain I had first experienced. Odd, muscle soreness and tension don't just disappear overnight. I sat upright and stared down at the wounds on my arms and legs. They were faint. The swelling had gone down almost entirely. Thankfully, I could see again, too. I still had some swelling around my eyes, but not like it had been.

A man's voice echoed throughout the room.

"Well, look who's awake."

I peered through the cell bars. A few men sat at the table in the room which encompassed my prison cell. But it was the man who stood that caught my attention. He was about six foot, muscular and lean, with broad shoulders. As he stared at me from under his brow, his thick, brunette hair fell in his face. His eyes were brown, his jaw square, and his skin well-tanned.

Beyond him was a refrigerator on the furthest wall and to the left of it a counter and cabinet that wrapped around the wall to their right. Built into the countertop was a small stove. On the counter sat a toaster, microwave, and coffeemaker. A rustic and lonely light hung from the ceiling in the middle of the room. This looked like some old break room.

One of the men who remained seated said, "Her face doesn't look like hamburger meat anymore."

He chuckled and glanced at the other guys.

Scowling, I looked him over. He was about five feet ten inches and slightly broader in the chest than the other man. He too was a lean and muscular man, but almost too lean. His brown hair was slicked back, his face chiseled.

The others stood up and approached me.

"Yeah, the face is healing much better," the second man said, looking confused. He glanced at the other guy.

"Did you...?"

The first man shook his head.

"She looks much better," another said from the shower room.

He had come out of nowhere. This guy was shorter, approximately five feet eight inches, with short blondish hair that was spiked and messy. The others had five o'clock shadow while he didn't look old enough to shave yet. He was thinner than them, his shoulders squared and broad. Considering the size of his shoulders, his head looked like it should have been on another man. He was lanky and even his feet seemed abnormally large for his size.

Disregarding him, I glanced from one to another, studying their clothing and their shoes. They all wore jeans and t-shirts except for one man, the one who did not move. He wore a slightly looser fitting grey button up shirt which was unbuttoned at the neck.

No guns hung from their hips nor could they conceal them within the clothes they wore. Most men with large hands have a tendency to carry larger grip guns which make the weapon stand out in their clothing. Since there were no outlines of an identifiable weapon, I presumed they didn't have any unless they were hidden in their shoes. My gaze shifted to their feet.

Though a couple of them wore hiking boots, gun concealment was next to impossible. The "hamburger meat" guy rubbed his boot on his leg in an attempt to scratch an itch. His jean leg caught high enough on the boot to reveal the low top. As for the taller, buttoned shirt man, the top of one hiking boot peeked out from under his jeans. The rest of them wore tennis shoes.

I peered up at him, the one who stood near the table, watching me.

I approached the cell wall and wrapped my hands around the bars.

I pressed my face into them. "Fuck you!"

The guy who made the hamburger remark turned and looked at me, his face pink.

"What'd you say?"

"You heard me," I said. I felt a hell of a lot better than I had.

He snapped at me. "I don't think you're in a position to be making remarks like that."

The other two stood next to him.

"Yeah, you got some balls, bitch," said the one to his right. "You want to put your skills to the test already?"

If I could get them to open the door, maybe I had a fighting chance to get out. My prison had two walls made of bars and the other two made of concrete. The one that separated us had the door to my prison. I remembered seeing a hallway which aligned with the concrete one to my back, between my cell and the training room.

I glanced back at the men. To the left of them was another hall or entry which aligned with the right concrete barrier of my prison. I had two options if I could get out of here. I just had to get them to open the door, and pray they didn't have guns.

Adrenaline began to pump through my veins. "Bring it on, asshole."

He stomped towards me.

The guy on the left, the short one, spoke up. "Uh, I don't know if you should be doing that." He made a grab for his friend. "She's egging you on, man."

"Shut up," spat the hamburger remark guy. With his angry eyes intent on mine, he continued to storm in. He shoved his hand in his pocket. As he fumbled to pull the keys out, coins and other miscellaneous stuff spilled out. His brow furrowed in as a look of contempt spread across his face.

"I wouldn't open that up." The man on the right backed away.

What the hell was he so scared for? Worried that a woman might kick his ass? So be it, then.

I ignored him and backed away from the bars. Flipping through the keys, hamburger meat guy approached the door. Just as he found the right one, he stopped and grinned.

"Ah, you almost got me, didn't you? You thought I was going to fall for it. I almost did. But I didn't," he said. He shook his hand at me.

"What are you talking about?" I tried to play stupid, but it wasn't going to work now.

"You were trying to get me to open the door so you could try to escape. You're clever but not that clever." He put the key back in his pocket and left.

The short guy looked at him, relieved that the door hadn't been opened.

I was scared, tired and hungry. I was emotionally and physically drained. My heart was heavy, for fear of what was to become of me.

Frustrated and aggravated, I demanded, "What do you want with me?"

No one spoke. They just glanced from one to another.

"Can somebody please answer me?" I looked at each one.

"In due time. Right now, we need to get you to work, so let's get some food in you." With that, the taller man moved toward the refrigerator.

"Who are you?" I clenched onto the bars again.

The tall guy gazed back at me and smiled.

"I suppose we could be on a first name basis. I'm Wayne," he said. He slicked his hair back with his hand. "This is Alex." He pointed to the hamburger comment guy. "And, this is Neil." This time, he pointed to the short guy.

"You are...?"

I started to say my name, but halted. I didn't know it. I tried to dig into my head and associate something with myself to remember my name or my life...but could not.

"I don't know," I mumbled.

I pushed the hair back out of my face. Thoughts of my life seemed distant.

"What's that?" Wayne took a step toward me and cocked his head. "I didn't catch your name."

I detected the sarcasm in his voice.

I glared back at him and repeated myself. "I don't remember it, okay, asshole?"

"Then give me a name, something we can call you," he said, grinning. "Uh, hmm..."

Before I decided on a name, Alex and Neil chimed up.

"How about Cher? I always liked Cher," Neil replied.

Alex and I frowned.

"Cher? Really? What the fuck? No, she looks more like a...hmm, Angela."

"Angela? That's just a common name. She needs something more interesting. I know, how about Rihanna?"

"Dude, really? What is your fascination with music icon names? She needs a better name than that."

Alex and Wayne appeared to study me.

"She needs a much better name," said Wayne. The next two words had a longer drawl, "Something worthy."

"How about Delilah?" Quite happy with his suggestion, Andrew smiled at everybody.

I rolled my eyes and tried harder to gain some recollection of my name.

"Delilah?" Wayne arched his brow.

The corner of Neil's lip dropped. "Uh, I don't like that."

When Alex didn't get the response he wanted, he asked, "What? What's wrong with that?"

"Okay, we're not doing a porno here," replied Wayne.

That was when Wayne asked, "What do you remember prior to being here? Maybe we can figure out what your name was and elaborate on it."

I tried to ignore Neil and Alex while I searched my memory. "I don't remember anything. All I remember is what happened here."

"Okay, then what do you remember here?"

"Um, waking up," I began. "My whole body hurt. I don't really know why or how I wound up here. I do remember the guy with the blue eyes, the one that helped me clean up…"

Wayne cut me off, "Clean up?"

Within a second, his cheeks were pink. A flash of something eerie and hostile appeared in his eyes. In another split second, it was gone, yet tension filled the air. Alex and Neil recoiled from him by taking a couple of steps back.

"What do you mean he helped you clean up?"

I hesitated, afraid to answer him. He took a step toward the cell.

Glancing back at Alex, he opened his hand.

"Give me the keys," he demanded.

Alex fished the keys out of his pocket and tossed them in his hand.

Prodding me, he asked again, "What do you mean he helped you clean up?"

As if threatening to come into the cell with me, he held the key up.

Something told me not to push him. Taking a couple of steps back, I abruptly answered, "He helped me wash my hair. That was it. He didn't do anything else."

I wasn't going to tell him about the weird vision I had while I was in the shower. Ah, yes, the vision. Blue Eyes and the way he'd handled my hair popped into my brain again. It was a pleasant memory despite my situation. I closed my eyes. He treated me like an exquisite jewel, the way you would handle a crystal. Hmm, crystal…I liked that.

I opened my eyes.

"Crystal. I like Crystal."

"Crystal, I like that too," Wayne said with a smile. "Sounds girlie, almost too girlie. The others may underestimate her. That'll work."

I cocked my head. "What do you mean, underestimate me?"

He didn't answer. Instead, he turned his back to me and rummaged through the refrigerator. The others sat down at the table, ignoring me.

I let my frustration get the better of me. "What do you mean, underestimate me?"

Silence again.

The temperature rose in my body while they continued to ignore me. My stomach growled. Then, my stomach lurched. Bile rose up in my throat. I didn't want to vomit so I choked it down.

The food tray opened and when it did I was on it within a second. It didn't take long for me to inhale two sandwiches, chips and water but while I did I glanced about the rooms.

All of the walls in the rooms beyond were concrete and cold. There were no windows.

As I went to take a drink, Alex gave me a sly smirk. Ignoring him, I finished my food and then leaned against the back wall with my eyes closed. Footsteps echoed within the corridor to my left. Out of my peripheral view, I watched a large, bald and very muscular man emerge from the hallway. When he entered the room, he peered at me through my cell bars. He was scary looking.

He continued to walk towards my cell and as he did, he bellowed out something in a heavy Irish accent. I raised my head when Wayne threw him the cell keys. I swallowed hard. Jesus, what did this clown want? He stopped in front of my door.

"Has she eaten yet?" His voice was low and menacing. Our eyes met.

"Yes," answered Wayne.

"Good."

Wayne stood up and walked towards my cell. He shoved his hands in his pockets and stared at me. At this point, I decided I would rather deal with Blue Eyes.

"Don't do anything stupid," replied Wayne.

The heavy clink of the key resounded in my cell, a sound I would never forget. The door opened.

The man's eyes focused in on mine. "Come on."

Taking my time, I hesitantly approached him. "I need to use the restroom."

He nodded, his mouth a rigid line. I drew in a deep breath and after a brief moment, I brushed by him. His hand slammed into the back of my shoulders. A groan escaped my lips. I caught myself before I fell and pulled my head up, squaring off my shoulders, and prepared for the worst.

I started walking but he grabbed my hair at the base of my neck. I tensed up, certain he was going to rip off my skin and hair. I leaned my head back into his hand so it didn't hurt so much. His knuckles buried in the hollow of my neck. The men followed close behind as he led me to the restroom. If I had any chance to run, I would have four men on my heels. My chances were slim, if any.

We stopped in the restroom before we moved onto the workout room. Only a rusty light hung from the ceiling. Once my eyes adapted to the lighting, I saw the older training equipment: heavy steel dumb bells, straight and curved bars, heavy bags, speed bags, mats, old stationary lockers, miscellaneous equipment, and even a boxing ring.

"When I get here, you train. Got it?" His brow narrowed in on me.

I was shocked at the fact I was here to train, and alarmed that I had to train with him, of all people. My eyes darted over each man, hoping that somebody would tell me that what I was hearing was not true.

"I don't mean to sound stupid, but you're training me? I'm working out?"

He huffed and narrowed his brows in on me.

I glanced at the door, where two of the men stood, guarding it. That was the only way out.

"No questions," he said. "And you do as I say. Got it?"

I peeked at the doorway again. Maybe I could push the men out of the way and escape.

My eyes trailed over him, locking in on his narrowed eyes.

Then I bolted.

Using my height to my advantage, I lowered myself at the last minute, driving one elbow into one man's ribs and my other elbow into the other's solar plexus. They doubled over in pain. Once I dashed through the doorway, I turned to my right, the same direction the muscle man had come through. I ran down the murky grey hallway, high on adrenaline. The walls seemed to converge on me as the echo of footsteps followed in my wake. I wanted to shout out, but I had a feeling it wouldn't matter.

Considering that there were no windows, it was dark and cold, and the air had an earthy smell to it, I was certain it wouldn't make a difference. I was positive my prison was underground.

I was slammed hard into the cold concrete wall. Something cracked on the left side of my face. I groaned, pain instantly radiating through my head. A forearm slammed into my upper back, his elbow connecting with my wounded shoulder. I howled.

The Irishman leaned into my ear and whispered, "Okay, we can do this the hard way."

He grabbed my hair and imbedded his fist in the crook of my neck. Tears clouded my eyes. Maybe trying to escape wasn't such a good idea after all. He pushed me down the hallway.

"Are you sure we have the right woman?" Neil asked.

"Just let Goldie work on her," Wayne replied. "She's suffered some trauma, so she's not quite the same right now. We're all just going to have to get tougher with her, including Goldie."

Goldie. Oh, chrome dome, the asshole who pushed me down the hall. Once in the training room, he shoved me into a heavy bag. At least it was softer than the wall. I tried to wrap my arms around the bag to keep myself on my feet when the Irishman came busting into the room behind me. I backed away.

"Look. I'm sorry, alright? I won't do it again. I promise."

I held my hands up in surrender. He rushed me again prompting me to back off. His right hand came straight from the hip and into my stomach. I doubled over, damn near falling over. His hand was still in my stomach, holding me up.

The Irishman whispered in my ear, "That's okay. We can do it your way."

I tried to object, to let him know that we could do it his way. Instead my lungs gave in, unable to let me breathe or talk. I struggled to find something to hold onto, but he was the only thing within my reach. So, I leaned my face against his shoulder, unable to move.

He scowled. "We'll toughen you up."

He pulled his arm back and I fell into him. As hard as I tried to push away, I found myself leaning on him for support while I struggled to breathe.

As soon as I caught my breath, he stepped away and let me fall to the mat. I wrapped my arms around my midriff and tried to curl up into a ball but every time I tried to move, my abdominal muscles cramped up.

I didn't want to get up for I feared training with the man. I closed my eyes. I tried to take in a deep breath, but only inhaled the foul stench of his sweat.

# TRAINING

Once I was able to get up and regain my composure, the Irishman started me out with some stretches. Next, he began a regimen of warm ups. I dropped into a horse stance at his request and proceeded with a vast array of strikes, blocks and kicks.

As I proceeded through more detailed movements, Goldie determined that I had taken some form of martial art. In retrospect to that, he tried to help me recall what I did know and what form of martial art I had taken. Although I didn't desire to work with him, just the idea of remembering something made me feel a little better.

In between warm ups, he had me drop and do push-ups and crunches. I focused on the training, but my mind still wandered to the thought of escaping.

"Have you ever sparred before?" he asked.

Before I had a chance to answer, he threw a pair of gloves at me. Oddly enough, I recognized them as martial arts sparring gloves.

He grabbed another pair and we strapped them on.

"Get in the ring," he said.

I climbed in and eyed him. I was leery he might sucker punch me from behind just to teach me a lesson in turning my back on someone. I dreaded the idea of fighting him.

I glanced up at him, frowning. "Why are you training me?"

We stood face to face inside the ring.

Goldie smiled. "Uh, she should know. She needs to be ready."

Wayne replied, "Yeah, that would probably be a good idea."

I didn't like where this was going.

Wayne turned to me.

"You have a fight this Friday night. You're the newbie, so everybody's looking at you."

His smile stretched from ear to ear.

I looked at him, my mouth hanging open.

"Me? Why me?"

"Because they already saw a piece of the action, and they want more. By the way, that vamp, uh, stripper you fought? She's dead. You killed her." His eyes lit up. "Do you remember that?"

"Huh? No, I don't remember that."

I killed someone? A stripper? Jesus, what the hell happened? My legs were weak and my stomach nauseous.

"Now we want to see more." Goldie bounced around like a boxer while I stood there.

"But I don't want to fight."

"Well, you're going to whether you like it or not." He put his face in mine.

I recoiled. I still couldn't get over the fact I killed someone and now they were going to force me to fight. No, no, I wasn't going to do it. This was not going to happen, not if I could help it.

I removed the straps on my gloves. "Then you're going to have to make me."

"No problem. You just won't see your kid." He hesitated and then added, "But if you don't want to fight, then we won't need him. We'll just kill him."

I stood motionless, my thoughts scrambled. I had a child - a child I couldn't remember.

Chills ran up my spine. I stared blindly back at Goldie, unaware of what to say or do. I wanted to run. But if I had a child, I didn't want to put him in danger.

I swallowed hard. "I have a child?"

My eyes searched his. He seemed content in his knowledge of my situation.

"Yes, don't you remember him?"

I shook my head.

"That's sad, a mom who doesn't even remember her own son. Well, it's your choice. What do you want to do? You want to fight, or would you prefer to leave and never see your kid again?" He stared at me, his face more serious than it had been.

Resentment and anger fueled up inside of me. Then tears erupted from my eyes. I hated him for what he was doing to me and to my child.

He started to bounce around again. "Now, if I were you, I think I'd fight." He pointed his gloved hand at me. "So, what do you say?"

"Yeah, wait," I stuttered.

His face turned red. "What?"

"If I fight this one fight, then I get him back, right? I can leave then?"

He thought about this for a moment.

"Yeah, sure," he said, cracking his neck.

I tightened the straps on my gloves. Okay, I could do this. One fight. I get my kid back and get the hell out of here.

"Anything goes. Got it?" replied Goldie.

I nodded. "Yeah, I got it."

If I was a martial artist, then I had to have some knowledge of how to fight an opponent. Or so I hoped. I fought not only for my life, but for my son.

Goldie was over six foot, so he had a better reach and longer strides than me. I moved around with him and blocked a couple of his wheel kicks with my left arm. I took several shots to my body before he rushed me with a right and then a left punch to the side of the head. My left arm came up and blocked his right arm. Just as I angled in towards him, I took a blow to the side of my face from his left glove. I delivered a right uppercut to his throat. My head rocked back, my left hand rebounding back from his arm. The glove strap peeled apart, scraped under his chin, and slid off the side of my hand. I struck him with a chop to his Adams apple, my actual hand connecting with his throat. His head snapped back and he bent over in pain, clutching at his throat. I stepped away while the other men came into the ring.

"Goldie, are you alright?"

Goldie coughed and choked. I stood motionless. My gaze shifted to the door. Nobody blocked the door. Instead, they were all in the ring. I had a chance to escape.

I ripped the other glove from my hand and started to climb out of the ring. Goldie grabbed my left leg. I held onto the ropes, turned, and with my right leg, kicked straight out. My foot struck him dead in the face, whipping his neck and driving him backwards. I ran through the room with the others in close pursuit. Neil grabbed and threw a five pound steel weight at me. It struck me in the back of the calf and sent me to the floor.

I rolled onto my back. Neil ran full speed at me. At the same time he jumped me, I raised my right leg and nailed him square in the chest. Broken bone echoed in my ears before he crumpled to the floor. Alex and Wayne were right behind him. About the same time Neil fell, Alex tripped over his shoulder and fell to the floor, half on and half off Neil. Wayne didn't stop.

He lurched over the top of Neil and right at me. I rolled to my left. He landed on the floor next to me. Wayne's hands grazed my shirt. I rolled on to my back to get away from him. Wayne stared at me with a wild, inhuman look in his eye. I staggered to my feet. A change tried to take forth in his body. He snarled, his lip curling back. His eyes changed from brown to a gold haze. I decided it was best to get him while he was down. I kicked him in the face a couple of times. Alex stood up and came at me again. I backed off towards the door. He threw a right punch. I barely eluded him by dodging it. As he neared me, I kicked him to the inside of his thigh, forcing his legs slightly apart. A kick to his knee forced his leg to weaken, threatening to throw him to the ground. I connected with another kick, only this time to the abdomen. He doubled over as I moved in towards him. Gripping his hair, I forced his face down. At the same time, I brought my knee up into his face. Something broke, but I didn't care.

My survival was the most important thing to me, so when I thought about running, I remembered him: my son. I was pissed and frustrated. The rush of adrenaline coursed harder through my body. I wanted to hurt my kidnappers more because of the position they'd put me in. I drove my elbow down into Alex's upper back. Then I screamed from frustration, knowing damn well that I fucked up. If I really did have a son, I just dug his grave with an attempted escape. Tears welled up in my eyes, a knot in my throat. I tried to swallow, but somebody threw me to the ground. Now they were all over me. Fear and hatred settled deep within my body. I surrendered to them, while blow after blow landed. I tried to fend off some of the attack, but I was weak and helpless.

§

They bound my wrists, dragged me to the cell and dropped me to the floor. The locked engaged.

From outside of my cell, Alex exclaimed, "That bitch! I think she broke my fucking nose."

"What the fuck are you complaining about? I think she broke my ribs," another groaned.

Footsteps reverberated off of the walls, followed by silence.

I lay with my head turned towards the back wall, my body in agony.

This was bullshit. I had to find out where my son was and get the hell out of here. If I had to fight, then I would do it. If I'd killed before, fuck it, I'll do it again. I struggled to my knees and glanced out into the room. I was alone, left bound, helpless, and confined within my prison.

I leaned against the bars and pulled myself up. The muscle in my calf was weak. I bit my lip to stifle my cries of pain. The bone flexed beneath my skin and threatened to give out underneath me. I hissed through my teeth and bore the pain of the weight on my legs. Tears streamed down my face. The bone had to have been broken.

I fought to hide the tears, and hopped on my good leg back to my bed. The vibration of the hops sent waves of pain into my bad leg. I sat down on my bed, my hands still bound behind my back, and leaned against the wall.

My shoulders ached. I started to give up my life for my son's when Goldie came around the corner, glaring at me. His eye sockets were multi-colored. I figured it was from the kick in the ring. I chuckled to myself as he came around to the front of my cell. I don't think it was just the look of his face that made me laugh. I think it was a combination of pain and frustration that made me lose it, too.

"What the hell are you laughing about?" With the discoloration, his face looked demonic. His lips pulled back into a sneer. "Bitch, I'm going to kill you."

"What's wrong, can't take a beating from a woman?" I stared back at him, my lip curled up.

That was all it took to set him off. He pulled the key out and opened my door. I jumped to my feet, the bone in my leg giving way.

He lunged for me at the same time I went down. He went over the top of me onto the cot and landed head first into the wall. Waddling on my elbows and my knees, I scrambled to get out of the cell. Once I emerged from it, I rolled over to shut the cell door. He stood next to the cot, blood on his face and hand. He stared at the blood, in shock.

"Bitch!" He ran at the door, but I slammed it shut. I held it closed with my feet though I knew I wasn't going to be able to hold it much longer. I struggled to find something to hold onto, but there was nothing. I was in trouble. He put his full weight into the door and shoved it partially open. The bone in my calf dug into my muscles. I gasped. My body slid backwards. Then Wayne walked into the room.

"What the hell!" He looked at me and then at Goldie.

"I'm killing that bitch!" Goldie slammed his fists into the door.

I shoved hard, but the door continued to inch open.

"The hell you are!" Wayne's eyes penetrated Goldie's. "I thought you were some badass, but you let her get the better of you. You are the most inept, incompetent person I have ever met!"

"Fuck you!" Goldie yelled at Wayne. His eyes were wild and horrific.

That was it. I couldn't hold on to the door any longer. I let go of the door and tried to back away, but it was too late. The steel door swung wide open and rebounded off my back. Pain flared up my spine. Then Goldie went after Wayne.

"Oh, shit," I muttered.

Several blows were exchanged between the two. Then the fight went to the ground. I scrambled to get back inside the cell. The snarls of a wild animal echoed through the room. Somebody screamed, and then something latched onto my foot.

I screamed.

Terrified, I struggled to fight off Goldie, who held onto my foot. Above him stood Wayne, whose body was in mid-transformation to something canine. Goldie proceeded to pull himself into my cell using my body. Wayne stalked him, as if contemplating his next move. Almost crushed to death under Goldie, I was useless to protect or defend myself.

Goldie managed to get inside my cell while I was still in the doorway, closest to Wayne. I tried to back away from Wayne, but Goldie shoved me out the door and into him. Wayne's gruesome fangs were in my face. I fell back onto the ground and turned away from him, waiting for the attack. But it wasn't me he was after.

A breeze wafted by my head. My cell door slammed shut and blood splashed on me. I kept my head buried against the concrete floor. I cried. I wanted out of this horrible nightmare. The sounds of mutilation echoed in my ears. Goldie's screams eventually died down. Then the canine moved above me: the sound of claws on concrete. I remained where I was, scared of what stood overhead.

§

Later that night, I awoke with a jolt, the memory of Wayne's face still vivid. I threw my hands out in front of me, in defense against an invisible creature. I remembered the splash of Goldie's blood. I touched my face, half expecting to find residue, but there was none.

Then Wayne came out of the darkness.

I backed into the wall.

He handed me a bottle of water, "Drink up. You need it to maintain your health."

"No, thank you."

"Drink it," he demanded. He set the water bottle on my lap. Then he stepped back and crossed his arms.

"Really, I'm okay." Curious about his transformation, I asked, "What was that about earlier? You changed into something. It wasn't a dog though. What was it, and why?"

The look in his eyes remained intent. "Don't worry about it. Just drink up. It's important that you stay hydrated."

I held the bottle up and gazed at the liquid inside. I contemplated drinking it, but my thoughts drifted to my son. I twisted the lid off.

"When do I get to talk to my son?"

"Later, just drink your water."

"But, I'd like to talk to him. Please, may I?" My voice cracked.

His voice became stern. "Another time, not now. Now, drink your goddamn water or I'm going to force feed it to you."

I put the bottle to my lips and took a sip. It tasted like diluted blood. I spit it back out.

"This isn't water. It tastes like blood." In horror, I stared up at him.

"It's not blood. It's vitamins and proteins. They taste like shit but you need them."

He lied to me.

I grimaced.

"Drink the fucking water, or so help me, I'll shove it down your throat."

I wasn't in shape to fight him. My body hurt. Instead, I chugged down the entire bottle. It left a horrid aftertaste in my mouth. My stomach churned until I gagged. I fought the urge to vomit.

Wayne took the water bottle and left my cell. I curled up under the covers.

I gagged again and glanced back at Wayne, who sat alone at the table. I caught a glimmer in his eyes, something that just didn't appear normal. It was eerily similar to what I'd witnessed earlier. When I recoiled, a small, thin grin spread across his face. I backed into the wall.

I buried myself under the covers and peeked out to keep my eye on him. I was afraid to turn away for even a second. I lay awake for what seemed like eternity.

Then he snored and a deep, menacing growl escaped his lips. I prayed that when I awoke this whole thing would have been a nightmare.

§

As I awoke, I detected male voices in the room. Normally, I would have listened to their conversation and tried to discern what was being said but this time I ignored them.

Rolling over, I pulled the covers with me and took in a deep breath. I inhaled the scent of eggs, hickory smoked bacon, toast, potatoes, onions, bell pepper, and coffee with a hint of Irish Crème. Oh, it smelled terrific!

The aroma put a smile on my face. Last night must have been a nightmare. I gazed at the back wall and sat up, turning toward the voices behind me. My smile faded away. It had not been a dream. I turned around, fixing my gaze upon them.

Doc, Wayne, Alex and Neil focused their attention on me. Wayne flashed a wide, toothy smile. I glanced at the others. I hoped to find something that would alert me to whatever danger lay ahead. I not only feared these men and the fight, I also feared more to this whole situation. Then Wayne caught me off guard.

"Breakfast is ready," he said.

He appeared in front of my cell with a plate of food and slid it through the food tray. I ambled over to it. When I reached the plate, comprehension settled in: I felt good. A new source of energy pulsed through my body, a feeling that almost set me on edge. I looked down at my leg. I was bearing weight on it without any pain.

"How do you feel?" He shut the tray door.

I looked at him. The bruises and swelling had completely vanished from my arms and legs. My vision and sense of smell were phenomenal.

He grinned at me.

"I feel good. Never better," I replied, questioning my own answer.

The others approached my cell and eyed me curiously.

Alex examined me through blackened eyes, his nose taped up. He looked more pissed than anything. Neil wore a brace around his midsection. Wayne looked fine, though I knew damn well I had hurt him. Doc stood amongst the men. He looked me over, scanning every inch of my body.

Then he advanced. "How are those stitches on your shoulder?"

I half turned my back to him while he reached through the bars to assist in lowering my shirt. He ran his hands over the smoothness of my bare skin. In shock, I peered back at him. Doc smiled.

Without turning his head, Wayne said, "Nobody must know about this."

When no one responded, he turned to look at the others. They nodded in agreement. He looked at me again.

My heart raced. "What the hell is happening?" I asked.

"With her fighting skills and this, she'll be just fine," Doc said. He smiled, "Great idea, Wayne."

My eyes flickered over to Wayne, who wore a shit eating grin. Doc walked away, grabbed his mug, and poured himself some coffee, a smug look on his face.

I gripped on to the bars. "Would you tell me what the hell is going on?"

They didn't respond. I was a damn guinea pig.

Neil met my eyes.

"You are truly amazing. Not just your beauty and your skills, but now this." He made a wide gesture with his hands.

I was getting more pissed by the second. I slammed my hands on the bars to get their full attention.

"Hey! What the hell is going on?" Still, no answer. Repeatedly, I slammed my fists against the bars. "Answer me! Damn you!"
Wayne advanced toward my cell. His face was turning beet red.

"Knock off the ruckus in there and eat your damn food! Or, I'm personally going to come in there and deal with you!"

As he moved in closer, I backed off. I thought about how he had turned into the rabid canine, or whatever the hell it was.

Once I backed off, he smiled and calmly replied, "You have a big day ahead of you. Now, I recommend that you eat your food like a good girl. You need your health."

My adrenaline coursed hard through my body. I turned to my food and closed my eyes. So I could calm myself, I took in a deep breath. My hands shook as I opened the cream and sugar. Most of it spilled onto the tray. I took in another deep breath and poured what was left of my sugar in to my coffee.

"I'm not going to do anything for you if you don't explain to me what the fuck…" I was too pissed to finish my sentence.

I threw my stir sticks down, grabbed my plate, and plopped myself down on the cot. I ate my food within seconds. The men whispered at the table.

After finishing my coffee, I approached the food tray with my plate. I eyed them.

"Can I get more coffee?"

Neil approached me.

"Yeah."

He reversed the tray and took the garbage. After he'd pulled the tray through, I offered my Styrofoam cup to him.

He turned his head as he reached through the bars to take the cup.

"Doc, can you throw these away? I'll get her coffee."

"Yeah, sure." Doc took them and walked off.

As Neil took my cup, I grabbed his wrist with my left hand and pulled him face first into the bars. The cup fell to the floor. A rush of air shot out of his mouth and into my face. I latched onto his Adams apple, squeezing it.

"Let...go...of...me..." he said, his voice muffled against the bars.

"I want some fucking answers now!" My fingers tightened on his throat.

He tried to pull away from me, so I locked my feet against the bars and twisted his arm. He screamed in pain and gawked at me. With the weight of my body, I held his arm in place, inching my face closer to his.

"You want to die, motherfucker?"

Only a gurgle escaped his throat.

Wayne was at Neil's side, his eyes fixed on mine.

"Let go of him," he demanded.

"Why should I?" I glared back at him. My grip tightened, my nails sinking deeper into Neil's skin.

Gritting his teeth, he grabbed the bars and leaned into them.

Angrily, he spat, "Let go of him, now!"

"No!"

Wayne's face turned red. Then he scowled.

"I'm coming in there."

Wayne unlocked my cell door. The others stood up from their chairs yet remained their distance.

I released Neil. A thin trail of blood ran down his neck. He fell backwards onto the floor, clutching at his throat.

Ready for an attack, I spun to face Wayne and shook my fists. "I want answers!"

I started toward him when he took a calm step toward me. I halted. There was something about his calm demeanor that unsettled me.

Wayne eyed me, his breath deepening. The stench of his sweat leaked from his pores. Just moments ago, Neil reeked of fear, and I swore I had heard his heartbeat escalate.

He licked his lips. "Don't do this."

"Why can I smell the sweat on you! I don't even see any!"

My olfactory sense was acute.

"What's wrong with me?"

I took two steps back. Tears filled my eyes. I started to put my face in my hands.

Wayne took another step forward, palm out towards me.

"We'll talk, but not now."

"Why!" My voice was shaky.

He let out a deep breath. I was tired of being locked up, beaten, and threatened. A surge of adrenaline shot through me and I rushed at him, knocking him back four feet into the cell wall. He pulled himself from the bars as though it were nothing. He cracked his neck, rolled his shoulders back, and squared off with me. I stopped in my tracks. The bars should have hurt a little when he hit his head on them. There was that glimmer in his eye again. I knew better than that. He sneered, a low snarl escaping his lips. A shuffle of feet left the room.

He strolled toward me.

"I just want answers, Wayne, please?"

He ignored my pleas and continued toward me.

"Wayne?"

I backed up farther and realized I pressed myself into a corner.

Unable to access anything to help me, I did the unthinkable. I reached out and punched him in the face. When I went to hit him again, he caught my fist.

"Shit," I muttered.

He pushed my hand down and moved his face closer to mine. My body molded into the corner.

"You really need to be nicer to me," he whispered into my ear.

I swallowed hard. He pressed hard against me, almost burying my face in his chest. I tried to recoil but could only turn my head. He took in a deep breath along my neck and shoulder. The rise and fall of his chest moved against mine. He reached out and grabbed the bars on either side of me, pulling in tighter.

"I'm strangely aroused," he snickered. He pulled back and cocked his head. Our eyes met.

What the hell? I pushed against his chest.

"Look, I don't have any clue what I did to turn you on, but I'm not interested."

"Show me what you got." He snarled through his teeth again.

"What...?"

His hand grabbed my jaw – hard – and turned me to face him. His mouth landed on mine, firm and angry. He pressed in tighter to prevent me from pushing him away.

"Stop...it," I said.

Each time I tried to turn away, he pushed his mouth harder into mine.

I dreaded what would happen next. He latched on, grabbing me harder with one arm. His other palm found my breast, his mouth now on my neck. Oh, hell, no, this was not happening. His hands were hard and rough as he wound his way under my bra. I managed to squeeze my arms in between us, but he was too powerful and too quick. His strength was inhuman.

My bra was loosened, my breasts spilling out. I groaned. I was not going to let him have his way with me. He wrapped his hands around my hips, hoisted me up, and braced me against the bars behind me. I grabbed onto the bars, ready to fight, but I didn't have the upper body strength to hold my body weight and fight him off at the same time.

Instead, I did the opposite. I latched onto him, my mouth pressed into his. Our eyes met for a brief moment before his hold tightened even more. I wrapped my arms and legs around him and let him carry me to the cot.

He dropped me to the mattress and pulled back to undo his pants. I locked my legs and ankles around his midsection. Then punched straight up into his nose. He grunted, and when he lowered his face to mine, I brought my elbow up and struck him.

"Fuck!" He clamped his nose shut to stop the blood from dripping down his face.

He tried to rise again and muttered, "Son of a bitch."

I continued to hold him with my legs while I struck him with a half fist to his throat. My hand slid around and hooked onto the left side of his neck, my forearm in tight against his throat. I brought my left palm in hard and struck him in the side of the ear, driving him to the right and off the side of the cot. I kept my legs wrapped around him so that when we landed, I came down hard on top of him.

A rush of air escaped his lips, followed by laughter. I started to get up when he pushed me off.

"Oh, that was good. Hurt, too. You could still use some work, but not bad."

I knelt in front of him, one leg up, and stared back at him in shock. "What the...?"

"Don't worry. You're not my type anyway." He tapped me on the cheek with his hand.

I cocked my head and glared at him, more pissed than before.

"When I said to show me what you got, I wasn't referring to your sexual skills, but you're fighting skills. I figured I'd get you riled up, and the best way to do that is to take advantage of a woman. No better way to get her pissed off," he said.

I remained in a kneeling position while he stood before me.

"Nice job. Now get up, I'll train you.

He offered his hand, but I was reluctant. He had an odd but friendly smile. Hesitating, I took it. My frown only seemed to put a broader grin on his face. A voice came out of nowhere, startling me.

"Uh, Wayne? We need to talk," Alex said.

Wayne nodded. "Go ahead."

Alex and Neil glanced at each other and then back at Wayne.

"Her fight's been moved to tonight."

Wayne whipped his head around. "Why?"

They swallowed hard.

"Because the big guy has a new fighter," Alex said, "and he wants more time with him. He figures since Crystal's experienced, she shouldn't have to wait. Wayne, he already scheduled it. There's no changing."

Wayne took a long look at me.

"Who's she fighting?"

"Lilly."

He nodded. "Crystal will be fine. But when it comes time to fight Kara, she'll have to be primed up." He scratched his chin. "Sure."

"Hold up. You guys said I only had one fight." I stared at Wayne.

A menacing grin expanded on his face. "Did we say that?"

"Yeah, Goldie did. Why can't you find somebody else instead of me? I don't want to fight!" I was on the verge of losing my sanity.

"Because you're special," his teeth gleamed.

My heart beat faster. My hands shook as I pushed the hair out of my face. Adrenaline pumped harder throughout my body.

"Let's go. I want to fill you in on the details and get some training in."

I followed him into the exercise room.

"Why me?"

He scratched his chin again. "For starts, you're a hell of a fighter. Never seen a woman as good as you."

I could only take so much of this. I would fight a couple fights if I had to, but I needed to escape.

"How did I get here?"

"You might say, courtesy of your friends." He seemed amused.

"My friends?"

"Yes, your friends."

Obviously, I didn't have good friends. Alex and Neil followed us in to the room and watched us while we trained.

§

Once we were done training, we leaned against the ropes, tired and sweaty.

"Listen carefully to me," Wayne said, sternly, "a lot of people are looking forward to this fight and are placing bets on you. That little bar fight you were in was just an amateur match. This is not. You've progressed to a real one. This isn't a game, Crystal."

"Okay," I muttered.

"The rules are there are no rules."

I arched my eyebrows. "No rules?"

"No, no rules. These fights aren't regulated. Got it?"

I looked at him. Then it registered in my head. "Oh, shit. You're talking illegal?"

A smirk appeared on his face. "If you want to call it that."

I was definitely in a heap of trouble. This wasn't good. Criminals, gangsters, and anybody else who lived an alternative lifestyle might be there. I cringed at the thought.

"Crystal, these fights are not only about winning." He stared hard into my eyes. "You'll fight to the death."

A lump stuck in my throat. The chills not only shot up my spine, but goose bumps percolated all over my skin. My heart raced, and the room seemed darker than before. I wanted to see the sun, feel the heat upon my skin and know I was still alive. Right now, I was dead, unworldly, hidden in the confines of this underground universe. Tears welled up in my eyes.

"I don't know if I can," I replied.

His hands were on my shoulders in an instant. "I know you can. As a matter of fact, I need you to muster up the adrenaline you had in you the other night. You were an animal. You took control of the situation and tapped into it. If you don't do it, you're not going to make it."

I tried to swallow the lump in my throat.

He turned to exit the ring, but stopped and spoke up again. "Remember, we have your kid. Don't think that we won't use him against you."

He left me alone in the ring. I was nauseous. My legs crumbled beneath me. I let them guide me down to the mat, and then I sat in silence, the ropes digging into my back. I wanted to cry, I wanted him to just give my son to the nearest living relative who could take care of him, and then shoot myself.

Tears streamed down my face. I tucked my head into my knees and cried like a baby for the next hour. My jail wardens let me have my sorrow. I didn't know where they were, but it didn't matter.

Wayne eventually walked me into the showers. He watched me periodically but I didn't care. I had no intention to attack, fight, or run from him. I was too busy trying to sort out my emotions and prioritize my thoughts. I leaned against the shower wall and wept.

# THE CIRCUIT

By the time I ate, I was in a somber mood. My captors had tried to converse with me, but I was not interested. They were nervous about the fight, but not for the same reasons. They were worried I would lose, and the fact that I was acting different unsettled them.

Me, well, I was coming to terms with my fate, and the fate of my child.

I had to make a decision and act on it. And that decision was to win tonight's fight. If I had to kill, I would. It would not be the result I wanted, but I would do it if necessary.

I asked my captors if they could play some music to get me in the mood. So, they turned on Rob Zombie and Marilyn Manson. Perfect, I sat with my back to them in a meditative style. That was my first step to taking action – mind over matter.

I focused my thoughts and all my energy on finding peace with myself and whatever actions I must take, despite the circumstances. I listened to the music behind me and let it push me into a deeper, darker place, a darker state of mind. A place where one could only find a killer deep inside their soul. Though my heart calmed itself, it found a rhythm, one that pulsated with new life. It was strange, strong, and vibrant. It gave me a new sensation, a new meaning to self reliance.

I sensed a presence. I opened my eyes and turned to gaze at the open doorway where Wayne stood. His eyes searched mine in the dim light. He anticipated an attack. He was wrong.

"Are you ready?" asked Wayne.

I stood up. I wasn't hesitant, and I wasn't reluctant. I was going to give this fight my all.

Wayne looked me over. I was dressed in black leather pants which were tight in the thighs but loose in the calves. A small zipper started at the ankles and went up to the knees. I had them zipped most of the way, which left four inches unzipped at the bottom. The pants accentuated my strong legs. The shirt was black with a silver dragon on it, tank top style, revealing my powerful shoulders. I wore black leather wrestling boots and had my hair pulled back into a pony tail. The outfit went well with my pale complexion. My new demeanor and clothing had him nodding in approval.

Alex and Neil led us to the farthest wall from my cell and through an archway to a set of stairs which I had not been able to see from my cell. Wayne followed as we ascended the concrete spiral steps that curved over my cell below. As I bumped into the wall, I noticed how old, cracked, and cold it was. At the top of the stairs stood a wooden door that creaked open. It sounded like something out of a horror movie.

We emerged into a small, empty concrete room which had two more doors. We exited the one opposite us. On the other side, distinct faint bellowing noises issued down the long concrete corridor. As we continued on, the sounds of music and people became clearer. We followed the winding passageway to another door. This one had a small, barred window in it. The bars in it were thick and sturdy.

We stopped by the door. I looked through it and beyond I noticed another similar door which also had another barred window in it. A tall, lanky man stood on the other side of that door. He spoke to a short, burly man who occupied the room that separated us. Lilly's name was mentioned. The man inside the room approached our door. He peered out at me through the small window. He sized me up.

"She's short," he commented.

I shot him a dirty look. What the hell did that matter?

"Ah, don't worry," Alex said, grinning. "She's a mean one."

The man in the room snickered. I rolled my eyes and glanced at the door to my right. My heart quickened. I was sure what lay beyond was the fighting arena. I ignored them and began to fidget. It started with a tapping of the foot. Then I began to rub my arms and legs. To overcome the nervousness, I decided to get my adrenaline going. So, I began to clench and unclench my fists. I stared at the door while the men discussed the fight. Wayne opened the door and walked me inside. His hands urged me on. I swallowed hard.

I stared beyond him at the large door which stood opposite the one I came through.

He turned me to face him. "Remember what I said?"

Our eyes met. I nodded. He exited out the door and locked it behind him.

Great, here we go. Now it was pitch black. It was warm in here and it smelled like dirt. Just beyond the door, people hooted and hollered. There was a large commotion of feet as they stomped them.

A voice boomed over the sound system. I recognized it as the short, burly man that Alex and Wayne had spoken to.

"Ladies and gentlemen!"

I cranked my neck to the side. A loud pop echoed in my ear.

"I'd like to introduce you to a new fighter! She's vicious, mean, and downright nasty. You might have seen her at The Ferocious Hog!"

Okay, now this was stupid. Ferocious Hog? What the hell kind of a name was that?

"Welcome Crystal!"

He was talking about me. My eyes widened and my body snapped to attention. This was it. It was time to fight.

Tremors vibrated through the ground beneath my feet. Light filtered through a set of bars in front of me and revealed a concrete slab that opened on a mechanical motor. The barred gate slid open, making the arena visible just on the other side. The smell of death filled my nostrils and stuck in my throat. My eyes watered and bile rose up in my throat. I struggled to keep it down.

I forced myself into the arena. Both the slab and the gate closed behind me with a loud clunk.

I ignored it and looked around the massive arena. The concrete walls were twelve feet high with faint red and brown blotches, blood from the fighters who'd battled numerous times prior to me. Above the walls were heavy duty crisscross bars, much like a chain link fence, that separated the audience from the arena.

The audience was packed closely together and a magnitude of individuals sat behind the bars, some dressed from one extreme to another. A lot of them were downright mean looking. Some screamed, some booed and some cheered. I wanted to crawl back into my cell and wither away.

"And, from Cuba, we welcome the dirtiest fighter to enter the ring! She's mean, she pulls hair, bites, and scratches and claws her opponents to death! Lilly!"

The clunk of another slab door opened to my left. I gazed back from where I'd come in. These two entrances were only for the fighters. When a woman screamed, I snapped my head around to watch Lilly emerge from the darkness.

She yelled again, urging her fans on while they screamed in response to her. I hoped I would remember whatever martial arts training I had.

As Lilly stepped onto the arena floor, dirt wafted up around her legs. Her dark, hip length hair was pulled back into a braid. She wore a gladiator outfit and stood about five feet eight inches. She was bigger than me but not nearly as muscular. I hoped that I had the speed advantage.

She strutted about the ring, raising her arms up and down to get the crowd going. There were more boos than cheers. I presumed she wasn't a fan favorite. She turned toward me with a sneer.

The lights above the audience went out. I glanced up into the darkness. Colored eyes burned above me. I stood hypnotized as they gazed down upon us.

I had seen eyes like that before. Jesus, Wayne was not one of a kind.

My gaze drifted over others in the crowd. The pupils ranged from golden to glowing red. What the hell was Wayne, and who the hell were they? Dread washed over me. Chills ran down my spine and goose bumps spread across my flesh. I wished I was not here.

Lilly came at me fast and hard. She drove her size nine boot straight into my face and knocked me to the ground. Her foot came down towards my sternum. I barely managed to roll out of her way and onto my knees when her foot struck ground.

I glanced back at her. She moved much quicker than I expected. Her right foot came up and struck me in the face. The impact of her kick sent me over backwards. A bone cracked in my face.

"Oh, fuck," I groaned. I reached for my face, and her foot struck my forearm. I was thankful that I had my arm up. Otherwise she would have struck me right in the nose, possibly driving bone into my brain. Her right foot came back up.

Ah, hell no, she was not going to beat me. She might have some advantage over me, but she was not going to win. I blocked her foot with my left hand. She stumbled. I punched straight up with a middle knuckle into the large, heart shaped muscle on the back of her calf. She groaned as her leg gave way and almost sent her down on top of me. I rolled in the opposite direction. She landed with a heavy thud.

I glared back at her from under my brow. Pain reverberated through my cheeks, but I ignored it and scrambled to my knees. She stood, her leg weak beneath her. I charged her and drove her backwards into the wall. Her head bounced against the wall and echoed throughout the arena. I backed away and looked at her. My stomach churned. The pain had to have hurt.

She was on me again. Her fist looped around and caught me in the temple. I struck her in the chest and knocked her back. My legs threatened to buckle underneath but I managed to stay on my feet. My eyes clouded over. I tried to blink it away while she circled me.

She rushed me, her arms forward, like she was going to tackle me. I turned towards her, and stepped shortly to my right. I delivered a left snap kick to her stomach while throwing my right elbow in front of me. My right forearm struck her in the side of the head, throwing her offline from hitting me dead on.

My forearm and elbow slid along the side of her face and caught her nose. I stepped back and twisted out, striking her with a right hand chop to the back of her neck. As her face jerked up, I reversed my hand and hit her with another hand chop, only to her throat. Lilly stumbled to the right, I jumped short and quick. My right foot connected with her inner calf of her injured leg. She went down in the dirt on her right side.

She rolled on to her back, her arm still in the air. As I caught her arm, my foot connected in the crook where her shoulder and torso met. I jerked it hard and fast, dislocating her shoulder. She screamed.

The audience went quiet. I twisted her arm which spun her shoulder around. Her wailing echoed in my head. By the time I dropped to my butt, her arm was completely twisted. I locked my foot into her armpit. She turned to face me.

"Make it quick, please," she muttered.

Adrenaline coursed harder through my body. I gritted my teeth, rolled her over, and straddled her back. Gripping her head, I cranked it to the side and snapped her neck. The crack of it was loud.

"The winner is Crystal!"

Stunned, I looked up at the audience. I glanced back down at my hands which were bloody, beaten and bruised.

The fans screamed and cheered. I stood up and stared down at her body, but anxiety took over. My heart beat faster and my stomach churned from the realization I had ended her life.

For me, there was no excitement. I wanted this over. I'd rather be in my cell right now, away from the noise and horror. I turned for the exit but caught sight of the commentator behind a barred window. He smiled at me. I simply turned away.

The slab door slid on its tracks.

Then the chants started. "Crystal! Crystal! Crystal!"

I glanced back at the audience, and then turned away. Though I had won over some of my opponent's fans, I was not enthralled with my outcome. Instead, I was disgusted. I was not proud of the fact that I killed Lilly. She was a human being. This was a horrifying game they were playing with us. I resented anyone who was affiliated with the arena, the fights and the managing of the fighters.

As fast as the adrenaline had come, it had gone. The doors closed behind me. Wayne, Alex and Neil stood on the other side with wide grins on their faces.

"Nice job," Neil said.

He raised his hand to give me a high five, but I ignored him.

"You did great!" Wayne gave me a hug. "Now, let's get the hell out of here."

The little man grinned. "Great job!"

Wayne grabbed my upper arm, rushing me back towards my cell. I glanced at the window on the other side of the commentator's office. Lilly's manager stood on the other side of it. He glared at me, his hazel eyes darkening.

That night, I cried myself to sleep and dreamt of Lilly. This time we didn't fight in the arena. Instead, we fought in a pool of blood.

§

The morning after, I awoke to the aroma of breakfast and coffee. The odor of it made my stomach churn. Ah, no, this was the last thing I needed now. I didn't want to be sick.

"Okay, snap to, Crystal. You need to eat and we need to get some more training in today. You have another fight tonight," said Wayne.

The food tray slid open.

I held my stomach for awhile longer, eventually curling up into a ball. It hurt. Hell, I hurt. With everything that happened over the past twenty-four hours, I couldn't deal with it.

"Crystal? Do you hear me? I'm talking to you."

I didn't move or speak. Instead, I was more worried that I would vomit, which I didn't want to do.

"Crystal, don't ignore me," demanded Wayne.

Damn it, force yourself up. At least do that, that way he doesn't think you're ignoring him. I pushed myself up. A wave of nausea overcame me. Okay, this wasn't good.

I propped the blankets up behind me to keep the cold wall from touching my back. Dizziness overwhelmed me. To keep from passing out, I opened my eyes wide and looked up at Wayne. His eyes were droopy and his skin slack from lack of sleep.

The dizziness lingered for a moment before dissipating.

"You look like shit," replied Wayne.

"Yeah, well so do you."

Neil and Alex chuckled.

The scent of a breakfast burrito wafted toward me. Damn, it smelled good. It had been awhile since I ate so maybe that was part of my problem.

I pushed myself up onto my feet when the wooziness hit me again. Only this time, I went down for the count.

"Oh, shit! Crystal!" screamed Wayne. He bolted to his feet.

"Doc, get in here now!" screamed Alex.

The metal clank of the door slid open and in ran Wayne and Alex.

My body was weak and my head continued to spin.

Wayne and Alex moved me to my bed. The other two joined us.

The only thing that felt good right now was the cool sheet upon my skin. I gathered it up in my hands, pressed my body into it and clung to it.

"Crystal? Crystal? Do you hear me?" asked Doc.

I rolled over, pulling the sheet around my body so I could have full contact with it. It wasn't that I didn't want to answer them instead I couldn't. I needed to escape into another world. A place where there was some normality.

"Do something, Doc?" demanded Wayne.

"Sure, you guys might want to hold her down though."

Wayne touched me. I screamed. Neil scrambled for the other arm while Alex scrambled for my legs. I flailed out, trying to push them away.

Once they gained hold of me, something sharp, cold and slick pricked my arm. The medication took a moment but when it did, it completely relaxed me. I settled down into the sheets again. I glanced up at the man who held the syringe.

It was Doc.

For the first time since my vision had cleared, I was actually able to see his face. Before, my vision had been to blurry. That and he wasn't always here like the others were.

His nose appeared longer than usual on his thin face. He wore his small wired glasses halfway down his nose and his long, gray hair pulled back into a ponytail. He was slightly smaller than the average sized guy. His small eyes were intimidating.

I closed my eyes.

"She's had an attack," said Doc.

His voice faded in and out. "A mix of mental…depression and anxiety. I've given her a sedative…needs rest…time…"

Then I was out.

§

I awoke to my kidnapper's voices but I lay unmoving, quiet and unnoticed. I contemplated rolling over but decided to pretend to be asleep for I didn't want to fight anymore.

"When is she going to wake up?" Alex asked. His voice carried over from the break room into my cell.

"Soon, I hope," replied Wayne. "Her fight is in less than an hour and a half."

"I suppose there's no way it can be rescheduled?" Neil asked.

"No, it can't. It's too late," Wayne said. "If she doesn't wake up soon, I'm going to have to drag her ass out there anyway."

"She's going to get her ass kicked if you do that." Alex scooted back in his chair and plopped his feet on the table.

"I know, and we can't have that." Wayne stood up and paced the floor.

"Maybe you need to give her some….you know?" Neil said.

What was he referring to? Come on, just say it!

"I think that might be one of the reasons why she's been so full of energy these past couple of days."

The other men agreed with Wayne.

Wayne sighed, "I'm going to have to. And if I do that now, it'll take a little while for it to kick in anyway. So the timing should work."

"Well, then you better get to it," Alex said.

Behind me, was a faint unrecognizable noise and then a groan. About the time I considered rolling over to find out what was going on, hands clamped onto me and turned me over. I struggled, but my resistance was weak. One of the hands covered my eyes. Warm liquid enveloped my mouth. I gagged on the blood, only this time it wasn't mixed with anything. I fought to spit it out, yet Wayne forced my jaw closed so I had no choice but to swallow it.

"Are you hungry?"

I gazed up at Wayne who stood at the head of my bed. I was pissed but couldn't do a damn thing about it because I didn't have enough strength to handle fighting them. My stomach churned and grumbled. I clutched on to my stomach. The nausea came back. Maybe I did need some food. It had been awhile since I last ate. Wayne kneeled on my bed, just to the right of me. I weakly nodded. He pulled back as my arms fell to the cot. They left my cell and conversed in the break room while they prepared my food.

"So will that affect her differently since you gave it to her straight?" Neil asked.

"Yes, it will take effect sooner, and she'll be much stronger," Wayne said. "Timing is critical tonight. She needs to be on her toes."

I weaved in and out of consciousness until they brought me my food. I ate my dinner and worked out again, but I wasn't up to my prime.

Halfway through a set of squats, Wayne struck me. I fell into the weight bench and groaned in pain. From the look on his face, I knew he was unhappy with my performance. I struggled to stand so that I could continue with my workout.

They watched, unimpressed.

Wayne assisted me with changing into my clothes. I didn't really care. I had no modesty at this point.

He whispered in my ear, "You need to get your shit together. We can't have you like this out there. They'll kill you."

"Maybe I'd be better off," I mumbled.

I gazed up at him. Anger resided in his eyes. To avoid his glare, I closed my eyes. My mind was still not right for I was a little too relaxed right now. It was a good feeling. I grinned stupidly at him, my eyes still closed.

Something whizzed across my face, stinging my cheek. I opened my eyes, his red face in front of mine. His hand was drawn back for a second wind up.

"You, bitch, are our ticket. You better fucking straighten up now. We need you. If you don't get your shit together, we're all dead. Do you understand me?"

I gritted my teeth. "Why am I so important? Am I worth something to you? Let me guess--money? Is that it?"

His eyes stared hard into mine.

"As much as I'd like to tell you, I can't. The less you know the better you are. Now, listen to me." Wayne jabbed his finger in my chest. "Within the first few minutes of your fight, you're going to find a sudden rush of adrenaline, power, and strength. You better use it to your advantage. If you don't tap into it, she's going to kill you in the first five minutes.

"So, you better get with it. I'm hoping that with my push, maybe we can move it along quicker. It's already in your bloodstream. It just needs to move through your body faster. So, let's get it going."

Then he punched me square in the jaw.

I recoiled. I was distant and weak. Then it hit me. I knew what he was after but I didn't quite have the adrenaline or even the energy to keep up with him.

"What the fuck is wrong with you, I can't fight you? I'm too drained from the sedative the doctor gave me."

"Well, sweetcakes, you better muster up some adrenaline soon?"

Then he hit me again, only on the left side this time. I stared at him in awe. He tried to push his blood faster through my system by getting my adrenaline pumped up.

I tried to relinquish to the cot behind me, but he wouldn't let me fall back.

When I fell into him, he grabbed on to my shirt. As before, the transformation in him took place. Not only was his nose and jaw line trying to change, but his eyes narrowed and the pupils turn a golden hue against the whites of his eyes.

What the....?

His lips curled back to reveal elongated canine teeth. I took a step back, fear stirring inside me. He pulled me into him again, chest to chest. I fought him and stumbled backwards onto the cot with him atop me. To get him away from me, I pushed against his chest. The heat from his body radiated through my hands.

For the first time, I realized we were alone. I trembled against him. He cranked my head to the side, exposing my bare neck to him. I fought to keep him away as he continued to transform.

I wanted to scream, but it took all of my effort just to keep him at arm's length. His mouth lowered, his growl vibrating against my flesh. His teeth sunk deep into my upper shoulder.

I screamed. I was going to be mauled to death with no chance of being rescued. No one would hear me.

I fought harder. He thrashed against me, shredding my skin. My arms fell limp at my side. He pulled back, releasing me. I moaned in agony, pain shooting through my upper body. Spasms ripped through my muscles. I pressed my hand to his chest to push him away. My fingers touched the abnormal growth of chest hair beneath his torn shirt.

I struggled to turn my head, the pain in my neck and shoulder revolting against me.

"Oh God," I mumbled.

He was re-positioning for a second attack when our eyes met. I screamed. Its teeth were fully formed in its massive jaw. His shirt was torn where the muscles strained against the fabric. Thick coarse grey and black hair protruded from his skin.

My mouth hung open.

"Don't, please don't," I whispered.

Tears leaked from the corner of my eyes.

I froze in mid push. His eyebrows came together as if in thought, and then his teeth and hair retracted. His eyes returned to their normal color, and his muscles condensed down to their original size.

I lay on the cot with my mouth agape. I had just been attacked by a werewolf, one that never gained full transformation or momentum. I was thankful that he never made the complete change. Blood poured from my wound and soaked my shirt. He stared at the blood, his eyes widening. He grabbed my shirt and ripped it off. I screamed as the cloth tore at my wounds.

"Fuck! Is Doc back yet!"

The sound of running footsteps reverberated through the hallway.

"No, he's not! Why?" asked Neil.

"What the fuck do you think!"

Alex and Neil appeared behind Wayne.

"Oh, shit," Alex muttered. His eyes were huge.

"Get me some wet and dry towels! And get me Doc's medical kit!" demanded Wayne.

Neil and Alex rushed around the break room, gathering the supplies. Wayne held his hand tight over my wound.

I groaned in pain, wondering whether I was going to bleed to death. My arms lay limp at my side.

"Um, I was kidding when I said maybe I'd be better off."

I tried to keep a sense of humor. Another spasm shot through my shoulder. Wayne groaned, but kept his eye on my wound. A stupid smirk adorned his face. I closed my eyes when he spoke up.

"Don't worry you're not going to die. You'll be just fine. I didn't bite you that bad."

Once the guys brought him the towels and medical supplies, he started cleaning my wound.

"So, am I going to turn into a werewolf?" I asked.

"No, it wasn't that bad. It was just a nibble. Had you been bitten worse, then maybe."

He called that a nibble? Another painful spasm reverberated down the muscles in my back. I bit my lip, stifling another groan.

"Oh, okay, that's comforting. I didn't think werewolves even existed."

He wiped down my skin and I shivered.

"Stay still. And, yes, they do. You got living proof in front of you."

I tried not to think about the pain. "Let me guess, you change when you're angry?"

"Yes, I do. It's either by full moon, anger, fear, jealousy, and sometimes when I'm sexually aroused. Don't believe the old wives tales that it's only the full moon that changes a person into a werewolf. Emotions come into play with this curse."

I snapped my head around to look at him. "Did you say sexually aroused?"

My eyes remained fixated on him, concerned about any woman he tried to bed.

He looked at me and then turned his attention back to my wound. He smiled. I lay my head back down, closing my eyes.

"Yes, I did. When you're like me, you have to be careful. Try to keep your emotions in check." Wayne threaded the needle. "It's not easy, especially during sex. It's better when you're with somebody like you. You know what you're capable of and what to expect from your lover."

A vivid image popped into my head. I tried to clear it from my brain. The needle pierced my flesh.

"Ow!" I screamed.

"Sorry, but we need to get this stitched up before you get out there, which is in about forty minutes. And I don't have time to wait for Doc to get this done."

I tried to relax, but it wasn't easy. Alex and Neil stood by, taking Wayne's orders. I turned my head away from the bite. I didn't want to see what it looked like. The pain was bad enough.

Once Wayne had finished, he tapped me on the cheek. "How you doing there?"

I opened my eyes.

"Peachy keen." I realized he was straddling my body, pinning my arms down with his knees.

"Good," he said.

He helped me sit up and cleaned off my shoulder again. Then he lowered himself to his knees in front of me. "I need you to listen carefully to me now."

I nodded.

"I stitched you up and bandaged your wound. We're going to give you another shirt to wear. Trust me, you don't want to smell like you just bathed in blood."

Smell like I bathed in blood? Did it really matter? I lowered my eyebrows, thinking about what he had said.

"You have got to get in there, get the job done, and get out," said Wayne. His voice softened, "I'm sorry I bit you. I had no intention of hurting you. Do you understand me so far?"

I nodded again. I asked no questions because all I had now were questions. I didn't want to get either one of us riled up at this time.

"Good. Try not to break those stitches. Otherwise you'll be in a world of hurt." He turned his head to Alex. "Are there pain meds in there?"

Alex shook out a couple of pills and handed them to Wayne.

"She might be okay though, right? I mean she's got your…stuff…in her."

"True, but we don't want to risk anything right now. She just needs to get in and get out." Wayne popped the pills into my mouth.

"Chew them up. They'll get into your bloodstream quicker."

I bit down on the pills. The chalky substance coated my mouth, and I wanted to gag. He handed me the rest of the bottle of water they had used. I sucked it down, rinsing the nasty residue out but still a bitter aftertaste lingered.

"It's time," Neil said.

Wayne helped me put on a plain black t-shirt. As he pulled it down, a surge of blood rushed through me from my head to my toes. The room spun, and I had to close my eyes to keep from getting sick. I literally held out my hands to keep my balance and grasped onto Wayne to maintain my stability. A current of heat radiated out from my face, down and throughout my body.

"Is she alright?" Neil's eyes widened.

My skin color must have changed or something. I opened my eyes, practically staring through him.

"It's working. We need to hurry up," Wayne said.

Though I really didn't need his help at this point, Wayne rushed me up the stairs and down the corridor. Alex and Neil couldn't keep up, so I knew they were mortal. Wayne's blood pumped harder through my system. Strength and power overtook me, making me practically invincible, almost Godlike. I approached the window where the commentator sat.

I spoke up instead of Wayne. "I'm ready."

Wayne shot me a look that told me to back down and let him handle things. I innocently smiled at him. His eyes narrowed before he turned towards the commentator.

The commentator peered up at me. When the door opened, I stepped inside and stood with my back to my captors. The door shut behind me, and I didn't look back.

I stood alone. The urge to bust down the wall and the iron gate became overwhelming. The commentator announced Xena as my opponent, and the concrete wall slid open. The crowd went wild. Thunderous music boomed about the arena and echoed off the concrete walls.

A wide, evil grin crossed my face. The extreme urge to take on everybody in the arena, fighters and fans included, became difficult for me to hold back.

Then Xena emerged from the darkness. She was much larger than my last opponent. She stood about the same height, but she was leaner and more muscular than me. Her long limbs would give her an advantage over me, but I didn't care. I could take her.

Her dark, tanned body moved in closer, her long braids hanging in front of her face. Her metallic bra and chastity-style belt clanked.

Okay, enough with the stupid comic outfits. It was time to get down and dirty. She strolled in front of me and crouched, ready to pounce. We grinned at each other.

Then I rushed her. Once I neared her, I jumped, turned, and delivered a full flying sidekick to her face. She flew back and hit the concrete barrier with a loud thud. I landed on my feet and looked on as she tried to pry her body from the wall.

Xena scrambled, wobbled and then stopped, grabbing her head. She tried to regain her composure. I decided to take advantage. I ran full force at her and delivered another flying sidekick to her face. Her head bounced off the wall again. A loud crack echoed in my ear. I grasped her by her hair and pulled her forward. She clutched weakly at my arms. I lowered her head and kicked her several times in the face with my knee. Another crack resounded.

I glanced at the wall beyond her. It was spattered with fresh blood. The smell of it stimulated the adrenaline inside me. I threw her head and body back hard into the wall. Blood sprayed my face.

I lurched into the air and kicked again. My foot connected with the bottom of her chin and cocked her head back against the wall. Another crack, and then there were the whites of her eyes as she fell, face first into the ground.

I stepped back, geared and wired for more, when the fight was over.

Dammit, no. I wanted more. So I turned with my hands up in the air and egged the audience on. Cheers and excitement escalated throughout the arena. They chanted my name. I turned and glanced back at Xena, who lay dead on the ground. Blood soaked the dirt underneath her. I hadn't had enough yet, and then I found myself on top of her, my feet applying enough pressure to snap her neck. Her face contorted at an ugly angle.

I still wanted more when the sound of steel moved above me. Gazing up at the audience, I caught sight of a steel bar. The bar protruded out of place in the barriers between me and the audience.

Then I remembered what Wayne had said: get the job done and get the hell out of there. I'm not exactly sure what that meant, but when Wayne said something, it usually wasn't wise to second guess him.

I exited the arena, the concrete wall and iron gate closing behind me. My fans still chanted my name. Damn, it was great! I was powerful and respected.

When I entered the corridor I caught sight of my captors. I ignored them and headed for my cell. Wayne didn't look happy. Once I exited the door at the end of the hall, he grabbed my arm and twisted me around. We stood face to face.

"What the hell was that all about?" he growled.

"What?" My adrenaline still pulsated through my body.

"You know exactly what I'm talking about." His voice was harsh and rough.

"I just did what you wanted." I turned away.

He jerked me back into him. I stepped closer, my face within inches of his. "You need to figure out what the fuck you want from me. I'm tired of your games. First, you want me to do one thing and then you want me to do another. I'm not playing them anymore. I'm going to do what I need to do to survive. I'm done with it."

I jerked my arm out of his hand, our eyes meeting before I turned away. But the cold hearted bastard stepped in front of me, his face hard as stone, his eyes beady and cold.

"You trying to get us fucking killed," he said. His fists clenched and unclenched.

I leaned in to him, almost to the point I could kiss him if I wanted.

"You know, I've tried to get a story out of you, but you keep telling me that I need to wait, that I'll find out later. I'm sick and tired of this shit, so -" – I enunciated the last two words for him – "fuck you. And, go ahead and bite me again, asshole. See what happens next."

He cocked his head and let out a chuckle that was nasty and menacing. Then he shoved me. I flew into the concrete wall behind me.

He tackled me to the ground, his hands wrapping around my throat.

"You got some balls, bitch. Don't think you can take me on."

My blood pulsed with his energy. I snapped my arms straight out and up at him. My fists connected with his middle abdomen before sliding up his chest. They stopped in an X position underneath his chin. Using all my power, I pressed him upwards, breaking his hold. I pulled my legs from underneath him and kicked him off completely. He fell to the floor. We scrambled to our feet at the same time.

"You want to fight, let's go, bitch."

He came in fast and hard, throwing a high kick to my chest. I was barely able to block it with both of my arms. When his foot touched the floor, he threw a right punch and caught me on the left side of my face. I stumbled backwards a few steps.

He was right there with another kick and punch. I blocked him, and then threw my right elbow into the side of his ribs. Tight against his body, I stepped to his rear and nailed him in the kidneys with my elbow. My left hand gripped the back of his shirt as my left elbow struck him again in the ribs. I pulled against his shirt while sweeping his legs out from under him.

He went down hard on his back. I brought my right leg up and nailed him in the side of the head. He grabbed at my ankle. Neil wrapped an arm around my neck and jerked me backwards.

I threw my left elbow back into Neil's ribs, and then swung my fist down into his groin. I side stepped him, and twisted my upper body to take him down with a left elbow to the chin and a fist to the solar plexus.

Wayne and Alex tackled me. As I fell, I landed atop Neil. They pulled me off of Neil and pummeled me with their fists, elbows, and knees. Then a hard blow to my kidneys weakened me and left me wanting no more. I lay in pain while they stood, Neil and Alex panting from exhaustion. Wayne just stared at me.

"Come on, get up." He motioned for me, but I couldn't move.

"She's a tough bitch," Neil said. "Jesus, that hurt."

"Pussy," Wayne mumbled, shooting Neil a stupid look.

"What'd you just call me?" Neil tried to look tough but it didn't go over well. Once Wayne turned and glared at him, Neil backed down and muttered, "You know I'm still human. There is a difference."

Wayne rolled his eyes and motioned for me to get up. "Come on, I'm not in the mood for games."

I rolled over onto my stomach. I was weak and hurt from the beating I took.

I started to stand when Neil kicked me in the stomach with his steel toed boots and dropped me to the floor. A groan escaped my lips. I lay on my face, clutching my stomach. Wayne's eyes dilated as they fixated on Neil.

"What the hell?" grumbled Wayne.

"What?"

Neil gave Wayne a cocky look and shrugged. Wayne reached out and decked him in the groin. He bent over in pain and stared back at Wayne, confused.

"What?" he squeaked.

"How's that for a cheap shot, Neil?" Wayne glared at him. "That wasn't necessary. She was already down."

Neil groaned and dropped to his knees in front of me, his face contorted into a horrendous look of pain. We were almost face to face when Wayne reached out and dragged him away from me. He tossed him to the floor like a rag doll, then reached out and grabbed my arm.

"No, no, no," I started to moan when he cut me off.

"Don't worry."

He threw me over his shoulder. The bone dug hard into my stomach.

The pain was horrible. He carried me down the stairs and tossed me onto the cot. I sank into the cool covers, allowing them to swallow me up. The coolness of the blankets was a small relief against my warm, swollen skin. Before I closed my eyes, Wayne stood above me, his hands on his hips, and shook his head.

I lay on my cot for a couple hours and thought about what had happened earlier. This was my second, well, third killing – since I don't remember my first.

I had taken it beyond killing tonight. I had taken it into madness. There was a sound inside my cell but I didn't identify it at first. My eyes snapped open. Even though the lights were out and the room dark, Neil appeared in my face.

He was the wounded puppy, the embarrassed and bullied child everyone picked on. I was nauseas.

"Hello," he said. A smirk stood out on his face.

Oh, shit, I really must have pissed him off. There he stood above me, at the head of my bed. Just then, I caught a glimmer of something shiny. The switchblade snapped open. I feared the look in his eyes. He lowered the blade next to my face. He wore a look of embarrassment and a loss of pride.

But wait – I thought only Wayne had the key.

The cool steel rested against my cheek. I started to raise my hands when the sharp blade pressed harder.

"Hey, Neil," I tried to keep calm and relaxed. "You don't really want to do that, do you?"

A flicker of pain slid across my cheek where the blade had been. Warm fluid emerged from the laceration. Okay, maybe that was a stupid question.

Then he lowered his face to mine, "You're a real badass, aren't you?"

I didn't answer, afraid that I might find myself in more trouble.

"And, you're probably one of the most beautiful women I've ever met."

Okay, now he was starting to make me a little nervous.

He laid his cheek against my bloodied face. "You're beautiful enough to fuck."

I swallowed hard. He rubbed the side of the blade down my throat.

"I bet you're good too. Aren't you?"

I didn't answer that one either. The blood began to stick, coating our skin.

I closed my eyes. A chill ran up my spine, the hair on my neck stood up, and goose bumps erupted on my skin. His hot breath warmed my neck. The coolness of the blade chilled my flesh. He rested it against the cleavage of my breasts.

"I remember when Wayne first brought you here. I thought, now that's the one I want. I want her to be my first."

This wasn't getting any better.

"I still want you to be my first. That is before I kill you."

The tip of the blade dipped down inside my shirt and bra, inching towards my nipple. I trembled. Goosebumps percolated across my skin. The sharp edge grazed my breast. I winced. He wasn't paying attention to the knife because he was too involved in his thoughts. I took a deep breath and held it, debating my options. Anything I did at this point could hurt me.

This guy was just a kid. Young, probably in his early twenties. I'm sure he thought if he could work with these guys, he was going to be a badass. Maybe even get a chance in the arena himself. I don't think he really knew what he'd gotten himself into.

He rubbed his cheek against mine again. Some of the blood trailed down my neck.

"Ooh, that's warm," he said, his voice low.

What the hell was he thinking? I had to do something, but I wasn't exactly in the position to do anything about it. He inched his face away from mine. As if wary of my actions, he kept his eye on my hands. Slowly, he moved over me.

Our eyes met, and in them, there was a child that had snapped, a lost innocence, a lost youth. He lowered his mouth to mine. The knife moved again, the blade shifting back towards my neck.

His mouth found mine while his free hand slipped inside my shirt and fondled my breast. I let him have me, if only for a moment. Then I reached up and wrapped my hands around his hair. I moaned in response to him, making him think I wanted him just as much. He dropped the knife and groped me with both hands. The knife struck the floor. Our mouths parted.

He asked, "What's it like to kill?"

Hmm, that's what excited him - the thrill of the kill.

He let me turn over to face him. I slinked onto my hands and knees, arching my back.

I whispered, "Do you really want to know?"

A slow smirk crossed his face. He nodded, and then a twisted expression spread across it.

I grinned. "Did you just realize you imprisoned yourself with a killer?"

We lunged for the knife. His hand wrapped around the handle and mine around the blade. He jerked it backwards, slicing my palm wide open. I gasped in pain, unable to open my hand, afraid of the amount of blood that would pour from it. The pain was excruciating.

He stared in fear of me. I clenched my fist and buried it in his face. He stood, in shock, unmoving, and took two more punches to the face. The knife sliced through the air. I narrowly dodged it, and re-positioned my body. Then I was able to block his hand from coming back at me.

I struck the inside of his arm with my injured fist. The knife clattered to the floor. I formed a half fist and struck him in the throat, stepping in as I did. His breath caught.

I circled my arm back down, ramming an elbow to his chest. His head shot forward, and I clawed his face. I took him down, dropping into a kneel stance. A loud thud and a grunt later, I was on top of him, my hands wrapped around his neck.

"You want to fuck me now, you son of a bitch!" I screamed.

Unable to breathe, he tried to grab onto my wrists.

"Come on, motherfucker! Try it now! Get your fucking knife and slice me now!"

A sick feeling came over me, my stomach twisting in knots. I tried to tell myself he was just an innocent young man, but my mind wouldn't accept it. He was a part of this whole thing. I would not allow him to get away with it, anymore than Wayne and Alex. They would all suffer one way or another. His body became limp beneath me.

The lights in the break room came on and then the cell door banged open. I was thrown into the far wall and struck my head hard against it. I lay there as Wayne and Alex stood above Neil. I stared down at my hand. Blood pumped wildly from the deep wound. I clenched my fist closed again.

Wayne turned to face me. I tried to regain my composure. I stifled the urge to cry and scream. I bit my lip, the pain in my hand unbearable.

Alex whispered in Wayne's ear, "He's dead."

They glanced back at me.

"What happened?" Alex asked.

I stifled my emotions the best I could, but my voice still shook. "Long story short. He told me he wanted to fuck me and kill me, put a knife to my face, and was going to rape me. He dropped the knife and that's when I killed him."

I exposed my wound to them, groaning in pain. They looked down at it.

"Wrap up her wound," said Wayne. "I'll take care of Neil."

Alex shifted his gaze from me to Wayne. He hesitated. He didn't want to be alone with me.

"Fine, I'll take care of her hand. You take care of Neil," said Wayne.

Wayne reached down, tore off part of Neil's shirt, and approached me. He worked on my hand while Alex struggled to drag Neil's body out of the cell. I should have felt guilty about the young man's death, but I wasn't.

I couldn't watch Alex drag him out so I averted my attention to Wayne.

It was sad; neither of the men really seemed to care that he was dead.

"You're going to have some war wounds after this whole thing is over."

I ignored Wayne's comment and instead stared out the cell bars. Would I ever be free again? What did the future have in store for me? What would I even do once I got out? Would I ever find my son?

I leaned my head back against the wall.

Wayne snapped his fingers. "Hey, are you okay?"

Maybe he did have a heart, or maybe it was another rhetorical question. I didn't answer.

He stopped bandaging my hand. "I'm not sure if you heard me or not, but are you okay?"

I looked at him. "Do you really want me to answer that question?"

He gave me that snide look.

"Do I look fucking okay to you?"

He took a deep breath, exhaled and got busy again.

"I think I'm going to be dead by the time this thing is over," I went on. "And not because I volunteered for this either."

He didn't answer that.

"I didn't, did I?"

He didn't answer me, but kept his attention focused on my cut.

We maintained our silence while he finished bandaging my hand. Alex came down the hallway and, as he stepped into the room, I glanced up at him. Blood caked his body. My mouth dropped open. Jesus, he looked like he'd jumped in a pool of the crimson liquid. Wayne shifted his gaze to Alex.

He stared at him, wide-eyed.

"What the hell….?"

"I took care of the body."

"What the…?" he began again when Alex cut him off.

"I'm showering here. I have some clean clothes I can change into."

He walked away, his face hardened.

I needed to use the restroom. But Alex was in there now stripping down.

Wayne must have detected something in me. "What's wrong?"

I squirmed a bit. "I need to use the bathroom."

He rolled his eyes. "Can't it wait?"

"I wish, but it's been a while since I've gone. I don't exactly have a toilet in my cell or any privacy even if I did."

He grabbed my arm and pulled me to my feet.

"Come on."

This wasn't the time, but I couldn't hold it. I had to go.

Outside the door, he yelled, "Hey, she needs to use the bathroom! Are you covered?"

"No, but I'm not worried about it! Maybe she'll see something she likes!"

Wayne stuck his head through the doorway before me and peered at him. "Hey, asshole!"

"Hey, dude, I was talking about her liking something, not you!"

Wayne shook his head and then walked me into the shower area. I tried to keep my head down while he led the way to the stalls.

"He's a dick," he said.

"Like you aren't?" I replied.

Wayne shot me a dirty look.

I caught a glimpse of Alex under the shower head at that moment. Water ran down his taut, glistening muscles. I took in the breathtaking view, my eyes scanning him from top to bottom.

Then he caught me red-handed, my gaze fixated on him when our eyes met. He grinned and winked at me. I blushed and snapped my head back around to avoid his gaze. Alex wasn't the only one who caught me looking, Wayne did too. I hurried towards the stalls with Wayne on my heels.

"Like what you see?" Alex asked.

I didn't answer. Instead, I kept my eyes forward.

"I'm better equipped than Neil was, you can bank on that."

I bet he was.

Alex had no modesty and after viewing his glorious, naked body, new feelings came over me. Feelings I hadn't had in – hell, I didn't know how long. I glanced back at him before walking into the stall area.

"Now how would you know about Neil's equipment?" I asked.

"Yeah, I'd like to know that myself," Wayne said with a grin.

Alex smiled. "Do you really want to know? How do you think I got all that blood on me?"

Then a visual came over me, and I didn't want to know anymore. I had a feeling that Neil was no longer in one piece. My stomach churned, and I had to rush to the bathroom.

I spent more time in there than what I should have, just to have a little privacy and to try to maintain my sanity. My stomach cramped up, and I wanted to vomit, but it didn't happen. While I sat there, I overheard their conversation. Alex confirmed my suspicions.

When I came out of the stall, I washed my hands and face, then ran water through my hair. While I bent over, Alex moved beside me, fingering the strands of it.

"Would you like a shower?" asked Alex. "It's been a while since you had one."

A shower did sound good. I wanted to let the water run down my body and relax my muscles. I straightened up, not knowing how close he was until I backed up into his bare wet chest. Turning around, I came face to face with him. I scanned the room, looking for Wayne. He was nowhere in sight.

"Where'd Wayne go?" I asked.

"He had to take a call." Alex looked me over, and then touched my cheek.

"You might have a thin scar from it, but nothing too bad."

He was a little too close for comfort, and I blushed again. I tried to avoid his eyes, but when I lowered them, I had to look away from staring at his groin.

"What did he do to you?" he asked.

Our eyes met. "Who?"

"Neil."

"Just what I told you."

The steam from his bare chest sunk into my skin. I couldn't move. I was stuck in between him and the sink.

"Did he hurt you?" His large brown eyes were curious.

"What do you think?"

He didn't answer me. I looked him in the eyes.

"He put a knife to my throat, and almost cut my breast off."

He lowered his gaze to my chest before meeting my eyes again.

"Would have been a shame. They're nice." Alex grinned. "Not too large, not too small, and not bolt-ons. I like them."

"Can we not talk about my breasts?"

"You're the one who brought them up. I'm just commenting on what you said."

"Are you for real?"

A wicked half grin formed on his face.

"Oh, yeah, all man. Nothing fake here, and, I'm not a damn werewolf either. I got the real deal."

"Really?"

He posed like a damn bodybuilder and completely caught me off guard. I turned away and started back through the shower area. He grabbed my shoulder.

I half turned towards him.

"Yeah, you're all man, alright."

He smiled and dried himself off while I stood by, my arms crossed in front of my chest.

"You want your shower?"

"Probably not a good idea right now," I said, glancing around.

"Why not? I gave you a show. You can give me one now."

I whirled my head around to glare at him.

"You're just as bad as Neil."

He threw his arms up in surrender.

"Hey, I didn't put a knife to your neck or try to slice your tits off."

True, but his ego was starting to get to me, despite his insanely masculine body.

"I'll wait."

He turned with his back to me and bent over, picking up his clothes. He did have a great ass. Jesus, I needed away from here. I turned away from him and leaned against the wall.

"It must have been an important call."

I peered over my shoulder.

He zipped up his jeans. "Yeah, it was. It was the big guy."

"Who's the big guy?"

"Somebody you don't want to know. Trust me, I don't even want to know him." He pulled his shirt on over his head.

"I take it he's not a nice guy."

"Mm, depends on what side you're on."

Crossing my arms, I leaned back against the wall.

He leaned against the partition wall and put on his shoes and socks.

"Does he have my son?"

He glanced in my direction, and then ignored me.

I approached him. "Does he have my son?"

"I don't know who has your son."

"When is this going to end? When am I going to be able to go home?"

"I can't answer that."

"Why?"

"Because I don't know," he said. Looking me over one last time, he straightened up.

From behind, Wayne entered the shower area. "Fight number three is tomorrow night," he said.

We peered over at him.

"It appears as though Crystal is an overnight sensation." Wayne smiled at me. "The fans are eager for your next fight."

"Jesus, there've never been that many fights in a row before," Alex said.

"No, there haven't. You should be proud of yourself, Crystal."

A new thought formed in my mind. This wasn't just about my fighting. This was about fighting to the death, and winning. If I died tomorrow night, they would find another fighter.

I needed to get out of here and find my son. I needed to strategize a plan.

I thought about the knife in my cell. Had they found it? I hoped not.

Later that evening, when I had the chance, I searched my cell but came up empty handed. I was doomed.

# CHANGE

I fought several times within the next four years, sometimes more than twice a week. I lost count of the number of opponents. I lost count at two-hundred and fifty. Wayne and Alex graduated me to battling against men too, progressing from smaller to bigger, weakest to strongest, slowest to fastest, and the worst to the best.

The matches became more brutal so Wayne was giving me a daily dose of his blood, just enough to heal my wounds. Before I entered the ring, he would give me another dose to keep me amped up. By the time I was done sparring, it was close to wearing off. It was never enough to fight Wayne if I had to.

I had nightmares too, ones that would wake me up in the middle of the night and keep me awake. I dreamt about the fights, about people changing into werewolves and attacking others.

I tried not to let the effects of killing get to me, but I swore I was losing my sanity. This wasn't a normal life for anyone, yet I accepted it. It was my life, whether I was here involuntarily or not.

I thought about my son a lot. I highly doubted they had kept him alive the entire time I was captured. I prayed every day I would see him or hear his voice but I never did. I also prayed for some memory recollection of him and again I never did. The thought of my son gave me something to fight for. There were many times I had debated on giving in and letting somebody take my life. I even tried to commit suicide by antagonizing Wayne, praying he would just kill me. Instead he fought his curse every time and would not.

My reality merged into my nightmares and my nightmares merged into my life.

§

One night, I laid on the cot in excruciating pain after a brutal match. My opponent had been large, and I had barely managed to take him out. Wayne had been insistent that I not take too much of his blood. There were concerns from the men who organized the fights that I might be under the influence of his life-force, so he backed off on the amount he gave me. Due to the severe pain I was in and some medication he had given me, I faded in and out of sleep. I had no clear understanding of what was real or not.

That night he had not given me any of his blood. He wanted my body to heal naturally. That was, until it happened.

I lay with my face to the cell wall, curled up under the covers as Alex and Wayne sat at the table in the break room. I was able to discern them under the low light.

"I need to back off, not give her as much or maybe even stop giving it to her," replied Wayne.

Alex whipped his head around, followed by a light scrape of the chair against the floor.

"What the hell are you thinking? As it is, you've been barely giving her anything. She's hurting, Wayne, and if you don't do something about it, you're going to get her killed." Irritation and frustration filled his voice.

"Granted, she's good, but I don't know how much longer she can keep going if you don't give her something."

Silence followed his comment. I closed my eyes.

"I'll think about it. Why don't you get out of here, Alex? Go get some rest. I'll stay here."

"Not a problem. I am tired. You," he said, "need to think about what I said, though. And, give her the real deal, Wayne. Stop mixing it in with drinks and shit. She might be bouncing off the walls for a few days, but it'll heal her."

"That's what I'm trying to avoid," Wayne stressed. His voice elevated. "I don't need the big guy coming down here and killing all of us, because she's high on wolf's blood!"

"If you give it to her now, she'll be good for her next fight in a few days. Don't cut her off though. You're going to hurt her. Do something, and do it now."

Wayne sighed. "Okay, I heard you. Now get the fuck out of here."

I detected irritation in his voice. Alex's footsteps faded out of the room. The pain in my muscles settled into my bones and joints. I groaned. At this point, I wish I did have some of his blood in me. Wayne turned the light off. I lay there in the dark, wishing I could sleep.

§

I swore I had been asleep for hours when he walked into my cell. My eyes shot open. About the time I went to get up, Wayne firmly pushed me back. He shot me a look of concern.

So, I slowly propped myself up, keeping an eye on him. Right now, was not the time to fight him. I was too weak and tired. "What do you want?"

"Listen to me," he said. One eyebrow raised up.

I nodded.

"Your body needs to heal." He sighed. "The only way it's going to get better is to drink my blood undiluted."

There was a moment of silence between us. Then I moved in closer to him and gently touched his hand. He was right, I needed his blood.

He glanced over at me, "There's one thing to consider..." He cleared his throat. "Your body is not used to the full blood so you may have a reaction to it. Let me help you to control it."

Our eyes met.

"I promise I won't hurt you."

I was hesitant, but it needed to be done. A knot formed in my throat.

"How are you going to help me control it?"

"By holding you," he answered. "Restraining you, so you don't hurt either of us." Compassion filled his eyes. "I've already seen what it can do to you when it's diluted. I'm concerned that your adrenaline might get the better of you which isn't a good thing."

I drew in a long deep breath and nodded.

"That's fine," I whispered.

Wayne bit into his wrist and then pumped his fist a few times. Blood oozed down his forearm.

Bile rose in my throat. I forced it back down.

Before he lowered his arm, I grabbed it and closed my eyes. It was time to get this over with. I licked up the blood from his forearm, wrapped my lips around his wound, and drank from him. The urge to vomit overwhelmed me. I gagged and pulled away.

But, not before he grabbed me and forced me to feed from him again. The liquid leaked from the corner of my mouth. It flowed down on to my chest.

"Drink it, Crystal," he demanded. "You know you need it."

He tightened his hold on me, his fist pressing against the back of my head.

The thick fluid coated the lining of my system. My body recognized the liquid, and this time it moved rapidly. It was a rush!

His breath was hot in my ear.

To try to slow down my reaction, I concentrated on his even breathing. The taste of his blood was disgusting.

It must have been the whole blood that sent me into convulsions. Wayne pushed me down on the cot and climbed atop me, pinning me down. He buried his nose in the nook of my neck and inhaled my scent. Though I tried to fight the tremors in my body, he told me to let go and let it happen. There was no stopping it.

My breath became short and erratic. Wayne locked his ankles around mine. He swept his tongue across my cheek and lapped up the blood that had spilled from my lips. His breath quickened.

Our eyes met. I swallowed hard, unsure of where this was going. His tongue slithered over my cheek again, only this time from my lips to my ear. His chest pounded against mine, his heart beating faster and stronger by the minute. I closed my eyes and pulled my head further back into the cot.

His lips brushed against my ear. I relinquished the side of my neck to him. His throat pulsated against it as his tongue snaked over my jaw line and back to my lips. I noticed he refrained from touching his lips to mine.

What was happening was not sexual, though I had an intense desire to have sex with him.

Wayne's tongue lapped over me again, raising the intensity inside me.

Instead of fighting him, I wrapped my hands around his head and pulled him into me, almost crushing his face into mine.

"Oh, Wayne," I moaned.

What the hell was I doing? Yet, I could feel it too. An unidentifiable emotion stirred within me. His breathing became heavy, and I recognized the rumble in his chest as a low growl. I moaned while his hands studied every inch of my body. The urge to bed him grew even stronger. But I told myself I could not give in. He continued to breathe in my scent, prowling on my territory.

Then he grabbed me around the hips and hoisted me onto his lap. I tried to stifle the moans but gasped in surprise when the hardness of his manhood pressed against me. The smell of his testosterone wafted up my nostrils, throwing my hormones into overdrive. I had to have him.

His fangs grazed my shoulder, and I winced. I curled into him, and buried my face in his neck, still leery of having sex with him. I pulled back. That was when our eyes met. I wanted his lips on mine. When I moved in closer, he turned his head, and pulled my face into his neck. I ran my tongue up the side of neck. His hardness pressed against me. He wanted me just as much.

I ran my hands down his chest and stomach, his muscles flinching against my touch. I kissed down to the hollow of his collarbone, unsnapping the button on his jeans. He pushed my hand away.

"No, we can't," he mumbled in my ear.

"You can't tell me you don't want me," I said, my lips against his chest.

I found the zipper on his jeans and slid it down.

He pushed my hand away again. "No, Crystal."

I ran my tongue up his neck and to his ear. "Look, I don't know the last time I had anything, but I can guarantee it's been awhile. Fuck me, Wayne."

He glanced at me. I moved in fast, my mouth enveloping his. He pushed me back.

"You don't understand…"

Frustrated, I pushed his arms away, and shoved him.

His eyes bore into mine.

When he tried to grab me, I shoved him again.

"No, obviously you don't understand. I need somebody to show some compassion towards me. I'm not asking for a fucking relationship with you." I jammed my finger into his chest a couple of times.

"Just give me something, anything…please." Gently, I touched his chest, and leaned into him. "All I ask is that you don't bite me."

He allowed me to push him back on the cot. But the moment he was down, he latched on and held me tight against him. I fought for him to release me, but he wouldn't let go.

I cried in his arms, wanting just one positive thing in my life regardless of what it was. Something other than this hellhole.

I lay lifeless in his embrace. Something stirred within me, and I felt it in him as well. Eventually, I fell asleep in his arms.

Sometime later in the evening, I awoke. When I turned over to face what I thought was him was instead a pillow pressed against my body. He was not there. The cell door remained shut and locked. No sound, no sight of him. I wasn't even sure if what had happened was real or not, though I swore it was. Even my body told me so because there was no more pain. I wrapped myself around the pillow. Something was missing from my previous life, even though I still couldn't remember what that had been.

The next day was a constant reminder that the feelings we both had the previous night was an illusion. Wayne displayed no feelings towards me, not even a hint of testosterone-based emotion. I remained confined within my shell, afraid to even mention it to him.

§

In the four years I had been here, I had lost about thirty pounds. When I wasn't sleeping, I was working out. I was becoming stronger, agile, more powerful, and more muscular. My belly fat was gone, flat, and well toned. The muscles in my legs and arms had expanded another couple of inches while my hips, waist, back and chest had decreased several inches, accentuating my figure.

During this time, I had learned nothing new about my son. Every time I asked to speak with him or see him, they wouldn't let me. They wouldn't tell me anything about him. I was beginning to think my son didn't really exist, that it was a lie to keep me here and keep me fighting. I pushed, prodded, and pried, but when I became too persistent, they left me alone. I hoped that if my son did exist that he was still alive, healthy, and taken care of. I still had my doubts about his existence.

After the four years I had been in the circuit, they scheduled my fight with Kara, one of the most elite and prominent fighters. She was apparently the best and biggest female fighter out there. Wayne and Alex had tried several times to arrange a fight with her but her manager would only schedule her with the best contenders. I finally made that list, so Wayne scheduled the fight.

I was told she was a professional cage fighter in the mortal world, but that she preferred underground fighting. I was eager to take her on. The day of the fight, I trained extensively. I pushed myself to go longer with the cardio, and I added more weight in my strength training.

The heavy bass and hard music pumped me up as I entered the arena. I threw my arms in the air to get my fans riled up. In the darkness, the crowd rose to their feet.

After the commentator announced Kara, the crowd chanted her name. Kara entered the arena. I had to admit, I stood in awe of the woman. She was at least a foot taller than me and exceptionally muscular. I looked like a midget compared to her. Her hair was straight, black, and shoulder length. She looked like she might have been on steroids.

I would have to get the upper hand early in the fight, then go low and take her down. As Kara and I faced off, our fans screamed.

Kara threw the first punch which I was able to dodge. I sidestepped her and caught her in the rib.

She groaned and doubled over.

I moved in, grabbed her by her hair and brought my knee up into her face.

That was when she wrapped her arms around me, and tried to take me to the ground.

Instead, I ran into the wall behind me. An uppercut rocked my head back, banging it against the wall. I groaned. I took a shot to the stomach before I was able to get her off of me.

While we fought, the fans slammed each other against the bars. The commentator made the announcement for the fight to stop. We glanced up at him.

Recognizing it was for the fans to stop, we returned to our business. I rushed her, going low for the legs, and slammed her into the barrier. Even though she struck the concrete wall, she was still able to elbow me in the middle of the back.

I yelped in pain. The riot started above us again. A corpse struck the bars. The snarls and growls escalated, catching our attention as they echoed throughout the arena. Kara and I glanced at each other and then at the chaos above. The bars had been bent.

Kara stood near the barrier, trying to focus in on the crowd. Blood poured out from the bars, drenching her from head to toe. She stared at me, wide-eyed, as if she knew the inevitable. My mouth fell open. Fear set deep inside me, and from this point on everything seemed to happen in slow motion.

Kara stood frozen in place. The bars moaned beneath the massive weight, continuing to bend in multiple areas behind the steel barrier. Fearful that the bars were going to split wide open, I took a couple of steps back, ready to run.

The bars exploded throughout the arena. I threw myself to the ground and covered my head. Steel echoed off of concrete walls, rebounding around me. Two of the bars struck me in the legs. They were heavy, but not heavy enough to seriously injure me.

I glanced behind me at Kara, who had fallen to the ground with a male corpse atop her. It had been torn to shreds. I gasped in horror. Blood soaked the dirt surrounding her and the body.

She barely managed to get the man off of her and stand up when several fans jumped into the arena. I pulled myself up, watching them circle Kara. Covered in blood and guts, she gave me the look which I recognized as defeat.

She was defenseless against the lot of them.

I took one step toward them, and then halted in terror. She was shredded within seconds. They devoured her, some still feeding off of her while she fell to the ground. More fans followed the others into the pit, coming towards me. Their lips curled back, revealing their elongated fangs.

I backed up, recognizing the difference between their fangs and Wayne's. At first I thought they were werewolves too, but their flesh was white and their eyes darker.

Then I made the connection: they were vampires.

I turned and ran straight for the open concrete door behind me, my heart pounding in my chest. I never ran so fast in my life.

Wayne stood just on the inside of the gate and yelled at me to hurry. There was no sign of Alex. My guess was that he had booked it, for he was mortal like me. He needed time advantage.

Something grazed my back. I screamed. The tiny hairs on my neck stood up. I was no match for these creatures. They were closing in on me. Wayne lurched forward and pulled me to safety behind the wall, gate, and door.

Some of the vampires got stuck in the small room that barricaded the corridor from the main arena. This didn't stop them, though. They tore through the door, blowing it apart. Pieces of it flew in all directions, striking us and the walls. We ran down the corridor.

Vampires shrieked behind us, followed by unhinged metal and something heavy rebounding against the wall. Wayne and I had already passed the commentator and were coming up fast behind Alex.

The commentator screamed. I presumed the heavy object had been the door to his small office. Blood sprayed the wall next to me.

Wayne let go of me and pressed me onward, before transforming into his alternate form.

Two of the vampires jumped him while he was still in mid-transformation. He slammed them into the walls.

I screamed. He received several bites before he fully transformed. His massive body took up most of the corridor, blocking us from all of the vampires except one. I ran through the door to our right, after Alex. The one vampire who was now amongst us jumped Alex just on the other side of the door.

Alex swung the door shut and fought back. He was thrown to the ground, the vampire atop him. I jumped on the vampire's back, wrapping my arm around its neck. The door broke into pieces around us. Wayne stormed in, still in wolf form, and bared his teeth. The creature threw me off of its back. I struck the wall behind me, my head rebounding off of it. The vampire glared at me. I thought for sure I was dead.

Wayne ran full stride at the vampire. His claws echoed off the concrete floor and drove him into a wall. Alex jumped to his feet, threw open another door, and pushed me into the dark room. Screams and other noises which I associated with being mauled escalated in the room behind us.

As we ran into the room, Alex flipped on the light switch. Wayne mutated into his human form and ran into the room after us. He slammed the door shut, separating us from the vampires.

The back of the door was made of metal and had several locks, chains and various other deadbolts. Alex moved in front of it, sliding and locking everything on the door before he glanced around.

"Is there an exit in here?"

I too, glanced about. There was no exit. We were trapped in a room with no windows and no doors. My mouth fell open. Wayne stood before me naked, blood dripping from his flesh.

"What the hell are we going to do?" I screamed.

Wayne tore the room apart, moving boxes and a desk away from one wall. The door bent under the weight of the vampires on the other side.

There was no stopping them. I stood defenseless next to Wayne. He ripped out a screwed on metal sheet from a large, dog size vent in the room.

"What the hell was that all about, anyway?" I folded my arms across my chest and stared at him.

"Vampires and werewolves place bets on the human underground fighting circuit. That's part of their entertainment. You're one of us. One of the werewolves' fighters. The vampires have their own fighters. Humans, of course." He looked at me.

"Now you know why we can't have you bleeding in the ring. The blood attracts the vampires, makes them want to fight and kill. Most of the werewolves can control themselves. Older vampires have learned to do this too, but the fighting circuit attracts most of the younger crowd. Needless to say, they don't know how to control themselves as much."

The door started to bulge in. I glanced about, looking for some sort of a weapon. There were miscellaneous boxes, books, papers and other office material. I rummaged through a box, and found nothing but papers. I moved on to another box.

"Wayne, you need to hurry up," said Alex. "We don't have time for explanations right now."

They exchanged looks. Both men had a look of concern on their face. This wasn't good.

I stared back at him. This was the end for me. I put my hands on my hips and paced the floor.

Wayne stepped in front of me and gripped my shoulders. "Listen to me carefully. You go through this vent. Go towards the top. Do not go towards the bottom. If we don't follow you, you keep going. Get the hell out of here."

I nodded my head. The screech of nails raked against the outside of the door. It bulged in further.

"Your son's name is Robert Bouchard. He's twenty-two and was born June twentieth, nineteen eighty-nine. If we lose contact, good luck," said Wayne.

He started to turn away, and then grabbed my shoulders again. "Stay on top of your training. You may still need it. Also, try to locate a man named Tristan Ayers, if you can. The werewolf community knows who he is. He's a hard man to find, but he'll help you and so will they."

The door caved in even more. The sound hurt my ears. I crawled into the vent, and then turned toward him.

"Wayne?" I was scared to be alone right now. Tears welled over my eyes.

"You need to go," he demanded.

"Why? Why me?"

He whispered in my ear, "Just find Robert. You need to be with him, now. I know you can find him."

"Seriously, Wayne! We don't have time for this shit!" screamed Alex.

Wayne turned toward Alex, "I know, Alex. Give me a fucking second."

"Is this going to be a sentimental fucking thing or what? She's just a goddamn…"

One of the vampires hit the door.

"Fuck, Wayne! Let's get this done!"

I reached out and grabbed his hand, "Come with me. What are you two going to do? Are you going to die in this hell hole? I don't want to be alone. I'm scared. I don't know where to go or what to do. I don't know how to find my son. And, why me? Why did you choose me?"

"Get out of here now, while you can." Gently, he tapped my cheek.

Wayne started to shove the metal cover back in place.

"Wayne?" I pushed against the metal cover but he continued to force it back into place.

"Answer my fucking question. Why me?" I beat against it, trying to get his attention but he ignored me.

"Wayne, please?" I begged.

"Stop, Crystal. You're going to get the vampires attention. They'll come after you. Go now."

The desk scraped across the floor as he shoved it in front of the vent. The deafening noise of the door caving in forced me to push farther away from the vent cover. Horrific sounds came from the other side. Someone was being mauled! I clamped my hand over my mouth. A new voice entered the room.

I backed away from the vent. I was on my own now. I decided it was best to carry on. Wayne had protected me, had put his life on the line for me. I wondered why.

As I made my way through the dark vent tunnel, I repeated my son's name and birth date to deposit it in my memory. I had a new mission: locate my son.

It was dark; only once in a while I would get a little light. Occasionally, hip hop music filtered in from somewhere within the building.

I followed the tunnel of the venting system. Some of the curves would lead me downward. There were a few times I had to backtrack in order to find the tunnels that led upward.

I kept an ear and an eye out for anybody who might be following me, but so far no one seemed to be. The metal of the tunnel walls was cool on my hands and arms. I tried to keep quiet because sound echoed through the venting system.

Then I came upon an upward curve, one that actually had steps. I proceeded along to a metal door, put my ear to it and listened. Silence.

I pushed the door open and peered beyond into the darkness of the night. I tried to get a visual before opening it completely. Fresh cool air wafted in, bringing with it the smell of grass, weeds, trees, and flowers. Oh my God, my sense of smell was overwhelming. Wayne's blood still flowed inside of me.

I opened the door farther, pulling myself out of the vent. A breeze swept through the air and brushed back my hair. It was like fingers caressing my flesh. I stood still and basked in it.

I took in a deep breath, the scent of the earth overpowering my senses. I wanted to lie down on the ground and kiss it, inhale and breathe mother earth. Another scent drifted through the air to the right of me. It was inhuman, deathly. It was time to leave.

I didn't know where I was going, but instinct told me to go to my left, so I followed it. I ran towards a group of trees and glanced over my shoulder from time to time. Once beyond the trees, I crouched behind them and scanned the area. The building I had exited was a bar with several cars parked in front and to the left of it. The customers would be entering from the opposite side, so I wasn't at risk of being seen.

A man emerged from the bar. He appeared to be looking for someone. I pressed against the tree in front of me, keeping my eye on him.

He was dressed in dark clothes and his pale skin clashed with the dark forest beyond him. He didn't look familiar and it was apparent he hadn't seen me.

He stood there for a while, surveying his surroundings.

I glanced around. There were no other buildings nearby.

Great, I was in nowhere land. I had no clue where to go or which direction to head. The man went back into the bar. I let out a deep breath. It was time to leave this place and move onward.

I turned, fell into a ditch about five feet deep and landed in muddy water, face first. Shit. I pushed myself up on my hands and knees and glared down at the water, cursing myself for not being more careful.

I attempted to stand when a foot slammed into my back, throwing me down to the earth. I ate mud. Groaning, I spit it out. It left a nasty taste. Ugh. This time when I tried to stand, I prepared for the worst. When his foot connected with my back again, I retaliated. As soon as I hit the ground, I turned, and brought my right arm backwards. I hooked it around his ankle, knocking him off balance.

At the same time he fell, I leapt to my feet and landed on his chest. He bolted upright, scaring the shit out of me. Fangs bared, he grabbed me by my head, and pulled me towards him. His pale skin was cold. His blonde hair was messy and his dark eyes intense. He glared at me. I shoved my arms outward and braced my hands against his throat, locking my elbows so he couldn't pull me in.

His grip tightened as we struggled against each other. The pressure in my head was horrendous. Then I realized he was trying to crush it. Fuck! I remembered I still had some of Wayne's blood in me. I wasn't sure if I could actually kill the vampire, but it was worth the risk.

I leaned my head in, his face closer to my neck. His mouth opened wide. As I let go of his neck, I shoved my fist straight into his mouth, breaking one of his fangs. My fist continued straight through to the back of his mouth, almost down his throat. His eyes widened in surprise and his mouth locked open. Almost half my forearm was down his throat. I had hoped that I was able to disengage his jaw to the point it couldn't shut. I pulled my arm out and stared down at him.

He clutched his jaw, trying to fix it. His face was hideous, like some deformed creature from an old horror movie. His mouth was abnormally large, stretched out into a grotesque grin. His dark eyes were wide and confused.

I found a thick branch nearby and went after him. About the same time he was able to shut his jaw, I stood over him, branch in hand. I drove the branch straight through his heart. He shrieked and writhed in the mud, his body decomposing down to ash. I was mortified. I wished I had still been one of these mortals who didn't know vampires and werewolves existed.

Worried that there were more vampires around, I gazed up at the dirt walls. I was waiting for more to jump me. As I deliberated about climbing the mound of dirt, I realized it was impossible. Besides, as a tactical advantage, maybe I should stay in it. I decided to follow the ditch to a lower point where I could get out of it. So, I continued onward, away from the bar.

There was no telling how many of those things were inside the building and I wasn't sure if I could enter it without somebody recognizing me and coming after me.

As I walked on through the ditch, the wind picked up. I wrapped my arms around my chest, trying to keep warm. Overhead, clouds rolled in from the mountains. They covered the moon, bringing in the sweet smell of rain. Although I would normally take pleasure in it, this was not the time. I would be stranded here in the middle of nowhere, drenched, hungry, and cold.

The ditch came to an end. At this point, I was able to climb the lower walls onto the side of the road. Glancing around, I surveyed my surroundings. I had lost sight of the bar. Though I almost regretted leaving the bar behind, it was my only chance for survival. So I continued along the side of the road.

The wind became more forceful, blowing my hair across my face. I gazed into the distance. I had walked much farther into the woods. So, I stopped, and looked back in the direction I had come from again. I wasn't sure if this was a good idea or not. I was getting worried now.

The tall trees loomed over me, threatening me with their density and massiveness.

Then the rain started. I eyed the paved road next to me.

Then something slammed into me, throwing me halfway across the road. I flipped several times across it before I went down, face first, onto the asphalt. Road burn raged through my skin. What the...?

I stood and, before I caught sight of what it was, it hit me again. It was very large and its heaviness rested on my back. Pain seared through my side. I wanted to turn around, but I was afraid to.

Howling bellowed through the forest. It was a little too close for comfort. The moment I started to push off of the ground, its hot breath brushed my hair. I halted. It snorted, blowing my hair into my face. A low growl echoed in my ear. I lay motionless, not knowing what to do. Wayne's blood had already worn off, so I was no match for a fully transformed werewolf.

Saliva dripped onto my neck. I cringed, trying to keep as still as possible. His gaping jaws lowered near my neck. A low rumble came from the near distance in the direction of the bar. I was thankful for the car that loomed around the curve in the road, but as it bore down on us, I became leery it wasn't going to stop. It was traveling much too fast.

The car came to a screeching halt, turning at the last minute and narrowly missing us. The werewolf bounded into the forest. I threw my arms over my head, curled into a fetal position, and squeezed my eyes shut. Doors flew open, and footsteps approached.

"Hey, you alright, lady?" asked a male voice.

I was sure they were from the bar. I worried about showing my face, unsure of whom they really were.

Then another male voice boomed in the night, "Is she alright?"

"I don't know," replied the first male.

One of the men grabbed my shoulder and flipped me onto my back. Four men stared down at me. I was thankful nobody looked familiar, but I was worried about who would recognize me.

With their faces partially hidden in the darkness, I allowed them to help me up. My muscles tensed. I was ready to fight, if I had to. Their massive bodies filled the space around us.

If I had more of Wayne's blood in me, I would have no problem taking them on, but without it, I was worthless.

A pain shot through my side. I bent over in agony.

One of the men said, "She's hurt. It looks like the wolf scratched her up pretty good."

The man in back spoke up. "Get her in the car. She needs medical attention."

I glanced up. His eyes glistened in the dark and his dark skin blended into the night. He grinned, revealing his white teeth.

§

I sensed a presence. My eyes shot open but it was too dark to see anything. Something beastly and masculine lingered in the room. My body was drained and lifeless. I closed my eyes again, afraid what I might see. I had no fight.

Then it touched me. Its finger traced an invisible line on my back. An icy chill ran through my spine. I cringed, my breath caught in my throat. The finger continued in a curvy and extensive design.

He withdrew his hand and rested it on the back of my head, his breath in my ear.

"Get some sleep, you need your rest," he whispered. Sleep overtook me again.

# THE DRAGON

From somewhere within the house, country music played. The song, Rough and Ready by Trace Adkins filtered into my room and penetrated my dreams. It was a familiar song. One that I relayed with an encounter prior to my kidnapping.

Visions of fights, blood and music flooded from my subconscious. It set off some sort of a mental button that restored part of my memory.

My husband and I walked into a bar with another couple on a cold rainy night. Rough and Ready played over the loud speakers. The song would become an omen to me. We were celebrating someone's birthday on a weekend trip to Payson, Arizona. The four of us were going to stay in a cabin that we owned.

Somebody in our group had heard about a bar on the outskirts of town, so we decided to meet up there. It was known to bring in a lot of out-of-towners.

I glanced around.

Animal heads lined the walls: deer, elk, and bear. The walls and floor were wooden, and the floor was also covered in sawdust. It appeared to be an ordinary country bar to me.

I moved with the music as we walked past the bar and into another area where female strippers danced on a stage. They were decked out, complete with cowboy hats, thongs, and chaps. I couldn't care less about them. We were out for the weekend, and we were going to have a good time. It didn't help that I'd left the restaurant with a few beers in my system already.

We found a table and were promptly served by a nearby waitress. We laughed and joked amongst ourselves while she tended to our drinks.

The stage was dimly lit. The dancers' hats and flying hair hid their faces as they gyrated against the floor, the poles, or other bar patrons.

While we talked, Ashley's husband, Abel leaned over, kissed her, and stuck a bill in her blouse. She laughed and kissed him back.

A stripper approached her, and gyrating her hips, danced for Ashley. The dancers' breasts moved before her face. Ashley blushed and laughing, glanced at me. I turned my attention back to my husband, who held a bill in the air, waving another stripper over for Abel. The dancers moved with the music. My husband's face lit up with amusement. I laughed at their goofiness. I reached over and squeezed his hand, glad just to get away from the everyday stress.

He squeezed back, then grabbed his beer and chugged it. I took a swallow of mine and leaned my face in towards him. Just when I went to kiss him, the stripper who was dancing for Abel came over and grabbed my husband's face. She pulled him away from me and leaned into him.

I peered up at her blonde head, the cowboy hat tilted on it. Her body and hips gyrated to the beat of the music. Her hips moved within inches of his face. I straightened up.

With a huge smile, he winked at Abel. I wished we hadn't come here.

To the left of me, two women stared in surprise at what had just happened. I was embarrassed and pissed at the same time. The stripper had some nerve. I hadn't come here to watch my man get hit on. I had come here to have fun. The temperature rose in my cheeks. I faked a smile. I glanced back at my man. The blonde shook her butt.

Oh, boy, I wasn't sure if I was going to make it through this. I told myself it was all in good fun, no need to get jealous or upset.

I stood up and headed for the bathroom to calm my nerves. Inside the restroom, I weaved in between the women who scrambled for the mirror. While I contemplated dragging him out of here, I worked my way through to the stall. Maybe we could hit up another bar where there weren't any strippers.

I left the stall and wound my way to the sink through patrons and strippers refreshing their makeup. As I washed and dried my hands, I eyed some of the strippers.

They were gorgeous, but their skin looked really pale. I left the room. Behind me, a scuffle broke out between some of the women who tried to get mirror time.

I strode down the hallway and back into the strippers' lounge. New dancers gyrated on the stage. I moved past them. My female audience had disappeared. Ashley's seat was empty, too.

Two dancers shook their asses on our husbands' laps. In the blonde's place was now a redhead. I rolled my eyes and headed for my seat. I stopped short. The blonde stripper was sitting there. She whispered something in my husband's ear, and he grinned like the Cheshire cat.

This wasn't playing well with me now. If she needed to take a break or something, then she needed to get away from him and find somebody else to bug, preferably a single man.

I wondered where Ashley was. I figured if I could grab her, then we could talk the guys into going to a different place. I scanned the bar looking for her. She wasn't there, so I assumed she must have been in the bathroom.

The big cowboy bartender glanced at me and then back at my husband. He frowned. By the look on his face, he appeared to expect trouble, most likely from me or possibly, the dancer. I didn't like that sign. I continued towards my husband when the blonde noticed I was coming. Leisurely she stood up, making a show of joining the redhead on his lap. Her leather chaps surrounded her long, lean legs. The blonde kept her eye on me, smiling. Straddling his free leg, she sat down. Both ladies rubbed against him, as though they were riding a mechanical bull.

The music switched over. A female voice belted out, "Let's Go Girls."

How about not? My blood boiled. Adrenaline pushed through my alcohol-infused blood.

When I approached, both women rubbed against his chest, his neck, and then his face. Then the women began groping each other. I stomped up behind him and jerked his head back by his hair.

"Ow," he groaned, his eyes widening. He peered up at me, his head extended over the back of the chair.

"You surprised to see me?" I asked. I glared at the blonde. She smiled. I shifted my gaze to him. His Adams apple bobbed up and down.

Yeah, I'd caught him off guard.

"Hi honey." He brought his hands up in a questioning gesture.

"I want to go," I said, staring fiercely at him. I crossed my arms in front of my chest.

"Well, hold on, honey. Abel paid for the lap dance, so I'd hate to waste his money."

I was shocked at his attitude about the whole incident.

"Yeah, I bet." I looked up at the strippers.

The redhead stood and went back to Abel. He had no money in his hands, so I knew the lap dance wasn't paid for. The blonde continued to sit on my husband's lap.

"Hey, why don't you give the rest of the dance to my wife?" he asked her.

A smirk crossed her face. She stood, and a huge smile spread out on his.

"Cute. I'm not interested," I said.

She walked around him and came towards me.

I put my hand up as a warning to back off.

"Look, bitch, I'm not interested. I just told you that, so go away."

I started to walk around her. She stepped in my path. She took off her hat and put it on my head, her dark eyes gleaming with delight. I glanced around the bar. The others were watching us, as if we were the show. The bartender chuckled. I started to remove the hat when I observed that my husband continued to lie with his head back, smiling at us.

"Are you enjoying this, asshole?" I asked him.

I caught a glimpse of Abel, who sat drunk and motionless in his chair. He had that same damn look on his face. The redhead buried her head in his neck, her body moving against him in rhythm with the music. My eyes fixed on the empty seat where my girlfriend had sat, and I wondered again where she was. It didn't take this long to go to the bathroom.

I decided it was time to grab the guys, find her, and get the hell out of here.

"Babe, let's go," I said, turning my attention back to my husband.

The blonde was on his lap again, her face buried in his shoulder.

"Look, bitch, get off him."

I walked around to the front of him, which was the back of her, and jerked her hair. She didn't even flinch. Her head remained tight to his neck.

What the hell?

I grabbed her by her hair and pulled back. The sound of ripped flesh echoed in my ears. Blood flowed from his mouth. A gurgle escaped his lips. The woman turned and hissed. Blood covered her face, and leaked down her chest. Her eyes were dark. My gaze shifted to my husband. Blood gushed down his neck and chest.

"What the…" I let go of her and pushed her off him. She fell to the floor, blood oozing from her mouth and down her breasts.

"Honey…"

I leaned in closer and examined the bite mark. Muscles and skin were shredded and torn away. I recoiled from him, tears welling up in my eyes. A knot stuck in my throat.

"Oh my God," I muttered.

Someone shifted to the right of me. I peered at her from the corner of my eye and caught sight of her on her knees, her head eerily and slowly looking up at me. Her lips curled back into a sneer, revealing fangs. Blood doused her face, neck, and bare chest. I stared into her eyes and recognized what she truly was -- a vampire.

"Jesus," I whispered.

I reached behind me, searching for Abel. My fingers located his arm so I latched on. Wait…it was smooth and cold. I spun around and faced the redhead who was still on his lap, feeding from him. I wound in between the chairs, backing away from them. The redhead threw her head backwards. Blood streaked the air and splattered onto everything in its wake. Her face was covered with Abel's blood. She hissed at me.

The blonde stood up, a menacing smile looming on her face. She came towards me, her eyes dark and fixated. The redhead brought her legs up onto Abel's chest, ready to lunge for the next victim. I didn't want to move. I was afraid they were going to attack me. A figure to the left of them tried to sneak by. The wooden floor beneath him creaked as he took his next step. Both women turned and lunged at him.

I surveyed the room. Several of the strippers fed on the patrons on both the floor and in their chairs. They thrashed around, eventually losing the battle. Those that were alive screamed. Some tried to fight back, and others ran for their lives. One stripper still danced onstage and gyrated against the bloody pole. Blood coated most everything in the bar. It looked like a slaughterhouse.

I stifled a scream. I bolted past the chairs and to the front door. The strippers continued to feed on the men who had been waiting for the next dance. I darted past the bar, keeping my eye on the bartender. His fangs protruded between his lips, and he sneered at me while he dried a glass in his hands.

Ah, shit. I ran as fast as I could. Some men were able to escape with their lives but once I neared the door, crowds of men blocked it as they fought to leave. I stopped and looked around for an alternate way out. The blonde approached. I glanced to the right. A large patio window overlooked the outside eating area.

I turned to grab a chair and throw it through the plate glass window. The blonde lurched at me, tackling me into the men who barricaded the door. I fell, knocking several men off their feet. Lucky for me, it blocked access to me, but not for them. I struggled to push them off of me. Their weight nearly crushed my chest, and made it difficult to breathe. Their bodies were flung from mine. They crashed into the bar, tables, and chairs behind the blonde. She grabbed me by my shirt and pulled me into her. A pool cue struck her on the right back side of her head. She let go of me and grabbed it from one of the patron's hands. Before he had a chance to defend himself, she snapped it in half and buried it in his chest.

Shit, this wasn't good.

I turned and grabbed another stick from the stand behind her and struck her on the left side of her face. A pool ball whizzed past us and smashed into the wall. She snapped her head around. She started to go after him when I struck her in the ribs with the stick. It didn't faze her. She stopped, and turned toward me. The moment her hand came up to snatch my cue, the man swung his. The hiss of air caught her attention. She spun, grabbed his, broke it and threw it to the floor. He ran off. Snarling, she pursued him.

I dropped the unbroken pool cue and grabbed the broken two. Since they were shorter, I figured it would be easier to fight the vampires off with them as compared to a longer stick. Somebody jumped on my back. Feminine hands wrapped around my neck. I threw myself backwards onto the ground, landing on my attacker, and then head butted her in the face. A crunch of bone sounded in my ear as I managed to swivel out of her grip. I turned and shoved one knee into her ribs. She lunged, her hands on my neck. With all my strength, I drove one of the sticks straight down into her heart. Blood spewed over us. I recoiled and stared at her in disbelief. Blood drenched us.

She gave in to eternal damnation, leaving ashes, dust, and skeletal remains. Eventually, her bones turned to dust.

Dying moans filled my ears, leaving vacant bodies to fill the room. I looked around and thought about the man who was chased down by the blonde. Where had he gone? And, where was Ashley? I walked around to the back side of the bar, and clasped my hand over my mouth. The man lay bleeding on the floor, his neck awkwardly wrong. I tiptoed around him and tried to avoid stepping in the pool of blood.

The screams and chaos of the mass attack had died down. Cautiously, I proceeded onward, surveying my surroundings. The vampires were gone.

I followed the hallway to my left that led to the bathrooms. It was dark. Water dripped from the faucet and the smell of blood permeated the air as I neared the women's restroom. I pushed at the door, but it barely opened. Bodies lay crumpled on the floor behind it.

I peeked in and looked around. Ashley wasn't in there. I let the door shut, and proceeded to the men's restroom, listening for movement behind me. The door at the end of the hall was open. Keeping my eye on it, I pushed the men's door open and peered in. I gasped. Ashley lay spread out on the floor, blood soaked into her clothes. Tears formed at the corners of my eyes, but this was not the time.

I stifled my emotions and looked behind me into the darkness of the bar. No sound. No movement. I proceeded toward Ashley. I wanted to touch her, to make her better, but I knew I couldn't. She was gone.

Tears escaped my eyes, but I bit back the sounds of crying. I covered my mouth with my hand. Time did not allow me to weep for her and my husband. I wiped at my eyes.

"Get the hell out of here," said the little voice inside. "Just get the hell out of here."

I backed up into the hallway and gazed down at both the bar and the back door, which were opposite each other.

That little voice spoke up again, "Go outside. Leave, now!" I neared the back door, but sounds of a struggle issued just beyond it.

I turned and headed back down the hallway. Though I tried to avoid stepping on the blood caked floor, I found it near impossible.

I kept my eyes open for the blonde. I detected no sign of her even though I knew she was nearby and waiting for me. I glanced in the bar area. Nobody was there. The smell of alcohol from broken bottles mixed with blood wafted into the air. I traipsed around the back of the bar again. The bar was dark; several of the hanging lights had been broken. Something caught my eye in the reflection of the plate glass window. I couldn't quite figure out what it was until I moved in closer.

Behind me, a Budweiser light hung from the ceiling above the pool table. The blonde had hidden atop the Budweiser light. I turned just in time to see her come out of her hiding place. She had been watching me from my reflection in the plate glass window the whole time.

She hit me hard and drove us both backwards through the window. Shards of glass rained down. We crashed onto one of the tables on the outside deck. When the table broke beneath us, glass penetrated our flesh. We fell to the ground and rolled into a large, clay pot, shattering it. I scrambled to my feet. Voices filled the air around us.

Both of the bartenders, some of the strippers, and some of the patrons stood nearby talking. I didn't quite understand what was going on until the blonde bolted to her feet and came after me again. Bets were placed on who was going to win the fight. I turned. Her fist connected with my jaw and dropped me to the muddy ground. I struggled to my feet. She jerked me by my hair to pull me onto my knees, my head and neck extended backwards. Rain washed over my face and body.

With my hair and the rain in my eyes, I was barely able to see her. She let go and punched me in the face again. I dropped to my side and stared up at the full moon, aware that we had visitors. The presence of something evil and monstrous neared us, raising the hairs on the back of my neck.

I braced my hands on the ground, pushing myself up on all fours. Snarls and growls broke the air. She hunkered down behind me, ready to attack. I raised my head. Werewolves surrounded us. They hunkered down, their hair standing on end. Their claws dug into the earth. They were also ready for battle.

I froze, afraid to move. I wasn't sure if they were all going to slaughter me. The vampires moved in closer behind me.

Great, I was done. Drop the casket and bury me now. If I was going to go die, I might as well go fighting. The blonde growled behind me, and the werewolves in front of me snarled. I was ready for action and ready to be killed. She stayed hunkered, staring the wolves down, her head about a foot above me. I kicked straight back into her face and rolled onto my back, driving my left foot into it when she came at me again. She recoiled for a split second and snapped her mouth at me, her fangs glistening in the moonlight. I brought my legs in and kicked out, striking her in the chest. She flew backwards into the roof of the bar, sliding down the awning. Her angered cries echoed in the night as she plummeted to the ground.

How the hell did I do that? I might have been practicing martial arts for twelve years but I didn't have that much strength. I glanced at the other vampires, who backed away from me.

"How the…" I began.

My gaze shifted to the others. They were staring at my arm. I looked down. Two puncture holes formed the vampire bite in my skin.

I could only guess it happened when the redhead attacked me. The other vampires backed off. Didn't vampires turn humans by biting them? She must have made me more powerful. I smiled.

I turned and looked back at the werewolves who remained several feet behind me, watching. They stood their ground, but didn't attack. The bushes near the bar rustled.

Hissing, the blonde bolted to her feet, teeth bared, ready to kill.

Faster than any mortal, I ran straight at her and tackled her, taking her down backwards into the wall of the bar, collapsing the part below the awning. The pillar still stood, but barely held the awning in place. We tumbled inside the building with some of the debris. She wrapped her hands in my shirt, her mouth closing in on my neck. I tried to pull away.

Oh, hell, no.

She rolled atop me, her mouth almost on my throat. I forced my right forearm in between my neck and hers, trying to put distance between us. My other hand sought out her hair and wrenched her head backwards. I drove my right fist into her throat several times before she let go of me.

Her hands found my throat. I wrapped my legs around her body and used all my strength to force her onto her back.

We fought, each trying to get the upper hand. A siren wailed in the distance. During our struggle, she somehow managed to twist around on to her stomach. I figured by the time law enforcement arrived, the beasts would probably be gone, and the hell if I was going to jail. I was getting out of here, one way or another. I grabbed her by the neck, forcing her head backwards.

Staring down into her face, I locked one hand around the bottom of her mouth and the other around the top. Her fangs gouged my hands as I fought to wrench her mouth open and back, disengaging the lower jaw from the upper. I remained straddled over her back. The crack of bone vibrated through my palms. Her eyes widened in horror.

My adrenaline pumped harder. Unfortunately, this alone was not going to take her out. I jerked her head back more and used all my force and momentum to snap her neck. Her body went limp beneath mine. Breathing hard, I sat up and stared out the window at the vampires and werewolves who stared back at me. I started to stand up. She trembled beneath me.

"Fuck!"

I reached out and grabbed one of the cue stick halves I'd dropped earlier and drove it into her heart through her back. Smoke billowed out from her body which disintegrated into dust and ash. My own body writhed in disgust. I stood.

The others were still in close proximity. I grabbed what large wooden debris I could and exited through the window. I scanned my surroundings, watching the vampires and the werewolves. I looked for the easiest exit I could find. The vampires were at my right, the werewolves in front of me, and part of the bar blocked an escape to my left. I was apprehensive of my actual escape plan. Everyone was going to be on top of me. I walked towards the werewolves, past the patio. As they backed off, they kept their gaze on me. I averted locking eyes with the vampires. Their teeth gleamed in the moonlight. I glanced in the direction of the werewolves, walking backwards to my left beyond the bar. They had vanished, their existence unknown to man.

A pair of hands grabbed me and threw me into the wall of the building. A forearm pressed hard into my upper back, forcing a groan out of me. Something ripped from beneath my skin, sending a horrid pain through my shoulder. Warm blood dripped down, coating my skin. I succumbed to the agony, my body weakening while he held me against the wall. I hissed through my teeth, tears escaping my eyes.

Then his hands were all over my body, searching. Somebody had called the police, and here they were searching me for weapons. Oh, this was a joke.

I struggled to turn my head in the direction of the vampires, wondering when they were going to attack. He grabbed me and threw me against the side of the county police car. My face was pressed against the cold, wet metal.

I struggled to get a better view of the vampires but they had disappeared. I wanted to cry.

"Deputy –"

"Shut up."

"But –"

"I said to shut up," he demanded.

I swallowed hard, wishing this was all a dream. I closed my eyes. The metal shackles closed on my wrists. Maybe I would wake up in the morning on my cool sheets.

He grabbed me by my cuffed wrists and the back of my neck, pulling me up. I hung my head low, hair sticking to my left cheek. I was going to hell. The car door opened. He started to shuffle me in, but I tried to turn around to warn him about the vampires.

He slammed me back into the side of the car.

"That's resisting arrest. Do you want to go for another count?" he whispered in my ear.

"No, but there's –"

"There's what?" he asked, sarcasm heavy in his voice.

"There are vampires…"

"Vampires? Oh, that's good."

"And werewolves…"

"Uh huh."

"No, Deputy, there really are…" I started.

Rain came down harder, drenching me. He turned me around, but the rain obstructed my view of his face. The Deputy grabbed my chin, forcing me to look at him.

"I don't think you really believe in vampires and werewolves, now do you?"

Our eyes met. His were a captivating blue, exquisitely beautiful. As he stared into mine, he moved in closer.

"Do you?" he whispered.

I tried to look away, but his gaze was hypnotic and mesmerizing. His voice penetrated my brain. Again, he asked if I really believed in the Gothic creatures. I tried to close my eyes, to break the trance he seemed to have on me, but could not.

"No," I answered.

"I didn't think you did," he whispered in my ear.

He shuffled me into the backseat of the patrol car and drove off. When we finally stopped, he helped me out the door. I glanced at the wooden building and the forest that surrounded it. A section of the building was dilapidated yet music filtered out from somewhere else within the structure.

The Deputy grabbed my arm and led me to the side of the building. The roof overhang was short. It was barely enough to keep us dry.

I peered up at him while he removed my handcuffs.

"Once you're inside, you'll go to sleep and you won't remember anything before you wake up again," he said. "Do you understand?"

"Yes." He was in control of my mind.

"In time, you'll remember everything on your own. Your conscious is going to be your only barrier, so learn to bear the weight of it. Do you understand?"

"Yes."

"Good, dragon. You'll do well."

Days later, I would awaken in a prison, where I was to train and fight for the sheer entertainment of the immortal world. For the creatures I wasn't supposed to believe in.

§

I opened my eyes in horror, aware that what I'd experienced was not just a dream. It was a memory of my prior life, my prior existence.

I glanced about the room, noticing a slight illumination from the moon through the window. Then I remembered him – the man who had saved me from the werewolf. The same one who had been in the room with me, tracing an intricate design down my back.

Was he still in the room?

I took a deep breath and turned my head to the right. I reached out, but came up empty handed. The dark skinned man was not there.

Then there came a voice – deep, threatening.

It was not the same man who had touched me earlier.

"You're awake? Jace will be glad to see that."

Abruptly, I sat up.

Aware I was only half dressed, I grasped at the blankets which covered my legs and pulled them to my chest. I stared into a dark corner where a man sat. I could not make out his features and I could not identify him by his voice alone.

He stood. Fear pulsed through my body. Sauntering into the moonlight, he moved closer to the bed, within a few feet from me. He stopped at the foot of it, half of his face still hidden by shadows. The man was tall, broad shouldered with a broad chest, his bald head pale. He stroked the thick hair on his chin, his dark pupils narrowing in on me. A lump formed in my throat. My instincts told me he was dangerous.

"Look, I don't know what you want." I swallowed again. My throat was dry.

"If you just let me go, then I won't say anything."

A hearty laugh escaped his lips.

"If you remember clearly, Jace saved your life. He took you in and gave you medical attention. You should be grateful." He smiled. His teeth gleamed in the moonlight.

He leaned over and braced his arms on the bed, his full face coming into view in front of mine. Sharp, white, sparkling teeth – almost fangs – emerged slightly from his lips. I shuddered and recoiled.

"Who are you?" I asked.

He leaned in closer and grinned. "I'm David."

I folded my knees to my chest and wrapped my arms around them. I glanced away, towards the left of me where a sliver of light shone under the door crack. He stood unmoving, stone-like, still leaning on the bed.

"How long have I been sleeping?"

Without hesitation, he said, "You've been out for about seventeen hours."

"Oh," I replied, realizing how quickly time had flown. Then I remembered I was half naked. "What did you do to me?"

I was afraid to know.

He straightened up, his arms crossing his thick chest. "Nothing you need to worry about. You're just fine."

I was wary of him as he backed up, receding into the shadows.

The heat rose in my face. I wanted to make a run for it, but then I remembered the others. Were they immortal, too?

"Where are my clothes?"

His head perked up, his lip and eye twitching. I realized he was only trying to be nice to me.

"You're naked because we had to strip you down, clean and medicate your wounds. You should be grateful. This was Jace's idea, not mine." He sneered. "I don't like your kind. You're weak, ungrateful, and stupid. You're a hell of a fighter, though. I'll give you that. But it doesn't matter what I think of you. All that matters is that Jace really likes you."

He lunged onto the bed, his massive body hunkering down over mine. I backed into the headboard and threw my arm up, covering my head. At the same time I threw a right punch, he grabbed my wrist to block it. He grabbed my other arm before I could react. His lips curled back, showing his fangs.

The door opened. I didn't dare look away from David, who remained hunkered over me. Our eyes were intent on each other.

"What's going on?" the new guy asked, his voice stern.

"She just woke up. I was welcoming her." David grinned at me, his fangs illuminated in the dark room.

"Well, Jace wants to see her now."

The man shut the door behind him, leaving us alone. I wished he hadn't left. While David continued to stare me down, I lowered the covers and swept my legs to the side, off of the bed. As I stood, waves of pain shot through my entire body. With every move I made, a moan escaped my lips.

David climbed down from the bed behind me. Looking down, I realized they had let me keep some modesty by not stripping my panties from me. His presence made me nervous, so I turned away from him, leery of his intentions. I crossed my arms to guard my bare breasts and glared back at him.

"Where are my clothes?" I scanned the room.

He moved slightly towards me. A sense of danger lurked within him. Though his eyes didn't wander anywhere else, I almost wished they had. Then I would have known what he wanted.

His voice was adamant, stern. "You need to take a shower first. There's everything you need in there, including feminine products, razor, et cetera. In the meantime, I'll get your clothes." He pointed to the corner at the back of the room where he had sat when I first woke up.

"The bathroom is in there. Use it."

I ran and closed the door behind me, reaching for the light switch. It didn't work. I stood in the dark and gazed at the window to the right. A dim light filtering through the glass block was enough to see what I was doing. I turned on the water in the shower and let it run to maintain temperature while I focused my attention on my reflection in the mirror. The multiple scars on my skin stared back at me.

To tally up all of the damage, I half turned in the mirror, pulling my hair forward on to my other shoulder. The huge tattoo on my back caught my attention. The head of the dragon started on my upper back with the serpentine body elongating down my spine. The wings slightly extended out along my shoulder blades and ribs, with the tail extending down my lower back. Multiple colors faded into each other. The head was raised up, teeth exposed, as if ready to attack.

# CONFRONTATION

I stepped out of the bathroom wrapped in a towel and sensed his presence. I glanced to the left where David sat, his feet propped up on the end of the bed. He motioned towards it.

"Jace got you some clothes. They should fit you."

In the moonlight, I was barely able to see the clothes on the end of the bed. Then I sensed his alertness, his eyes attuned to my actions.

"You're bleeding."

It was not a question, but a statement.

I started to turn toward him but he grabbed my arm. I closed my eyes, my back to him, and remembered what he looked like earlier. The animalistic side of him.

He caressed my arm, and he inhaled my scent. He knelt down behind me and tugged at the towel at my waist.

I glanced down at him.

He examined the deep marks on my side. The wound had opened up and was dribbling blood. His hold on me tightened. I took in a deep breath, my muscles tensing up. The blood flowed from my wound while he focused in on it, his shoulders rolling, ready to feed. I wrenched myself from his grip and ran for the door. He lunged at me, sending me sprawling to the floor with him on my back.

The door opened.

I froze, afraid to look up. David's weight lifted off of my back. I lay motionless, and out of the corner of my eye, watched him stand.

A deep, smooth voice spoke up. "Cover yourself and get up."

Without looking at the speaker, I stood, wrapping the towel tighter around me.

He spoke up again. "David, you need to behave yourself. I put you in charge of a delicate situation, and I expect it to be handled with care."

"She's bleeding," David insisted.

"Ah, yes, she is, isn't she? Hmm."

He craned his neck toward me, an almost eerie presence overcoming him. I stood up next to the bed, my back to the man in the doorway. I turned around, leery that he too might attack.

"Yes, she could make a creature difficult to control himself."

I turned to look at him. A smile spread across his face. Both stood approximately the same in height at about six foot four. Only the man who had just entered the room was dark complected with his hair in a crew cut, his shoulders and chest broad but his body lean and muscular. David was bigger around in the chest than the man in the doorway. The dark skinned man was dressed in khaki pants, a white button up shirt, and tan house shoes. David was dressed in blue workout pants, a grey t-shirt, and tennis shoes. I was certain that David was his right hand man.

"I'm sorry we had to meet under such horrible circumstances. I'm Jace Templeton." The man in the doorway put his hand out, and I accepted it. I locked my towel in place around my breasts.

"I'm Crystal."

He squeezed my hand. "Nice to meet you."

He glanced at David and then at me. "I see you've met David."

I nodded. David obviously didn't care that he had messed up a "delicate" situation.

"David takes care of some of my most delicate treasures."

I wasn't quite sure what to say. I wasn't sure if he was referring to me or something else, so I refrained from saying anything. I also wondered why he put David in charge of his *delicate* situations since it seemed like David screwed them up. I wasn't looking forward to having an ongoing relationship with David, and I really hoped I didn't have to.

"How about I have David leave? You can change your clothes in the bathroom, and I'll wait here for you. I'd like you to meet my friends. Besides, we need to have Doc take a look at that wound for you."

"That's fine."

With that, I turned, grabbed my clothes, and rushed to the bathroom. David left the room about the same time I shut the door behind me. I dressed, thinking about what Jace had said. Doc? I remembered Doc, somebody who had dressed my wounds before. Was this the same man? I finished dressing into the clothes he'd given me: a pair of solid black workout pants, a purple camisole, socks, and a pair of tennis shoes. Once dressed, I glanced at the block window. How I wished it was a regular window, one I could escape through. I appreciated Jace's hospitality but wondered why he'd really helped me. They did not seem to be men of a generous nature but I decided to give him the benefit of the doubt.

I came out of the bathroom and met Jace at the open bedroom door. Beyond it, there were male voices. Lynyrd Skynyrd's Simple blared in the background. He pushed the door open wider and stepped aside. I flashed him a vague smile, hoping the night would allow for the same. As I stepped through into the dark curved hallway, I watched for others who might spring at me from some dark room.

The doors to my right were shut, all except for one which stood open. On the walls in between two of the doors were sconces which were lit up in a fiery orange. They cast eerie shadows down the hallway, reminding me of old horror movies.

Movement caught my attention to my left. I snapped my head around as Jace moved beside me.

"Follow me," he said.

I followed him down the old Spanish tile hallway, taking a right turn into a large living room with walled mirrors, sconces, and a chandelier hanging from the ceiling. I glanced about. There were no reflections in the mirrors except mine and that of one other man.

Suspicious of this, I scanned the rest of the room. On one wall was a massage table draped with a bloody sheet, and a tall square table next to it with medical tools. Against another wall was a large L-shaped black suede couch. Draped over the couch was a leopard blanket. Before the couch, was a leopard rug and a glass coffee table with a black panther as the base. On the wall opposite the couch was a large entertainment system, set up with state-of-the-art TV, stereo, and surround sound. To the left of me there was another entry way that led further into the house.

All voices dropped to a whisper when I entered the room with Jace behind me. I knew he was right behind me but when I looked in the mirror, I did not see him. It was obvious they didn't have many visitors who didn't know what they were, or else I doubted they would have designed the room this way.

One man in particular caught my attention, the one who reflected in the mirror – Doc. He was the same doctor who had been in my prison.

Jace spoke up. "Doc, the wound on her side opened up. We need you to re-stitch it."

Doc looked me over. He hesitated before he stood. I wondered whether Jace caught sight of it, and if so, what his reaction was. Doc approached, a mild expression on his face. We recognized each other but neither of us spoke. Thoughts of him and Blue Eyes flooded into my brain. I remembered the time he stitched me up while I was pinned down on the cot.

I thought of how he treated me. Then my anger sought to control me. Why was he here?

Being in a house alone with vampires and a doctor I'd met previously in a horrid situation struck me as odd. The arrest at the bar popped into my head. Then I remembered the Deputy's eyes. It was Blue Eyes. He was the cop who had arrested me, and driven me to the prison.

This didn't make any sense. I had the eerie suspicion if anybody knew what was going on, it would be Blue Eyes. But since he wasn't here, I couldn't question him. Instead, I would ask the doctor.

The doctor's face appeared in mine. He had pulled out a light and flashed it in my eyes. I had a lot of questions for him and struggled with the thought of whether to hold back or ask now. He seemed hesitant toward me when I first walked in the room, so I took it as a sign he didn't want anybody to know who he was.

I drew in a deep breath while I contemplated this. I studied his every action and every reflex. He swallowed hard, his Adams apple bobbing up and down. He was trying to avoid meeting my eyes.

He cleared his throat. "How are you doing?"

I gritted my teeth, thoughts of my prison overwhelming me.

"I'm good," I lied.

"Good. Can I have you lay on the table and pull your shirt up so I can look at that wound?"

Turning away, he ambled toward the massage table. I wanted to reveal his evil deeds. I needed to know why I was here, why had I been taken to the prison, and why my life seemed to revolve around these creatures.

As I followed him to the table, I noticed his eyes seemed to never leave my face in the reflection of the mirror. He was scared of me. There was fear in his eyes.

"Lie down on the table," he said, his voice shaky.

The vampires had all convened at the couch and were talking amongst themselves, which left me some alone time with the doctor.

I inched in closer to him, watching him pick up a medical tool. He held it in between us as if he was going to protect himself with it. My eyes narrowed in on him and his choice of weapon.

"Who are you?"

He surveyed the others before turning back to me again.

"They call me Doc. So you should too."

I took a step toward him. "You know what I mean, Doc."

He took a step back.

I closed the distance between us. "Are you a real doctor?"

"Of course, I am. They wouldn't have me here for any other reason." He lowered his gaze. He was lying, and I knew it. He also knew I was smarter than that, which was why he avoided my gaze.

"Are you sure about that?"

His grey hair fell over his eyes. He dared not meet mine, for I remembered a brave man who had knocked a bottle of water out of my hands and called me a bitch to my face in my cell. A wave of heat spread through my body while I continued to stare him down. I inched in closer, coming in contact with him. He stood still, his hand with the medical tool pressed in between us.

"Is there a problem?" Jace yelled.

A breeze whisked through the room as Jace appeared at my side. He glanced from one to the other. The presence of the men lingered amongst us.

Doc spoke up, "No, she was just getting ready to lie down."

We exchanged looks with Jace. His eyes narrowed in on us. I gazed up at him and smiled a warm, confident, yet discreet, grin.

"I was just asking why the sheet on the table was bloody, but he hadn't answered me yet."

Jace looked at me, a disconcerting look on his face.

"That's all yours. That was from when he doctored you up the other night."

"Oh."

Due to the massive amount of dried blood on the sheet, I wondered if somebody else had actually been on the table besides me. If so, where was the body?

The vampires convened around us. The hairs on the back of my neck stood up. The urge to run away overcame me, but I didn't have the speed to escape them. I stood there, procrastinating about getting on the table.

"Can I get a clean sheet, please?" I muttered.

"Of course. How thoughtless of me," Jace snapped his fingers.

One of the men reached into a hidden closet and pulled out a clean white sheet. That was a little too convenient for me.

Doc removed the bloody sheet and put the clean one on, stuffing the crusted one under the table. I glanced back at the men before climbing on.

The men continued to stand before me. Their eyes beckoned and their fangs protruded from their lips as if preparing to attack. I wanted them away from me right now. I decided it was best to let Doc doctor me up and not press the subject of the prison yet. I still had intentions of interrogating him, but not now.

Trying to act more innocent, I changed my attitude and the tone of my voice.

"I'm sorry, but I'm a little self conscious. Would you mind?"

I did a little flip of my hand to wave them off, worried they wouldn't leave my side after the incident.

Jace glanced at Doc.

"Yeah, that might be a good idea. It would be easier for me too," Doc said, almost pleading. His head lowered, his eyes barely meeting Jace's.

They all walked away and resumed their positions on the couch. I lay on the table and listened to their conversation while the doctor worked on me. Somebody bragged about a kill and laughed about it. I decided it was best to tune them out. I didn't particularly want to hear about somebody being slaughtered.

As I grimaced from the pain in my side, thoughts about the prison scrambled around in my brain. My life was like a damn puzzle. I needed to pick up the pieces and fit them together.

I closed my eyes. How I wished my life would return to normal? Or maybe this was normal for me. Hell if I knew. I just wanted a simple life. I was tired of the bullshit.

Then it hit me: my son. My eyes shot open. What the fuck was I doing here? I needed to get out and find my son.

Instead I lay on a table, getting medical attention in a vampire's home. What the hell was this all about? Why were they stitching me up instead of making a meal out of me? Something was definitely wrong with this picture. My heart beat so fast and hard, I thought it was going to erupt from my chest. Obviously, they had other intentions for me.

Again my brain struggled to remember. A long span of time had elapsed while I had been imprisoned. My son was born in 1989.

"Doc?" I whispered.

"Yeah."

"What year is it?"

"What?"

"What year is it?"

Confusion arose in his voice. "Don't you know?"

"No. What's the goddamn year?"

"It's two-thousand twelve."

Everybody's voice came to a halt. I detected their eyes upon us again but I ignored them, calculating numbers in my head. I had been hidden from mortal civilization for approximately four to five years, and my son would be about twenty-two or twenty-three. My heart was broken.

I was alone and lost within. Tears welled up in my eyes. The knot in my throat constricted my breathing. His father had been killed and so had he. My heart told me so.

"Done," Doc said.

That was good, because so was I.

I pushed myself up on my knees and lunged for him. We fell against the mirrored wall and then crashed to the floor, sending the massage table toppling sideways. I wrapped my hands around his throat, my thumbs pressing into the hollow of his throat.

"Who killed him!" I screamed at the top of my lungs. "Tell me, who killed him?"

I was ready to kill anybody and everybody who had a part in my family's death and my kidnapping. And that was when it struck me. My husband and my son's death had been no accident. It was intentional. They had been murdered. Whether it had been by vampires or not, it was murder. There was definitely more to my life than what I knew.

David grabbed me around the waist, and pulled me away from Doc like it was nothing. As he threw me over his shoulder, Doc grabbed his throat and attempted to sit up. Then Jace slammed his foot into the doctor's chest, pushing him right back to the floor. I struggled against David's abnormal strength, but I had no chance of escaping him. I continued to pummel his back with my fists and kicked him, anyway. He wrapped his thick arms around my upper legs, constricting my ability to move.

"Let me go!"

Jace's deep voice bellowed out, "Now, now, Miss Crystal, there does seem to be some issue we're not aware of. Would you care to relay this to me? Or do I need to question Doc here?"

David turned sideways so Jace could look me in the face. I took in a deep breath. It was not the kind, serene face I had seen earlier. Instead, a menacing, deformed scowl masked it. His fangs protruded grotesquely against his lips. I stared at him, aware I was committing suicide by vampire. I really didn't want his fangs sinking into my skin.

"Are you going to answer my question? Or do I have to ask Doc?"

He gazed down at Doc, his foot still atop Doc's chest. Doc's eyes widened in horror, his arms limp beside him.

"Well, Doc, what's the problem?"

Doc's lips parted, but no sound came out. He simply lay there, unmoving, quiet and nervous.

"Mm, are we going to have a problem? Now you know I can't hurt her, but I can hurt you. You're dispensable. She's not."

I struggled to come up with some sort of answer without divulging my personal life. If I managed to live through this, I didn't want them coming after me or my son. I stared back at Doc, realizing I was being selfish, but by then it was too late. Jace continued to drive his foot harder into Doc's chest until bone cracked. I attempted to hide my face, but one of the men jerked my head up and forced me to watch. Doc screamed in pain while bone punctured his skin and organs.

Tears formed at the corners of my eyes as I contained my and my son's secret. I had been concerned Doc would tell my private life to Jace, but he had not and now I wondered why. Why didn't he reveal them to Jace? Or did he even know everything? Might he have been an innocent mortal in the realms of the immortal? Now, I was disturbed that an innocent man may have been killed.

Doc grasped his chest, as if trying to push his body back into place. He screamed in agony, his sickening cries filling the room.

"Please stop!" I cried out.

Jace peered back at me, his fangs pressed against his lower lip hard enough to pierce it.

"Stop, please!"

Blood dribbled down his chin. A tight curl formed at the corner of his mouth. He glared at me.

"No!" I pleaded.

"Why do you dare save this man's life?"

I stumbled over my words. "Because…I think he's an innocent man. He was just a bystander."

"Whose death were you questioning?"

I hesitated. "My husband. He was killed."

Jace seemed satisfied with this answer. He gazed back at Doc. "So who killed her husband?"

Doc raised his hand, pointing it upwards towards Jace, before letting it fall back to the floor. The words, "You did" escaped his lips before he lost his life.

I stifled a cry and stared back at Jace. The other vampire let go of my face and stepped back.

In a most awkward and vulnerable position, I tried to push off of David again. He willingly lowered me to my feet while Jace stepped off of Doc. I tried to speak, but my voice stuck in my throat. Doc had told him Jace took my husband's life, but I knew a female vampire had killed my husband. Just as I had thought, there was more to the story.

Jace advanced on me. I stepped backwards, coming into contact with David again. He stiffened up behind me, and now I understood what he was used for. I was one of those *delicate* situations right now. David was ordered to *take care* of it, whether it was to kill me, hurt me, or otherwise. David was Jace's right hand man. His feelings and emotions didn't come into play.

At this moment, I wasn't sure whom to fear worse, David or Jace. Then, I remembered a comment which had been made back when I was in the prison.

Wayne had spoken of the big guy, the man who ran the underground fighting rings. Was Jace that man?

"You know, I really didn't need him after all. I'm glad you helped me make that decision."

I glanced beyond him at the horrid sight of Doc. While I debated the thought of suicide by vampire, Jace's fingers wrapped around my chin and lifted my face to meet his.

"Now you, on the other hand, are not dispensable. I need you." An evil grin crossed his face.

I needed to know if my husband's death had something to do with this man. My thoughts wandered to my son as well. Had he been killed because of something we were involved in? And why not kill me as well? Why only kill my husband and my son?

Maybe death by vampire was the solution. Let him get it done and over with. He was strong and quick. He could kill me within seconds.

He inched in closer to me. I recoiled, hitting my head on David's rock hard chest. I was desperate to get away from him, but he held on tightly.

"I hear they call you the Dragon. The Crystal Dragon. Exquisite and detailed in your fighting skills and abilities. Strong, defiant and, of course…undefeated."

That was a first for me. I hadn't heard the term, Crystal Dragon. Neither Wayne nor Alex had spoken of it.

"I like the name. It fits you well," he said.

He turned away from me and glanced back at the mirror. Wishing he cast a reflection within it, I averted my eyes to the mirror. But all that stared back at me was the reflection of the room.

"It was fate that brought you to me," he said. "You were destined to be mine!"

He turned, his face transformed into a demonic image. His eyes had narrowed into dark slits. The corners of his lips crept up into a jagged and toothy grin. Both fangs pierced his own lips, producing enough blood to drench his chin. I tried to step away from him, but David held me in place around my waist.

I turned away. Jace's new demeanor had put a change on the others faces. They too, had mutated into an evil form. I dreaded being here and wished David would just snap my neck now. They all advanced on me with Jace in the lead. I squirmed to get away from David, but he pulled me back into his arms. Jace turned my face to his. His long nails dug into my cheek, causing me to bleed.

In between haggard breaths, he whispered, "Your first fight is tomorrow night. You will be prepared. Do you understand me?"

My eyes widened in horror. My previous captors had transformed me into a killing machine, but that was not who I was deep inside. Our faces inches away, Jace's eyes widened in excitement. Tears welled up in mine.

"Yes," I muttered.

"Do not cross me at any time. You'll regret it."

I didn't know what he meant, and I didn't care. My instinct told me just to stay on his good side. I looked beyond him at the others who stood by, ready for Jace's word to attack. But he had not given it, nor was he going to.

He turned away. The others backed down as well. I was sure that Jace was the big man whom Wayne spoke of, that he was the man who ran the underground fighting. With his back to me, he straightened out his shirt, his voice and temper eerily calm.

"Now, David, I would like you to take Miss Crystal down to the workout room." He turned around, his face staggeringly normal compared to only seconds before. "Miss Crystal, you will live, breathe, and die in that room, if you cross me. Do not attempt anything with me or any of my men. Do you understand?"

I nodded.

"I've seen you fight. I know what you can do. These men that you see here today are my business partners. This man to my left is Woodrow." I recognized him as the one who forced me to watch Doc die. He was a little younger than Jace, probably in his mid-thirties. He had dark hair, almost shoulder length and slicked back. He was leaner and muscular. His dark eyes narrowed on mine. I presumed he was second behind David to take care of the *delicate* situations.

"These other two men are Devon and Falcon."

I stared at them and wondered where the hell Jace had gotten these men, *clonemonsterousmotherfuckers.com*? They all stood well over six foot compared to my five foot three frame. They had to have made these men in a warehouse, they were just too damn big. Devon and Falcon were both broad-shouldered men. Devon's blond hair was pulled back into a short ponytail, and Falcon's dark hair was more of a military cut. Their bulk made them look massive. I presumed they were in their mid-thirties as compared to Jace, who looked like he might be in his early forties.

I glanced back at Jace. I was thankful his demeanor had changed, because the attitude in his business partners had changed, too. I swallowed hard, realizing David still gripped my arms. Noticing my arms were turning red, I gazed up at David, who seemed ignorant to the fact.

"You're hurting me."

Jace nodded his head for David to release me. Once he did, I rubbed them, trying to increase the blood flow again.

"You will do what I say," said Jace. "Is that understood?"

I turned back to Jace, the others still nearby. "Yes."

I nodded, and then lowered my head when I noticed Woodrow and Devon glaring at me. The last thing I wanted to do was piss anybody off.

"And you'll sleep in the same room you woke up in."

His finger was on my cheek, though he had stood just three feet away. He was quick; they all were. Oh, how I wish I had not been found in the road. I would rather have suffered a horrible death by the werewolf who had attacked me.

"You're a beautiful woman. I don't wish to ignore that."

I gazed at him through the corner of my eye and caught him smiling at me. His good looks were charming in an evil way. I dreaded the thoughts that consumed him.

The growling from my stomach was the perfect opportunity to change the subject.

"Can I eat before I work out? I'm hungry. I haven't eaten in awhile."

The conversational shift put a curious grin on his face. "Yes, you must be. Let's get you some food and get you training."

Jace led the way through the hallway and into the kitchen. The dining room and kitchen were huge with a massive island in the middle. I wondered what they actually stocked up on, considering they didn't eat human food. Or did they make a spread of their victims on the island

and table for feasting upon? My stomach lurched at the thought. I tried to push the idea out of my mind as I looked around.

The others followed and sat down at the long, medieval looking table. It was made of a heavy wood and was decorated with a bowl of fruit and two red candlesticks. I walked past it and glanced at the large glass window.

The dark and thick curtains were open, casting a view upon the backyard. The large porch was set up with a nice wood table and chairs, and overlooked the grassy yard and the elongated crystal blue pool. The moon cast its reflection upon it, the water rippling at the surface. Trees and bushes lined the brick fence.

I glanced at the back door which was made from a mahogany wood with old style medieval-looking locks. It was obvious that whomever they brought into their home was not getting out. That included me.

I walked to the island where Jace and David now convened.

"You need to eat healthy, so we got you some food for your enjoyment," Jace said.

I wanted to laugh. I hardly pictured vampires and werewolves shopping for food and drinks. The thought of a human shopping mart appeared in my head. The image stopped me from laughing. It was a good thing because David glared at me as he threw a chicken club salad and dressing down in front of me.

"Can I get a fork?" I asked.

He threw one across the counter of the island.

"Thank you."

I ate my food, practically inhaling it without gracefulness. A bottle of water appeared before me. I grabbed it and sucked half of it down in one gulp. Jace placed another one before me.

"I didn't realize you were so hungry and thirsty."

Wiping my mouth with the back of my hand, I replied, "Yeah, I can't remember the last time I ate or drank anything. Sorry."

"Yeah, your manners aren't the best either," David replied.

Now, just who the hell was he to judge my manners? He was a fucking vampire.

"Sorry, I've been locked up. I ate only when I was given the chance, so my manners have gone to hell. I didn't have to impress anybody. I apologize."

David gave me a napkin. With a stupid grin on my face, I grabbed it and cleaned myself up, wondering if, when he was done sucking the blood out of a victim, he wiped his mouth.

"Apology accepted," Jace said. "Are you still hungry?"

"Yes." I looked down at my empty bowl.

Jace took my bowl and filled it back up with more salad. I ate my food within seconds again and opened my second bottle of water. I chugged it down, then swiveled the barstool towards the others.

"Can I use your restroom, Jace?"

He seemed caught off guard.

"Uh, yes, it's…"

"Thanks."

As I walked out of the room, Devon spoke up.

"Are you going to put a leash on her?" he asked.

I came to a halt just out of their sight but still within earshot. I wanted to know what his answer was.

"Are you questioning me?" asked Jace.

"No," Devon replied.

My bladder reminded me that I needed to use the toilet, so I hurried through the bedroom to the bathroom.

I thought about their conversation as I flipped on the light in the bathroom. I was convinced Jace was the big guy. If this were the case, then this could be more dangerous than what I had thought. If it weren't and they were only a pack, there might be a chance one of the others might attack or kill me at any time. If Jace was a leader, then his men wouldn't be as apt to question him or go behind his back.

But he did mention they were business partners. What did he mean by business partners? What kind of a business were they in? He told me I had a fight tomorrow night. Did this business have anything to do with the underground fighting? I pondered these thoughts while I was in the bathroom. When I was finished, I turned off the light and stepped out into the dim room.

A light illuminated it.

Jace stood in the doorway. I scanned the room. It was the one I had woken up in. A large king size canopy style bed occupied the middle of the room. Red and cream colors flowed throughout the room from the blankets and the canopy material, to the drapes on the window.

I had memories of a man lying next to me, whose fingers trailed lines down my back. Disturbed that I had woken up with a man, my curiosity arose. I glanced at it, and then Jace. Our eyes met.

"Don't worry. I won't be sleeping with you. The bed isn't for sleeping in."

Crossing my arms over my chest, I rubbed them. Then, I fidgeted. My eyes moved from him, and back to the bed. I stared at it. "I was almost naked when I woke up."

"Yes, you were. We did not have sex, if that's what you're concerned about," he replied, his voice unconcerned. "We merely dressed your wounds. I'm a gentleman, not a monster."

He could have fooled me.

"Why didn't you re-dress me then, if you're a gentleman?"

"Because your body needs air and oxygen to heal. It shouldn't always be confined within dressings. I did not take advantage of you." He glared at me.

Apparently, he didn't appreciate my concerns.

I decided to change the subject.

"Where's this workout room you have?"

An enigmatic smile spread across his face. It seemed apparent that my eagerness struck his curiosity.

"Follow me." He sauntered over to the door.

I glanced about the room before following him out of the door and down the hall. At the end of the hallway, stood a closed door. Jace opened the door, leading the way to a murky stairwell. The staircase walls were dark. A pungent smell wafted up them. The stairs curled down and to the right, leading into a large, open gym.

The other men were already below and were waiting for us when we came in.

The gym itself was old, much like the one at my previous prison, only with a couple of newer items. Bags hung from beams and a couple of old lights hung from the ceiling. The gym was complete with free weights, heavy bags, speed bags, stationary benches, incline benches, and more.

As I approached the equipment, I remembered Wayne used to give me some of his blood to assist in the healing process of my wounds and to help with my speed and agility. Though I was a tough fighter, I worried I might disappoint Jace and his buddies since I no longer had Wayne's blood in me.

I walked over to one of the mats and started my stretches while they stood by and talked amongst themselves. From their discussion, I understood all of them to live in the house. So there must have been at least six bedrooms in it.

The gym was a basement, though there weren't many homes in Arizona made with basements unless it was in a northern part of the state.

I stopped and thought about this. If I remembered correctly, I lived in Phoenix, Arizona. My husband and I, with our friends, had gone to Payson for a weekend getaway when we ran into trouble at the bar.

So, to my knowledge, I was still in Payson, which meant our cabin was somewhere nearby, hopefully.

Unless the vampires had taken me somewhere else, of course.

I decided to try to play this off and hope for the right opportunity to get away. These guys were big, strong, and just too many for one of me to handle, regardless of my martial arts training. I could defend myself to an extreme, but against five men, all of whom were either vampires or werewolves, I didn't have much of a chance.

I had one advantage here over my prior situation: I wasn't caged up in a cell. That upped my chance of escape. Now, it was a matter of opportunity. I was going to use everything to my advantage.

I decided against suicide by vampire since I was not locked up. I just had to stay on their good side. But that was a different story.

Once I finished my stretches, I moved on to the incline bench. The others watched me from time to time. At least they weren't on top of me, pushing me to do more or work harder like Goldie and Wayne. I was on my own. I guess they figured I wasn't going to try anything stupid. While I worked out, I looked around the room to see if there were any windows or doors which may lead to the outside. I located what might have previously been a window, but was currently boarded up with heavy wood. There were no slats and none of the boards were broken. The window was too high up, making it inaccessible.

I continued to scan the room for escape routes but was unable to locate any. Sweating profusely near the end of my workout, I stopped and bent over to catch my breath. Woodrow threw me a couple of water bottles. I chugged one down.

Jace turned to David, "What time is it?"

David looked at his watch. "It's eleven."

"Hmm, we have three hours. I think we should go." Jace motioned towards me, and then they all stood up.

# BACKLASH

Jace threw a towel at me. "Wipe your sweat off and fix your hair. We have somewhere to go."

"Would you like me to do my makeup too?" I said sarcastically.

Both Jace and David shot me dirty looks.

"Don't be a smartass," David said.

"I'm sorry, I'm just asking." I smiled at him innocently. It didn't pan over well because they all gave me that same dirty look.

They were all hardwired guys and didn't seem to have a sense of humor. I approached them, smiling. Woodrow reached out and grabbed me by my arm, pulling me along with them.

"Just because you're not expendable doesn't mean you're not going to get hurt."

I looked up at him, playing innocent.

"I'm sorry."

He huffed, still holding my arm, and walked me up the stairs. Jace and David led the way.

He leaned in closer and whispered in my ear, "Stop playing stupid; otherwise I might push you down. Then we'll see how well you can fight. Hell, Jace may kill you himself if you can't fight."

I shut my mouth and let him lead me up to the first floor. I really didn't want to be killed in the middle of a bunch of vampires. I shuddered at the thought. In the hallway, we stopped as they blindfolded me and wrapped a blanket around my shoulders. Then they led me out of the house.

Once outside, the cool breeze brushed against the sweat on my body and chilled me to the bone. Goosebumps spread out all over my skin as they escorted me into a car. They sat me in between a couple of them. Their cold skin grazed my arms. I grabbed the blanket and wrapped it tighter around my shoulders.

The car started up and took us down a bumpy road which eventually smoothed out. A few minutes into our ride, the blindfold was torn off my head. I looked about at our surroundings, but was unable to see beyond the tinted windows. I sat complacent for the entire ride, only speaking up once to question why we were taking a car instead of traveling by foot to our destination. Jace's comment was that we needed to remain incognito in case we happened upon mortals while out and about. There were times when they preferred to remain unknown, and this was one of those times.

As the car came to a halt about fifteen minutes later, I tried to look out the window beyond the vampires. It was too dark. Jace stepped out the door and reached back in, taking my hand in his. I let him guide me out of the car. I decided it was best to take him up on his gentlemanly qualities because I didn't know when I would see them again. I left the blanket in the car and stepped out into the cold. The sound of rhythm and blues blared into the night. The others joined us.

Jace smiled at me. "Now, be a good girl."

I resented that remark. Never the less, I followed him to the door.

The sign read: The Southern Belle. The name sounded more like a country bar to me. Once inside, I looked about. Several patrons and waitresses stared at us. I guess I could figure out why. My friends were not only large, but also abnormally pale compared to the rest of the people inside.

I glanced around, wondering where the next exit was when Woodrow glared at me. The hairs stood on the back of my neck. For an unknown reason, the tension among my newfound friends grew within a matter of seconds. David's eyes darkened, his jaw tightening. He stood up straighter, jutting his chest out, and flexing his arms, his hands clenched into fists. He was agitated. I didn't understand why. Then, I glanced at the others. Their faces were on the verge of changing into their demonic form. A voice caught my attention.

"Well, look who it is."

I turned to my left. Jace snapped his head around, too. The newcomer was darker than Jace in skin color, but not as tall and not as stocky. His facial features held an almost boyish charm. His dark hair was also cut shorter than Jace's.

"I haven't seen you in awhile," he said, watching the others.

Jace approached him, "No, you haven't. Have you?"

The tension rose between the two.

"So, what brings you here?" the stranger asked. His eyes narrowed on me.

Goosebumps spread out on my arms. I sensed danger. From beyond him, other vampires approached.

"Business, strictly business. Where's Bryant?" Jace's eyes moved to and fro, searching for somebody.

"Bryant doesn't run the business anymore. I do. What is it you want?" The man examined Jace's men.

They turned and focused on the vampires behind the newcomer, their hands curling up into fists. Their muscles flexed, straining against their clothing.

I turned back in the man's direction. Some of the patrons and waitresses were closing in on us. I swallowed hard.

"What happened to Bryant?" Jace seemed angry at the fact Bryant wasn't the owner anymore.

"Bryant left us in spirit. I'm in charge now. What business is it you want, Jace?"

I presumed his comment meant Bryant was dead. I wondered whether Bryant was a vampire or if he was mortal.

"I have a new investment." He averted his gaze back to me.

*New investment?* Although I knew what I was, I really didn't like the sound of it. The man approached me, looking me over as if he were getting ready to test drive a new car.

With just the tip of his finger, the man pushed my chin up to look me over. When I recoiled from him, his finger grazed my cheek. I didn't want him touching me any more than I wanted Jace to touch me.

"She has a sense of charm," said the man.

I glanced up at Jace, who grinned at me.

"Yes, she does," replied Jace.

"Is she good?"

The man walked around me, his eyes scouring my entire body. Feeling like a piece of meat ready for devouring, I watched him. I didn't trust him anymore than I trusted Jace. He stopped in front of me, eyeing me curiously.

"She should be? She's the Crystal Dragon."

The man's eyes opened wider. "No shit. How the hell...?"

Before he could finish, Jace answered. "There's been a turn of events. She's paying off her husbands' debt through me now."

"No shit." The guy eyed me again. "How did you...?"

"That's between me and the dogs. It's none of your concern."

My brain took everything in. My husband's debt? The dogs? I presumed the dogs meant the werewolves. Was I paying off my husband's debt through the werewolves? What kind of debt was he talking about?

Now was not the time to question Jace. That would have to be done behind closed doors. If I questioned him here and now, I would be killed in front of everybody much to their delight. On the other hand, had I not fought in front of the vampires before? Surely, there wouldn't be much difference. But, getting the immortals riled up could put human lives in jeopardy. I sure as hell didn't want to do that. I decided it best to wait. I would put only my life in danger, not the lives of innocent bystanders.

The white lights throughout the bar switched to multi-colors, casting an ominous glow upon the customers. I glanced around, studying my surroundings. Several of the patrons were not alert to what was happening around them. A voice brought me back to the situation at hand.

"Nice to meet you, Crystal. I'm Steve."

The man put his hand out.

I looked him over, and then up at his face. Such an ordinary name for such an ordinary vampire. His face was too boyish and charming. I didn't like it, and I didn't trust it. He reminded me a little too much of Neil, only in an immortal body.

I refused to shake his hand. How could I guarantee he wouldn't maul me right here in front of everybody? I stared back at Jace, his eyes upon me. I sensed the tension mounting between all of us. Something was up here, more than just retaliation for my husband's debt. When I glanced back at Steve, everything seemed to move in slow motion. He pulled his hand back.

"She needs to learn some manners."

Then his hand came up and hit me hard in the face, almost knocking me off my feet. Bone shattered within. I rebounded. He backhanded me on my right cheek. The thought of this asshole hitting me without any confrontation infuriated me. My eyes swelled with tears. Adrenaline fueled its way through my body.

I struck him in the face. Arms wrapped around me and pulled me back. When he struck at me again, the blare of a saxophone screamed through the air. Jace caught his fist in mid air before it reached me. I struggled against the arms that confined me. I wanted a piece of this man, this ordinary vampire, who seemed like the leech of the clan. Granted, I didn't shake his hand but he had no right to strike me, to try to put me in place, especially before Jace. He had some fucking nerve. He might beat his fighters around but he sure as hell wasn't going to do it with me. It was one of the rare times I was glad to have Jace by my side.

Jace glared back at Steve. "No, she's not fighting you. Sign us up with your fighter."

Steve's anger seemed to take over his body. His teeth protruded from his mouth. I managed to escape David's thick arms, whether he had let me or not, and advanced on Steve. Jace put his hand up in front of my face.

Jace cocked his head and glared at me. "Did you hear what I said, Crystal?"

Before I had a chance to respond, he said, "You'll murder his fighter. I have no doubt about that."

In response to Jace's comment, Steve's eyes lit up with resentment. "My fighter will kick her ass."

Devilish as it was, Jace's grin was darkly elegant beneath the colored lights. "You think so? I have the Crystal Dragon, almost five years undefeated. What do you have?"

Steve said nothing, his fang having bitten through his own lip.

"Tomorrow night at one," said Jace. He glanced around at the clan behind Steve.

"One it is. My fighter will kick her ass, you can damn well guarantee that," Steve mumbled.

His clan backed down while David, Woodrow, Devon, and Falcon hovered nearby. Their presence made the hairs on the back of my neck stand up.

"Your fighter better be ready for the challenge," Jace said.

Steve stood in silence. Jace started towards the front door. Then he stopped and glanced back.

"Oh, and this fight is for the deed." He motioned with his hand towards the bar. "You know, the deed to the bar."

Steve didn't move. I knew he wanted a piece of me. Apparently, I had made a name for myself in the circuit and wasn't even aware until now. I walked up to him and held out my arm. What a look of confusion on his face as he reached for my hand.

I struck him in the mouth, breaking one of his fangs off and burying it in his lip. Blood flowed from the open wound.

"You fucking..."

Jace separated us, his eyes darting from one to the other. Steve shut up and turned away. I walked around Jace, heading into the night.

The cool breeze hit me hard, taking away my breath. Tree limbs whipped through the dark sky, reminding me that I didn't have a jacket on.

As I hurried to the car, I smiled. Yeah, I sucker punched him, but he deserved it. If I got the chance I was going to take him down, along with his fighter. My clan followed behind me and kept an eye out for any backlash from Steve's pack, but nobody followed. I didn't glance back. I didn't care what they thought, didn't care about what happened prior to my joining them. I was going to take the challenge and own it. With a smile on my face, I got in the car, and the others climbed in behind me.

I stared out the window into the darkness. Jace sat opposite me. The door shut and killed the light inside, hiding his face in blackness.

"What the hell was that for?"

I continued to stare out the window. "For the hell of it."

"If something's going to be done for the hell of it, it's going to be by me, not you. Do you understand?"

"Yes." I gave in. It wasn't worth the fight. I sat in silence for the ride.

"That went well, don't you think?" Devon asked, glancing at Jace.

Jace glared at him, unappreciative of the sarcasm.

I grinned, my eyes still fixated on the darkness beyond the car. I appreciated his sarcasm. It lightened up the mood a little bit, at least for me. The car started up and rolled down the road.

"Look at me," Falcon demanded.

Falcon sat next to me. I turned to him. The blindfold was in his hands.

"Is that really necessary? I can't see shit anyway."

"Yes, it is," he said, holding it up.

I turned my head so he could put it on. Once he was done, I leaned back against the leather seat.

"I don't see the necessity in this. I could easily take this thing off."

I felt their eyes upon me. Since I didn't get an answer, I figured it wasn't worth the effort and shut up. I closed my eyes and concentrated on my breathing, trying to temporarily forget about the scene at the bar. We drove for another fifteen minutes in silence. Then something hit the car hard. It swerved from side to side.

"What the fuck...?"

Not caring what they thought, I pulled the blindfold off my face. The car came to a screeching halt, throwing Falcon, Devon, and me forward into the others. I scrambled off Jace as he rolled the window down and looked out. I backed off, allowing him all the room I could so if anything came through, he had first dibs. The cool night air wafted in. I glanced back at Falcon and Devon, who sat to my left. Devon also rolled down his window and gazed out at the night air. Then, both Devon and Jace stepped out. Just when I started to take my seat again, David and Woodrow pushed me down to the floorboard.

"Stay there," David said.

"Okay, no problem."

Unaware of what they were afraid of, I stayed right where I was. Then Falcon opened the sunroof of the vehicle and peered out. He pulled himself up and onto the roof.

"Come out, come out wherever you are!" His boots thudded on the top of the car.

"Who's afraid of the big bad --?"

A blood-curdling scream filled the vehicle as Falcon was thrown backwards off of the roof. Blood poured in from the sunroof and devoured me. I bent forward, trying to hide my face, but it was too late. I was drenched in blood.

"Get her out of here!" Jace yelled. "You two stay with her. Devon and I are going to track it."

"You got it," David said.

The doors slammed shut.

"Uh, what the hell?" I started to lift my head, but Woodrow pushed it back down.

"You'll get it in your eyes. Keep your head down," he said.

"I already got it in my eyes." I lifted my head abruptly. "What the hell was that all about?"

"The wolves, I'm sure," David said. "They're probably pissed off at us."

"The wolves? What the hell did you do to piss them off so much!"

Woodrow beat on the window behind the front seat. "Take us home."

The driver nodded, and floored the gas pedal.

"Who's that?"

David glanced back at me. His mouth twitched, "That's Ezzie. He's the hired help around the house."

"Oh."

Ezzie and I caught a glimpse of each other through the rearview mirror. An eerie grin rested on his face.

I remained on the floorboard and gazed through the back window. Blood covered the glass, making it next to impossible to see anything.

My eyes averted over to David and Woodrow, both of whom fought their appetite to rip me apart. After all, I had Falcon's blood all over me. I'm sure wasted blood whether it be human or not, would be intolerable to a vampire. I kept my eyes on them and backed myself into the seat behind me. Their eyes fixated on mine, their fangs now protracted from their lips. They sneered.

Ah shit, this wasn't good, and I was stuck in a damn car with them. My only option at this point was to jump from the car or fight them in such a confined space. My eyes met Ezzie's in the rearview mirror. He couldn't see the change in their faces so he had no clue what was about to happen.

They inched their way near me. I drew my legs onto the seat. I figured if they were going to attack, I could at least try to kick them in the process. Woodrow slinked forward, wrapping his hand around my ankle. His tongue flicked out at the exposed skin on my leg. David grabbed my other ankle, and inhaled the scent of blood along my calf. At the same time I kicked Woodrow in the face, something hit the car again. The car flew across the road and rolled onto its side. Metal screeched across the road, tangling us within its mess.

From behind, Woodrow's arms wrapped around me. I struggled against his hold and attempted to crawl out of the tangled heap of metal.

David's arm reached through the side window. Once he had a hold of me, he yanked me out into the cold. He climbed onto what should have been the roof of the car, but was now the side, his arm wrapped around me. He held me close. Wary that he was going to attack, I struggled against him. I glanced around, catching a glimpse of David. Then Woodrow flew out of the window and onto the side of the car with us. I recoiled into David's chest, his hold on me tightening.

David turned in circles, surveying the trees around us. I fought to push my bloody hair out of my eyes so I could see, but it stuck to my face.

"Come on, motherfucker! Let's see your face, you piece of shit! Got no balls, now do –"

Something struck us, knocking us backwards into Woodrow. I slipped out of David's arms as we fell to the ground. I struggled to my feet. Woodrow and David were already standing. They were practically glued to my side. I stood up, mud coating my skin.

"Fuck!" I screamed. This was bullshit. If it wasn't one thing, it was another.

A low rumble came from the right. I snapped my head around and looked into the eyes of our attacker. I had never seen anything so huge in my life. His back stood about three and a half foot tall, his body about five to six feet long. His dark grey hair stood on end. He snarled at us, saliva dripping from his huge mouth. I froze, watching him watch us. His dark eyes moved from one to the other.

David and Woodrow stood on either side of me, hunkered down, staring at him, their fangs bared, ready to lunge if the werewolf attacked. The werewolf paced back and forth before circling us. David and Woodrow changed positions, keeping the wolf in their sights. Their hands curled into fists.

To keep my eye on it, I considered changing positions but any movement from me might trigger the wolf to attack. Hell, I was the one with the blood on me. I'm sure it was me he wanted, not them.

By twisting only my torso, I kept him in my line of sight but only to a certain degree. I dreaded moving any further. More snarls and growls erupted behind me, and I couldn't tell who it was.

I swiveled around to face the wolf again. Then it lunged at me. With no destination in mind, other than the direction we had traveled, I took off on a dead run. A scuffle ensued behind me. Even though we had been on a dirt road prior to it turning into pavement, there would be no trees blocking my view. I would be able to see anything coming at me from almost any direction.

I wasn't the fastest runner, never had been. But with the adrenaline fueling through me, I was doing pretty well. The breeze fought against me and sent a chill through my bones.

Then something grabbed me. I tried to fight it but was swept off the ground. The leaves and tree limbs brushed against us.

We flew through the air. A heavy branch caught me on my foot and knocked me out of his arms. I flipped in mid air and tumbled headfirst towards the ground. Woodrow flew at me, catching me in mid-air. I screamed.

He slammed us into a tree trunk, perching us atop a heavy branch. Luckily, his arm took most of the brute force instead of my back. My breath came in heavy gasps. I opened my eyes to look Woodrow in the face.

"Are you okay?"

I stared back at him. Now, that was the stupidest question he had asked me.

"Yes, I'm fine and dandy. Of course not. What the hell do you think?" I closed my eyes, and leaned back against the tree.

What a night! I was ready for a bottle of Jack Daniels. A voice spoke from above. My eyes snapped open. David was looking down at me.

"Sorry."

"Asshole." I closed my eyes. Then, Woodrow whisked me into the air, again.

I clung onto Woodrow for dear life the entire way home. When he stopped, I was still wrapped around him, my face buried in his neck. He let go of me, but I didn't budge.

"We're home," he said.

I lifted my head, glancing about the front of the house. I thanked God I was still alive and in one piece. Then, I undraped myself from him.

"Thank you," I said.

Woodrow shrugged his shoulders. I'm sure the evening had put a damper on his mood, with his friend being killed and all. I wondered whether vampires had a sense of compassion. If so, I could almost sense it in him now. He walked towards the house. David appeared behind us with Ezzie draped over his shoulder.

The big man walked toward the house. I looked at him. "David?"

He stopped in his tracks and looked at me. "Yeah?"

"Thank you."

"Don't mention it."

I followed Woodrow into the house. All the lights were off, so I couldn't see a thing. I grabbed onto the back of Woodrow's shirt so I could follow him to the few rooms I did know.

Once in the living room, David laid Ezzie on the massage table. Ezzie had been knocked unconscious when the car rolled onto its side. The driver's side window had broken and had cut his face. Unaware that Woodrow was behind me, I recoiled from the sight and backed into him. I turned away, fear settling inside me. I took a deep breath.

Woodrow looked me over. "You're a mess. You need a shower."

"Yes, I do."

"Come with me."

Woodrow walked me back into the room I had slept in and flipped on the light. "You have clothes in the dresser."

The dresser was mahogany, almost matching the color of the drapes, canopy, and covers on the bed. I walked over to it, my eyes fleeting back to his.

"Woodrow?"

He looked at me. "Yeah?"

His face almost looked heartbroken.

"I'm sorry about your friend," I said.

He nodded. "Thanks."

As he grabbed the doorknob, I called his name again. He lifted his head and looked at me.

"I really do appreciate you and David saving my life."

"Yeah." The door closed behind him.

# HYBRID

I enjoyed the warmth of the water cascading down my skin, washing away the drying mess of mud and blood that caked my body. I scrubbed hard, leaving red scratch marks on my skin.

As I dried off in the bedroom, I thought about Jace and Devon. I wondered how their search had gone, whether they were able to catch up with the creature that had attacked us.

I broke down in tears, realizing how close I had come to being killed. I needed to get out of here right away. My chances of being harmed increased with every second spent with my new friends. Even others of their kind seemed to have confrontations with them. This frightened me. It made me more susceptible and vulnerable to being killed. And, tomorrow night I had to prove my worthiness to them. I was not looking forward to it, considering I had none of Wayne's blood in me.

Jace burst into the bedroom. He approached me fast and hard.

Clothed in only my panties and bra, I backed myself into the wall, confused as to why he was angry with me. His eyes were almost as black as the night. My instincts kicked in. I threw an uppercut but Jace caught my fist. He grabbed my chin and shoved my head backwards, against the wall. Upon impact, I bit my tongue. The taste of blood filled my mouth. I grabbed his wrist, struggling to loosen his grip.

His voice was deep and rough. He whispered, "You're mine, do you understand me?"

"Yes," I muttered. I tried to turn away but his fingers dug deeper into my cheeks.

"You will do as I say. No smartass comments and no fighting whom I do not tell you to fight," he demanded. "Understand?"

"Yes." I nodded.

"Say it!"

I cringed. "I understand."

He pulled his face away, his body still molded into mine. Lowering his eyes, he looked me over. I fought to control my breathing, watching him, leery of his intentions.

I didn't like where this was heading. His presumptuous need to fulfill his ego and his sexual desire disgusted me.

I hesitated. "What did I do to upset you?"

His eyes bore through mine. "Stop questioning me!"

The fullness of his mouth was upon mine, his tongue exploring the inside. Stealthily, he wrapped his arms around me, confining my body against his. I struggled against him. Finally able to loosen one hand, I struck him.

Our lip lock broke. Only a smirk arose on his face, giving rise to the fact he was amused by my feistiness. The slap had been a mistake. Jace thought it was some kinky foreplay. It was not.

At some point during my struggle for dominance, he threw me onto the bed, his thirst undeniable. Fearful that he would gouge me with his fangs, I continued to fight.

His mouth settled on mine, his tongue deep inside. When I tried to scramble out from beneath him, he latched onto my bra and my panties and ripped them away, leaving a severe welt on my thigh.

"Get off of me," I demanded.

"You're making this much more difficult than this has to be," he responded.

Our eyes met, and somehow I was under his spell.

"I don't..."

"Like me," he said, finishing the sentence. "That's fine, but you're still mine and I will have you one way or another." He unbuttoned his pants.

His body pulsated against mine. I really wished I hadn't been found. Not only did I have to fight against my will, but I had to pleasure him, too. The problem was, I wasn't sure if I could resist the urge. A form of hypnosis overtook me. It convinced me that I desired and enjoyed his insatiable appetite.

He caressed me, from my ribcage to my hips. Then he was inside me, his fingernails digging into my buttocks.

Against my free will, I gasped. I did not want to have pleasure with him. I bit my lip, trying to maintain my silence. I told myself no, but something said yes. His lips traveled down my neck and shoulder.

It had been a long time since I was with a man, and I regretted it. If I had been with one sooner, maybe I wouldn't have caved in this time.

Our eyes met again. I wrapped my legs around his, and I experienced the ecstasy I had forgotten. My fingers flitted over his massive biceps, then up and around his neck. I pulled him in to me, relishing the moment. The moans I sought to control now escaped my lips.

He nipped at my ear. I wrapped tighter around him, reaching greater heights of ecstasy.

"Oh, Crystal, I've wanted you for a long time. How delightful it is to finally have you," he whispered.

Gripping my hips, he guided us to our full peak. Arching his back, he plunged deep inside one last time. His mouth widened and his fangs came down at me.

I screamed. The fangs pierced my flesh, sending a wave of pleasure and pain through me at the same time. As quick as the convulsions begun, he pinned me down and drank of my blood.

Jace left me with select memories of tonight. Had it have been my choice, I would not have remembered any of it. Then, sleep threatened to overwhelm me.

Jace stood up, dressed, and then draped the covers over me before he left the room.

My eyelids fluttered. The moment my eyes closed, I forced them back open. No, I would not sleep. I had to get out of here.

I rolled onto my side, facing the door. Through blurred vision, I watched him leave. I tried to crawl out of bed, but found I didn't have the energy. I was barely able to reach the edge before I passed out.

§

When I awoke, my energy was renewed with a fresh life of its own. I glanced around the room and stretched, unavoidably and carelessly touching myself. The slight caress was sensual and brought back reminiscences of my sexual encounter with Jace, for which I cursed myself.

Sighing, I rolled onto my back. I'd be damned if I was going to let him turn me into a whore, or a vampire for that matter.

My gaze followed the red canopy drapery from one end of the bed to another. A slight movement behind me caught my attention. Jace appeared in full view above me.

A sly grin spread across his face. "How are you doing?"

"I'm good," I lied. I forced a smile.

I was not good. Actually, the more I thought about our tryst, the more I became confused and agitated. I did not recall wanting him sexually. He had pleasured me and I had enjoyed it, that I remembered. Yet, my conscience told me I did not enjoy it. This confused me.

I started to turn over, but he grabbed my bare breasts. The chill of his skin penetrating my flesh.

"You're like ice," I said. I folded my arms over my chest in an attempt to warm myself up. The plumpness of my breasts swelled, drawing the attention of his eyes.

"You keep that up, and we're going to have another go around," he said.

My fake smile disappeared. Maybe life as a vampire would be easier, but I was not a cold ruthless person. I was far from it, despite my past. That was one thing I was sure of.

His smile faded.

"I see you don't want that."

Afraid to aggravate him after last night's turn of events, I chose my words carefully.

"I didn't say I didn't want it."

"You don't have to say it. Your actions speak louder than your words." He moved to the door.

With his back to me, he replied, "Please dress and meet us in the living room."

Following the soft click of the door was silence.

*My actions.* The words lingered in my head. I was going to have to be careful if I was going to survive this. After all, I didn't know when there would be a chance of escape. I crawled out of bed and found my panties – shredded. I needed to get the hell out of here!

More sex with him would either kill me or turn me into a monster.

I rummaged through the dresser, found some clothes, and dressed.

With a heavy sigh, I opened the door. Wary of what this was about, I vigilantly walked down the hallway to the living room. Jace and his counterparts sat in the room.

As I sat, I glanced around. The massage table was gone, along with remnants of Ezzie and his blood. That peculiar knot in my throat reappeared. Eager to not keep them waiting much longer, I turned my attention to them.

"Please, sit down," commanded Jace.

Jace motioned for me to join him and the others on the couch.

Remaining cautious, I walked toward them. Tension filled the air though it was not as strong as it was at the bar.

I squeezed in between Jace and Devon. The leather moaned beneath me. Woodrow and David sat opposite us. The others stared morbidly at me, their eyes somewhat downcast yet dark and intent.

"What's going on?" I asked.

"We're concerned about the werewolves," answered Jace.

"So, what does that mean?" I prompted.

"We think they're going to attack again, and that they're going to try to take you."

"Why?" I exchanged glances with them. "I don't understand why they would take me when they could just kill me."

"That's a possibility too," said David.

I was worried about this new development.

Woodrow leaned forward. "Actually, I think that was their intent."

I was somewhat startled about this revelation, yet I wasn't. Was this really any different than being held prisoner by Wayne? I didn't think so. After all, the vampires did try to kill Wayne and I.

"Am I in the middle of some war or something?"

"You could say that. They know we have you and they don't want us to have you, whether you live or die," David said.

"Uh-huh…," I muttered.

I still didn't understand the situation.

"They would prefer to have you alive, but they're not going to take unnecessary precautions to keep you alive," added Jace.

"So, please explain this to me?" I leaned forward, burying my face in my hands. I dreaded the answer but I had to know.

"They have a vested interest in you," Devon said.

I looked at him.

"Let's just say that they lost you somehow. I don't know how, though I am curious," Jace said, with an inquisitive tone. "Regardless, you were their fighter. Now, you're ours." He patted his chest. "They have to find somebody new or get you back, if they can."

"And obviously, word has gotten out you're no longer with the wolves. You're with our clan," David said.

Great! I was with a clan nobody liked.

"So, if word's gotten out, wouldn't it spark an interest if the wolves suddenly lost me and the vampires had me?"

They looked at me.

"Yes, you're right, it would," Woodrow replied. "And, I'm curious, how did the wolves manage to lose you?"

I lowered my eyes, and debated on how to answer the question. I wasn't sure if the truth was a good thing or not.

"Honestly, I couldn't tell you. I don't remember much," I lied.
Everyone looked at me.

"When we're out, you need to be on guard," Jace said. "Usually our kind doesn't mix well with the werewolves, but sometimes there tends to be some camaraderie between a vampire and a dog. This happens sometimes when a vampire or a dog doesn't form a friendship with a clan."

I suspected the word dog was their choice of words for somebody lower than them, specifically the werewolves.

I sat back, listening.

"We're presuming this might have been the case with the wolf that attacked us," Devon replied. "We don't need you or any other stupid mortal pissing off our enemies which sometimes happens to be the case, especially when it comes to our fighters."

Devon stuck his finger in my face. "You damn mortals think that once you win a few fights, that you're a badass. Well, you're not, and I will gladly put you back in your place," he hissed.

Jace pushed Devon's hand down. "Now, now, we don't know if that's the case here."

While Jace and Devon rambled on, I thought about my confrontation with Steve.

"So, instead of sending out a member from his own clan, will the leader ask loners to fight or kill someone for them?"

Jace looked at me. "Yes, sometimes the leaders will hire a loner to do the dirty work, especially if they don't want the death linked back to them. Some vampires or werewolves have a high standing in the community. You'd be surprised at some of the things that are kept secret." A devilish grin appeared on his face.

"Oh," I whispered.

Then, Jace winked at me.

I blushed. A reminder of our sex temporarily distracted me from the conversation we were having. Was that considered a secret as well? For some reason, I doubted it.

I looked away. Though, I tried not to look at his friends, they caught my eye. I tried to block the sex out by forcing myself to think about Steve. Did he send the werewolf after us?

"So, do they get inducted into the clan at that point?"

"No, generally they don't," Woodrow interrupted. "Unless for some reason, the head vampire or werewolf decides to let them in, but that depends on the leader and the clan," he explained, gesturing to his brotherhood. "Like gangs and clubs in the mortal world, they usually vote on their members, and sometimes, they have to pass a test. Packs and clans are the same way. So, even this could have been a random test for a clan member. It's hard to say."

"Which is quite possible," David replied.

"I think we're getting a little off subject here," Jace said. He and Woodrow exchanged looks.

Being curious as ever, I asked, "So, do you think Steve sent one of his own kind or one of your kind persuaded him to attack us?"

"Yes," Jace answered. "It's quite possible."

"Well, then do you think Steve talked that werewolf into attacking us? I'm only asking because of what happened earlier tonight."

"It's possible, but highly unlikely," David replied. "For it to be Steve, he would have had to react fairly quickly."

"Oh." I sat back.

"And, it was last night that you were attacked, not tonight," commented Devon.

Had I slept that long? I looked at Jace for confirmation.

"You fell asleep for over twelve hours," he responded.

I couldn't keep losing track of time! I needed to get a hold of myself. Goose bumps erupted on my skin. My gaze drifted up to the air conditioning vents. The cool night air wafted in through the slats. I rubbed my arms to create some heat. To avoid thinking about how the hell I was going to get out of here, I changed the subject. I didn't want them to think I was preoccupied with escaping.

"So, were you able to catch up with the werewolf?"

A smug yet annoyed look stood out on Devon's face. It was evident that I had offended him. Sarcastically, he replied, "Of course."

"Sorry, I was just asking."

"Do you want to know what we did with him too?" he asked, his eyes large and wild.

I guess I had pushed the right button to fuel his fire.

"No, that's okay." I backed off with the questioning.

I could only imagine what they did to him, probably something equally disturbing to what the werewolf had done to Falcon. Then my gaze shifted to where the massage table had been. Their cleanup left no evidence behind.

Jace and Devon picked up on what I was focused on.

"Do you want to know about him, too?" Devon asked.

I shrugged my shoulders. Was he okay? Did they try to stitch him up? Or did he become their midnight snack? My vivid imagination created a scene I didn't want to think about.

"No, I don't."

I mulled over everything they had told me and tried to fit it into my own life. The fact that I still didn't have a clue about my fate was equally disturbing.

The vampires sat in silence.

Finally, David returned to the original topic. "We still need to find out who it was."

"I know, and I have an idea who it is, but I can't verify it," Jace said. "I need to ask around. We'll start tonight at the fight."

Oh yes, that's right. I had two fights scheduled tonight. My stomach rumbled, confirming I hadn't eaten in over twelve hours.

"Yes, you need to eat," Jace remarked. "You have a couple of fights tonight. We need to get you ready."

Jace led me into the kitchen. Behind us, a deep male voice escaped the stereo speakers on the wall. Elvis Presley's Are You Lonesome Tonight filled the room. I scrounged through the refrigerator while Jace sat at the island.

The soft lyrics made me think of my lonesomeness in a lonely and strange world. I wished I had somebody normal, preferably mortal, whom I could talk to. Ezzie could have been that friend, at least so I suspected, but he was no longer around. I regretted the chance I would not get to really know him.

I shut the door to the refrigerator, empty handed, and turned to look at Jace. He looked back at me quizzically. David and Devon walked in.

"I'd eat now while you can. You need your energy," Devon said.

"Yeah, I know, but can I get something I like? I know it's not healthy, but I'm seriously craving a huge, nasty burger."

Devon's face twisted into something horrific. "Ugh, you like that shit?"

"Yeah, I like that shit. Can I please get a big, fat burger? I've had nothing but health food the entire time I've been cooped up."

Jace chuckled, "Devon, would you mind?"

"Me, why me?"

Jace stared at him.

"Fine," Devon said. "There's a fast food place down the street. What do you want?"

"I want a double meat burger, no tomatoes, large fries, and a large Coke."

"You're not hungry, are you?" David asked.

"Yes, I am, and can I get two hamburgers? Please?"

They were appalled, except for Jace, who seemed amused.

"David, go with him," Jace demanded.

David and Devon left the house.

"In the meantime, you can start your workout. I realize you don't have any food in you, but you can at least get warmed up. They shouldn't take too long," Jace said.

We started to leave the room when Woodrow walked in, blood dripping down his mangled neck and shoulder. Unsure of what attacked him, I took a step back and ran into Jace. Though his arm was cold, I allowed him to comfort me.

Who attacked Woodrow? And, were they in the house?

My heartbeat escalated at this thought.

I peered back at Woodrow. The living room lights to the right of Woodrow remained lit but beyond him lay a darkened hallway.

Jace shoved me behind him.

"What's this?" Jace asked.

"It's Ezzie."

I was relived to hear Ezzie was alive, yet concerned. How could he tear Woodrow up like that? Was he a vampire, too? No human could rip open a vampire's flesh like that, unless…

"Ah, where is he now?" Jace asked.

"He got out of his room."

Jace shot Woodrow a nasty look. "And?"

"He's hiding in the house as we speak," Woodrow answered. His wounds were healing up, the blood drying against his skin.

After Woodrow's remark, I was sure Ezzie was human. They probably kept him locked up. If so, then maybe Woodrow attacked Ezzie out of hunger. If that was the case, then Ezzie would certainly fight back. He wouldn't want to be found. Anybody in his situation would put up a brutal fight which made good sense why Woodrow's neck and shoulder were mangled.

Deep in my heart, I knew Woodrow attacked him. I was afraid to know the answer, but I had to ask, "Is he hurt?"

"Don't worry about it. I'm sure Ezzie is fine," Jace said. Then he turned to Woodrow. "You take her down to the workout room and then come help me locate him."

"You got it." Woodrow glared at me. He snatched me by the arm and escorted me downstairs.

I glanced up at him, my footsteps echoing in the stairwell.

I had to know, so I asked again, "Did you hurt him?"

Distracted, he answered, "Like Jace said, it's none of your concern."

Still angry over my questions, he met my gaze.

"You should be fine. He never did like it in here. It always reminded him of a crypt."

I stepped onto the ground floor and thought about what he said. It reminded me of a crypt, too.

"I'll be back," he said, bounding up the stairs.

I stared after him, wary of being down here alone.

A scratch issued from a far corner. I spun around, searching for someone hiding within. I swallowed hard and considered searching the room but decided against it. It was best to retreat up the stairs, so I backtracked, the low light hiding shadows in the corners and walls. About a quarter of the way up the winding stairs, a face swung down from the ceiling, appearing in front of me. Apparently, he was hanging from a rafter.

I shrieked, stepped back, and missed the stair behind me. I fell down the stairs, and my head hit the floor. A groan escaped my lips. Upon impact, my hands flew to my head. The headache was instantaneous. I opened my eyes, my vision blurred. A pair of eyes stared down at me.

I screamed. The creature, who now stood over me, grabbed me by my shirt and swept me into the air with him. Afraid of what was going to happen next, I shut my eyes. Footsteps and voices entered the room.

"Put her down!" Jace yelled.

Upon hearing his command, I opened my eyes. I was hopeful that he would be able to convince the creature to put me down. Then I recognized the creature who held me tightly against him. It was Ezzie. His dark crimson eyes were menacing, his skin cold and pale, his dark hair slicked back, his fingers transformed into claws. I recoiled and gazed beyond him at the black wings which extended from his back.

"What the...?"

He bared his teeth, his awkward looking fangs protruding out. They were neither the typical vampire nor the typical werewolf fangs. He snapped at me while I struggled within his grasp. With his arm still wrapped around my waist from behind, I stared down toward the floor at the others. His leathery black wings beat rhythmically behind me. The warmth from his breath lit my blood on fire. His teeth gnashed, barely missing me. A flash of movement caught my eye.

Jace lunged for Ezzie, and the three of us slammed into the ceiling. Ezzie took most of the impact. Plaster and debris sprayed around us. Ezzie dropped me, and I plummeted to my death. Devon's arms opened wide. He caught me and gently brought me down to the ground.

David flung a food bag at me. "Go eat. Your drink is upstairs."

"Huh?"

He and Woodrow were upon Ezzie. Blood splattered the walls as they tore Ezzie's wings from his back. Pieces of black leather littered the room.

"What...?" I stared in horror, unable to draw myself away. I was devastated. Tears leaked from my eyes. "No! No! Don't...!"

I started toward the middle of the room but Devon latched on to me. He rushed me up the stairs, the bag of food still in my hands. Within seconds, he had me sitting down, placing a straw in my drink. But I was no longer hungry.

"You need to eat up. You need all the energy you can get right now."

I looked at him. He acted as though nothing had happened. Then he grabbed my bag, emptied it, and laid my food out before me. The stairwell door opened, followed by footsteps.

I turned to find out what was happening. "Devon...."

Devon came around the counter and stepped into my line of view. "Don't concern yourself with them. Eat your food. You need to get ready for your fight."

"What was that all about? What happened to him?" I asked in shock.

"He's a hybrid. We're not exactly sure with what, other than he's half vampire."

"Hybrid?"

"Yeah, unfortunately, there have been a few circumstances where somebody has been attacked by more than one animal at a time. Usually, it's a werewolf and a vampire, but not always. Anyway, when two animals' poison gets inside a mortal at about the same time, they change into whatever attacked them. It usually happens when two animals are fighting for a piece of meat."

With my hamburger in hand, I stared at it. His comment of meat fueled my distaste for food at the moment.

"Are they going to kill him?" I dreaded knowing, but felt the need to ask.

"No, they're not," Devon said. "This has been about the fourth time they've had to rip his wings from his body so he can't fly."

I set my hamburger down. "You mean they've done this before?"

"Yeah, it's how we keep him under control. We're trying to find out what other creature turned him, but we haven't been able to figure it out yet." Devon ripped a piece of meat off of my hamburger. "Unfortunately, Ezzie doesn't know either." He put the meat in his mouth and chomped down on it. "We originally found him on the side of the road, maimed from an animal attack." He gagged and spit the meat out into his hand. "Ugh, that's some nasty shit. I really don't know how humans can eat this crap."

I glanced at the morsel in his hand, and then back at him.

"Anyway, that's when we presumed it happened. Ezzie only recollects a vampire attacking him. We picked you up for the same reason," he went on. "We weren't sure if just a werewolf attacked you or something else."

"So you're studying me? Like you are Ezzie? Does Ezzie know this?" I opened a package of ketchup, squeezed it out on the paper, and dipped a fry in it.

"Yeah, he does. And, he's agreed to it."

A scuffle ensued in the hallway. I dared not to look that way. I didn't want to see the blood.

Ezzie's cries broke my heart. Tears welled up again. I really had to get out of here. I had the distinct feeling these vampires were up to something more than studying Ezzie, and I didn't want to be a part of it.

I slurped down some of my soda. "And what will you do with him once you do find out what changed him?" I ate more fries.

"Then we find the alpha dog and kill him. He's making monsters with these creatures."

"And what about you? Are you not a monster? Look at what you do." I pulled part of the hamburger off and stared at it.

Devon nodded. "Yes, you're right, but these monsters are worse. You saw him. He had no sense of right or wrong. Even we know how to control ourselves. At least most of us do."

Devon grabbed one of my fries and took a bite out of it.

"Crystal, they're going to get all of us in trouble." His face scrunched up. "Yuck, even this is gross." He threw the remainder of the fry back into the pile.

He could have thrown the fry anywhere else, but no, he didn't. That disgusted me. I set my hamburger down.

"Even the werewolves are concerned about them. That's when you know there's a problem."

My gaze shifted to the fry. It had come in contact with four others. There went five fries I wouldn't be touching. While he rambled on, I moved the other fries away from them. He didn't even notice.

"They've been seen in the daylight."

Hmm, hybrids in the daylight?

"Mortals have already seen them. Apparently, the sunlight has no effect on them."

I took in everything that he said.

Devon ripped another piece off of my hamburger. Instead of eating it, he stared at it.

What the hell was he doing? It was like he couldn't keep his hands to himself. Asshole. Predicting that he might try the soda now, I wrapped my hand around it so he couldn't take it.

"They are going to destroy all mortal life as we know it." He shook the hand that held the food in it. "And that cannot happen."

Before Devon had a chance to touch the other hamburger, I grabbed it, unwrapped it, and bit into it. I wasn't putting this one down.

In a way I understood, what he was saying. The cycle of life was necessary. If mortal life were destroyed, then their food source would be destroyed.

David, Woodrow, and Jace appeared behind me, new clothes on, hair in place, each looking just as spectacular as the other. They sat on the chairs next to me.

"Eat up," Jace said.

I put a fry in my mouth and glanced at him. A sly grin spread across his face.

"Is Ezzie put away?" Devon asked.

"Yes, he won't be out for awhile," David replied.

So apparently there was a reason for my not seeing Ezzie until the other night. I took another bite and wondered if there was any other weird shit I was going to learn while I was here. Was this life in Payson, Arizona, or was this happening all over the world and nobody simply knew about it?

I finished my untouched fries and hamburger, leaving the five fries and the dissected hamburger for Devon to mutilate some more. Then I worked out, showered, and changed my clothes. The workout room was nice and clean, except for the smell of blood.

# ON THE LOOKOUT

Jace told me to keep a lookout, no matter what I was doing, and I intended to do just that. My life was in danger, along with theirs. If they were killed, that would leave me vulnerable and my chance of survival slim. I was a good fighter – strong and skilled – but I was still mortal.

We arrived at the first bar outside of Payson on foot, which seemed like the typical around-the-corner bar. A mixture of southern rock and heavy metal blared through the speakers as we walked in. Upon entrance, Jace consorted with the bartender. Nothing was out of character and most everybody was cheerful.

We stood next to the bar. A man in his early fifties joined us, shaking hands with Jace. He glanced at me a couple of times, as if unimpressed with me.

"She's kind of short, don't you think?" asked the man, frowning.

Jace and I exchanged looks. The smile on his face widened.

"Trust me, she's a wildcat. You get her in the ring, and she'll demolish everyone," Jace replied.

"Hmm, well, her enemies will probably underestimate her. Alright, come on," he said. He waved for us to follow him.

I trailed after Jace and Woodrow, with Devon and David in the rear, down a hidden stairwell to a barred fighting ring. The fans sat behind steeled bars overlooking a ring. It almost looked like the one I had fought in while I was imprisoned. The only difference was the height of the spectator seating area and there was no announcer's box. The man led us through a steel door with steel locks. Once the man explained everything to me, he locked me in a room with David and Woodrow.

Jace and Devon stood on the outside, on guard, in case something were to happen.

I was practicing my jabs when a pair of hands landed on me.

David leaned in to my ear while he massaged my shoulders, "Don't let Jace down. You kick this bitch's ass."

"No problem," I muttered.

The announcer's voice came over the loud speaker, introducing my opponent, Sophie.

Woodrow whispered, "She's new, so you shouldn't have any problems with her."

Great, that made me feel good. Kill the woman during her first fight. I took a deep breath when my name was announced. The steel door in front of me opened.

I ran out, and my fans chanted my name. I glanced at the bleachers, trying to look beyond the lights. Some of my fans stood up, their fangs protruding. I wondered if Sophie knew about the audience, if she was as naive as I was when I first started.

If fights broke out in the audience tonight, I would head back to my friends right away.

Just as I turned, Sophie struck me. It stung. Okay, I deserved that. Stupid me, I was more interested in the audience when I should have been more involved with the fight. I faced her. Her kick connected with my stomach.

I threw my arm down and out, hitting her in the shin bone. She howled in pain. Her leg rebounded, coming down in front of her, off angle, throwing her forward into me. I punched her in the jaw. I tried to ignore her screams. I nailed her in the side of her knee, driving her back to the ground. Her shin bone split and protruded out of her skin. My mouth dropped open. Her kneecap was broken, her leg twisted beneath her.

Her eyes widened in horror. She didn't move. Instead, she lay there, waiting for me to finish her off. Her blonde hair was a tangled mess, and almost pink from the gash on her face. Her jaw and cheek bone were almost torn from their hinges.

She brought her arm up in defense and tried to block her face.

I knew what I had to do…and I regretted every second of it. I glanced up at the audience.

Their angry chant resounded throughout the arena. "Kill her! Kill her!"

The adrenaline pumped through my vessels again. It was the poison Jace had injected into me the night before. The power took over my body. I grabbed her by her head, jerked her to her knees, and snapped her neck. The bone popped beneath my hands. I closed my eyes.

Euphoria took over my entire body. Chills ran down my spine and spread to my limbs. If only one bite from a vampire could do this to any mortal, I wondered how much more euphoric I would feel if I were bitten a hundred times more. I was in total control of myself. When I opened my eyes, I dropped her to the ground. I looked out at my fans who cheered me on.

I turned and walked back to the already opening steel door. On the other side, Woodrow and David patted me on the back and told me how good of a job I did. Their fangs glistened in the dimly lit room.

Another rush of euphoria pumped through me as the exit opened. Jace and Devon stood beyond the door.

Several of the fans stood on the outer side of the block window opposite us. Vampires and werewolves alike yelled through the glass, cheering and jeering.

I glanced back at them. A man was pushed into the window. His face was contorted. He tried to scream, but could not. The massive crowd rushed at the pane, crushing him. Blood sprayed across the window as his body smashed into pieces against it.

Jace grabbed me by my arm and rushed me out of the arena.

We stopped in an office before leaving and met up with the owner of the bar again. Two of his bouncers stood on either side of his desk, and the man sat behind it, holding a wad of bills in his hand. His eyes fixed on Jace.

Jace stood in front of me, almost hiding me.

"She's good, I'll give you that," the man said. "She has exceptional power. I'm actually quite surprised at her strength."

A smile cracked on Jace's face.

"Yes, she does."

The man stood up and strolled around the side of the desk, the bills still in his hand. He shuffled them from one hand to another, and then he stopped just short of Jace. He gazed beyond him, at me, his beady eyes on mine.

"On that note, I question her intoxication."

"What do you mean?" Jace turned towards the man, stiffening up.

"Does she take drugs? Because you know the rules, Jace. Anybody who is intoxicated in any way is disqualified from fighting."

He walked closer to me, one of his bodyguards following.

"This includes vampire and wolf blood. If she's suspected of either of the two, she's subjected to a blood test."

Jace put his hand on the man's shoulder, and the other bodyguard stepped up. Jace confronted the man on the left.

"I wouldn't do that if I were you."

The bouncer bared his fangs at Jace.

Jace curled back his lip to reveal his.

"Tell your man to back off," Jace said. Then he pointed at David, who stood on the other side of me. "Or that man there is going to rip his head off, literally."

The owner looked at his bouncer, putting his hand up. The bouncer stepped back but remained, ready for the attack.

Jace's hand remained on the owner's shoulder, forcing him to look at me. "Now, now, Parker, you know I'm always on the up and up. Do you really question my integrity? Look at the woman. Does she really look like she's high on vampire blood?"

"No. But the rule is she is to be a full mortal woman, with no drug interaction. I have to give a blood test." Fear settled in his voice. I wondered whether he was a mortal man. And, if so, why would he push the issue?

"Really?" Jace turned Parker to face him. "Is that really necessary now? She's already fought. She's already won the fight. What are you going to do, have your fighter regain her life and fight Crystal again? She's already dead."

Parker swallowed hard, backing away from Jace.

"Now do you still want to question my integrity?" Jace followed the man, his facial features gradually changing.

"No sir. I don't...need...um, guys..."

The bouncers backed Jace into a wall, sneering, revealing lengthened fangs. One of the bouncers attempted to grab Jace by his shoulder. David appeared behind him, grabbed him by the top of his head, and yanked backwards. The man attempted to step back to regain his footing. David pulled fast and hard. The man's neck snapped, the vertebrae giving out. David latched onto his neck and drove him backwards onto the desk. The man flailed about, his blood spraying everybody and everything in the room.

Devon yanked me behind him. Woodrow advanced at the other bouncer still at Parker's side, grabbed him, and threw him against the wall. The man rebounded and rushed Woodrow, driving him through the entire wall. Plaster and wood flew out into the open hallway.

Then Woodrow's mouth closed on the bouncer's throat, draining his life. Then he ripped the man's head from his body and threw it at Parker's feet. The head rolled up alongside the head David had torn off of the other man. The man stared in horror at Jace, holding the money up with his right hand.

"Here, take it, it's yours! She won fair and square," he cried.

"Why, thank you," Jace replied. With a sly grin, he took the money from his hand.

"Now, for future reference, don't question my integrity. It's not worth it, is it?"

"No," Parker mumbled.

Jace let go of him. Parker fell into a crumpled heap on the floor, weeping.

Jace stepped over the debris and glanced down the hallway at the patrons who stared at him in shock. I, too, glanced down the hallway. I could almost guarantee most of the patrons in this bar were mortal and of those who saw what happened here in Parkers office, well, they wouldn't live to talk about it. Devon rushed me down a different hallway which led to a back door.

Nothing was said as we traveled back to the Southern Belle, the same bar we had visited the night before. We stopped just on the outskirts of the forest surrounding the bar. There were a few cars in the parking lot but nothing compared to the amount of patrons inside the bar.

Jace turned to the rest of us. "Don't forget to be on the lookout in here. The other bar really didn't seem to have many of our kind or the wolves. So, I'm not as concerned about that place. This one I am. Crystal, be alert."

"Yeah, I will." I was nervous that someone may have followed us so I glanced around.

"And, it's not Steve I'm concerned about. I'm concerned about some of the customers."

"No problem," David replied.

Woodrow and Devon nodded.

"Crystal." Jace came forward and grabbed my chin. "Don't tempt fate in here. There are some customers that frequent this bar who I don't trust."

"You should know not to trust a vampire anyway," Woodrow remarked.

My eyes turned towards him.

"Or a werewolf for that matter."

Jace met his eyes. "Let's go."

I contemplated what Woodrow said as I followed them into the bar. Not like I really did trust them, but they seemed to have some protection for me because I was an asset.

Jace stopped in front of the bar and glanced at the bartender. The bartender nodded, and grabbed a phone next to him. I assumed he was contacting Steve.

I scanned the place, looking for anybody who might have noticed us. Movement to the right caught my attention. I turned. Steve headed toward us followed closely by a tall, dark-skinned woman.

She came around the side of the bar, her hair pulled tight against her scalp, her physique strong and well developed. She was dressed in a black button-up shirt that was tied just below the rib cage, a gold mini skirt, and gold high heels that accented her hourglass shape. She had long, lean legs and voluptuous breasts.

Something about her set me off but I didn't know what it was or how to bring it to their attention without Steve hearing.

"Hello, again," Steve said, awkwardly.

"Hi Steve. Did you bring your contract?" Jace asked.

"Yes, I did, but I don't think we'll need it tonight," he said, shooting me a disdained look.

I caught a glimpse of the woman again, noticing a weird dilation of her eyes. She was one of them. I was going to die here tonight. I stared back at Jace and the others. If they had picked up on her vampirism, they didn't say anything. Maybe they thought I could take her on.

I still had some of Jace's poison in me, but I was sure some of it was wearing off. Or maybe I needed to wait for another attack of adrenaline.

"Crystal, this is Patrice. Patrice, Crystal," Steve said.

I decided to use my manners this time, and extended my hand towards her. "Nice to meet you."

She stared at me, her arm limp at her side, and gave me a quirky grin.

"Looks like she needs to learn some manners," Jace said.

His eyes moved from Steve to her and back to me. I let my hand fall, peering at Steve.

"I apologize," he said with a sarcastic tone. "She doesn't play nice with others."

The dilation appeared in her eyes again, before she and Steve turned, walking away. We followed but I fell back in the line, hoping to get somebody's attention. Woodrow grabbed my arm and pulled me in tight next to him.

"Stay on your toes with her," he said.

"I will, but Woodrow, listen, I think –"

"I know what you're thinking. And, unfortunately, it doesn't matter right now. Stay on top of your game."

"Woodrow, I think –"

He slowed down, grabbed both of my arms, and pulled me in to him. He glanced at the others before turning back to me.

"If we say something about her, then they're going to test you, just for the hell of it. We both know you have Jace's blood in you, and you don't want to be tested. They'll disqualify you, and Jace won't have a chance to fight for the contract."

"So my life is on the line?"

"Your life has always been on the line, honey. You just have to fight this bitch, kill her, and win the contract for Jace." He tapped my cheek a couple of times. "I have faith in you."

With that, he turned and walked towards the others. Everybody stopped and stared at us. Jace held a look of suspicion on his face. I contemplated what Woodrow had said, then hesitantly followed in their footsteps. Jace nodded to Woodrow. Words weren't needed to identify the question.

"I was offering her words of encouragement," Woodrow said with a smile.

I frowned. I gazed at the others. We followed them through a dark hallway into another room. A desk resided in it. On one wall was a door that led to the back of the bar, and another led to the left.

One man sat behind the desk, and another man stood to the right. The man behind the desk wore a black felt hat and thick eyeglasses that made his eyes look bigger than what they were. The other man stood next to the desk keeping guard, his arms crossed over his chest.

Hidden red lights barely lit up the room. He stamped their hands and directed them towards the door to the left. Steve and Patrice walked to the door behind the desk.

Steve turned towards the man. "That woman is the other fighter, Crystal."

"Okay," he replied.

As we crossed the room, the guard spoke up, "You guys have to pay."

"We're with the lady," David said.

Jace joined me at the door.

"Doesn't matter. The manager is the only one allowed in without pay other than the fighter. All others pay at the door," the man behind the desk said.

"Really?" David turned to Steve.

"We'll make an exception," Steve said. He turned away, a scowl on his face.

The man sneered back at David. He stamped each of their hands. A stupid grin spread out on David's face. We followed Steve and Patrice through the door down a long, dark hallway. Steel bars caged us, and a large, black leather cloth covered the outside of the bars, enclosing the hallway. We followed Steve and Patrice, the sound of hard music and chanting coming from the next room. At the end of the hallway which separated us from the arena was a large, steel gate.

Beyond the gate, the audience sat in the stands. The only thing that separated the audience from the arena was a half concrete barrier separating the bleachers from the dirt ground.

I was leery about this fight. Jace pulled my face up to meet his.

"Don't worry," he whispered.

My eyes flickered to Steve and Patrice, who stood with their backs to us.

"There's something wrong."

He shook his head. "No, there's not."

"Yes..." I started. Her name was announced over the loudspeaker and the gate swung open.

"Jace..."

She jumped out in the middle of the arena, and ripped off her skirt and blouse, exposing skimpy boxer shorts and a bikini top. She kicked her high heels to the side. Her fans cheered loud and stomped their feet. The sound echoed throughout the arena.

Jace turned and looked at me. "Don't worry."

"I have a bad feeling about this," I said, my voice cracking.

The announcer bellowed my name through the loudspeakers.

"You need to go." He patted me on the back, and nudged me forward.

I swallowed hard and looked back at Jace. Woodrow and Devon stared after me, wide eyed at the arena, possibly thinking the same thing I was. Hell, I didn't need to worry about someone trying to kill me or kidnap me when I wasn't looking. It was going to happen in front of everyone. The person we were searching for was probably in the audience.

I stepped into the open with hundreds of vampires and werewolves watching, the light damn near blinding me. My fans cheered me on and stomped their feet.

My heart beat fast, thoughts surfacing on how I was going to be killed. Would Patrice do it? Or would one of our fans claim that duty? How was I going to die tonight, by vampire or by werewolf?

Regardless, I could guarantee I wasn't leaving here alive.

The gate closed behind me. My clan stood behind the bars. Would they make it out of here, too? Or would Steve have them eliminated?

I turned my head, just in time to receive a foot straight into my chest, knocking me backwards to the ground. Pain shot through me as my chest bone cracked. I lay there, finding it difficult to move or breathe. Then, she approached me, her foot aimed at my throat. I rolled away, barely missing her.

I forced myself to get up on my hands and knees. Patrice kicked out, aiming for my face. I knelt with one foot braced on the ground, ready for the impact. About the time her foot almost came in contact with me, I threw my left elbow down and out with all my power, connecting with her shin and ankle. Her bone cracked. I thanked God I still had his poison in me. I just needed to take care of her before I lost the juice again.

As her left leg came down, I came up full force with a right hand punch to her sternum. Her fist narrowly missed my face. Another crack and her breath escaped her lips. She stared wild eyed, and bared her fangs.

I grabbed her shoulders and pulled her in towards me. My right knee came in contact with her stomach. Her left fist came up, striking me in the rib. Her right fist struck me on the other side. My ribs fractured under her power. I pulled my arm down to protect my unbroken ribs.

As she threw a left uppercut, I swung my other arm up quick and hard. I was able to block her forearm and strike her in the head at the same time.

Again, she flashed me her fangs. The side of her face where I had hit her was partially caved in. Our arms wrapped up, delivering strikes and blocks. We pushed each other, sending the other flying to the ground. The crowd went silent. We bolted to our feet.

She came at me with a spinning rear kick. I slid to the ground knocking her leg out from underneath her, sending her face first into the ground.

I jumped on her back and grabbed her hair, jerking her head toward me. She snarled and threw us backwards into the barricade. I hit hard, debris and concrete flying everywhere. She fell atop me. I swore my ribs were going to break out of my skin. The rest of the barricade beneath us gave way, dropping us to the ground. I lay buried beneath her and debris, almost totally under the bleachers. Chaos broke out while I tried to push her off of me. Patrice jerked back and forth. Then it dawned on me, at least two vampires or werewolves had a hold of her.

The audience screamed, "Vampire! Vampire!"

They had figured out what she was and weren't happy about it.

I scrambled to push her off me, trying to get away from the audience. As I did so, I had pushed myself beneath the bleachers. I pulled my hair out of my eyes and stared back, horrified. The werewolves tore Patrice apart literally limb by limb. Her screams echoed throughout the arena. Then, the vampires and werewolves started fighting over her. Blood and body parts flew everywhere.

I backed myself against the wall, trying to remain quiet. I held my breath. My heart beat faster. The adrenaline pushed the poison harder through my system. I stared back at the horrific scene, praying they would not notice I was missing amongst the chaos and mayhem. I presumed the creatures wouldn't remember who destroyed whom.

Panic escalated to my right. The audience ran out the doors next to the bleachers. I headed that way. I pulled my hair tie out and smoothed my hair to conceal my face. I crawled farther, locating a deep blue pull-on sweater somebody had lost. I looked up, praying nobody was going to come looking for it and slipped it on over my other shirt. The bleachers were vacating so I would have to hurry if I planned on making an escape. A commotion continued where Patrice had been.

I wanted to merge with the crowd so I hurried towards the aisle. As I neared the edge of the bleachers, the smell of blood spread throughout the arena. A massacre had taken place. Vampires and werewolves lay in mangled heaps. Others fought within the confines of the arena.

Without looking back, I pulled myself up to a standing position beneath the bleachers. I wrapped myself around the door jamb of the emergency exit, trying to sneak out undetected.

I inhaled the cool night air. Pain submerged deep in my ribs, causing me to stop quick and hard. I nearly doubled over. Somebody ran into my back practically knocking me off my feet.

"Watch what you're doing, lady," a man exclaimed. He pulled a woman along with him in a hurry.

I didn't look back. I sighed, looking for the quickest way out. I could do it by foot or vehicle, but either way was dangerous. By foot, I was slow and there was no way to know what I was going to run into in the middle of the forest.

By vehicle, I would have to hijack someone else's transportation. Either way I was screwed, but I needed to seize the opportunity before I was caught by either Jace or Steve's crew. This was probably my only opportunity to get away.

I considered hijacking or hiding in a car. My only problem was I didn't know what vehicle belonged to whom. I dreaded being stuck in a house with another vampire. Jace's crew had already proven me wrong on one count, and that was that vampires don't travel by car. I checked that one off my list.

I pulled the hood up on my sweater, covering most of my head. The cold penetrated my face.

I peered at the cars, looking for the easiest and least conspicuous. I ran through the parking lot surveying them. A reflection caught my attention. A set of keys dangled in a young man's hand. He laid face down and motionless on the ground, blood surrounding him. I rushed over to him, hoping nobody was watching. I grabbed at the keys. He gripped them tighter.

I gasped in shock. He twisted his neck to stare at me.

"No," he whispered.

Considering the amount of blood, I was surprised he was still alive. My eyes settled on the bite mark on his neck. Shit, he had been bitten. I wrenched the keys from his tightening fist.

He clutched on to my wrist. "Help me, please."

"Oh, God," I muttered. I looked around. Almost everyone had disappeared into the night.

His voice became louder, "Help me, please."

I scanned the area and prayed nobody heard him.

"Please!"

I regretted the decision I had to make. I drove my fist into his upper back. Blood shot up everywhere. His rib cage caved in, breaking off fragments of his ribs and driving pieces through major organs. I clamped down on his heart and squeezed it between my fingers. His body grew limp beneath me.

"Ugh," I moaned.

I wiped my hand off on the back of his shirt where it wasn't bloody. Still kneeling down, I picked through the keys, and found the black rubber truck key, noting the maker of the vehicle. I pressed the unlock button. The lights on the Toyota Tundra flashed. With one last glance around the parking lot, I ran straight for it, climbed in and scanned the backseat. So far, no surprises. The truck came to life, and so did I.

Regardless of the direction I was headed, I was optimistic that I would find my son.

# INVESTIGATION

Deputy Robert Drake Bouchard sat in his county police car. In one hand, he held a radar gun, and in the other, he held a photograph. The picture reflected his mother, Brandy Crystal Bouchard, at the age of thirty-three, sitting near a creek in the forest. Her long dark hair draped elegantly over her shoulder. Her large brown eyes and demure smile lit her face up.

Robert recognized the background. It was a place his grandmother took him to often, the same town Brandy had disappeared, Payson, Arizona. This was the only picture he had for the rest had burnt in a house fire.

He eventually crumpled it up and tossed it to the floorboard. Robert leaned his head back and gazed up at the ceiling of the car. He was about ready to give up. He had not been able to find the victim and was getting more irritated by the moment.

Deputy Torrance peered in through the open window.

"Damn, dude, you need to relax."

Deputy Robert met his eyes, barely picking his head up.

"Yeah, you're right. I do. I've been thinking about moving the family, maybe making a fresh start."

"Again?" Torrance looked at him. "I don't think that's a good idea, man. You've already moved your family twice in the past year and a half."

"Yeah, you're probably right. But I think this would be for the best. Rebecca and I aren't doing so well right now."

Robert scrunched up his face, thinking about the frustration of his marriage.

"And you think moving is going to help?"

Torrance leaned on the window, almost putting his head inside the patrol car.

"It's only going to cause more problems. You can't keep packing up and moving the family. It's not just hard on you and Rebecca. What about the kids? And your sister? Is she still living with you?"

"Yeah, Jennifer's been having some anger issues. She's actually been going to counseling."

"Really? It's been that hard on her?"

"Yeah, ever since Mom and Dad died, she can't handle it."

Robert looked up at Torrance.

"I've tried to console her, but it doesn't work. And, you know Grandma died. That made it worse."

"Yeah, I know, but it's been what, two years now?"

"Yeah, it doesn't matter. Grandma was like a mother to her. She's practically raised her since Mom disappeared. Hell, she wasn't doing well at the time. Jennifer was in the hospital when everything happened."

"I'm sorry, man."

Robert wiped a tear from his eye.

"You got to stop looking for her, Robert. It's been too long. We'll probably never find her body."

"Yeah, I tell myself that all the time, but I keep looking. It's as though she's still out there, somewhere." He looked beyond Torrance at the forest.

"Robert, her body is decomposing. The elements and the animals would have gotten to her. We'll be lucky if we can identify her.

Torrance slicked his blonde hair back. "Hell, I still think she was one of the women at the bar. The medical examiner couldn't identify half of them." Torrance shook his finger at Robert. "I'm telling you, she was there."

Robert wrinkled his nose at him and wiped his dark hair back. Everybody always told him he had his mother's large, dark eyes and short, cute nose. That followed him around his entire life. He swore if he ever came across her body, he would recognize her, decomposed or not.

"How are the babies doing?" Torrance's hair fell over his large forehead.

"Good, when they're not being a handful. They're getting big."

"I bet. I'll have to come over and see them. It's been a while. Hey, maybe you can hook me up with your sister?"

"Torrance, she's only sixteen. You're a cop turning into a pedophile. That's not cool." Robert stared hard at him. Torrance knew better.

Torrance cast his eyes down on the ground. "Sorry, I always think she's older than what she is. These damn sixteen year olds don't look like sixteen year olds anymore. They're supposed to look like kids, not twenty-one year old women."

"I agree. Trust me, I wished she looked like a kid too. It would save me a heap of problems," Robert sighed. "I always have to bail her out."

"She been getting into trouble?"

"Not literally. It's mostly the boys. She's my little sister. I practically have to sit on the front porch with my rifle, waiting for their dumb asses. I feel like her Dad instead of her brother half the time." Robert glanced about the parking lot.

"Yeah, well, she's a looker." Torrance smiled.

"You keep that in check," Robert snapped. "I'll kick your ass if you touch my sister."

"You know I won't do that."

"Yeah, well, you better not."

Torrance grinned.

Robert peered out the window at something moving along the foot of the forest.

Torrance glanced back, smelling the pine in the air. Something rustled behind him. "What's that?"

Robert peered at the small creature. "Looks like a squirrel."

"Oh, yeah?"

The furry creature caught their attention as it ran up the tree.

"God, I love Flagstaff," Robert mused aloud. "I really love the atmosphere here."

"Yeah, and that's another reason you need to stay. Make me a promise, Robert. Don't move. Life is good here. It's beautiful, serene, quiet, just fucking fabulous."

"Yeah, I agree. I feel great."

Torrance straightened up, tapping on the roof of the car. "By the way, you never said what was going on with you and Rebecca."

"Um, I'm not sure if I want to go there."

"Why? What's up?"

Robert shrugged his shoulders.

"Come on, Robert, we're friends. You can talk to me."

"It's a little difficult."

"Did you catch her with another man?"

"No."

"Because if you did, just shoot the son of a bitch and hide the body."

"Oh, that's cute, Torrance." Robert snickered. "Not only are you turning into a pedophile, you're turning into a murderer."

"I'm trying to get you to laugh, Robert. Your sense of humor seems to have vanished. I need you here with me busting criminals, and because you have a serious job, you need to laugh once in a while."

Robert nodded. "Yeah, you're right."

"So, what's up with the wife?" Torrance leaned on the car.

"I'm not real sure. She's just been weird."

"Like?"

"I don't know how to explain it."

"Drugs? Alcohol? Another man?"

"No, I don't think it's any of the above."

"Okay, then what else is there? Oh, another woman?" Torrance winked. "What's so bad about that?"

"It's not another woman." Robert shook his head. He put down the radar gun. "Good Lord, let me out of this car. I really have to take a piss."

Torrance opened the door for him, grinning. "All you had to do was ask, man!"

Robert ran behind some trees and unzipped his pants.

"You know, I could nail you for indecent exposure!"

"You do that!"

"What the hell got you all fired up?"

"I just really had to take a piss. I couldn't wait. What the hell is –?"

Torrance waited for Robert to finish his sentence, but he didn't.

"What the hell is what?" Torrance asked.

Robert cocked his head.

Torrance walked up behind Robert, and whispered in his ear, "What the...?"

Robert snapped his head around. "Don't do that."

"Do what?"

"I don't like you whispering in my ear, especially while I'm taking a piss. What the hell are you doing?" Robert stepped away from Torrance and glared back at him.

"I'm just coming to see what you're looking at." Torrance stared ahead.

Robert pointed to the edge of the woods about one hundred yards in the opposite direction of where they were standing. "Look over there, on the ground by the dead tree."

"Yeah?" Torrance squinted.

Robert zipped up his pants. "Does that look like a body to you?"

"Holy shit! There's more than one body. Let's go!"

Torrance ran towards the tree with Robert following close behind, his hand on his gun holster, ready to flip it open and draw his weapon. As they came within ten yards of the bodies, a horrible stench filled Robert's nostrils.

"What the hell?" Torrance closed his hand on his nose.

"They've been burned." Robert neared the bodies.

"Who the hell would do that? Much less to what – I guess, ten people. Jesus!"

Torrance backed away from the bodies.

Robert closed in, wrinkling his nose in disgust. The bodies had burned to a crisp sometime in the night. All that was left of the fire were burnt bodies, a rancid smell, and a light smoke that wafted into the cold air.

Robert glanced back at the car, surprised they hadn't seen this earlier. The patrol car was hidden from view behind some trees. They wouldn't have seen the bodies from there, had he not needed to go to the bathroom.

"Hey, come here, Torrance."

"Why?"

"Because you're a Deputy, and I need you to verify something."

Reluctant, he joined Robert. Torrance recoiled from the smell, grabbing his nose.

"What?" he asked in a nasal voice.

Robert glanced back at him. "Look at that right there, on the arm. That's a bite mark. Is it not?"

Torrance leaned in, eyeing the arm.

"Yes, it is." He gazed back at Robert and took in a deep breath. "We got another one."

"Yep, only this time somebody tried to burn the evidence. But who and why? This isn't an animal attack. Animals don't burn bodies."

"Yeah, I'm calling it in."

Torrance quickly and gladly left the evidence for Robert to analyze.

# DAYLIGHT

The chirping of birds and a cool breeze wafting in through the cracked open window woke me up. Although my body ached from the previous night and the freezing air, I was thankful I had not awoken confined in a prison or in bed with a vampire.

I lay crumpled in the backseat of the Toyota Tundra, beneath a blanket that smelt of dog. I didn't care. It was the closest I had been to independence in a long time.

The man I took the truck from practically lived in it. There were empty fast food bags, empty cups, and other miscellaneous trash. I pushed my achy body up to a sitting position and surveyed the vehicle. I leaned back against the seat cushion, closing my eyes. My head was groggy.

I had decisions to make.

My eyes shot open. I threw the blanket off of me, pulled my shirt up, and looked my body over. I pressed in on my ribs, assessing my wounds from the fight. No pain, only pressure.

A cheesy grin crossed my face. My ribs were intact, my bruises gone, and my cuts healed up. The only sign of a fight was some blood which remained on my stomach, arms, chest, and face.

I noticed a camouflage hat on the front passenger seat. Crawling over the middle console, I searched the floor, the glove box, and the compartments between the front seats.

I sat down in the back again and rummaged through the garbage and items on the floorboard. An ammunition box caught my attention. It would be helpful if only I could find a rifle to go along with it. I dug some more, finding everything but a gun or knife.

The man was a hunter. I recognized the camouflage accessories in the truck. He should have some weapons around here.

I scrounged through the rest of the backseat, finding another hat, jacket, calls, a t-shirt, and a pistol holster.

A pistol holster. That meant there might be a gun in the truck, preferably a smaller one for self defense. I climbed out, found a place to empty my bladder, and returned to the vehicle to do a thorough search.

After searching the cab and the bed, I still had not found a gun. Damn! What the hell kind of a hunter kept ammo in his truck but no weapons, not even a hunting knife?

So, instead of searching for more weapons, I decided it best to try to blend in with the scenery. I located all the camouflage clothing I could find and put it on. The owner had been a little bigger than me, so when I put on the outerwear, it worked out well with all the clothing I had on already.

I rummaged through the food and drinks, woofed down a can of pop-top sausages, some crackers, and canned raviolis along with a soda and water.

I reveled in the smell of the pine and stared up at the sky while sitting in the back. The forest was beautiful and from now on, I planned on taking life day by day because from here on out, I didn't know if it was going to be my last.

I climbed out of the bed, slid behind the wheel, and shut the door behind me. I started the engine, rolled down the window, turned the radio on, and pulled onto muddy terrain, hoping to find blacktop.

Sometime later, my gaze located the gas gauge. It was getting close to empty. I followed the terrain onward, hoping to at least run into a hunter or somebody – anybody – before I ran out of gas. I turned the music down, hoping to hear gunfire. Boy, I never thought I would say that, but right now gunfire was a welcoming sound to me.

The gas gauge dropped from a quarter of a tank to empty, and the truck stalled. I was still on mountain terrain and when I surveyed my surroundings, I wondered how I was going to travel on the rocky footing. My shoes were not made for hiking, so this was going to tear up and injure my feet.

"Shit."

I jumped out and rummaged through the bed of the truck, hoping to find a gas can the owner may have filled up, but there was none to be found.

Why didn't he have a gas can? Weren't hunters supposed to be resourceful, especially out here in the middle of bum fuck Egypt?

I kicked the tire and leaned my head on the side of the truck, cursing some more.

I raised my head, realizing I didn't have much of a choice but to walk. Then I thought of the toolbox. Maybe he had other resources I could take with me. Even a simple tool such as a screwdriver might be used for self defense.

I grabbed the keys out of the ignition again and opened the toolbox on the bed of the truck, throwing everything out in the process. Just like I thought, the screwdriver was the only thing worth taking. Everything else was too heavy or too bulky.

I had hoped to find more in the truck, though. Anything like a backpack or a canteen would have been helpful. I was growing more frustrated by the second.

"Dammitt! Dammitt!"

I sat down hard, and my butt hit something. I grabbed it and threw the object across the truck.

"Fuck. Shit. Dammitt! Dammitt!"

I buried my head in my hands, ready to cry. I didn't even recall seeing a compass in the truck anywhere. At least with that, I would know which direction I needed to head to find the nearest town. I tried to identify the location of the sun, but that didn't help either. It looked like it was straight over the top of me.

Frustrated, I figured I'd better at least get a head start now while I could. It was early, so I still had the remainder of the day to look for help.

I searched the truck one last time for anything I could use for a bag. Nothing. So, I gathered food instead, stuffing granola bars, trail mix, a couple cans of pop top sausages, and water into my pockets. I didn't have much and it wasn't going to last long. I grabbed the hat and shoved it on my head. On a whim, I headed down what seemed the most traveled road.

I traveled throughout the day, stopping on a few occasions to empty my bladder, rest, drink some water, and grab a bite to eat. On the way, I saw a couple of trucks and headed towards them hoping to find the owner, but they were unoccupied. When I had stopped on both occasions, I checked their cooler to verify they were recent stops, which both were. The coolers still had ice, food and drinks in them. The vehicles were locked but I was able to crack open the sliding rear windows and confirm the keys were not in the ignition. I helped myself to a water bottle and some other food to help me in rationing my own food for my trip. They had more than I did and a working truck, so their journeys couldn't be as difficult as mine. I waited for almost an hour before moving on. I hoped to hear something, whether it was one of those annoying calls or even gunfire.

Eventually, I came upon a blacktop road. I found a nearby rock, and sat on it. Clouds were forming overhead. I chugged down some water, and then halted. I needed to ration it. Only one bottle remained after this one. I closed it up and shoved it back into the inside pocket, staring down the road. My fair skin was burning up, my cheeks taking the brunt of the sun. The rest of my body was almost entirely covered by clothing, but even with the hat on, my face was still exposed. I sat for what seemed like an eternity, hoping a car would pass by.

Eventually, I gave up and started down the road to my right, following the blacktop. Two cars passed me but did not stop, and as day turned into night, I regretted leaving the truck. I was alone in the dark and fearful of what it might bring. Remaining cautious, I headed towards the biggest tree I could find.

Broken limbs lie on the ground next to the tree. A few small branches jutted out of it, giving me the difficult task of climbing it. With my toes barely supporting my weight, I began my ascent. I grasped on to the branch roots while I maneuvered up the tree. The bark dug into my hands, cutting them. I lost my grip three different times, and every time, I fell to the ground. After three unsuccessful attempts, I made it to the top.

Once I made myself comfortable on a high branch, I ate a few crackers and sipped on my water. I kept my ears open, listening for the sounds of the wild. Then I lay on the branch, positioning myself so I could not fall from the tree. Throughout the night, the wolves, owls, and wild cats alerted me to their whereabouts. At one point, I thought I smelled a dead animal approaching. But, as the smell neared me, it turned out to be a black bear. I held my breath and hoped he wouldn't climb my tree, or I would be in a world of hurt. The bark scraped against my skin, leaving red marks. I got comfortable as best as I could, but this was no bed. My legs managed to stay locked in position around the tree limb for most of the night. A couple of times they slipped and woke me up, almost throwing me from the tree. Thankfully, I made it through the night alive and able to talk about it, with only visions of vampires and werewolves in my dreams.

# SEARCHING

"Have you seen this woman?"

Deputy Robert held up the picture for the cashier.

It was the crinkled up picture of the woman he had stared at in his car every day for almost five years now. He smoothed it out and held it up for her.

She barely glanced at the picture before handing a bag of items to a grey haired lady.

"I'm sorry, Deputy, I don't recognize her."

Robert huffed. He held it up for the old lady, who shook her head.

"Excuse me, ma'am. What about you? Do you recognize this woman?"

"No," she said and walked on. He showed it to the cashier again.

"Are you sure? I don't think you really looked at this picture," he said, irritated by her high pitch voice.

The cashier fixed her eyes on him and then at the picture.

"Who is she?"

"She's either missing or dead. She hasn't been seen from in almost five years now. Can you please just answer the question?" Robert said, frustrated.

"Don't you guys usually close cases like that in what, like a year or two?"

She eyed him, and then took a fleeting look at the picture.

"Her husband was killed and she hasn't been found. Now, have you seen her?" Frustrated, he asked the question again.

She rang up another customer and bagged his stuff while Robert stood there, annoyed. He was tired of people who didn't want to get involved. As the elderly gentleman turned to leave, Robert held it up again.

"I apologize for bothering you, sir, but have you seen this woman?"

The old man focused on the picture through his thick glasses. "Nope, sorry."

He turned and walked out, the bell above the door chiming behind him.

"Never mind, forget it." Robert started to leave when the cashier spoke up.

"Is she in trouble?"

He turned, nodded, and raised the picture up in front of her eyes again. She looked from the picture back to him. Her blue eyes questioned his. "You know, you two look alike. Are you related?"

He dropped the picture from her view, sighing. "Can you please answer the question?"

"No, she doesn't look familiar. But if you give me your business card and I see her, I'll call you."

"Thank you," he said, handing it to her.

"Deputy, what's her name?"

He turned, hoping she changed her mind and recognized her.

"Brandy Bouchard."

With that, he walked away. He had been down this road many times looking for her, hoping someday somebody would recognize her. Somebody had to know something. She was missing for too long. In a small town like this, everybody knew everybody's business. But even he had to admit, the town was growing and it wasn't what it used to be. He would hate to see it grow into a big city like Phoenix.

He knew Phoenix well. That was where he had been born. But that's not where his mother went missing. She disappeared in Payson, when she, Dad, and another couple went up there for a weekend getaway. His father and their friends died, but not his Mom. She had disappeared.

The local police covered up most of the story, but folks in town suspected tourists killed some patrons at the bar that night. Payson was a good town with good people, and so it was a hard thing to imagine a multiple slaying occurring at one of the bars up there. Townsfolk said they started hearing weird things at night, and some even mentioned seeing some weird things deep in the forest. Deer were killed the same night, but that was blamed on wild animals. Yeah, wild animals did kill one another, but not like this. Both the patrons at the bar and the deer had been *massacred* by something.

He walked down the street, going into every store, questioning everybody, looking for somebody who may have seen her, but everybody shook him off. The townsfolk thought he was a nutcase for asking the same question repeatedly. Robert just blew it off.

He walked outside and sat down on the bench, leaned his head back, and gazed into the sky. It was overcast, and the weatherman had predicted storms for the weekend. Torrance was probably right. Robert would never find her. She had likely been killed and disposed of, her remains washed away years ago when the horrendous storms had torpedoed through the area. He stood up, head hung low, and walked into the ice cream shop around the corner.

The shop was set up in fifties memorabilia with a vintage jukebox in the corner, black and white checkered floor, red cushioned seats, and pictures of celebrities from the fifties and sixties. He glanced at the pictures and then walked over to the counter.

"How can I help you?" the young lady asked.

Her long, brown hair was swept back into pigtails, her eyes green and mesmerizing, and her lashes long. She was dressed in a pink sweater and poodle skirt. He didn't recall seeing her here before. Maybe, she was new.

He placed the picture on the counter and ordered a double scoop chocolate ice cream in a cone. As she came back with his order, he rummaged through his pocket for the money. She looked down at the picture.

"I hear she's really good." Her eyes beamed with delight. "Are you going to the fights?"

"Excuse me?" His brows narrowed in as he handed her the money.

"The fight? Are you going?"

"What fight?" His eyes searched hers, seeking answers.

She glanced down at the picture again.

"Well, who else? Crystal?"

He stared down at it and then back at her. "You know her? You've seen her?"

"Well, yeah, some of us know who she is. I figured you did too, since you have a picture of her. Personally, I haven't gone to the fights, but my brother does. He says they can get pretty intense."

He stared back at her pretty smile, in shock.

Yes, his search had paid off. Somebody did know something. Then she studied it again.

"She looks a lot younger in that picture. Where did you get it? My brother would love to have a copy."

"I, uh, a friend gave it to me. I'm not sure where he got it." He decided to play into it with her. "I heard she's really good, too, but I haven't seen her fight. So, your brother is a huge fan, huh?" he asked, prodding her.

"Yeah, he loves Crystal. I heard she's over four years undefeated."

"Four? Wow!"

Four or five years would be about right. She disappeared right around his eighteenth birthday.

But, what was this about fighting? Then it dawned on him. He remembered his mother used to teach martial arts classes. She had competed and won in State, National, and International competitions in the Chinese Kenpo style.

"You know, I'd like to see this fight." He licked his ice cream. "Do you know when and where it is?"

"Um, sorry. I figured you knew, since you had her picture." The cashier opened the napkin holder. "I don't go to the fights. My brother won't let me." Grabbing a bundle of napkins, she stocked the napkin holder. "But he would know. I can ask him when he gets off work."

"That would be great. What time does he get off?" Robert was anxious. An energetic surge enveloped him, making his stomach queasy. The thought of seeing his mother alive made it difficult for him to contain his excitement.

"Five, but I probably won't be able to get a hold of him until almost five-thirty."

"Do you think you could get ask him for me? I'd love to see the fight."

He was getting too eager, and he noticed it when she started to back down.

"Um, I can try. I hear the fights are pretty gruesome though."

He leaned in a little closer. "That's okay. I can deal with gruesome."

His lips peeled back to reveal a cheesy, toothy grin. He was excited about this turn of events. As if catapulting to the finish line in a race, his heart beat faster, almost too fast. Robert found himself overly anxious. He needed to calm down some before he gave away the real reason he was here.

"Come back around five-forty tonight, and I'll see what I can find out for you."

"Great, thanks." With that, he turned and started out the door. Then he glanced back at her. "I'm sorry. I didn't catch your name."

"It's Gina."

"Thanks, Gina."

"You're welcome."

He walked out the door. The bells rang behind him as he left.

His mother's name was Crystal now, and she was fighting. Hmm, interesting. Why would his mother leave her family to compete around the state? She was able to complete statewide and raise a family with no problems before. She was a better mother than that. She wouldn't have left them. She loved her family. Then there was the massacre. Something didn't set right with him. The whole vibe sounded *wrong*. He walked back to the truck. And, gruesome fights? What the hell did that mean?

He finished his ice cream, threw the wrapper away, and then jumped in to his vehicle. He started the engine and drove home, eager to meet up with Gina again and get the details.

§

About twenty minutes later, Robert pulled into his driveway. He paused to take in the view. His two story log cabin style house stood before him. Most of the wooded land in the area was bought up in acres, so it would stretch for a quarter of a mile to a mile before he would come upon his neighbor's house. The forest swallowed up the pouring rain. In the distance, mountains flowed into one another, appearing as though they were one.

The moment he stepped out of his truck, he was drenched.

"Ah, yeah, this is going to be a good day." He just knew it. He enjoyed walking in the rain up to his house.

He traipsed through the front door. His daughters were sitting calmly, watching cartoons.

"How's Daddy's girls!" Robert threw his arms open to hug them.

They all screamed, running up to him and grabbing on to him. His wife, Rebecca, appeared in the hallway.

"Now you gonna go and get them riled up and leave again." Her disheveled hair stood on end, and sweat poured down her face and neck.

"I'm glad to see you too."

He leaned in and kissed her. Her hands never left her hips. She only stared back at him. She was a beauty but today exhaustion overwhelmed her face, especially her exotic eyes. She was dark skinned, stood about five foot five, not too skinny and not too fat. Just right, he always said.

She had full lips, and a long thin nose. Her dark hair was pulled back into a braid, and her t-shirt and Capri's were dirty. She must have been cleaning the house.

"I love you," he whispered.

Just then, Katie climbed up his legs and pulled herself into his arms. He scooped her up, looking his wife in the eyes.

"I love you too."

She scowled back at him, crossing her arms on her chest.

"I have some good news."

Using his pants and shirt as climbing gear, Leah and Tisa maneuvered up him. He looked at them. "Hey, stop it. You're going to rip my clothes. I really don't know how the hell you guys manage to climb up like you do."

"They take after their father. Very active. And you know they're always calm until you get home. I don't know why, but every time, they turn into monsters." She stared down at the youngest, Tisa.

As if Tisa knew Rebecca was primarily talking about her, she looked at her Mom and put her hands out, making grunting noises.

"Is that how you ask to be picked up?" Rebecca asked.

"Up, pease," Tisa said.

"Oh, how can I resist?" Rebecca picked up her daughter and followed Robert to the couch. She sat down next to him and propped her feet up on the coffee table. "So, what's the good news? We're not moving again, are we?"

"No, of course not. I wouldn't do that to you again," he said, remembering his conversation with Torrance.

Leah scrambled in between them and tried to get comfortable.

"I think I found a lead on my Mom," he said, smiling.

Rebecca frowned. "Robert, what did I tell you? I said to drop it. This isn't good. I told you bad things would come, but you're not listening to me."

He shot her a nasty look, "Look, I know you have your family. I want to have mine, too." He sighed. "I need to know what happened to my Mom, whether she's dead or alive."

Rebecca's hand moved to his. "I know you need closure, and I'm not trying to be negative, but it's been over four years. Honestly, what are the chances of her being alive?"

"I know. Slim, next to nothing." He put Katie down on the floor and her big eyes gazed into his. "What do you want?"

She put her hands out and gestured for him to pick her back up.

"Go play, sweetheart." With a gesture of his hand, he shooed her away.

In a split second, Katie bolted around the table, grabbed her toys, and brought them back to him.

Robert stared at her. "What the...?"

"I told you, when you come home, they go crazy. She only does that when you're around. But the problem is, you're always too busy to notice anything unless it happens right in front of you." Rebecca leaned forward, and grabbed his hands. "Pay attention to us, especially your children. They're growing up fast, Robert."

He nodded, and dropped his gaze to the kids. "I'm sorry, Rebecca. I've just been so busy with work."

She interrupted, "That's no excuse. You have a life outside of your job, and it's called your family. Before you realize it, they're going to be grown and you're going to wonder where the time went that you were supposed to be spending with them."

Frowning, he rubbed her hands, "You're right, and I'm sorry."

He glanced at his daughters. Their innocent brown eyes stared back at him. He agreed. He wasn't spending as much time with them like he should.

Turning back to Rebecca, he said, "You're right. I haven't. I'll fix that."

Her eyes brightened up. "Good."

"I'd like to get the kids in to some sports, like softball or something, though. I think it would be fun."

"That would be good. Anyway, what I was saying is, I know you want to find your mom, but I have a bad feeling about it. Stop pursuing it." She pulled her hands away and propped her leg up on the couch, setting down Tisa.

"I can't, not now." He turned towards her, mimicking her posture, and placing his arm on the back of the couch. "I have a lead, and this one says she's alive."

Her mouth hung open. "And is this a good lead? Somebody you can trust and count on?"

He lowered his eyes. "I hope so."

She reached out and touched his cheek. "You can't always count on hopes and dreams. They don't always work out."

"Rebecca —"

"No, listen to me." She retracted her hand. "You need to stop pursuing this. She's dead, Robert, and there's nothing you can do about it."

"She's not dead." He leaned forward, resting his elbows on his knees. "My gut instinct says so."

Rebecca followed his lead by leaning forward, resting her forearms on her knees. "Robert, even if you do find her, she's going to bring terrible things to our home, to our family." She leaned back, and rubbed her temple. "Do you –"

"Rebecca, she's my mother!" Abruptly, he stood. He paced the floor.

Her eyes narrowed in on him. "I don't care! I know what I know, Robert."

"Really!" He stopped pacing and glanced at the kids. They were running around, throwing their toys and yelling. "Girls, stop that!"

"Robert!"

He whipped his head around. "Rebecca, I don't know who you've been talking to, or what you do when I'm not around, but whatever you've been doing is affecting not just our relationship, but our family. I don't know where you get this crazy shit from, but you're starting to piss me off!"

It had been a long time since he had become angry with her. The horrid emotion rose within him, and the trembling sensations he used to get when his emotions took over were coming back.

He closed his eyes and sat back down, trying to calm himself.

"Look, you got the girls all riled up again."

Robert's eyes popped open. He eyed their children. Their table and chairs were lying upside down with the legs popped out.

"I didn't do anything to get them riled up," he muttered. He glared at his wife. "Back off."

"It's your anger. You really need to control it."

He forced a smile, pushing his frustration deep inside. If she thought that was bad, then just wait until she saw him when he was really pissed off. She wouldn't like it. He even scared even himself.

# LOST AND FOUND

Dehydrated and lightheaded, I moved on, following the road along the edge of the forest. I had not come upon a town yet. There was a car here and there, but nobody willing to stop for a strange woman looking like a transient in camouflage.

My hair was disheveled so I stopped again, and wrapped it back up in a ponytail.

I was sweating from head to toe. I even thought about getting rid of the jacket, but decided against it. If night came before I had a chance to find somebody willing to pick me up, then I would freeze to death without it. So, I kept it on.

I slowed down, feet dragging, then stumbled and fell face first into the ground. Pine needles poked my face. Not caring about the pain, I lay there, unable to move. I was tired, and I was becoming unmotivated.

A loud rumble echoed through the forest in the distance. A light drizzle of rain came down. So, I rolled over onto my back, opened my mouth, and drank the rain water.

The rumble moved through the forest. I struggled to my feet and spun around to face the road behind me. The rain came down harder. I put my arm out, thumb up and leaned my head back, trying to take in the water from the angry sky. I jerked my head forward, the black motorcycle barreling down the road next to me.

I wished he would notice me and stop. Instead, he ignored me and continued past, taking the curve in the road.

I hung my head, turned back around and continued onward, the rain drenching my body. The coat became heavy, and I decided it was best to take it off after all. It was only going to slow me down. Before moving on, I stopped and hung my head back again, drinking up the heavenly rain. Then I continued onward, eventually coming up to the curve in the road. As I rounded it, the motorcycle sat on the side of the blacktop. The rider emerged from the woods. His dark helmet and black leather jacket kept the water from drenching the upper part of his body. Only his pants managed to soak up the rain.

I stopped and peeked up at him. He didn't seem interested in helping me, so I thought it best to avoid him. I continued onward, keeping a watchful eye on him. He got on his bike, rummaged through his saddlebags, and pulled out a bottle of water. I averted my eyes from him while he twisted the cap off. I didn't need to watch him drink his water. It would only fuel my desire for more.

My foot hit a rock and almost sent me sprawling to the ground. Cute! Now, I looked like a clumsy fool.

I straightened up and started to pass him when his arm shot out in front of me, water bottle in hand. I stopped, my eyes moving from the bottle to him. He turned and looked at me.

"You're slow," he commented from under the face guard.

"Yeah, well, I hurt," I replied.

I looked at the water bottle, wanting to take it and guzzle it down, but I didn't want to be rude either.

"You're thirsty, right?" He extended the bottle out farther.

"Yes, I am. Thank you."

I took it but didn't drink it right away. I was leery about why he'd opened it for me instead of just giving it to me.

He noticed my apprehension. "You look tired and weak. I thought I would open it for you. If you don't want it, I'll grab you a different one."

"No, that's fine. Thank you."

I guzzled the water down. When I finished it, he took the empty container and hid it within the other side of his saddlebag.

"Thank you," I said.

He seemed the type who didn't want to be bothered, so I started on, hoping somebody else would drive by soon.

"Where are you going?"

I looked back at him. "Anywhere there's water and food."

I turned around, the sound of the V twins blaring behind me. I waited for him to blow by me, to smell his exhaust and fumes.

Instead he pulled up next to me, rolling along while I walked.

"That's where I'm headed."

"Yeah, must be nice." I stared at the long road ahead of me.

"What are you doing out here?"

"It's a long story."

"I have all the time in the world."

I stopped, my eyes traveling to him. "What do you want?"

"Same thing you want."

My eyes fixed on him, "And, that would be...?"

I wanted to see his eyes. I could usually tell what somebody was thinking by the look of their eyes.

"Food, water, and preferably some shelter," he said.

We eyed each other before any more words were said.

"Look, do you want a ride or not? I saw you back there trying to hitch a ride, and you look like you could use some food and drink."

I thought about the time Jace and his henchmen found me and the situation I wound up in then. But that was also in the middle of the night, and they turned out to be thugs of a different kind. So, how could I tell if the biker was any different from them? I couldn't. They looked like normal men. Nothing special, just men. My luck over the past few years was atrocious so what were my odds of coming across another monster? Probably fifty-fifty. I was apprehensive.

I gazed back at the road from where he had come. He was alone, at least for now. I looked him over. He didn't appear to wear colors, so hopefully I wouldn't wind up in biker territory or rival problems.

"I'm sure you're debating whether you want to come with me or not, and that's fine. But it's raining, and I don't want to get sick, and I'm sure you don't either. So how about you make a decision quickly? Those shoes don't look like they're going to last much longer out here."

I glanced down at my shoes. He had a point. They were going to fall apart soon. My trip through the rocky terrain had put quite a strain on them. I was lucky they'd lasted as long as they had.

"Yes, I'd like a ride, please."

He shifted forward in the seat, allowing me to climb on the back.

When my butt hit the seat, I had an overwhelming feeling of relief. My feet throbbed. I sighed heavily, feeling the weight of stress free itself from my body.

He must have heard me.

"Are you okay back there?"

"Yes, I am. Thank you."

Then his arm reached around the outside of my leg, and his upper back, shoulder, and arm leaned into me. He opened the saddlebag. I braced to defend myself. He pulled out a pair of sunglasses and handed them to me.

"Put these on…safety…for your eyes." His voice broke out over the sound of the motorcycle.

I wrapped my arms around his waist, and leaned in to him, turning my head sideways to avoid the wind and rain as much as possible. He was oddly warm, so I nuzzled into his back, hoping he didn't think I was getting too friendly. I inhaled his musky, manly scent. The smell of pine wafted through the wind as I drifted off to sleep, comforted against the body of a stranger.

§

I awoke to him patting my hands. I raised my head to look around, noticing the silence of the engine. I didn't want to let him go. He was warm, and I was comfortable, but I had to.

I un-wrapped my arms from his body, yawned, and stretched out. He climbed off the bike. We were at a motel. It wasn't the best, but it also wasn't the worst.

He took off his helmet, his keys in hand. I figured he was close to my age – in his early forties, – and approximately five feet eleven inches. His hair was brown and cropped to his head, with a receding hairline and five o'clock shadow on his taut face. His eyes were large, brown, and almost menacing without meaning to look it.

"You stay here. I'm taking my keys and my helmet. I trust you to not mess with my stuff."

"Do I really look like I could get far?"

He cocked his head, and then nodded. He turned and walked into the motel, leaving me alone on his bike.

I took in the breathtaking view of the mountains beyond the town. Snowcap stood on the top, and several streams of white snow highlighted the mountain. The scenery seemed familiar to me, but I couldn't place it.

Clouds rolled in, bringing a gust of wind with them. Now I was not only wet, but cold as the wind shuffled past me, chafing my lips and my face. I wrapped my arms around my body. A door shut to my left.

He headed towards me as he put on his helmet. I pushed myself back so he could climb on. He drove the bike to a different parking spot, closer to the room, and cut the engine. I figured it was time for me to bail so I climbed off the bike and handed him his glasses.

"Thanks for the ride."

He locked them up in the saddlebag. I started in the opposite direction of the motel, looking for a place to eat. Why was I bothering to look for a restaurant? I had no money. I stopped and rummaged through the pockets, pissed off, not knowing what the hell I was going to do. I had no identification, no credit cards, no money, no phone, not a Goddamn thing. Shit!

"Where are you going?"

"I'm not sure," I answered.

I really didn't know what I was going to do.

"Listen, I don't have a whole lot to help you with, but you can stay in the room with me tonight. It's a queen bed. That was all they had."

"I appreciate the thought, but I can't. I don't really know you. Thanks, though." I didn't want to soak him for his hospitality.

"What's your name?"

"Brandy." It was the first name that popped in my head without giving away my trade name. "Yours?"

"Warrant." He took his helmet off. "Now you know me? Stay the night. You need some rest. Besides, you need food, a hot shower, and a change of clothes. I'm not a creeper. I'm not going to do anything to hurt you."

I glanced up at him, feeling pretty low at this point. "Thanks, but I don't have anything to pay you back with."

I maneuvered around to walk away. I hung my head, wondering if I should have stayed with Jace, where at least I had food, clothes, and shelter. Somebody was willing to provide for me, but my sacrifice was my life.

Warrant's hand was on my shoulder, turning me back around. I threw his hand off of me.

"Sorry," he said. He held his arms out, surrendering to me. "I wasn't trying to hurt you."

I looked into his eyes. Something other than contempt and intimidation stared back at me. Sympathy, maybe.

He put his hands on his hips. "You're a stubborn woman."

"That I am."

He snickered. "Look, I've been in the position you're in now. Actually, worse, I was left for dead, and then somebody helped me. I'd like to help you. I'm not going to hurt you. You don't know where you're going."

He shrugged his shoulders and looked around, as if trying to emphasize his statement.

Dumbfounded, I focused on him. He was right.

"If you want a place to stay, come see me. I'm in that room right there."

He pointed to the door in front of him. He grabbed some stuff out of his saddlebags and hurried towards the motel.

I scanned the area one more time, and then followed him to the room. He had left the door open. I stepped over the threshold. Thinking about the vampires and werewolves, I locked the door behind me. I made a point to protect my ass.

I turned and found him watching me. "What?"

"Nothing." He peered at the door.

"Sorry, I'm just overprotective."

"It shows."

Ignoring his remark, I walked farther into the room. The décor inside was log cabin style, complete with a black wrought iron furnace. The room was small with the queen size bed, TV, table, chairs, and two end tables. It was nothing exquisite.

He put his stuff down on the floor and took off his leather jacket. Underneath, he wore a flannel with a thermal shirt beneath it. He looked over his shoulder at me, catching me watching him.

I glanced away. "Sorry."

He approached me. "You really should take that jacket off. You're going to catch a death of a cold."

I attempted to take it off, and our hands brushed together. I didn't realize he was going to help me with my jacket. Our eyes met as we both stopped.

"I'm just trying to help."

"Yeah," I whispered, allowing him to help me take it off. He draped it over the back of the chair. "Thank you."

"Not many men have been nice to you, have they?" His eyes were piercing and they seemed to bore right through me.

"Not lately." I started to sit down when he spoke up.

"Uh, your clothes are really dirty."

"Oh, sorry," I said, straightening up, debris falling from my clothes. "I didn't realize I was *that* dirty."

"That's okay. Listen, why don't you take a long, hot shower, and I'll get us some food. How does that sound?"

"That sounds really good. I could use a shower." I brushed past him, heading to the bathroom, then I stopped short and looked into his face. "I really want to say thank you. I haven't had very many friends lately – well, actually none at all – and you've definitely been the nicest to me."

He rested his hands on my shoulders.

"Don't worry about it. And do me a favor – stop thanking me."

He walked out of the room, locking the door behind him.

I stared after him before sitting down on the chair. I took my shoes and socks off, and stretched my feet out and wiggled my toes.

"Ah, yeah."

After sitting there for a couple of minutes, I proceeded to the bathroom and locked the door behind me.

I gazed at myself in the mirror, realizing how horrible I looked; then, turned the water on in the shower, getting it warmed up before I got in. I ripped the ponytail holder out of my hair and peeled my clothes from my body, noticing the debris fall from them. I grabbed the small toiletry bottles from the countertop, a washcloth and got in the shower. It was still a little too cool, so I turned it up. I scrubbed my body from head to toe, making sure to get every single part of my body before savoring the water, enjoying its spray.

I stood there for quite a while before I turned it off. Then a thought hit me, I had no clean clothes to wear. Oh, this was going to suck. I just got clean, and now I had to put on dirty clothes.

I would rather run around naked in front of him before putting those nasty clothes back on again. My hopes of being clean were destroyed. I sighed, pulled the curtain back and looked down at the tangled heap of clothes. Oh, yuck.

I reached out, grabbed a towel, and started patting myself dry. I stopped and stared at the clothes on the countertop. Atop, the clothes was a new hairbrush. I glanced back at the doorknob. It was still locked. How the hell...? I looked back at the clothes, reached out, and picked up the pajama pants, top, and panties. If he got my size, I would be surprised.

I pulled on the black cotton panties. They were just one size too big but they would do. Then I put the black pajamas on. The top was a camisole style with gray buttons near the top. Not bad. The pajamas were one size too big too, but that was okay. I'd rather have them too loose than too tight. Once I put the clothes on, I brushed my hair, smiling, happy I looked like a real human being now. I kicked my clothes under the sink and turned to the door. I would deal with them tomorrow. Right now, I wanted food and a bed. I unlocked the door and stepped out into the dimly lit room. Warrant sat on the bed watching TV. Food lay scattered about the table, along with drinks and some beer. He looked up from the TV.

"Wow! You clean up nice." He stood up and smiled.

I blushed, sighing. I hoped it wasn't a sign of a night to come. That was the last thing I wanted. I remembered my rendezvous with Jace and it wasn't the most pleasant. We headed toward the table. He pulled the chair out for me.

"You really don't have to go through all this trouble," I said.

"What do you mean?"

"I'm talking about the compliments and the chair. Thanks for –"

"I said not to thank me anymore, and I'm sorry if I offended you." He sat down and opened the bags of food.

"You didn't offend me, I just....oh, never mind." I glanced at the tacos, rice, and beans that lay before us. "It looks good."

"Well, I don't know what you like, so I just got a variety of food."

"That's fine with me."

"Here, we have tacos. There's some chimichanga here. Then there's flautas, rice, beans, burritos. Pick what you want and I'll eat what's left over. I like it all."

"Okay." I picked out my portion, setting it on a paper plate. "You got a lot."

"Well, there are two hungry people here. At least I know I am. I don't know about you."

"I'm starving, almost literally."

I smiled, watching him help dish out my food. I looked over at the drinks.

"Grab whatever you want," he said, scooping some rice on to his plate.

"I'm going for the beer. Do you want one?"

"Oh, yeah," he said with a grin.

"I haven't had a beer in forever," I said.

"Then you get drunk and get some sleep." He chomped down on the taco.

I grabbed two beers and set them on the table, laughing. It was the first real laugh I'd had in a long time and it felt good. I slurped some beer and then dug into my food.

"Oh, my God, that tastes so good."

"Oh, yeah."

He popped his bottle open and took a swig of it.

I took another gulp of mine, my eyes on him, "By the way, how did you unlock the bathroom?"

He grinned. "You noticed that, huh?"

"Well, how could I not?"

"I have my secrets."

"Mm, I'll remember you said that."

"How's the food?"

"Delicious."

We finished eating in silence. I ate almost enough for two men and downed three beers. Now I was bloated, tipsy, and tired. I sat back and belched out loud, surprising myself.

"Oh, my God! Excuse me."

He laughed. "Don't worry about it. Now, if you'll excuse me, I have to take a piss and a shower."

He grabbed his bag and headed to the bathroom.

I staggered towards the bed, glancing at the front door. Still locked. Nothing would be sneaking in tonight. My eyelids were tired, my vision blurry. Just as I neared the bed, my legs gave out and down I went. Instead of struggling to get up, I lay there, happy to be out of the cold. I curled up on the carpet and fell asleep.

§

Sometime later, I awoke in haste, Warrant's arms upon me. I struggled against him.

"Relax," he said, his voice calm and soothing.

I gazed up at the man who held up his arms in surrender. Then, I remembered I was lying on the motel floor.

"I'm just trying to help you get to the bed. I've been trying to wake you up for five minutes."

"Sorry," I mumbled.

I fought to keep my eyes open as I got to my hands and knees. Pins and needles shot up my arms. Then they gave out, pitching me face first into the carpet.

"Here, let me assist you."

He wrapped his arms around my waist, and helped me up. Our bodies brushed against one another, his warm skin against my cold flesh. Our eyes met as we stood, face to face.

"Damn, you're cold," he commented.

"Damn, you're hot," I replied.

A cheesy grin spread across his face.

"I only meant that your skin is hot," I slurred.

"I know, don't worry about it." He helped me to the bed. "And, don't worry, I only meant your skin was cold."

I snickered. "You're funny."

"Thanks, now lie down. You're drunk and tired. You need some sleep."

He placed the covers over me. I curled up under them.

Warrant was lean and muscular, with broad shoulders. His stomach and waist narrowed into his shorts. His hair was still wet. Water dripped onto his chest, and evaporated into thin air.

He started to turn away. I grabbed his hand, stopping him.

"I know you don't want to hear it, but thank you for being so nice, Warrant."

"No problem. Now, go to sleep." He started to pull away again. I latched onto his hand harder.

"You promise you're not going to hurt me or anything." I muttered.

I tried to focus on his face, my vision still blurry.

He sat on the edge of the bed, placed his hand on mine, and looked me in the face.

"Brandy, I'm not going to hurt you. I'm not that type of a guy. I'm not a rapist and I'm not a murderer. Now, get some sleep." He pulled my hand out of his and laid it on the bed.

He turned the lights off and climbed in next to me. I rolled over and faced him in the dark.

"You know, you're the first man I've slept with in a long time." I giggled.

"Great," he said sarcastically.

"I meant that literally, not sexually."

His hot breath was on my face. "You're really drunk. Now go to sleep."

His hand touched my face, as if reassuring me. It was nice and warm, comfortable. For some reason, I knew I could trust him. I wasn't sure why, but I decided to trust my instincts.

When he started to pull his hand away, I pushed it back down on my cheek.

"Can you just leave your hand there for a second? You're really warm. It feels good."

"You're still really cold. You must have been out there for a while."

I nodded.

"Are you feeling okay?"

"I'm just cold."

"Now, I'm not hitting on you, alright?"

"Okay?"

The covers rustled a bit, and then his body was next to mine. He jumped.

"Jesus!" His voice was shrill. "You are cold. Why didn't you say something a while ago?"

"Because I was hungry and didn't care about it at the time."

Within the confines of the blanket, the heat vaporized from his body and mingled with my mine. I nestled against him.

"You're really hot."

"I've always had a warmer body temperature than most people." He rubbed my arms with his hands, then my back. "Here, wrap your arms around me. It'll help to regulate your body temperature, and I can work on the rest of your body."

"Sure," I mumbled.

I enclosed my arms around him. The heat from his body was already soaking into mine.

He reminded me of someone I'd known before, but I couldn't place who.

I molded into him, and started to doze off. With my head on his arm, I let my body sink further into the mattress. His breath was hot against my face. My heartbeat slowed to a gentle rhythm but his heart beat fast against my chest.

No sounds in the room, only his quickening breath. Lying here, I knew only comfort. The dark welcomed me, the heat shunning the cold. I faded into dreamland.

From somewhere in the darkness, there was a low rumble. His hands stroked my back, his legs draping over mine.

§

I awoke sometime within the night. I recalled how quickly his heart had beaten before I fell asleep. Now, our heartbeats matched, slow and rhythmic. I concentrated on it and fell back asleep.

# MORNING

Robert watched the squirrels play in the tree while he waited for his truck to heat up. He sat in the driveway, still upset about last night.

He'd shown up at the ice cream shop just as Gina had told him to, but she had left already. He presumed she suspected his over eagerness as something more than a missing person investigation. That, or her brother had told her to avoid him, that he might be some sort of creep. This would be his luck. He was not the best of actors, but he was a hell of a Deputy.

Rebecca hadn't been too bothered, though. She said it was probably for the best. He was upset she wasn't backing him and supporting him like a wife should. After all, she had a family and he didn't. Most of his family had passed away, leaving him with nobody left to turn to. His mother's disappearance left a vacancy in his heart and something yet to yearn for.

He prayed she was still alive and healthy. If he found her and she was alive, he would unlock those secrets and find out why she never came home to her children.

This morning, he had every intention of driving down to the ice cream shop and waiting for Gina. He planned on doing his best to pry the information out of her without interrogating her. If that didn't work, then he planned on finding out who her brother was and what he was up to. He would find out one way or another.

He put his truck in gear and pulled out of the driveway. The early morning fog covered the ground like a blanket. He drove to the ice cream shop and parked, the fog enveloping his car. He walked to the shop and tried to open the door. It didn't budge.

He glanced at his watch and then at the times on the door. Just as he figured, he should have waited a little longer. Then he turned and walked down to the coffee shop on the corner.

He opened the door, and the smell of fresh coffee wafted through the air. Ah, yes, warm coffee to warm the body. A couple of customers sat at the tables inside, sipping coffee and eating breakfast. He walked up to the counter and glanced through the window. The clouds darkened the sky. A light drizzle came down.

"Can I help you?"

He turned and looked at the woman.

"Yes, I'll take a medium mocha cappuccino."

"One medium mocha cappuccino?"

"Yes."

Somebody else behind the counter made his coffee while he counted the money in his hand.

Movement outside the window caught his attention. He glanced over and saw Gina walk by the window, heading towards the ice cream shop with a man in tow. He studied both her and the man. They had the same nose. The man looked upset. He stepped up his pace, grabbed Gina by the arm, and rushed her along.

"Sir? Sir? You're holding up the line."

Robert looked back at the line forming behind him.

"Sorry about that."

He handed her the money in exchange for the coffee.

"Thanks."

He walked towards the door and opened it, allowing a couple of women to leave before him. Robert slowed his pace and sipped his coffee. He watched them hurry up the sidewalk. Looking around one last time, the man continued to guide her into the store. Fury had settled into his eyes, and his jaw had tightened, drawing his mouth into a slim line.

Robert kept an eye on his surroundings as he neared the shop. He stopped, the rain soaking into his clothing, and watched her through the window. He could tell the man was still in the store with her because she turned her head a couple of times as if listening to something that was being said.

Robert nudged the door, expecting it to be locked. Instead it opened. He entered the store, the bell above the door announcing his entrance. Gina stood up from behind the counter, and looked in his direction. Her eyes widened.

"I'm sorry, we're not open yet."

She came around the counter and advanced towards the door.

"I thought I locked that."

"Well, you didn't."

She continued towards him.

"And, technically, you should be…"

"It's not time," she said. Her eyes flickered towards the back room. She pushed on his arm to get him to leave.

Robert played stupid and took a glimpse at his watch.

"It's after 10."

"Sir?"

She pushed him harder on the back, trying to get him to move towards the door. He grabbed her arm and spun her towards him, pulling her near his face.

"You told me you would meet me here yesterday, but when I got here, you were gone. Why?" He whispered low so the man wouldn't hear him.

Her eyes moved to the back room again. "You need to leave."

"Talk to me," he said, frustrated.

"You almost got me in trouble with him."

"Who?"

"My brother Jerry."

"Why? What did I do?"

She glanced about the room. Moisture welled up over her eyes. "Can you let me go? You're starting to hurt me."

He lowered his gaze to her arm. It was pink. He hadn't meant to squeeze her that hard.

"I'm sorry, but you need to answer me. Is it over that woman?"

Gina nodded.

"Why?"

"You should know." Her eyes searched his, looking for the answer she thought he knew.

"I don't. I've been looking for that woman for almost five years now. Now, tell me what the hell is going on? How did I get you in trouble?"

She swallowed hard. "I can't."

"Why not?"

"He'll hurt me."

"No, he won't. He's your brother. Now, answer the question."

He was letting his frustration get the better of him. He loosened his grip again and leaned in towards her.

"If I say anything, he'll send the others to hurt me."

"What others? Listen, you need to come clean with me. I'm a Deputy and I can protect you."

Tears dripped down her cheek.

"You don't understand. They'll kill me, and there's nothing you'll be able to do about it."

"Then you're coming with me." He grabbed her arm.

"No, I can't. Please let me go," she whispered.

He pulled her toward the door, her feet sliding on the tile floor. Gina struggled to get away so Robert jerked her into him.

"I only want you for questioning, but if you keep fighting me I'm going to nail you for resisting arrest. Let's go." He growled in her face.

Somebody peeked around the corner. The movement caught Robert's attention. He recognized him as the woman's brother, Jerry.

Jerry came out within full view and proceeded towards Robert. He was about five foot ten, thin, and scraggly. Something about him set Robert off.

"Let her go!" Jerry screamed.

"No problem."

Robert released her and pushed her backwards into one of the booths, hoping it would partially protect her from any danger she might come into.

"That's my sister."

"Yeah? Then you should know what she knows. I have some questions about the fight."

Robert stood guard, ready for any retaliation from the man.

The man stopped about six feet away, leering at Robert.

"What fight?"

"Don't play stupid with me. I just want to see the woman fight."

Jerry looked Robert over, his hands curling into a fist. He cocked his head at him.

"Really? You sure about that?"

"Yeah."

"How much?" He jutted his chin up, tempting Robert.

"What's the wager?"

Jerry smiled. "Man, you just barked up the wrong tree."

Then he turned and ran. Jerry darted through the kitchen and out of the building, with Robert in hot pursuit.

Robert chased after Jerry, through the street and into the woods beyond. Jerry gained footing on the forest floor. Despite the fog, Robert was able to see him. He stayed close behind. The rain pelted against his body.

Robert sped up. Mud, pine needles, and rocks flew out from under his feet. The wind whistled past him as he raced up the hill, shedding his jacket.

Jerry glanced back. The hill grew into a mountain of rocky terrain. He sprinted faster. He leapt over the top of the mountain and took an immediate route to his right.

Robert bounded up, reaching the top within seconds. Jerry was nowhere in sight. Robert stopped. He peered into the trees and brush lining the mountain. He took a deep breath, inhaling Jerry's scent. This led him to his right. He turned, ready to draw his gun. A huge werewolf leapt at him from the heavy brush.

# WELCOME

I awoke the next morning with Warrant's arms wrapped around my stomach, my back to his chest. His face was buried in the crook of my neck.

Even though we had a heater in the room, it either wasn't working or it was set at a very low temperature. Luckily, I had Warrant to help warm my body throughout the night. Every time I turned to get comfortable, I always wound up back in his arms.

When I awoke, I was snoring like an old dog. Warrant's hand was practically glued to my stomach. I peeled it away and laid it down on the blanket. Yawning, I sat up and stretched. Shelter wouldn't last much longer, so I decided to enjoy it while I could. I set the coffee pot to brew and peered through the window at the parking lot.

I was still concerned that Jace, David, Woodrow or Devon would find me. In some odd way, I was curious to know what had happened to them. I was not aware whether they had tried to pursue me back at the bar. If they had, they might have been mutilated by some unscrupulous werewolves or vampires. Wouldn't that be a blessing in disguise? Could it be the same coincidence Wayne ran into back at the prison? I guess that was paying the price for embarking on the wrong track.

This was now my third chance at life without vampires and werewolves, hopefully. How I seemed to find them, I don't know, but I seemed to attract them like no other.

He rustled behind me.

"How'd you sleep?" His voice was gruff.

I smiled with my back to him. "Wonderful!"

I faced him.

Warrant scratched his head and stretched. He threw the covers off of him and sat up on the edge of the bed. Dirt and grass lay on the bottom sheet.

I stared at the mess.

"What?"

"There's crap on the bed?" I scrunched my face.

He glanced at the bed and then peered at me.

"Oh that probably happened when I lay on it last night, you know, before my shower."

I tried to picture him on the bed the night before. I was quite sure he hadn't pulled back the sheets, but I could not be positive about it.

I disregarded the gut instinct in my stomach and poured myself some coffee. "Would you like some?"

"No, thanks," he said.

He walked over to the table, grabbed a water bottle and chugged it down. I glanced at the other empty water bottles on the table. There were probably seven in all. I didn't recall either one of us drinking that much water within the last twelve hours. Even with myself being dehydrated, I still hadn't drunk that much water.

Silly, I thought. Why question whether somebody drank so much? What reason did I have to question it? Odd, maybe, especially that many in one night. Why be paranoid over water bottles? And, dirt in the bed?

Staring at the debris, I sat in the chair and sipped on my coffee, my knees folded into my body. Warrant sat opposite me, in shorts, rubbing his eyes and scratching his scalp.

"So, if you don't mind my asking, what are your intentions?" He watched me through one eye, the other hid behind the palm of his hand.

"I'm thinking about going to the sheriff's office and seeing if they can help me."

He moved his hand. "Help you? As in...how?" He shook his head.

I thought about how I was going to mention my plight, but decided against most of the details. After everything that happened with Wayne and then with Jace, I didn't know how well I could trust another stranger. It was probably best to get to know him a little bit better, especially after finding dirt and grass in the bed.

Maybe he couldn't sleep last night. Maybe he went for a walk.

Why am I giving this man the benefit of the doubt? Because something told me he's not like the others.

I leaned my head against my knees.

"I...um...believe I used to live in Phoenix. I suffered some amnesia or loss of memory, and don't remember a whole lot. I want to try to find my family."

"Oh?" His eyes lit up. "And, you just wound up here in Flagstaff?"

"I guess. Is this Flagstaff?"

"Yeah. You really don't remember much, do you?"

"No," I lied. I sipped on my coffee some more.

"Do you know how you got here?"

"No."

Slivers of daylight drifted in through the window, striking the wall above the bed.

"Well, if you want I can take you to the sheriff's office. Maybe they can help you?"

"Wow!" He leaned on the table, his arms crossed on the tabletop. "You must have really been through something."

"Yeah, and I wish I could remember."

He leaned back in his chair and folded his arms across his chest. "So, why do you think you come from Phoenix?"

"Something just tells me. Intuition, I guess." This was partially true.

"Huh...Well, maybe they can cross-link their information and see if they can find a missing woman with your description."

"Yeah, that's kind of what I'm hoping for."

"And, what if they can't?"

I looked down at my lap. "Then I don't know. I don't know anybody, at least that I remember."

I thought about this. Honestly, I didn't know what I was going to do, other than talk to the sheriff's department and see if they could help me.

"Well, tell you what. Why don't you get dressed, we'll go get some breakfast and I'll take you to the sheriff's office. I need to run a couple of errands in the meantime, so you can talk to them while I do that. After a couple of hours, I'll swing by and pick you up, find out what's going on, and we'll take it from there."

Our eyes met. "Really? You'd do that for me?"

"Yeah, I would. I hate to see anybody lose their family." He leaned forward again, "Listen, I'm from out of town, on business. You're more than welcome to stay with me in the meantime. I'll probably be here for most of the week. I do have work to tend to, but you can come in and out as you want. They actually gave me two keys, so you can have the extra one."

"Thank you." I was grateful for his help.

He whipped the extra key out of his wallet and threw it within reach on the table.

"I only ask that you don't bring anybody here. I don't know the townsfolk and I prefer to keep it that way."

"Then why did you help me?"

His eyes lowered to the table. "Like I said, I was left for dead."

I avoided his statement and let him continue.

"Also, please do not question me. If I have somewhere to go, leave it alone. Otherwise, you're going to find yourself back on the side of the road."

"Alright." Our eyes met yet again. I was now officially leery of him.

"Also, please watch your back. I don't want visitors."

"I understand –"

He cut me off, his voice stern. "No, I'm not talking about having friends over. Just watch your back."

"Can I ask one question?"

"What's that?"

"Are you running from the law?"

He snickered, his mouth curled up at the ends. "No, I'm not a criminal."

I finished my coffee and set the cup down. "Anything else?"

"I think I covered most everything."

I thought about our conversation, wondering who he really was. Was he a cop or some other law enforcement agent? If so, he probably would have said something when I mentioned I was going to the sheriff.

He stood up, grabbed a bag from the floor, and held it out to me.

"What's this?" I took it, looking up at him.

"Clothes. Your other clothes are looking pretty ragged."

"Oh, thank you," I said.

It was the last thing I expected from him. Hell, it wasn't like he knew me; we were practically strangers.

"You've been awfully nice to me."

"Don't mention it." He sat down again and leaned his arms on the table.

"Why don't you get dressed and let's get some food. I'm starving."

"Sounds good."

With the bag in hand, I relocated to the bathroom. It was a miserable feeling to have a perfect stranger buying me clothes and food, and providing my shelter without the inability to give back.

In the bathroom, I put on the black panties. They had a red rose on the hip. I prayed this wasn't another sign of things to come. I held the jeans up. They were too long, which was typical for a woman of my height. I pulled the shirt out. A bra and socks spilled out on the floor. I was feeling pretty low at this point.

What stranger bought clothes for another, not expecting anything in return? There had to have been a catch somewhere…and then I wondered if he had something to do with the fights. A gulp of air stuck in my throat. Maybe that was why he didn't want visitors or people following me? Maybe it had something to do with that. Maybe instead of taking me hostage and keeping me under wraps, they were using a different method, like tempting the bee with the honey – kindness instead of anger and hostility.

Maybe he had something to do with Jace…I would just have to stay on guard. I didn't have any other options so I hoped that wasn't the case.

I put on the black lace bra and then pulled the shirt over it. It was a long sleeve, black, button-up shirt with a layered tank look underneath. It was warm and cozy.

Setting the socks aside, I glanced at myself in the mirror. My eyes were looking a little better, not as tired as they were last night. I turned the water on and ran it over my face, hoping it wouldn't be the last time. I dried off and brushed my hair, scooping it back into a ponytail. Then I grabbed the socks and left the bathroom.

I sat at the table to put them on. Warrant set a box down in front of me. I glanced at the box, then up at him.

"They're not top dollar, but they're better than the other shoes you had on. Something a little more durable for the weather and terrain out here."

I stared at him for a minute before opening the lid. Inside was a pair of black hiking boots. I pulled them out and played with the strings before fixing my eyes on him again.

"Honestly, why are you doing this? Are you expecting something in return?"

His eyes studied mine.

"I don't know what you went through out there, and I'm not sure if I want to know. Obviously, something bad happened to you. And, if anything else happens to you, then you need to be prepared."

I sat there, holding one of the shoes in my lap.

Warrant replied, "Like I told you, I was left for dead. Something terrible happened to me, and a stranger took me into his home and helped me. He fed me, clothed me, and provided a shelter over my head before I left his home for good. If it hadn't have been for him, I would have died. Nobody deserves to die like that. Nobody deserves to live like that."

Why did I have to think he wanted something in return? Maybe I was in the wrong. I started stringing the shoes, peering up at him.

"I'm sorry. I didn't mean to be rude."

He knelt down in front of me, his eyes upon mine.

"Listen to me." He cradled my hands in his. The shoe tumbled from my lap. "I don't want anything from you."

"Alright." I started to reach for the shoe when he handed it to me.

"I'm guessing you had a bad situation with a man."

I nodded. Oh, if he only knew.

"And, I'm sorry to hear that. I hope you can move on with your life and that you can try to get past whatever happened to you."

I forced back tears, flashing a weak smile.

"Thanks," I muttered.

He stood up, grabbed his clothes, and moved towards the bathroom.

A bad situation with a man? More like monsters. I strung my shoes and put them on while Warrant dressed.

# CONFRONTATION OF THE WOLVES

Robert grinned from ear to ear, staring at the hideous creature which bore down on him. A burning sensation ripped through his own body. Every muscle and tendon pulsated as his blood pumped harder and faster, taking on a new form. His muscles enlarged, ripping his clothes. Hair sprouted, creating a thick layer over his skin. His mouth and nose elongated and his massive jaw opened, baring his new teeth and fangs. Robert's eyes deepened and darkened, glaring back at the creature who rushed him. He dropped to all fours on the ground, his back arching as a growl escaped his throat.

Fully developed into his alter ego, he reared back on his haunches and leapt into the air. The other wolf hit him. Robert charged. Their bodies collided in midair before gravity took them down to the ground. They scrambled to their feet. Then, they lunged at one another again, their vicious mouths snapping. Their claws struck the other, ripping large gashes across their chests and stomachs.

They came down upon the earth again. Robert's mouth clamped down hard on Jerry's neck, pinning him to the ground. Jerry's claws raked across Robert's chest, spewing blood over the mountainside.

Determined not to let him get away, Robert clamped down harder on his neck. But the pain from the wound spread throughout his pectoral muscles, forcing him to let go. Jerry spun around on his feet and took off running, blood dripping from his wounded neck.

Robert licked his wounds before launching himself after Jerry again. The rocky terrain provided little comfort to the wounds which resonated throughout his body. His nose sought out the coppery scent, taking him to a hidden cave within the mountains.

Robert studied his surroundings before lingering inside, detecting Jerry's presence within. Something whimpered. Leaving himself within his alter ego, he followed the sound. The cave provided little light, so he relied on his senses. He moved deeper into the cave, sensing another beast lurking inside besides just Jerry.

Robert wrinkled his nose in distaste from the smell of dead animal. A large shadow moved to his left. He whipped his head around, growling low and deep. The large black bear stood above him atop a rock ledge. The bear raised its limbs rose above its head, trying to convince Robert he was the alpha male. An even deeper growl echoed throughout the cave.

Robert rose up on his haunches and lunged at the bear above him, driving him and the black bear down to the ground, next to the wounded Jerry. The rocky ground drove hard into his back. Jerry scrambled to his feet and launched himself at the bear.

Robert's mouth came down upon the animal's back. Jerry snapped his mouth shut upon its throat. The bear howled in pain.

The bear's lifeless body fell to the ground as Jerry continued to maul at its neck. Robert spun his head around towards Jerry, another low growl erupting through the empty air. Jerry backed off of the bear as Robert advanced on him. Robert was ready for his prey to give in or die trying to live. He circled in towards Jerry, who backed toward the cave entrance.

Blood flowed from the gash Robert had left on Jerry's shoulder.

He lunged at Jerry, sending the two of them sprawling out of the cave. Jerry fell backwards into the tree trunk, coming to rest at the base. He lay, unmoving. Robert proceeded toward him.

Jerry transformed back into human shape. The blood that had coated his fur now coated his human skin. He struggled to pull himself up the tree, and stared back at Robert, groaning in pain. Robert stood in wolf form, inches from his face.

Jerry said between groans, "Who…the…hell are…you?" His injuries began to knit together.

Robert let his human form take over, blood dripping from his chest. He moved in close. Robert drove his fingers into the bloody hole, preventing it from healing. Jerry screamed.

"You motherfucker!"

Jerry squirmed.

"What do you know about that woman?"

"I ain't telling you anything!" he spat out.

Robert drove his fingers in deeper, causing it to bleed more.

Jerry screamed again.

"Answer the fucking question!"

Robert inched closer, watching Jerry's body try to transform back into his alter ego. Jerry's beast bounced back and forth, his jaw and eyes changing but never taking full form.

"Answer the fucking question, or I'm going to torture you the whole day! I'll fuck you over, drag your body in that cave, and leave you to rot!"

His fingers bore deeper into the man's skin.

"I don't know much, I swear!"

"Tell me what you do know."

Tears welled up in Jerry's eyes. His voice cracked. "Rumor has it she fought and killed a vampire in a bar fight."

Robert thought about this. Bar fight? Was it the same bar fight his father died in?

"Go on."

"She's some martial arts expert, impressed somebody within the circuit."

Robert's curiosity got the better of him.

"Where are these fights?"

The guy took a deep breath, coughing. "Everywhere."

"What do you mean, everywhere?"

Jerry winced. "I'm serious, man. I don't know all of them, but some bars have underground cage fighting."

Robert raised his eyebrow. "Really?"

"Yeah, the vamps and the werewolves bet on them. Once in a blue moon, we get mortals who find out about them and come to the fights, but they usually don't make it out alive," Jerry said. "The vamps usually detect them and get rid of them. And, if not them, then the wolves take care of the mortals."

"And…"

"Both the wolves or the vamps bring their mortal champions, and they fight to the death."

To the death…Shit, that wasn't good. Robert recoiled, pulling his finger back just a little.

"To the death?"

"Yes. Crystal has been reigning champion for over four years. Everybody wants their champion to fight her, because they all believe theirs can beat her, but nobody's been able to."

"No shit." Robert looked the man over. "You're not fucking with me, are you?"

He pushed his finger deeper inside. Jerry whined beneath his pressure.

"No, I swear. Please…"

Robert loosened up again.

"She's good, really fucking good," Jerry went on. "So much that everybody wants her for their champion, but she's hard to find. They've kept her hidden for years."

"What do you mean, kept her hidden?"

"Listen, man, I'm gonna get in trouble."

"If you don't answer the question, you're really going to be in trouble. Answer the question!"

"One of the wolves in the circuit kept her prisoner and then she got loose. Now the vamps have her, and the wolves want her back."

"Who has her?"

"I don't know. Somebody."

"Who has her!" Robert held back, trying to keep his emotions in check.

"I don't know the vamp's name…" He groaned in pain.

Robert's finger dug deeper. More blood shot out.

"Some vamp and his associates. They're some loner group. They don't associate with many other vamps unless it has to do with fighting, and even then they're usually not welcomed," Jerry said.

"They've done some illegal stuff within the community. I'm not exactly sure what. That's why the other vamps aren't too happy with them right now."

"What did they do?"

"I don't know! I'm not privy to that information. I'm a fucking wolf. You think they're going to welcome me into their private circle? Hell no."

"When's the next fight?"

"Tonight. Crystal's supposed to be fighting."

Robert pulled his finger out of the man's wound. "You're taking me with you."

"Oh, hell no."

"Yes, you are. If you don't, I'm going to find you and kill you myself, along with your pretty little sister."

Jerry's face twisted. "Don't you touch her."

"Likewise, asshole. I saw you manhandling her. You better watch your step. I'm a Deputy, and I'll bust your ass in a heartbeat."

"What!" Jerry stared back at him.

"Yeah, and I have links within the community. Don't fuck with me."

Jerry sighed and leaned his head against the tree trunk. "Tonight, meet me at the ice cream shop, seven o'clock. We'll go together. Starting price is a hundred a person. You can't get in if you don't bet."

"I'll have my money."

Robert gazed down at the gash on Jerry's shoulder. It had already started healing. Blood crusted the skin. "You should be back to normal soon."

Jerry peered up at him. "Yeah, I think I know that, asshole."

Robert grinned and walked away, leaving the man to be. His body was naked under the warm sun. He tromped through the grass to where his clothes lay on the ground. Scooping them up, he glanced back. Jerry was nowhere in sight. Robert walked on, back to the edge of the forest. He scanned the area, making sure nobody was around, and then ran back to his car. He threw his clothes in the trunk and pulled out a duffel bag. He jumped in the car and dressed inside of it, still keeping an eye out.

# SHERIFF'S OFFICE

Warrant took me to breakfast at a local restaurant and then dropped me off in front of the Coconino County Sheriff's Department, leaving me alone to ponder how I was going to approach them. I walked in and glanced around the facility, taking in a deep breath. I approached the man behind the front desk. His grey hair was thin and receding.

"How can I help you?"

He had a friendly voice, yet I found myself having to force a smile.

I looked around one more time, and then our eyes met. "I, uh, need some help."

He cocked his head. "Well, that's what we're here for. What is it you need, Miss?"

Hardly any activity was in sight. Flagstaff was a moderate-sized town and, from what I remembered, the crime rate was extremely low.

"I really don't know how to explain...I don't remember much, but I believe I used to live in Phoenix. At least, I think I did at one time."

His brow creased.

"I, uh, don't know my name either, but I was told I need to find a Robert Bouchard. He was born June twentieth, nineteen eighty nine."

The cop at the desk cleared his throat.

"Robert Bouchard?" He peered at me under his arched brow.

"Yes."

"And, who told you to find him?"

I thought about how to answer this question. "Um, somebody I met. They said he might be able to help me."

Somebody flew in the front door behind me. I turned, my eyes focusing on the Deputy who had walked in. He was busy adjusting his belt and shirt when the wind blew the door wide open, slamming it into the wall. He peeled it from the drywall and shut it.

Our eyes met for a brief moment before he turned and walked around me.

"You're late," the cop behind the desk said.

"Yeah, well, I had something to take care of, and Robert said we might have a lead…"

Before I turned to resume with the man behind the desk, the late cop did a double take, his eyes fixed on mine. His mouth hung open.

"Can I help you?" I asked, a little bothered by his expression.

"Actually, *he* can help *you*. Torrance, why don't you assist the lady?"

"Uh…Yes, I can do that. Thanks, Sid."

"No problem." A funny look crossed the desk cop's face.

I wasn't quite sure what to make of it.

Torrance continued to stare at me. He was stunned, at least from what I could tell.

"Well, then, are you going to help me?"

"Yes, yes, let's go." He looked me over before leading me to a different desk.

He lowered to the chair while I dropped into mine. He took a deep breath, folding his hands in front of his face.

"Are you okay?" I asked.

"Yeah, I'm great. How about you?"

He leaned forward, his elbows crossed in front of him. He seemed a little too eager to me. It seemed as though everybody I met lately was a little odd, in some way or another.

"I'm doing alright, I guess." I watched every move he made.

"You need something to drink? Coffee, water, soda?"

"No, thank you, I'm good."

"Okay, well then how can I help you?" he asked, fidgeting with his pen.

At this point, I thought I should have been more nervous than him.

I remained cautious of what I was going to tell him. "Well, I, um, don't know how to explain this. It might be a little weird, but my memory is pretty much gone, so I can't even begin to tell you what I do remember. Anyway, somebody came to my aid and told me to look for a Robert Bouchard. He was born June twentieth, nineteen eighty-nine." I had his name and date embedded in my brain. "The man said Robert could help me."

"Robert Bouchard?" He slowly pronounced the name, almost the same way the desk cop had.

"Yeah."

"And, did this person say how he could help you?"

"No, he didn't. Listen, I don't know why – maybe it's just intuition and I might be wrong – but something tells me I lived in Phoenix before I lived here. I think I might find family there. Is there any way to do a search on Robert Bouchard?"

"Uh, yeah…Hey can you hold on one second?" His voice cracked as he stood.

"Yeah." He was making me more uneasy by the second.

"I'll be right back."

"Alright."

He rounded the corner, disappearing from sight.

§

Robert was in his car, heading for his house, when his cell phone rang. It was Torrance. He flipped open his phone.

"Yeah?"

Torrance's excited voice came across the phone.

"Robert, you need to get to the station now!"

"I can't. I already told you, it'll be a little while."

"You don't understand. It's –"

"Torrance, I have something I've got to do. Bye."

Robert hung up the phone. He had a lead on his Mom and he wasn't going to ruin it for anything. He was going to do everything he could to find her. He didn't need to be bothered with other bullshit right now, even if it was related to work. It was his day off and, by God, he was going to use his day off for personal reasons.

His phone rang again. Robert glanced at his phone. Fuck, it would be Torrance. No, he was not going to answer his phone.

"Asshole, I'm not answering your call. You can wait."

He threw the phone in the console and drove onward. Eventually the phone stopped and then it beeped, telling him there was a voicemail. Then a few seconds later, the phone rang again.

"I'm not going to answer you right now, Torrance," he said to himself. It was soon followed up by another beep.

He continued to drive. The wind hit the side of his truck, almost sending him into another lane. Then the phone rang a third time. Okay, this definitely was not the time. Why the hell was Torrance bothering him so damn much?

He picked up the phone again and flipped it open.

"This better be–"

"It's your mother," Torrance interrupted.

Robert pulled over to the right lane, cutting off another car as he came to a sudden halt on the shoulder of the road. "My mother?"

He glanced around, the honk of the car whizzing past him.

"Yeah, she's here in the sheriff's office," Torrance whispered.

"What! I'll be right there." Robert shut the phone, threw it in the console, and peeled out, narrowly missing another car as he pulled onto the highway. Robert searched for the next exit.

Within ten minutes, he pulled into the parking lot of the station and whipped into a parking space, slamming on his brakes. He jumped out of his car and ran into the station, a gust of wind nearly knocking him off of his feet. The wind caught the door behind him and almost slammed the door into the wall, but luckily his cat-like reflexes stopped the door before it did. He shut the door.

"Hey, Robert –" the desk cop started.

"Not now, later." He turned the corner. Torrance sat at his desk, arms crossed, glaring.

"You really need to answer your fucking phone when I call you," Torrance said. His face was serious, his mouth drawn tight and straight.

"Where is she?" Robert looked around before heading toward the desk. Then Torrance approached him, and put his hand on his friend's shoulder. Robert brushed it away.

"Where the fuck is she?" He stared back in his eyes.

"She's gone. She fucking took off…"

"Where the hell did she go?" Robert turned to leave but Torrance grabbed him by his shoulder again.

"Hey, stop a second."

Robert spun around, glaring at him. "What?"

"You need to calm down."

"And, next time something important like this comes up again, you need to tell me." Robert brushed his hands off of him again.

"I tried, but you hung up on me, and then you wouldn't answer your phone."

Robert took a deep breath. "Listen…"

"No, you listen. I tried to tell you and you wouldn't talk to me. Do I normally call you repeatedly when it's your day off? No, I don't. You should have immediately asked me what the fuck was going on. Now, I'm not saying this is your fault, but had you responded to me, then she might still be here."

Robert glanced around.

"How long ago did she leave?"

Torrance sighed. "Probably five, seven minutes ago. After we got off the phone and I was heading back to my desk, I noticed she was gone. I'm sorry, man. I was trying to get her to wait, but –"

Robert was out the door, running around the perimeter of the parking lot, hoping for a slim chance to see her, somewhere. Clouds billowed up in the sky, darkening it, threatening to provide more showers for the day.

"Fuck! Fuck! Shit!" He finally threw his arms up in defeat and wailed. "No, dammitt, no!"

He fell on his knees on the wet ground, tears in his eyes. He was so close, and to lose it all within minutes – hell, seconds. Tears streamed down his face. Angry and frustrated, his alter ego tried to take over, pumping more adrenaline through his system. He strained to control the disease, his hands clenching and unclenching next to him. His fingers threatened to expose the claws.

Then a hand patted his shoulder.

Torrance knelt down next to Robert. "Hey, man, you okay?"

Robert snapped his head around. "Do I look fucking okay to you?"

Robert peered back at Torrance through wild eyes.

Torrance recoiled. "I need you to relax. You're making me nervous. I don't think you realize what it's like for a mortal to work with a werewolf. It's a little unnerving sometimes."

Robert closed his eyes, lowering his head. "I'm sorry."

Torrance patted him on the shoulder again.

"I'm really sorry. I shouldn't have yelled at you," Robert said.

"It's okay. I'm alright. It's you I'm really worried about. You know, I really thought she was dead," Torrance said. "Nothing personal, I mean – honestly – it's been over four years. When somebody's missing that long, they usually don't show up, at least not alive."

"I know. Trust me, I've had my doubts from time to time, but I'd never stop looking for her."

"I know it's been difficult for you, and your family. Rarely, does anybody keep searching for a loved one that long."

"I've put my family through hell." Robert glanced up and looked around the parking lot, knowing she was long gone by now. "My wife practically hates me, my sister damn near belongs in a mental ward, and my kids – well, I'm barely managing with them. They always get so damn hyper when I'm around. They never calm down for me. They do for Rebecca, but not me. It's probably the tension and stress they get off me."

Torrance looked at the ground. "You're getting yourself wet there. You might want to stand up before anybody notices. You look like you've been sucking dick with those dirty knees."

Robert snickered.

"There you go. That's what I want to see."

They stood up and glanced at the stores across the street. Torrance wrapped his arm around Robert's shoulder.

"We'll find her. And, hey, she's alive. That's a good thing! That's a real good thing."

"Yes, it is." Robert turned to Torrance. "How did she look?"

Torrance smiled. "She looked good. Really good, actually."

"Good, I'm glad to hear that." Robert still had something to look forward to. His mom was within the area, so he might still have a chance of finding her.

"Yeah, she looks like she's been working out. She's kind of buff now. Not real buff, but well toned."

"Really?" Dread filled his heart. Were the fight stories true, then?

Robert peered across the street, wondering if she was within walking distance.

"We need to talk. You need to fill me in on what's going on. Come on, let's take a walk," Torrance said.

As they took a stroll around the perimeter of the sheriff's office, they exchanged information, from both Jerry and the brief conversation Torrance had with Crystal.

# RUNNING SCARED

Since I had no phone and no vehicle, I decided it was best to get to the motel, away from what could actually be more dangerous possibilities. I guess no place was safe at this point, and that included the sheriff's office.

As I walked along the sidewalk, I thought back to the Deputy at the sheriff's office. Once Torrance left with his cell phone in hand, I presumed the worst and decided it was best to leave. Hell, he could be one of the wolves, alerting the others to my location so I bailed out of the sheriff's office.

Hell, I didn't know whom to trust anymore.

I swayed with the wind, proceeding towards the motel. I worried that if any cop were to see me, he would think I was drunk and try to haul me in. I walked, sometimes breaking into a run, cautious of my surroundings.

Almost two miles down the road, I noticed a truck speeding in that direction. I ignored it and pulled my hood up over my head, hoping nobody could see my face.

I was beginning to wonder if I should just head to Phoenix and pursue my mission there. Hell, my son wasn't up here, why the hell should he be?

Then the hail started. Great! I put my arms over my head and walked faster until I was practically running. Water splashed my pant legs. My arms stung from the hail slung upon me. Then the thunder cracked and lightning lit up the sky. Nice.

As I shuffled through the water, an engine roared behind me. I dared not look back. Knowing my luck, it was the whacko cop. I picked up my pace and caught a glimpse of the car next to me. I tried to ignore it but then a female voice drifted out of it.

"Hey, do you need a ride!"

Hesitant, I turned, and peered into the car at her.

She had rolled down the window and was leaning over, trying to maintain speed to stay next to my side. She was a young brunette, high school age.

"The weather's supposed to get real nasty. I don't know if I'd be walking in it!"

I glanced at the older red mustang. She couldn't be any weirder than the people I've been running into lately.

"Are you sure! You don't know me! Didn't your mother teach you not to give rides to strangers?"

The girl smiled. "Just get in. You're getting soaked, and you're going to get sick! Would you rather wind up in the hospital with pneumonia?"

Well, hell, if I did, then I'd have a place to stay for awhile, but who knew what the doctors were like. They may have been worse than the sheriff's department.

"I'm going to soak the seat," I said, climbing into the comfort of her car. It was nice – dry and warm.

"That's okay. I can clean it up later."

We glanced at each other as she sped up.

"Thank you."

"Don't mention it. I'd hate to see you get sick or get hurt out there." Her warm brown eyes smiled back at me, her cheeks full and rosy. "Normally, I don't pick up strangers, but you look like you were getting pelted out there. They leave any marks on you?"

"Oh, I don't know." I pulled my sleeves up and noticed the red welts. I guess they did.

"It looks like it hurts," she said.

"I've been through worse. Thanks for your concern, though."

"So, where are you going?"

I started to tell her where I was staying, but thought better of it. A restaurant was close by. I would just have her drop me off there, and then walk from the restaurant to the motel.

"The restaurant on the corner up ahead. I'm supposed to meet a friend."

"So what are you doing walking? It's kind of wet out there."

"Well, I was supposed to get a ride, but my ride bailed."

"Ah, that sucks."

"Yeah, you're telling me."

"I'm Jennifer, by the way."

I glanced at her before remembering the name I'd given Warrant. "I'm....Brandy."

"Ooh, I like your name."

"Thanks." I turned, my eyes focusing on the road up ahead. "So, shouldn't you be in school or something?" I asked.

She looked awfully young.

"Yeah, well, I had a doctor's appointment. I was headed back to school and then I saw you, decided you might need a ride."

"Oh, well, thank you." The warm air heated up my skin. "That was very nice of you."

"No problem."

I looked around the refurbished mustang. "I like your car."

"Thanks! My brother did all the work on it."

"He did a good job."

"Yeah? I think so too. He actually wanted me to get a truck or an SUV. He said it would be more practical."

"It probably would up here."

"But I like Mustangs, and it use to be my Mom's, so he fixed it up for me. I paid for the parts and he did the work."

"Good for you." Even though I didn't know her, I had some respect for her. She was a young, hard working woman, respectable and compassionate. "So where do you work?"

"That pizza place we just passed. That's where I work."

"Oh, see that restaurant right there?"

"Yeah?"

"You can drop me off there."

She pulled into the parking lot right in front. "It was really nice meeting you," she said.

"It was nice meeting you, too. You take care and keep on working like you are. You'll get somewhere with that kind of perseverance."

She had a glimmer in her eyes. "Thanks. I hope your date shows up."

"He's not really my date, but thanks."

I smiled and stepped out of the car. The hail had stopped but I still had to walk in the rain.

We waved at each other through the window. I was happy I finally met some normal people for a change instead of the usual vampires and werewolves. So that she would think I was going inside the restaurant, I stepped up onto the sidewalk next to it and stood by the door. I watched her drive away.

I waited for a couple of minutes before I stepped back onto the wet asphalt. Now I would have to back track down the road and around the corner, but luckily it wasn't too far. A rumble barreled around the corner. Warrant pulled into the parking lot, directly in front of me. His helmet hid his eyes, but I knew he was looking at me.

"How the..."

"Just get on."

I climbed onto his bike, my arms wrapping around his waist. I buried my head into his leather jacket. I didn't like the tone in his voice. He sounded pissed off. I lay still against him on the ride to the motel. The warmth from his body kept me warm.

Within a couple of minutes, we were at the motel. He helped me off the bike, his helmet still on his head as we walked to the room. I wondered how he'd found me.

He threw the door wide open, slamming it against the wall. He flung his wallet and hotel key across the room.

Yeah, he definitely wasn't in a good mood. I cringed.

His helmet flew across the floor. I started to ask him what the problem was when he slung the door shut behind me. It narrowly missed hitting my back. He backed me into the wall, his face halting within inches of mine. I stared at him, not understanding what the issue was.

"What the...?" I began.

He clutched me by my face and pressed me hard into the wall. I tried to pry his hands away, bending his fingers back, ready to break them. To my shock, they stayed intact. I stared at him. At this point, I would have broken the average person's fingers.

"Who were you talking to?" he breathed in my face. His eyes burrowed into mine, his voice gruff and menacing.

"Just some teenage girl. What is your –?"

"Who is she?"

His hands slid from my chin, farther down my jaw line to the top of my neck. I struggled against him but he only moved in tighter against me.

"I don't know. She offered me a ride. Look, I only asked her to drop me off at the restaurant. I knew better than to have her drop me off here."

His hand was on my throat, cutting off my oxygen. I grabbed at his hands.

"I thought I told you to wait for me."

"I...I..."

I tried to gasp for air but could not. I used what little strength I had and punched him near the elbow on the inside of his arm. My hand slid down his forearm, releasing his hold on me. My fist rebounded up and struck him in the chest, pushing him away.

Regaining my breath, I staggered away from him and the wall. I grasped at my throat, the heat from his hands still radiating on my skin. I kept my eye on him and tried to take in a deep breath. Instead I had a coughing fit.

"Stay….the…fuck….away from me," I managed to say. I continued to back away, coming in contact with a chair.

"I'm sorry, I really didn't mean –"

"Just stay away from me."

I straightened up the best I could and pulled the chair around in front of me, trying to block him from approaching. It wasn't much, but it was something to stand in the way. If I could regain my strength, I was going to chuck it at him.

He finally stopped and stared back at me. "I'm truly sorry. I didn't mean to hurt you."

"Yeah, whatever. Tell you what, let me give you your stuff and I'll get the hell out of here. I'd prefer to be on my own, lost and hungry in the woods, than stuck in a motel room with a violent son-of-a-bitch, or whatever the hell you are."

I took off my wet shirt and threw it at him, purposely hitting him in the face with it. Water sloshed all over him.

He grabbed at the shirt and wrenched it off his face. "No, don't…"

"No, really, you can have your shit."

I peeled the boots off and threw them at him, trying to hit him again. He removed the shirt, and caught one boot as it was headed for his chest. The second boot caught him in the groin. He tried to stifle a groan, but he doubled over. With him too busy to approach me, I pried off my jeans.

"Don't, really…" he began.

I advanced on him, took the jeans I had in my hands and wrapped them around his neck, squeezing hard. I kneed him in the face, and nailed him in the nose. He groaned again.

He wrapped his arms around my waist and drove me backwards into the wall, like he was trying to tackle me. I slammed into it hard. My hands slipped off of the jeans, and my head rocked back, striking the wall. I groaned. I grabbed onto his head like I was cradling a football, and kneed him again, this time in the stomach. He straightened up so I held on tighter.

He was much stronger than me. Even though I still held his head, he picked me up off of my feet, into the air and over his shoulder, tossing me backwards onto the bed behind him. I struggled to maintain contact with the ground, but my efforts were fruitless.

The moment I hit the bed, I glanced up and over my shoulder at him. He looked back at me.

"Okay, maybe I deserved that. Actually, I did deserve that. I shouldn't have grabbed you like I did. I'm really sorry," said Warrant.

I turned myself over on all fours, facing him. "Damn straight, you deserved that. You could have killed me. I'm still leaving. I'm not going to be around somebody who can't control his temper."

I started to get off the end of the bed.

He reached out and grabbed my arm. "Wait."

I looked down at his hand, "You better remove that."

He let go. "Can you forgive me? Please. I've never hurt a woman like that before, I swear to God. I really didn't mean to hurt you. I just let my anger get the best of me. I had a really horrible business deal, and I took it out on you. I'm really sorry."

Our eyes met, and then I realized I was down to my skivvies.

He looked me over before his eyes locked on mine. "I'm really sorry. Can I make it up to you?"

He walked a little closer and reached out to take my hand. I recoiled, wary of his intentions. I stared him in the eyes, swallowing hard, ready for him to attack again. His eyes were almost glassy. So much so, I could see my reflection in them.

I looked away as he picked up my hand. I faced him again.

"What the hell got you so riled up?" I was stern, and determined not to let him pull the same shit again.

He avoided my gaze.

"I really don't want to talk about it right now," he muttered.

"Oh, that's right. I can't ask you about anything, can I? Sorry, I forgot," I said sarcastically. I tried to pull away but his grip tightened.

He caressed my hand, partially enclosing mine in his. He traced the veins on the back of my hand, the heat from his finger radiating everywhere he touched me. My blood boiled. It was strangely erotic, a feeling I tried to disassociate myself from.

"Can you please not do that?" I asked.

His eyes were upon mine.

"Sorry, I was just mesmerized for a moment."

He still held onto my hand, his finger trailing down my arm before losing contact with my skin.

"I haven't been with a woman in awhile."

Oh, this was the last thing I needed right now.

"You don't know how hard it was for me to sleep in the same bed with you. I actually had to get up and go for a walk. That's why you saw the dirt in the bed."

That made sense. Unfortunately, my mind had wandered to stranger, more unusual circumstances.

"I really wish you would reconsider, though. It's dangerous out there. There are weirdos and animals out there."

"I've survived before, I'm sure I can do it again." I went to get my clothes.

"They're wet, and you're going to get sick. Do you want to wind up in the hospital?"

"No, I don't, but I can make it."

I went to the bathroom and grabbed my old clothes. Then, I sensed him behind me.

"It's going to get really cold out there. You have a chance in hell of making it one night in those."

He was probably right, but I would rather die in the cold than be strangled to death in my sleep. I stood up, facing him, my stuff in my hands.

"Besides, you can't even make it one night in a room with a broken heater. You were all over me trying to warm up," he went on.

I stared back, resentful I had curled up next to him. "It was strictly for warmth, nothing else."

"See, you just admitted it," he said, a sly grin on his face.

"So?"

"It's going to be five degrees out there tonight, and in here it was only thirty degrees. You need warmth and shelter. I promise I won't touch you."

"Do you think I'm some kind of fool? Why are you so damn hell-bent on making me stay here with you?"

"Fine." He motioned with his hands towards the door. "Go on out, freeze to death. See if I care."

He left me alone in the bathroom while he went to the bed and turned on the TV. That was fine. I didn't need him. I could make it out there again on my own.

The smell of mold wafted up into my nose. My clothes were still wet.

I wrinkled my nose in disgust and pulled my wet pants on my suddenly-freezing skin. Oh, God, the clothes were slick, almost fishlike. I was disgusted and, hesitantly, put my freezing wet shirt on. My nipples hardened. I thought they were going to fall off.

I picked up my shoes, which were slimy and gross now, too. I've been through worse, so what the fuck difference was this?

I walked out of the bathroom and sat down at the table. I was putting on my shoes when a loud thud filled the room.

"Oh, hell!" he yelled.

I looked up.

He had slammed the remote control down on the nightstand. "You are one stubborn bitch, aren't you?"

"Fuck you!" I pulled one shoe on and switched feet when he bolted toward me.

"What are you doing!" I screamed.

He wrenched the shoe out of my hand and pulled me to my feet, staring me in the face. "Jesus, you're freezing!"

"Yeah, so what do you care!"

"Enough to pull you in from the rain, shelter you, feed you, and clothe you. Stop being so fucking stubborn and get out of those clothes." He folded his arms in front of his chest.

"Yeah, I'm sure you'd like that." I was tired of him and his macho attitude. "I'm sure you enjoyed the show earlier too."

"Well, I am a man and it has been a long time. I'll admit it, yes. I enjoyed watching you bounce around the damn room earlier. As a matter of fact, I got a fucking hard-on the minute you took your shoes off."

I shook my head at him, my hands on my hips. Goose bumps and chills broke out on my flesh.

He sighed and calmed down. "Take your clothes off."

"No."

Our eyes met, mine hard and defiant, ready to win this fight. His were irritated and tired.

"Come on, stop being stubborn. You're going to freeze to death."

"No. Now can I have my shoe back?" I put out my hand.

"No." He threw the shoe behind him, striking the wall seven feet away.

"What do you really want from me?"

"What I really want from you right now is to stop being hard headed. Do I need to get physical with you?"

"What…"

He grabbed me, pulling me into his arms. My clothes soaked his, the smell of mildew mingling between us. I pushed him back.

"Oh, that's nasty." He gagged. He let go of me, wrinkling his face.

"Thanks, asshole."

I tried to walk around him when he pulled me back into his arms again, my back against his chest.

"I wasn't talking about you. I was talking about the clothes. Jesus, how the hell can you wear those?"

He grabbed the bottom of my shirt, and yanked it up to my nose, forcing me to smell it. I admit, I wanted to gag. And, the smell would eventually get worse.

"See, I told you," he said. "Don't you women ever listen?"

"Fuck you," I said.

He wrenched the shirt over my head and threw it to the side. I froze so badly I thought my bones were going to crack. I stood there, unable to move.

"Are you alright?"

"No, I'm really fucking cold." I wrapped my arms around my chest, trying to warm up, not caring I was partially undressed and wearing wet, slick pants.

Reaching around my waist to undo my pants, he sighed.

"No, don't," I said, my teeth chattering. "I'll – I'll do it."

His breath was hot in my ear. "Don't worry about it, I got it."

Pressing his cheek to my ear, he wrapped his hands around my hips and grabbed my pants. Warrant pushed my pants over my hips, leaving a trail of heat halfway down my backside. He slid his hands around to the front and gently slipped them inside. The warmth of his hands sunk in through the soft fabric, the heat radiating down through my pelvis, stroking every erogenous zone in my body.

I closed my eyes, aware I was now leaning back against him. The warmth from his chest burned through my back. He pressed hard against me, and his hands extended farther inside and circled around to my back, pulling my pants down over my rear. He slid them down to my ankles.

Everywhere his hands went, he left a trail of fire burning deep inside me. I wrapped my arms backwards and around his neck. His hands moved up and over me, caressing me. One hand circled over my stomach while his other brushed my hair to one side, leaving my neck bare. He pressed me back into him, until I felt his ever-increasing desire.

I took in a deep breath, wanting it just as much as he did.

He kissed me on the neck, and then his tongue flicked over my skin. I gave in, willingly, and took a deep breath. His hand cupped my breast, his mouth nearing my ear. His heat radiated throughout my body, my skin sweating from his warmth.

I shouldn't have given in to him after our earlier confrontation, but oh, did he feel good. I turned towards him, my mouth brushing against his.

Our eyes met.

He removed my hand from the back of his neck, and with his hand on my lower back, he spun me around. He pushed me into him, his lips on mine. It was soft and inviting but escalated into a sense of urgency. I grabbed onto his shirt, suddenly wanting it off of him.

I went for the buttons on his wet shirt, and then realized the water was not from the rain, but from him. The sweat from his body had soaked right through. He was extremely hot.

I fumbled with the buttons, trying to get a grip on them, and then decided otherwise. I grabbed onto his shirt and ripped it open. Buttons flew everywhere. He scooped me up in his arms and took me to the bed.

I sought out the button and zipper on his pants, barely getting them undone before he was on top of me. Then my hands moved to the top of his pants and pushed them down as we connected again. His mouth was burning up. The rest of our clothing trailed off our bodies while he slipped in between my legs.

He slid inside of me, holding tight onto my hips. I wrapped my legs around him. His mouth latched my neck, his hands exploring my body. Oh, yeah. I thought I was going to burn up, his body steamy and hot against mine. He pulled me harder to him, thrusting slow and rhythmically, our hips moving as one.

I expected him to be harder and rougher with me, considering he hadn't been with a woman in a while. Instead, he seemed to want it to last just as long as I did. I arched my back, my breasts swelling up in front of his face. Rolling my head back, I noticed a strange physical change in his face but I was too enthralled in the moment to give it a second thought.

As he lowered his head to mine, a wild groan escaped his lips. Welcoming his animalistic side, I responded, our thrusts becoming harder and more intensified. His grip tightened on my hips. Another growl bellowed in my ear. I didn't care, thought nothing of it. Instead, I reveled in our moment together.

Moaning, he pulled back. Our eyes met again. One of his hands sought the pillow next to my head. He held me tight with one arm as we came together, his last thrust throbbing inside me. He buried his face in the pillow next to my ear. His body trembled against mine, weakening within my arms.

I ran my hands up and down his back, the tension in his muscles relaxing. He lay with his face still buried in the pillow, his heartbeat now against mine.

"You okay?" I asked, grinning.

He lay quiet for a moment. Then he lifted his head and glanced at me. Something drifted in the air to his right. I didn't really pay attention to it until I looked at him. Pillow stuffing stuck to the side of his mouth. I laughed, not really meaning to.

"Wow!" I laughed. "I never met a man that got that excited. Does it help with the release?"

A smug smile crossed his face. "Sorry, it gets pretty intense for me, as I'm sure it does for you, too."

"Well, of course, but not enough to bite a pillow. I hope it was that good."

"Oh, yeah." He smiled.

Then a thought crossed my mind. I tried to disregard it, but it seemed to stay in place. Sheer terror filled my mind. My smile faded. I lay there, and stared at him, not knowing what to say. The look on my face wiped the smile from his.

"What's wrong?" he asked.

I panicked, pushed him off me and leapt from the bed, wanting to be as far away from him as possible. My heart beat faster. My hands shook. It was best to leave. He sat up.

"What's wrong?" he asked again. He moved to the edge of the bed and reached for my hands.

I recoiled from him.

"You're one of them. One of those fucking werewolves..." I spat out.

I scrambled for my clothes, glancing back at him. I was worried he was going to attack me.

The smile had vanished, his mouth now a thin line. He stood and strolled over to me. I struggled into the wet jeans, the ones he had bought. He stepped in front of me, just as I stumbled and nearly fell into him.

He lifted my chin. "Do you think I'm a monster?"

Leery of how to interpret his question, I glanced away.

"Well, aren't you?"

He let go.

"Well, I guess I am, in a sense."

I swallowed hard, moved away from him, and looked around for my bra. Then, when he approached me again, something registered on his face.

"That's actually kind of funny, now that I think about it. I never mentioned anything about werewolves, and most people don't believe in them. How was it you knew what I was?" He cocked his head, his hands on his hips.

I fumbled with my bra clasp, stating, "I just guessed."

I stepped back. He took a step closer.

"I'm sorry, nobody just guesses that. What gave you the idea I was a werewolf?" He became stern and demanding.

"Maybe it was the fact that you attacked a pillow while we were having sex instead of attacking me. Why? I'm not exactly sure, but…"

I remembered something Wayne had told me. He'd mentioned he had to control himself, whether it was anger, jealousy, or sex. Warrant could have easily killed me, but he didn't. Why not?

"What is it?" He stood naked before me, his hands still on his hips.

My curiosity arose. "Why didn't you kill me?"

"Is that what you want? Because if it is, I can take care of that for you."

I grimaced. He could have easily torn me apart and left me here for the maid to find, blood and guts spewed all over the room. But, again, he didn't.

"Who are you?" I asked.

Agitated, he said, "You know my name. It's Warrant." He was frustrated with my questions.

"No, not your name. Who are you?" My voice rose and cracked at the same time.

"Why don't you tell me why it's so important to you, Brandy?"

We stood in silence before either of us moved or spoke.

His voice lowered. "Or is that your real name?"

At that, I ran for the door. I jumped over the bed and bounded across the room. In a split second, he was blocking my only way out.

I ran for the window but he was quicker than me. He stood in front of it, arms folded across his chest. I decided to make another attempt for the door, which was behind me. Instead, I turned and bounced right off of his chest.

He pulled me up into him, my feet leaving the ground and my face inches from his.

"How do you know about us?" he asked, his voice stern.

I didn't want to give him all the details.

From what I knew, all the vampires and werewolves were horrible people. Not one of them seemed to be decent. Not like I really expected them to be.

"I had an issue with one," I mumbled.

His eyes bore into mine. "With a werewolf?"

"Yes."

He narrowed his eyes in on me and wrinkled his nose. "Anybody else?"

"No." Again, he wasn't satisfied with my answer.

"You're lying."

"No, I'm not."

"Yes, you are. Who else did you run into while you were out in the wild?"

Pins and needles shot up my arms.

"You know, Brandy, we can sit here all day and wait it out. I don't have any issues with that. Or do I need to offer some persuasion?"

He sat me down on the edge of the bed and knelt in front of me, his hands resting firmly on my knees. His eye color transformed from deep brown to a golden hue.

I recoiled, afraid to move too fast. Warrant spread my knees apart and moved in between them. I tried to hide the fear, but I was sure he could smell it. He moved in close to me.

"Do I need to hurt you for you to answer me? Is that what it's going to take?"

He leapt on top of me, driving me down on the bed, his body fully transformed above me.

I stared up into the face of horror, unmoving, in fear for my life. I held my hands out in surrender.

"If you can understand me, then please change back," I whispered. "I'll tell you what I know. Please." The horrific werewolf face lingered before me.

We lay there, our gaze intent on one another. Warrant changed back, his naked body straddling mine. Even though he scared me, it was probably the most amazing thing I had seen in a long time.

His eyes still held mine, and as he spoke to me, I explored his body. My hands and fingers trailed along his chest, shoulders, and back in wonder of how the change really took its effect on him.

"Well, talk," he said.

I didn't say anything. Frustration appeared in his face.

"Do I really need to go through with this again?"

My breathing sped up, my heartbeat racing. "Yes, please."

His brows narrowed together. "What?"

"Please change again. You can still understand me when you're in your other form?"

"Yeah, why?"

"Please change again," I said.

"What the hell for?"

"Please."

He changed into his alternate form, his monstrous face in mine.

"Can I touch you like this?" I asked.

He nodded. Confusion registered in his eyes. I touched him, my fingers intertwining with his fur. The warmth from his body penetrated my skin. As I caressed the wild beast, shivers shot up my spine. The closer I inched my hands near his face, the more my arms shook. My heart raced. I tried to hide my fear, but I knew I could not.

The shaking in my hands got worse. I stroked his face, getting a little too close to his muzzle. His lip twitched, a low growl resounding in his throat. I swallowed hard, unsure whether he was going to attack or not. Though he was dangerous, I enjoyed touching the werewolf. Beneath my hand, he transformed back into his human self.

The heat from his skin radiated into my flesh. Our kisses were urgent and passionate. He tore the remainder of my clothes off of my body and we made love. Only this time, he left large gashes in the mattress with his claws, and tore up the other pillow with his fangs.

Later, as we lay sleeping, him partially atop me, I tried to remove his hand from my breast.

He lifted his head, shifted, and stared down at me. "What the hell was that about?"

"Sorry. I just thought it was magnificent watching you change like that. I wanted to see it again, and I, uh, wanted to touch you."

"You know, it's dangerous to touch me like that."

"You didn't seem to mind."

"That's because I can control myself better than others. You have a date with danger or something?"

That was an understatement. It was more like death. I didn't answer him, just stared back, wondering what his issue was as well. He propped his elbow up on the bed, and leaned his head on his hand.

"Now, that I officially have you pinned down...You're going to answer my question."

"And what was that?"

He didn't seem to have a sense of humor right now. "Really? You know what the question is."

"Refresh me." I gazed back into his lethal eyes.

"How do you know about us, and who else did you run into out there in the forest? It's obvious you know something, but you're not talking. I want to know. No, wait – let me rephrase that. I need to know what you know."

"Why is it so important to you? Why can't you just let it go? Why is it you can ask me, but I can't ask you?"

"Stop with the bullshit and answer me."

I swallowed hard, thinking about my past four to five years. What should I really avoid telling him? And, what should I really tell him? Even though we had some magnificent sex, why could I not trust him?

Running my finger along the side of his face, I asked, "How do I know I can trust you?"

He smiled. "What are you hiding?"

"What are you hiding?" I smiled back.

He grabbed my hand, pulling my finger away.

"How do I know I can trust you?"

We both had dilemmas – something we were both hiding and not willing to give up.

"Look, it appears we both have secrets," he said.

"You think?" I replied.

The smile disappeared from his face.

"Brandy, we're both going to need to trust each other somehow. Technically, my job…. Hmm, how do I explain this?" He drew in a deep breath. "Look, I don't run with a pack. I don't really have any friends – a couple here and there, but nobody really close. I don't confide anything in anybody. As a matter of fact, it's been a long time since I've been with a woman. I'm talking over two years. I don't trust anybody. I can't, not with my job."

"So, what is it you do for a living?"

He wrinkled his brow. "Okay, um, I can't tell you completely, but what I can tell you is this. You know how you have cops in the mortal world?"

I nodded.

"I'm not exactly a cop, but I'm like a cop. I can't tell you my exact job title. Otherwise I could be killed."

"Alright…"

"I'm after somebody," he explained.

"Somebody like you?"

"Sort of."

"Hmm." I tried to make sense of what he was saying.

"He is, but he isn't?" He was trying to clue me in on something but wouldn't, or couldn't, tell me.

"He's not a werewolf?"

He shook his head.

Then, I understood. "He's a vampire."

He nodded.

"So, you're after a vampire. Wait, are you like – Oh, shit – what did he tell me? Dammit, somebody told me that vampires and werewolves who are loners sometimes turn on their own kind, or become reckless against their own kind. Is that true? Are you like that?"

Warrant looked at me. "I do what I have to do to survive. I get paid very well for it, too."

I thought about what he said, how he worded it: he got paid to do what he does. "You're like a sniper, or a bounty hunter. Do you have to kill him or capture him?"

"I don't think you really need to know this part."

That answered my question. He was a sniper, out to hunt vampires. But why?

"So, why are you after this vampire?"

A look of concern crossed his face. "In our world, just as yours is, we have morals and ethics. You might not think so, but we do. Sometimes lines are crossed. Some vampires or werewolves cross that line, because they're reckless, or they don't care, or they're angry, or whatever else. Basically, they're doing something unethical, or morally wrong, or are involved in other criminal activity."

Well, that made sense.

"So, you have to find this vampire and kill him?"

Warrant rolled his eyes. "Something like that."

"Oh?" I took all of this in. "Now, are there vampires who have jobs like yours?"

"Oh, yeah, we're not the only ones. They also have snipers and bounty hunters."

"Interesting. Do you sometimes have to go after your own kind?"

"Yes, they're not any more protected than anybody else."

"And, you're considered one of the loners?"

"Yes," he answered, and then he thought for a second. "You mentioned somebody told you about the loners?"

"Yes."

"Who was this?"

"Somebody I met." I tried to leave out the details because I didn't want to wind up in a cell again. Especially once he found out I had belonged to the wolves originally. I didn't know if Warrant would be assigned to bring me back or not.

"Oh? And who was this?"

"Just some guy. He told me the story of the wolves and the vampires."

As I spoke, Warrant peeked at my neck and shoulders. Then his eyes met mine.

"You've been bitten." His voice was stern.

I hesitated. "Yes."

"And, this…" He eyed the wound on my side where I had been attacked on the road. "You've been attacked."

I couldn't hide it. I decided I was going to have to tell him something…however incomplete or slightly off-detailed the account was.

I explained that I had been out at a bar and wandered away into the night when a fight between the vampires and the wolves erupted inside. As I ran from the bar, a wolf attacked me until a car came along and scared it off. Then I explained that somebody tried to help me – took me into his home, sheltered me, fed me, and clothed me – but then took me out one night when another fight erupted. Only, this time when I ran off, I got lost in the woods. That was where I left it. I didn't say anything about the fights or how I had been captured and held against my will.

His cell phone rang.

"Excuse me one minute." He stood and grabbed his phone from the dresser.

"Hello."

His eyes lit up. "Are you sure about this? Uh-huh, interesting. Tonight? Is he…yeah, yeah…Where at? And you're certain he's going to be there?"

He paced the floor, his muscles taut and magnificent. "Well, that might be what he says, but are you sure? I don't want to blow this. Well, I know he doesn't know me, but that doesn't matter. I don't want to be seen everywhere and him not be there. He'll become suspicious of me." He glanced my way, his nude body facing me.

Maybe I could trust him. Maybe? But, I wasn't sure yet – and I didn't want to find out the hard way. He turned away.

"I could, but…I don't think that's a good idea. Yeah, you might think so, but I don't want anybody else getting hurt who's not involved. You know what I mean? Yeah, well that was my decision. I know, I know. Yeah, I know. Are you done yet?"

The frustration in his voice escalated.

"You don't need to know. Somebody...A friend. A long-time friend. Goodbye." He slammed his phone shut and threw it on the bed.

"What's wrong?"

He turned, his eyes narrowing in on mine. "They sent backup, and they know you're with me." He walked to the window and put his hands on his hips.

I swallowed hard, concerned about what was to come. "Who knows?"

"My boss and my colleagues," he said.

I sat up.

He slid onto the bed, next to me. "Do not leave this room unless you are with me. Do you understand?"

"Yeah." Now he was making me nervous. His eyes darted around the room. I grabbed his arm. "Warrant?"

"Yeah." He turned and looked at me.

"Who are they? Are they more wolves or vampires?"

He touched the side of my face. "I don't know. He didn't say."

"Is there any way to find out?"

I became worried Jace might have something to do with this. My grip on Warrant's arm tightened.

"Maybe." He eyed me. "Why? What's up?"

I looked down at the bed, my thoughts racing on what to do. If they were werewolves, they could be watching at any time and could follow me wherever I went. If they were vampires, they would be out at night and would attack then. The wolves wouldn't be so brave as to attack in the middle of the day unless I were alone somewhere, or they might just try to kidnap me again.

My heart started racing, fear settling deep inside. I didn't want anyone to find me again. I had to be able to trust Warrant, and hope his intentions were good.

I looked up at him, suspicious of what his reaction was going to be.

"Warrant? I have something to tell you and I pray to God you can help me. You're my only hope."

His eyes focused in on mine as I explained everything, including the kidnapping, my son, and Jace. He listened to what I said, his eyes never leaving mine.

When I had finished, I straightened up, waiting for his reaction. He drew me into him, his arms wrapping around me, and held me for what seemed like an eternity. It was the first time I received compassion from another human being in a long time. I yearned for this, and I finally broke down. My tears flowed freely, dissipating into Warrant's warm skin, his flesh taking on my pain and my hurt.

"I'm so sorry you had to go through that. Jesus," he said, leaning his head on mine. Continuing to hold me tight, he pressed his lips against my forehead. "You must have gone through hell."

"Yeah," I said, sniffling. "Remember when you asked me if I had a date with danger. Well, I've had a date with death for a while."

His muscles tensed up, his body tightening. "Jesus."

"What?" Lifting my head from his chest, I gazed at him.

He grabbed my chin, a horrid look on his face. "Do you know what's going on tonight?"

"No. What?" I had no clue what he was referring to.

"There's a fight tonight, and you're suppose to be fighting."

My mouth dropped open, my eyes wide. "What?"

"Yeah, now I don't know if this guy Jace never canceled it, or if he's hiding the fact that you're missing. Maybe he already replaced you with somebody, or maybe he's going to introduce somebody else tonight. Either way, your name is still being promoted for the fight. So something's up, and I'm not quite sure what. Maybe? Hmm, just maybe…."

My voice rose, frustration escalating. "Maybe what?"

"Maybe he's leaving your name on there for a reason. Maybe somebody is supposed to be there, like he said."

"Like who said?"

"One of my colleagues. He said the guy I'm after is supposed to be at the fight tonight."

"Really? Well, this is a good thing for you."

"Yeah, but now my curiosity is really aroused. Why didn't this guy cancel the fight? Or…" Then he looked at me. "Maybe he's waiting for you to appear. Maybe he thinks somebody else took you, like one of us, and they're going to turn up with you for the fight."

"You're thinking an ambush."

"Yes, I am. Or, maybe he has somebody stalking you, waiting for the right opportunity to strike, so they can turn you over to him," he said. "If that's the case, then it means we're being watched. And, it could mean, they know who I am. Son of a bitch!"

Great, this whole situation was getting worse.

"So, what are you going to do?"

"Well, I'm going to show up for starts." He rubbed his chin. "It would be nice though, if I had a female agent who looked like you to take with me, somebody we could use as bait."

Warrant grabbed his phone and flipped it open.

"What are you doing?"

He jabbed two of the keys before he glanced up at me. "I'm calling the agency."

My voice cracked. "Why?"

"So, we can get a female agent here to help out." He pressed another key.

"Do you think that's a good idea?"

"We're agents, Brandy. We're not amateurs." He pushed another key.

I thought back to what we were talking about. "Warrant, what do you think they're going to do?"

"Brandy, you're distracting me. Let me make this call."

"No, Warrant. I want something answered first."

I grabbed his phone, shut it, and held onto it.

He clenched his jaw, and peered up at me.

"And, what if they get a hold of her? What do you think they will do?"

He reached for the phone. I jerked it away.

"No, Warrant. Please answer the question first."

"I don't have time for this shit. Give me my phone, or I'll take it from you," he demanded.

"Answer the question, Warrant! If they think she's me, will they kill her?"

Our eyes met. I didn't like the look in them. He had no sense of compassion in them, no empathy, and no remorse.

"I'm not going to sugar coat it for you. I don't know Jace and I don't know what his agenda is at this point. This whole fight may be a ruse just to get you there and kill you in public, in front of everyone, all because you managed to get away from him."

He leaned in closer, and pointed his finger at me.

"*You* escaped him. A mortal humiliated *him* - a vampire. Think of how that looks in the vampire community."

I swallowed hard.

"He may only be out for revenge now." He snatched his phone. "If he decides to make a move while we're looking for our guy, we can take him out."

He started to plug the number into the phone again.

"Our only problem is, we don't know what he looks like. Only you do. So, even with a female agent there, we can't do anything unless we get his name first which I doubt he's going to do."

He shut his phone again. "Fuck! I don't need anything fucking up my mission, much less this jackass."

He looked directly into my eyes. "Miss. Brandy, you're screwed." He raised his left eyebrow. "Unless of course you come with me. That's a thought, but I'm not sure if you want to go after everything you've been through but that's your choice, not mine."

Warrant rested his head in his hand.

I deliberated. Should I? He did say that he might be able to take Jace out. With Jace gone, I'd be able to move on with my life and find my son without him tracking me everywhere.

But, what if I wound up in a predicament? Would his backup be there? Would they help me? Or would they only help Warrant? And, would Warrant help me find my son in exchange for helping him?

"Warrant?"

He raised his head. "Yes."

"Will your backup be there to help you?"

"Yes, they will."

"And, what about anybody else you might have with you?"

His brows narrowed in. "They'll be there to protect whomever the agency or I tell them to. Why do you ask?"

"Granted, I really don't want to do this, but if I go and I do fight, would it allow for more opportunity to find this vampire?"

"Yeah. But I'm going to warn you now – my backup is not strictly the wolves. There will be vampires as well. And you won't know who they are, so if there is any chaos and we get broken up somehow, you'd have to rely on somebody you don't know.

He added, "There's a distinct possibility the vampires you don't want to have anything to do with might come forth and either kill you or try to take you again. The same goes for the wolves."

"Your backup will help me though?"

"Yeah, they will help you. But you would really have to be on your toes. Really keep an eye out on everybody and everything."

I leaned my head on his shoulder. "Is this man dangerous? I mean, is he anymore dangerous than the other vampires?"

"Brandy, you don't know the half of it. He's extremely dangerous, and we definitely don't want you falling into his hands. He might be a fan, but there's no telling what he might do to you anymore than Jace will. He's an extremist."

I lifted my head. "Warrant, if it does any good, I'll fight tonight."

He sighed. "There's no guarantee on this. You're risking your life. You need to ask yourself, is it worth it?"

"Life with my son is worth it. A life with no vampires or werewolves forcing me to fight. I need to find my son. He's the only thing worth living for."

Tears cascaded down my cheeks.

Warrant looked down at me. He caressed my cheek.

"If you survive tonight, I'll help you find your son. That's a promise."

My eyes lit up. A glimmer of hope filled my heart.

"Really? You will? You promise?"

Tears poured down my face.

With a cheesy grin, he nodded. "Yes, I promise. I have a lot of connections. I'm sure we can find him."

I smiled, and threw my arms around him, knocking him backwards on the mattress.

"That means everything to me, Warrant. Thank you so much!"

I didn't want to let him go. He held me in his arms, and let me cry on his shoulder.

After I finally calmed down, I whispered, "You can call me Crystal."

# THE CLASH OF THE BEASTS

Warrant continued to remind me of what could happen during the fight, but I wouldn't listen. We ate, and then went out into the woods.

He forewarned me the others would be here soon, but they wouldn't show themselves. It was one of the rules for the snipers and the bounty hunters – not to reveal themselves to anyone. I found out he'd broken that rule with me. He told me he wasn't supposed to consort with anybody local. In a sense he had broken that one with me too, even though I really wasn't a local.

In the woods, he began a training regimen to get me psyched up for tonight, once again warning me of what could happen. I understood that I was putting my life on the line. I was grateful for his companionship, even though it would be short-lived. He would have to move on. His home was not here, and he couldn't stay in one place for long.

Warrant had me training "old school" by requesting me to run up and down the mountainside, then carrying and lifting tree limbs and heavy rocks. As day turned into night, I detected the presence of the others, even though I could not see them. At one point, something blue shimmered nearby. I halted, thinking of somebody I had met before, someone with brilliant Blue Eyes. When I tried to focus on the blue circular objects, they disappeared. So, I disregarded it as a figment of my imagination.

Warrant touched my shoulder. "Are you alright?"

He startled me.

"Yeah, yeah, I am. I just thought I saw something." I peered up in the direction of the tree. Warrant's gaze followed mine.

"They're out there, Crystal. They're going to look out for you, too. This vampire is highly dangerous. There are others looking for him. I'm not the only one."

I nodded.

"What you're doing is brave. Not many mortals would put themselves on the line for any of us."

"Thanks," I said.

"I want you to understand something, Crystal. I can't stay here."

"I know, you told me." I looked down. He touched his forehead to mine. Our faces were a fraction of an inch apart.

"I've enjoyed spending my time with you, even when I wasn't the best company."

I looked up at the sky. The dark clouds threatened the night. If there was any time I wished it would rain, it was now because it would hide the tears welling up.

"I know. I've enjoyed your friendship. Thank you for everything."

"If you ever need anything, please let me know. I'll always be there for you."

I really wished it would rain now. I hadn't had a true friendship in a long time, whether or not it evolved into something more.

"Thank you."

"By the way, I have some stuff for you. I bought you some clothes for tonight…"

"You really didn't have to do that, but thank you."

"Yeah, I did. Your other clothes look like shit."

I kind of nodded, choking back tears.

"That, and um, this."

He reached in his pocket, pulled out a little black flip phone, and placed it in my hand. I looked at it, and then back up at him.

"I can't take this," I said, my voice cracking.

"Yes, you can."

I swallowed hard. "You really shouldn't have."

"You never know when you might need it. Besides, I've already paid for the service. All I ask is that you don't abuse it or I might shut it off." He smiled.

I couldn't prevent it anymore. Tears trickled down my face. I looked down at the phone. He lifted my chin.

"Don't do that," he whispered.

"Trust me, I'm trying not to." I sniffled, and wiped away my tears. "Honestly, why are you doing this for me?"

"You need a second chance at life. Somebody gave it to me, and I want to give it to you."

Then he wrapped his arms around me.

I hugged him back and cried like a baby. "Aren't you worried about the others watching?"

"No."

"Won't you get in trouble?"

"I could get in trouble for a lot of things. This is one I don't mind getting in trouble for. Besides, they're all rooting for you. All I have to say is I'm giving you a few words of encouragement and a hug for inspiration." He chuckled in my ear. "And, I'm sorry for being such an ass. I was more concerned for our safety."

"I understand."

I buried my head in his chest, comforted by his warmth. I really did wish he could stay, wished we could be friends, maybe more. But it wasn't possible, so I tried to get my emotions in check. I didn't want to scare him off or get him in more trouble with his employer. But I needed a lot of comfort and security right now, to help me and protect me. I needed a friend.

Something brushed past me. I lifted my head and looked behind me. Nothing. Warrant clutched my arm.

"It's time to go."

While he escorted me off, I scanned the area where we had been standing and caught a faint glimpse of somebody standing in the shadows.

I gazed up at the sky. A slight drizzle followed us as we rode on his bike. We stopped and paid for some fast food to bring back to the hotel. We ate in silence, staring at the muted TV.

At almost seven-thirty, I jumped in the shower. I relaxed under the water, letting it run down my body. The bathroom door opened. I paid no attention to it, knowing full well it was Warrant, but when his hand touched my back I about jumped out of my skin. I spun around. He moved in closer to me within the shower.

"Do you mind?"

Before I had a chance to respond, he grabbed the nape of my neck and pulled me in to him.

Our lips locked. He was all over me, his hands and mouth exploring my breasts, my buttocks, and every other pleasurable spot he could find. He backed me into the wall, his fingers sliding inside me. He pushed deeper into me, his fingers moving rapidly inside, sending waves of pleasure through my body.

"Oh, Warrant." I wanted more of him inside me. The real him. I went to wrap my leg around him, but he pulled his fingers out and pushed me away from him. His mouth left mine.

As I touched his chest, he pushed my hand away.

"I'm not in the mood." He took a step back.

I stared back at him, confused. "What the hell?" I threw my arms up. "Then why were you all over me?"

He smiled back. "Haven't you ever heard the saying, no sex before the fight?"

My eyes narrowed.

He chuckled. "I'm sorry, that was mean of me. I just wanted to get you amped up before the match." He smiled and stepped out of the shower. "It'll make you meaner, trust me. And that's what we want – a mean Crystal."

"You suck, Warrant."

I turned the water off and pulled open the shower curtain. He stood before me, wrapped in a towel, still grinning.

"I know."

"Besides, I know that you really wanted it. I could feel it, deep inside me," I said, enunciating the words *deep inside me* slowly.

He eyed me as I brushed past him, naked and wet, to grab the towel off the rack next to him.

"Oh, excuse me." I pushed my chest out, wrapping the towel around my back to dry it, leaving my front exposed.

He faced me and purposely dropped his towel, revealing his genuine interest.

"You're not funny," he said.

My gaze dropped. He did want me. Yet, he turned and left the bathroom.

I sighed. "Ah, dammit."

I wrapped the towel around my body, sexually frustrated at this point. That was not cool. I left the bathroom and found him standing next to the bed, still naked, with a bag in his hand. That changed everything.

"This is for you."

The man had no modesty. He didn't seem to mind running around naked. I approached him, taking the bag, eyeing his assets before gazing into his eyes. He obviously noted my full attention was not on the bag but on something else. A cheesy grin spread across his face.

"If that's what you want, then you're going to have to wait. Right now, you need to get ready for the fight."

"That was really cruel of you."

"I know. Come on." He grabbed the bag from me and emptied it on the bed, his back to me. I bit my lip, trying to divert my attention. Instead, I leaned on his side and squeezed his butt.

"What are you doing?" He gazed into my eyes.

"Nothing, I'm just standing here, waiting for you to finish."

He straightened up causing me to nearly fall over.

Amused, he turned and faced me. "Are you enjoying yourself?"

"Not nearly as much as you are. That was really fucking cruel. Now, you got me all hard up for you, dammit."

He patted my cheek. "I'm really sorry, and you're right, I shouldn't have done that to you. I should make it up to you..."

He leaned in and kissed me. "...but not now. Now's not the time." Then he picked up a pair of panties with his finger and dangled them in front of me.

I sighed. "You really do suck."

I grabbed the panties and put them on.

"You do look good in those," he said, staring at my butt.

"Just give me the rest of the fucking clothes so I can get dressed," I said, trying to avert my eyes from him.

He laughed and sat down on the edge of the bed. "Fine, if that's the way you're going to be."

The smile on his face spread into a devilish grin. I yanked the bra off his finger and started to put it on.

"Here, let me help you." He stood up.

"No, you're not touching me." I proceeded to put it on, watching his eyes move over my body. Then I took the black workout pants and slid them over my legs, turning away from him, my butt exposed. I caught him out of my peripheral view with that cheesy look.

"I think you're enjoying this a little too much," I said, spinning around so my butt wasn't nearly in his face.

"Um, you sure look good."

"Yeah, you keep saying that. Keep stoking my fire, asshole. You're not helping me in any way at all."

"Oh, yeah, I am. You're getting more pissed off at me."

He was right about that. I huffed, pulled the shirt out of his hand, and put it on. It was a black front-zip workout top that had one pink slimming stripe down each side. The sleeves were quarter length, enough to keep me warm, but not long enough to get caught up in anything. Then I put on the socks and shoes.

"You look like you're ready to kick some ass."

I flipped my head to the side, my hair flying over my shoulder.

"Yeah, and it's going to be yours." I jumped him, throwing him backwards on the bed and straddling his body.

He wrapped his arms around my waist.

"You know, for someone who really didn't want to be bothered, you sure are enjoying the company."

"Of course I am. I got a beautiful woman in my arms. I think it was after you took your first shower here that I thought, I could get accustomed to this."

"You're an asshole," I said with a smirk.

"Yeah, and I'm good at it."

I leaned into his face. His warmth penetrated my clothing.

"Yeah, you're a little too good at it." I leaned in and kissed him, his hands rubbing my butt. Even though I didn't want to, I pulled away.

I climbed off of him and watched him get dressed.

"You know, I could help you with that," I commented.

"Nope, no go."

"Why not?"

"Because I know it'll turn into something else. And, I'm not going to let you."

I walked away, grabbed a bottle of water, and slammed it down. I needed to cool off. I was getting a little too feisty.

"What time is the fight?" I asked.

"Nine."

I glanced at the clock. It was ten after eight.

"How long will it take us to get there?" I asked.

"About thirty minutes. And, by the way, we're not taking the bike."

I turned and stared at him, sitting down on the chair by the table. "Why not?"

"Too risky."

"Then how are we getting there?"

"By foot."

"What? We're walking?"

"No. I'm running, you're riding."

"Huh?" I looked at him. "I don't understand."

He chuckled at my naïveté. "We're going to leave here and go into the woods, somewhere no one can see us. Then I'm changing into a werewolf, and you're riding on my back."

Well, that was a new one.

"And, how often do you do this?"

"Believe me, with somebody on my back, not very often. And, that reminds me, we need something for you to hold onto. My fur may not be enough. With my speed, you could easily fall off and get lost behind me."

"Sounds interesting."

"Trust me, you'll enjoy it. Everyone else that's ridden on my back has enjoyed it. It's just a little bumpy, considering the terrain."

I eyed him. "And, who else has ridden on your back?"

"Don't worry about it, oh jealous one." He grinned. Then he sat back on the bed and leaned against the headboard.

"I'm not jealous."

"Oh, no, not Miss. Rosy Cheeks." He laughed.

I approached the bed and crawled onto it from the footboard.

"So, what am I? Another notch in your strap?"

He laughed again. A sparkle lit up his eyes. It was nice to see him in such a good mood.

He leaned forward. "Yeah, along with the other thousand women I've been with."

"Oh, I'm sure." I giggled.

"Honestly, no. I haven't picked up any other hitchhiking women, only werewolf women. They're what really turn me on."

"Haha, you're funny," I said, sitting up.

Then he grabbed me by my arm and pulled me in towards him. The look on his face turned serious, his eyes focusing on mine.

"Are you going to get sentimental on me now?" I asked.

"Yeah, I guess I am."

I swallowed hard.

"I really don't want you to do this. You could get killed," he said.

"I know." I was scared to be alone, again. I didn't want to fight either, but just the thought of being able to crawl back into his arms after the fight meant something. We formed an emotional bond with one another, and I didn't want to lose it.

"I haven't met anybody like you in a long time."

"You're just saying that," I replied, my eyes intent on his.

"No, I'm not. I really have enjoyed my time with you, and I really wish I could spend more of it with you."

"Well, then, I guess when you're in town, you're going to have to call me."

"And I will."

As we smiled at each other, the butterflies in my stomach fluttered and my heart ached. I had to remember this was only a temporary thing. It was better to ignore what my heart felt, so I did.

"I programmed my number in the phone for you," he said.

"Thank you," I replied.

Then a ticking of the bedside clock caught his attention. He turned and looked at it. It was closer to 8:15 now.

"We need to get out of here. Are you sure about this?"

"Yes," I said, though still hesitant.

Standing up, he nodded his head and scanned the room. He picked up a plastic bag, his wallet, and his phone. He shoved everything in his pockets.

"Are you ready?"

"Yeah," I said, scooping up my phone.

He watched me tuck it inside my bra. "So, what else do you hide in there?"

"Oh, wouldn't you like to know."

"I bet I can find out."

"I bet you could, too."

We left the motel and walked deep into the woods, leaving his bike in the parking lot. The presence of a strong, immortal was nearby, so strong it had to be more than one individual. Even though I couldn't see his colleagues, I knew they were there.

He handed everything from his pockets to me, and then stripped.

"Now listen to me. That belt, you're going to wrap around my neck. And I want you to hold on tight. It will be a little loose, but you'll still be able to hold on."

I nodded.

"If you need to, you may even be able to wrap one of your arms through and hook your elbow inside, so that you're not using all of your hand strength." He hooked his arm around the belt, and demonstrated how to do it. "It'll be easier on you...Or, if you can find another way, then do it. But you're not going to be able to wrap your legs around my body. Don't worry about choking me. I'll be fine. Also, don't sit up on me. Try to lie down the best that you can," he said, showing the position he recommended.

"Alright."

He put his shoes, socks and shirt in the bag.

"I'll need you to hold onto the bag, so don't lose my stuff."

"Okay."

He put his jeans inside. "Are you ready?"

"Yeah."

Once Warrant changed into his alter ego, I harnessed him like he recommended, and then climbed on.

When I was ready, I leaned into him. "Go."

He took off slowly at first, and then gradually built up his speed so I wouldn't fly off backwards. I stayed stuck to his body like a leech. I leaned my head in close to him, the cold wind brushing past my skin. His thick fur kept me warm.

He leapt across rugged terrain. The woods drew us in deeper. The night sky closed in. The darker it became, the more I worried about something jumping out of the brush.

When the trees became less dense, I glanced up at the building approximately one hundred feet away. It didn't seem like it had been long since we had left the motel until now. Warrant trotted to a stop just before the edge of the forest, inside a group of trees. Trying to maintain my balance, I climbed off. He changed into his human form.

I pulled his clothes out. His naked body was coated with sweat. I watched him dress, taking one article at a time from my hands. His eyes caught mine.

"Keep staring, I might get a complex." He laughed.

I was nervous about what was going to happen, and worried that maybe I shouldn't be doing this. What if Jace were here? What was he going to do if he saw me? He would probably have his henchmen with him, whereas I only had Warrant.

Then I thought about the snipers and bounty hunters who were supposed to be here. Would they make themselves visible to the public inside, or would they stay invisible in the night? I surveyed our surroundings, while he finished dressing. He patted my shoulder.

"You're *sure* you want to do this?" he asked again, his eyes searching mine.

"Yes, I'm sure," I replied.

We headed towards the establishment. This was a larger bar. In the distance I could barely make out the lights of the businesses that were still open in the mortal world. If they only knew what really happened at night when they went home and tucked their children in bed, they would never sleep.

We walked in behind some other people. The dim lights illuminated the crowded room. A heavy bass thumped hard against the walls of the bar, and a guitar screeched through the room, making my ears cringe. Red, white, and blue strobe lights bounced off the dance floor and shone upon the patrons who moved to the music. People crowded the bar, the edge of the dance floor, and the tables. There were way too many to count, and I doubted they were all here just to have a few drinks. Warrant wrapped his arm around my waist and pulled me into him, his mouth near my ear.

"Stay close. Do not leave my side."

I nodded. He gripped on to my hand. He wound through the mass of people, looking for a sign of some sort.

Other people crowded in, their bodies mashing into mine as they followed in pursuit. If I hadn't looked back, I would have sworn it was somebody coming after us. Instead, they were other patrons who obviously knew what to look for.

Behind me were a couple, and then a trio of men who also seemed to know where they were going. Warrant launched me forward in front of him. He yanked me to the left and wrapped his arm around me. A group of young adults screamed.

"Crystal! Crystal! Crystal!"

My fans had recognized me. Great, this was definitely not what I needed. I was trying to remain somewhat incognito, but it wasn't working. Several other people then joined in.

I peered behind me, debating about just getting the hell out of here. A trio of men tried to wind past a couple. The couple were getting aggravated with the men and continued to purposely stand in their way, blocking their view. Maybe that was a good thing.

A voice to the left caught my attention.

"This way, Crystal."

Warrant and I both spun our heads around.

The man who stood before me was a scrawny little balding man, completely un-intimidating. My eyes met Warrant's, who joined me in pushing past the mass and into an almost empty hallway.

The man was able to shut a door behind us despite the crowd, and then turned to face us. "Wow! We are so lucky to have you here tonight! You can see the number of fans you have here. Everybody's anxious to see you fight."

"Thank you," I said, noticing a line of sweat dripping down his brow.

Being human, he was more than likely nervous as hell about a group of immortals in his establishment which led me to believe that the entire bar might be strictly mortals. It was the perfect place for a night feast for the creatures.

I glanced back at Warrant, nervous about the night ahead, when a light above Warrant's head went out.

"Ah, shit, I just replaced that damn bulb. It keeps blowing out," said the balding man.

Warrant glanced back at me, his eyes darting. He was nervous too.

"Warrant?" I whispered.

"Shh," he replied.

I shut my mouth.

"Turn around," he whispered in my ear.

I turned back to the man.

"Come, follow me." He led us through the dark hallway and into a dressing room, complete with vanity, chairs, and a dressing screen. The light in here was as low as it was in the main bar. Shutting the door behind us, he turned to face me again. I was glad Warrant stayed glued to my side.

"If you'd like to do anything special with yourself in here, this is your room for the time you are here tonight."

"Thank you."

"And I will come get you when I am ready, okay?"

"Okay."

He disappeared behind a door next to the vanity, opposite the room's entrance. I turned to look at Warrant. He surveyed the room.

"Do you recognize anybody yet?" I asked.

"No," he said. "How about you?"

"Uh-uh."

"You haven't seen that guy Jace yet?"

"No."

"You let me know when you do."

"I will."

Then the light above the vanity blew out. I stepped in closer to Warrant, and he wrapped his arms around me. I was beginning to think this was a setup. I looked around the room and noticed the two closets. Neither was completely closed.

Warrant obviously noticed I was wary of the doors. He left my side and glanced inside each closet, then shut the doors behind him. He walked up to me just when the little man reappeared.

"We're ready," the man said with a smile on his face. He patted his forehead with a handkerchief.

"Can we have a moment?"

The man seemed to think about it, and then smiled. "Yeah, you have two minutes."

He shut the door, leaving us alone.

Warrant lifted my chin. He took in a deep breath and slowly exhaled. His Adam's apple bobbed up and down.

"I don't have a good feeling about this," he said.

"Neither do I," I replied.

"Stay on your toes out there. And, get the upper hand early."

"I will."

"This place is a massacre waiting to happen."

"I just want to get this done and get the hell out of here," I said.

"Good," he said. "So, do I."

We faked smiles but neither of us were convincing enough. It was a meat market out there.

I turned and approached the door, wishing I had not agreed to this. Then I reached out and grabbed the cold heavy brass handle. I opened it slowly, Warrant right by my side. The little man stood looking at me.

"Are you ready?" he asked.

"Yes, I'm ready."

The man turned and walked me down a dimly lit hallway. I glanced up. Splotches stained the walls towards the ceiling. I looked away, detecting a faint smell which caught Warrant's attention, too. His nose shriveled as he looked about.

Before we got to the end of the hall, the little man opened a door to the right of us, stepping back.

"This is as far as I go."

He stood behind, pressing himself against the wall. We walked up to the door and peered inside. Before I even had the chance to walk in, Warrant brushed me aside. He stepped into the room, and looked it over. He waved me in.

Blocking the doorway, I peered around Warrant, and tried to get a visual before entering. Then, a hand shoved me hard into the room. The door slammed behind me. We turned and stared at the door.

"I don't like this," he muttered.

"Neither do I."

I looked about the grayish room and was reminded of a previous experience in my life I didn't want to be reminded of. My eyes widened as I studied the concrete walls and floor. Warrant turned and looked at me, his brows narrowed in.

"What? What's wrong?"

"I…this reminds me of the prison…"

Then a voice boomed over a hidden speaker in the room. "Hello, Crystal, it's so nice to see you…again."

It was Jace.

"Oh, God," I croaked.

Warrant turned to survey the room again. It was bare. One other door stood before us. It resembled one I had seen before. It was made of heavy steel and had a small barred window on it.

"I see you brought a friend with you," Jace said.

He could see us? Was there a camera in the room?

I looked back at Warrant. His face was stern, his jaw locked tight. The hue of his pupils turned a faint yellow.

"What do you want, Jace?"

Warrant continued to survey the room.

"I was really hoping you would show up. Something told me you would be here tonight. Only I have a special surprise for you." He let out a deep, menacing laugh.

"What is it you want!"

The steel door opened, slightly ajar.

"Take a walk down the hallway, and you'll see."

I started towards the door, but Warrant pushed me out of the way. He opened the door and stepped into the darkness. I followed close him.

From somewhere nearby, an audience stomped their feet and clapped their hands. The door slammed shut behind us, confining us within a room. A blue light illuminated carcasses of dead people.

Eyes wide, I clamped my hand over my mouth. I recognized the clothing they wore and identified them as previous fighters. I closed my eyes, fearful of what was soon to become of me.

"Oh, God," I gasped.

"Don't let him scare you. He's just a piece of shit!" Warrant screamed.

Jace didn't respond. No sound, nothing. Warrant shoved me into a dark corner.

"What are you...?" I struggled against him.

"Shh," he whispered.

"War..."

He pushed his wrist against my mouth, constricting my breathing, almost suffocating me. Then, the taste of blood filled my mouth. I gave in, relinquishing my mouth to him, savoring every morsel of it. He was preparing me for whatever lay beyond this room, whatever surprise Jace had in store for me.

I gripped harder onto his arm and pressed his wrist against my mouth, seeking every drop. As I clamped down harder on his wrist, he groaned in my ear. He grabbed me by my hair and yanked my head back.

"That's enough. You're going to make me weak," he whispered.

I licked my lips. I gazed up into his eyes, and recognized the look. His mouth found mine. His tongue trailed over it and down my chin. I leaned my head back, his mouth on my neck. His fangs grazed my skin, sending an erotic sensation through my body.

"Warrant," I began.

I wanted to wrap my legs around him right now, but it was definitely not the time. Then he pulled away, licking his lips.

He smiled back at me, fangs glistening, and eyes gleaming in the darkness.

"I think I got it all now."

A sudden rush of blood shot through my veins and to my head. The rush was so intense, I was nauseated and woozy. I doubled over, too weary to continue down the hallway. Warrant had to help me stand.

"Are you okay?" he asked.

A rush of adrenaline pounded through my body, causing my eyes to dart to and fro.

"What the hell...?" He pulled me into him and muttered in my ear, "You've had wolf's blood before, haven't you?"

I trembled against him, closing my eyes and wishing he hadn't intoxicated me with his blood.

"Relax, Crystal," he said, kneading my back.

The warmth and security in his embrace comforted me.

"We need you calm right now, or they'll know your under the influence. Do you understand me?"

I nodded, reluctant to open my mouth. I worried something more than words would come out.

"Easy, Crystal, easy."

The fluid stroke of his hand calmed my nerves somewhat.

"When you're in the ring, you should be fine. You can let the adrenaline out. Do you understand what's happening to you right now?"

I shook my head. I had consumed wolf's blood before, but had never had an experience quite like this. It was almost as if I'd taken an overdose of drugs.

"Once you consume wolf's blood a few times, your body starts to accept the blood faster. The only problem is that it pumps the blood through your system faster and harder, and your body has a reaction. You probably feel sick to your stomach?"

I nodded.

"You should be fine. Only one in twenty actually get sick from this reaction."

Well, apparently, I was that one in twenty. Spasms of gut-wrenching pain shot through my stomach. I doubled over again.

"This will be over soon. Right now, we need to get you to the ring, or else they're going to know something's up."

I nodded. He helped me down the dimly lit hallway, pain now wracking my entire body. Once we reached the only door in the hall, I fell to my knees as pain tore through my chest. I thought I was going to have a heart attack.

Warrant knelt next to me, "I know it hurts, but if you're going to do this, then we need to do it now. When you get in the ring, you can let it out. Come on."

He helped me to my feet again, reaching for the door. His hand clamped around the steel handle and slowly opened it. On the other side, the audience screamed in anticipation.

Here we go again. I stepped out into an enclosed arena. Just as my foot landed on the sand, the door shut behind me. I spun to see several panes of the hallway walls disappear, revealing increments of the glass panes. Warrant dove behind the steel panes.

I stumbled to my knees and pain shot through my body again. I gazed up at the audience. Glass panes sectioned the audience off from the arena. Behind the glass panes, the arena was divided into sections by steel walls, separating the vampires, the werewolves and the mortals from each other.

Above me, a voice boomed over the loudspeaker, announcing my entrance. I knelt on my hands and knees, my head hung low.

A presence appeared above me. I raised my head. A foot slammed into my stomach, lifted me in the air, and threw me on my back. I pulled my arms into my gut, my breath barely escaping my lips.

As I looked up at the man who stood above me, his foot smashed into the side of my face, knocking me down.

I rolled over, and then pushed myself harder to roll onto my stomach. He rushed me again. As he lifted his foot, I pushed myself up on all fours. I kicked out to my right, connecting with his left knee. His right foot came up while his left knee gave way. I rolled to my right atop his left leg as fast as I could and struck him in the back of his knee with my fist. He landed with a thud. I came up over him, punching him in the groin.

Groaning, he clutched at his manhood. I punched him in the lower abdomen where his bladder was located. I maneuvered up and over him, staring down at the asshole. It was Wayne, the man who had imprisoned me for over four years.

"Crystal…"

I slugged him in the face. Not once, twice, or three times, but four times before he grabbed my arms. He threw me off of him, rolling onto me.

"Crystal, I need –" he began.

I spat in his face. "Fuck you."

Then I head butted him, threw him off of me, and was on top of him, beating him with my fists. I didn't care if he was a werewolf or not. He had held me against my will and forced me to fight to the death. I was not proud of what I had done. I had done it strictly for survival. Their needs were met; mine were not.

Below me, he fought to keep his transformation human though his body tried otherwise. I presumed Jace knew who he was to me. This was my surprise. But for him to bring an actual werewolf into a mortal's game was against the rules, unless there was more to this fight than the others.

What would Jace gain from this battle? His fighter back – me? Or was he going to enjoy the match between mortal and immortal? Did Jace want me killed? Or was I to kill Wayne for their enjoyment?

There had to be more of a reason for this fight. He had to have known Wayne was a werewolf…Or did he?

Wayne snarled, and threw me off of him. I flew back about ten feet, smashing hard into the glass pane separating us from the audience. The impact didn't hurt, but only seemed to push the adrenaline harder through my body. I slid down onto the ground and caught a glimpse of a fan standing above me behind the glass. He must have been a die-hard fan. A look of horror spread across the young man's face.

I glanced at him again. My brain tried to pull a piece of memory. Wayne slammed hard into me from behind. He spun me around, his elbow lodging into my throat.

"I really need to…" He trailed off.

Something had caught his attention in the crowd behind me. I turned my head to see what he was looking at, but only saw the much-anguished fan.

A distraught look appeared on Wayne's face. I presumed the fan might be a sniper or a bounty hunter. I smiled, impressed by his acting abilities. He was good, but not good enough to hide his disguise from Wayne. Wayne obviously picked up who he was and seemed a little worried about his near future.

"Is there a problem, Wayne?"

Wayne glanced from him to me and then back again. I took the opportunity to advance on him. I grabbed his hand, wrenched it back, and pried his arm off of me. The bone gave way. I shoved with all my strength, driving him back fifteen feet, and then throwing him into the glass-paned hall. Beyond the glass, Warrant hid, keeping an eye on me.

Wayne's body struck the pane hard. A thin crack trailed off the initial starred impact on the glass. He started to slide off. I rushed him, driving hard and fast. The glass shattered behind him, landing us into the hallway.

Warrant back off into a hidden corner. I turned my head towards him.

"Well?" I asked.

"Not him," he answered.

Wayne spun his head around, searching the darkness for Warrant. I grabbed Wayne by his neck and wrenched his face back towards me, before he could get a good view of Warrant. I pulled Wayne out of the hallway.

We fell to the ground, him atop me. Wayne broke away and jumped up to the broken glass pane flooring of the hall. A flurry of snarls and growls echoed in the hallway.

Just as I jumped up on the floor, Wayne was thrown thirty feet back into the glass panel of the audience barrier. He struck me in the process, knocking me to the ground.

The glass starred and then cracked. Blood dripped down the glass. I struggled to my feet and leapt at him again, when I caught a glimpse of brilliant blue eyes to my right. I stopped in my tracks. They disappeared into thin air.

I stared into the massive crowd, looking for the blue eyes. I had seen them before. Aware that I was no longer concentrating on my fight, I turned my attention back to Wayne, who lay crumpled to the ground ten feet in front of me. Blood coated his back. Shards of glass protruded from his skin.

I started to advance on him again. The glass shattered. I stopped in my tracks about five feet away from the audience barrier. The distinct smell of blood caught my attention. Wayne's blood. An army of vampires stood un-restrained and ready for battle.

I swallowed hard. Several vampires slinked across the barricades. Then, David emerged from the audience. I backed off, moving towards the hallway.

David approached Wayne. Even though I despised Wayne, I hoped at this point that he was dead and wouldn't have to suffer at the hands of David.

I turned away, not wanting to witness the horror David was going to deliver. The glass that separated the wolves shattered.

My gaze shifted to the transformations taking place within their section of the arena.

In fear for my life, I ran for the hallway. Behind me, the creatures clashed, bearing down upon one another. I prayed they weren't on my heels.

I glanced back. The vampires who had been nearest me were confronted by the four-legged beasts.

My gaze settled on the ground where Wayne had been. Only now he was gone, along with David.

Aware I had slowed almost to a stop, I turned to continue onward. Invisible arms wrapped around my waist, whisking me up into the air. I cringed in horror, dangling from the unknown person. I didn't know whether I should struggle or let it carry me away.

I cast my eyes down upon the room, hoping Warrant would come after me. The anguished fan now stood, staring at me in awe. Two other men stood with him. One I recognized as the Deputy at the sheriff's office. The other I did not know.

A long blonde-haired vampire lurched at us, jarring the man who held me. As I slipped from his grip, a shriek escaped my lips.

I was worried I was going to fall so I clung to him. I slid down his body, my grip tightening around his waist.

The invisible man latched on to my arm.

The blonde vampire turned his attention toward me. His dark maniacal eyes focused in on mine. He snarled, and swiped at me with his clawed hand. I recoiled.

Maybe it was a good thing that I held his attention because what happened next was quick and grueling.

With two swipes of one clawed hand, my savior took the vampire's head off. Blood splashed across the three of us. The vampire crashed to the floor.

My savior pulled me up into his arms. He drew me farther up into the air towards a skylight, and then buried my face in his chest.

Below, Warrant was nowhere to be seen as the audience erupted into a frenzy.

My anguished fan and the Deputy rushed out of the arena. Other creatures and mortals fought to leave, while others stayed to fight to the death.

Above me, there was a crash. Shards of glass rained upon us while the invisible person continued to hold my head down. He flew me out into the night, the cool air whisking past us. I shivered, struggling to warm my body against his but only found the coldness of his skin. I glanced down at the earth and caught a glimpse of my fan and the Deputy before they disappeared into the woods.

He flew me up and over the trees. The smell of pine and juniper permeated the air.

"Who are you?" I asked, still leery of his connection with the fight. Although I had already gotten a sense he was one of the snipers or bounty hunters Warrant knew, I hoped he wouldn't hurt me. Hopefully.

He didn't say anything, instead he halted on the top branch of a tree. He glanced back in the direction we came from, and cocked his head, as if listening.

I presume he was making sure we weren't being followed.

After a moment of surveying our surroundings, we continued on, away from the fight.

As he was lowering us closer to the ground near a clearing something struck us. It jarred me. The impact threw me out of his arms. I landed with a solid thud, and hit my head on a fallen tree.

Staggering to my feet, I cupped my hand to my head and searched for a bloodied wound that wasn't there. I scanned the area, looking for the invisible man, but only the werewolf and Deputy stood there.

My intuition had been right. The cops were involved in the fighting circuit just as the werewolves and vampires had been. The werewolf and Deputy looked at me. The wolf's jaw was slack, as if smiling, and its eyes gleamed. Weird, I thought. He looked at me as if he wanted to make friends, not like I could be his next meal. I was leery of this creature.

The plain-clothed Deputy watched me. I wondered if he was investigating the fights, but something told me otherwise. The Deputy sauntered over to me. I recoiled. The half moon cast shadows in the darkness and faint illuminations on their faces.

"Where's your friend?" the Deputy asked, looking around.

"I don't know." I wished the invisible man would pick me up and take me away.

"What's his name?"

"I don't know," I answered, backing off.

The wolf walked over.

"Okay. Well then, who is he?"

"I don't know."

He chuckled. "Do you always let strange men take you away in the night?"

"Not if I can help it," I answered, glancing back at the wolf. Where the hell was my invisible stranger? "What do you want?"

They stopped. Hesitantly, so did I.

"We'd just like to introduce ourselves," he answered.

"I already know who you are, Deputy Torrance. Just tell me who the hell he is and get to the point," I demanded.

I was in no condition to be demanding, but I wasn't about to be hauled off to the sheriff's office either, or wherever they were going to take me. And why the hell wouldn't his friend change to his human form?

Oh, that's right, he or she would be naked.

Before Deputy Torrance had a chance to answer, a low noise erupted nearby. I presumed it was my invisible savior, but just then a dark-grayed hair werewolf appeared in the distance. I recognized it as Warrant due to the belt looped around its neck. The one with the Deputy sensed Warrant, turned, and glared at the creature. He sneered, and bared his teeth at the dark-grayed haired wolf. Tension filled the air. Torrance took a couple of steps back. Warrant drew closer. The silver wolf circled around Torrance. He was protecting the Deputy, I assumed.

The wolves bared their teeth at each other. Warrant glanced at me. I recoiled, wondering where the hell my savior had gone to. As Warrant circled around in front of me, I backed up into the dense brush. Hiding was my best option, at least until Warrant or my savior could get me the hell out of here.

The wolves snarled and leapt at each other, colliding in mid air before they fell to the ground. I gasped as their claws struck one another, their mouths snapping. Growls and the gnashing of teeth echoed throughout the night. A hand covered my mouth and pulled me further into the woods.

I started to scream, but Jace's voice filled my ear.

"Shh! We don't want to upset them, now do we? Just imagine what they could do to you," Jace whispered.

I cringed in horror. If there was one creature that scared me the most, it was Jace. I would have preferred to fight with Wayne again. His cold, hard body pressed closer into mine, and his hand gripped my arm. I eyed the wolves in the clearing, the dark grey one slamming into a fallen tree trunk. Jace leaned in closer to my ear.

"See that cop over there," he whispered, pointing to the Deputy who now stood on the other side of the clearing. "He isn't going to be a cop anymore."

I swallowed hard.

The Deputy stared in my direction, scratching his head. I presumed he didn't see me hidden within the dark brush. The Deputy crept toward me. Periodically, he glanced back at the wolves. Then, he stopped at the edge of the clearing and peered about five feet to the right of me.

He didn't see me.

He was afraid to enter the foliage of the forest. He stood frozen. Then, he took two steps back.

I was sick to my stomach, a knot forming in my throat. Even though I wanted nothing to do with the Deputy, I didn't believe he deserved what was going to happen to him.

I struggled with Jace, trying to get free, to yell something to the Deputy, but Jace restrained me. My voice came out in low muffles, constricted against his body.

Somebody emerged from the trees above him. I stared in horror at Devon, his blonde hair pulled back tightly in a ponytail, rushing towards the Deputy. I wanted to scream, to warn him The Deputy was about to die if he didn't do something. Devon approached the Deputy from behind, his hands ready to latch onto him. The Deputy turned with his gun drawn.

Devon's head snapped back, his body leaning backwards in an obscure, horizontal dance-like pose. It wasn't a natural look for anybody. Blood sprayed, raining down upon Devon, the Deputy, and the invisible man. The rain of blood spattered the invisible man, revealing a vague human shape. His face was indiscernible but I could tell he was looking at the Deputy. He dropped Devon's headless body to the ground.

Before Deputy Torrance had a chance to fire his weapon, the invisible man ripped it from his grip and threw it to the ground. The invisible man's eyes changed, reflecting a beautiful blue. I swallowed hard. I remembered those eyes, but was unable to identify a face to go with them.

I resumed struggling with Jace in the shadows of the trees. The wolves were still battling, unaware of Jace's presence in the night.

"Who are you?" the Deputy asked.

The invisible man didn't answer but stared at the Deputy as he advanced toward him.

I continued to struggle with Jace, sensing he was unaware of the invisible man.

Finally, I was able to free my arm and throw it back, my elbow connecting with Jace's ribs. A slight grunt escaped his lips. I spun forward and out, grabbed onto the wrist that had held my mouth closed, and kicked him in the stomach. As Jace bent forward, I delivered a sidekick, connecting with his face.

I ran towards the battlefield, screaming, hoping to gain Warrant's attention. The other beast was atop him, his mouth latched onto the back of Warrant's neck.

"No! Stop it! Don't kill him!"

I ran into the midst of the two, glancing back at where Jace had been. He was gone. I turned and glared at the Deputy and the blood-splattered invisible creature. The Deputy stood still, but the invisible creature ran full force at me.

I turned to run. Both wolves slammed down to the ground in front of me, the grey wolf atop the silver one, his teeth gnashing. The invisible arms wrapped around me again.

"No! Let me go!"

I pried at his hands, trying to loosen them. I beat his hands and arms with my fists.

"Please let me go!"

I tried to turn my head to find Warrant but leaves brushed against my face. We left Warrant and the battlefield behind. I struggled with the invisible man as he bound from tree to tree.

The blood on his body also covered his face. When he finally stopped in the branches, I caught a glimpse of his cheek, nose, and forehead. He pressed me into the side of the tree, his blue eyes glaring into mine.

"You trying to get us killed?" he sneered.

If I could have recoiled I would have, but I couldn't move.

"Who are you?" I asked.

Instead of answering, he continued to glare at me. "If you don't settle down, I'm going to personally rip your head off. Got it?"

I nodded. About three pine trees away, there was a whisper of leaves. We turned our heads and peered into the trees behind us. I held my breath, listening to the night. The clearing was silent.

I worried about Warrant. I wanted to go back and check on him, but I knew better. Apparently my savior felt the same way.

The night became abnormally quiet, the leaves becoming still. I glanced around. I was wary. The woods were not meant to be quiet. As if knowing what I was thinking, he wrapped his arm tight around my waist.

I dared not look down, afraid I would make a sound. Instead, I turned back to the man who held me in his arms and tried to make out his face. I let out a breath, my body trembling from the cold.

He pressed harder into me, eyeing something beyond the tree. His body was hard and cold against mine. I took another deep breath. My teeth chattered, and I tried to stifle the noise. I caught the scent of the blood on his body and gulped. When I tried to peer behind me at whatever he had been looking at, we came face to face.

He whispered in my ear, "We need to go. Can you keep it quiet?"

"Yes," I said.

I wrapped my arms around him and held on tight. Quiet and stealthy, he flew out of the tree. The breeze rushed past our bodies. I glanced back in the direction of the clearing, praying that Warrant was unharmed.

§

Sometime in the night, the invisible man brought me down to the earth. Once our feet touched the ground, he peered around, still holding me. The crunch of pine cones and the crack of breaking branches emerged from the brush nearby. Warrant, in his beast form, appeared out of the darkness.

He stared at me with those menacing eyes. Saliva dripped from his mouth. Despite the terrifying look on his face, I smiled. He stopped about fifteen feet away, next to a tree. I pulled myself from the invisible man's grasp and headed toward Warrant. The invisible man latched on to me, confining me against him.

"What…?" I struggled against him, throwing an elbow into his rib.

"You need to stay calm. He's been hurt and because of that, he could hurt you right now. You can't be near him yet."

I settled down and gazed back at Warrant. He lay on his side, panting and growling. He glared at me like I was his next meal. Shocked to see the look on his face, I let the invisible man take me into his arms again.

"You've gotten too close to her and you're going to put us all in danger," the invisible man said.

Warrant had several scratch marks all over his chest and back. Blood soaked his fur. He eyed the man, ready to attack.

"Warrant?" I called out.

His lip curled back revealing canine teeth. A growl escaped his throat.

"Can he hear me?" I asked.

"Yes, he can hear you, but that doesn't mean a Goddamn thing. He's an animal, wounded and bleeding. He needs to change first."

"Well, then, why doesn't he do it?" I watched Warrant inch forward on his belly towards us. I backed up farther into my savior.

"Because he's wounded. He needs to gain control of himself first. He's too weak."

The invisible man pulled me back farther. The wolf continued to inch forward, trying to regain his footing. I worried that if he did, he would attack.

"Can you help him?" I asked.

"No, he's the only one who can help himself right now."

The blood around his wounds dried up, allowing his injuries to close. As they did, his momentum progressed. He moved nearer, his growls deepening.

I bit my lip, realizing the quicker he healed, the faster he could attack, and the quicker he would regain himself. A lump formed in my throat, making it difficult to swallow.

Turning to the man, my back to Warrant, I asked, "Can you..."

I needn't say anymore. He whisked me away into the forest. The pounding of paws struck the ground behind us. Warrant advanced upon us, blood dripping from his chest.

His wounds were closing, but not quick enough. He had gained some of his power and strength back, but not enough to control his emotions.

The wind brushed past us, carrying the smell of other creatures in the air. I tried to glance through the forest but was unable to locate an actual shape until it was too late. Something slammed into my invisible savior, throwing him into a large pine tree.

I screamed. My savior pulled me in tighter to his chest. Then something slammed into him. As he managed to spin himself around, we struck the tree. His back took most of the impact, and not my head. The jarring of our bodies sent waves of pain through mine. Jace approached. The invisible man let go of me. I slid down him to the ground.

My eyes darted from him to the scene behind him where Warrant and David fought amongst the trees. David's powerful and massive vampire form was even more threatening than Warrant's both as human and immortal.

Their monstrous bodies clashed, each throwing the other to the ground. I looked at Jace and then my savior, aware that Woodrow was not present. As I stood, the invisible man pushed me back down to the ground.

Jace leapt at him. Yet, the invisible man jumped straight up, higher and a millisecond faster than Jace. He delivered a sidekick to Jace's face. The impact sent Jace flying past the wolves' battle and into a pine tree, splitting it. The twenty foot tall tree cracked and tumbled forward, coming straight down on top of Jace, the wolves—and me.

"Shit."

Afraid that it was going to flatten me, I ran. An unpredictable gust of wind pitched me forward, almost knocking me off of my feet. Through my peripheral vision, I caught a glimpse of Jace. He not only managed to catch the tree, but also hurled it at the invisible man. My savior caught it and tossed it to the side.

I ran in the opposite direction we had come from. The bottom part of the tree landed. The impact of it rocked the earth. The top part of the tree came toward me. I was sure it was going to hit me. Then, my foot struck soft dirt. The dirt gave way beneath my feet, and down I went.

I tumbled down the side of a ravine, crashing to the ground and hitting my head on a rock in a small creek. Water splashed up, soaking my face.

I moaned, sitting up, unsure whether the liquid was just water or if I were bleeding, too. I touched the wound on my head, catching a glimpse of the werewolf behind me. My eyes widened in terror. It crept forward. A voice came out of the darkness.

"We apologize. He didn't mean to hurt you."

I gazed at the creature, watching the mouth, whose lips never moved. It couldn't talk. Oh, hell no. It wasn't the creature who was speaking. It was Deputy Torrance, who walked around the side of him.

"Are you okay?" He came closer, extending his hand to mine.

"You? What the fuck do you want with me? Why do you keep following me!" I didn't take his hand. I stood up on my own, staring back at the werewolf, my feet sloshing in the water below me.

"Look, I said we're sorry. He was trying to help you, not hurt you." I gazed back at him in shock, and then peered over at the wolf.

"Why does he want to help me? And what the fuck do you want with me?"

I eyed the wolf, worried it was going to attack, when I noticed the dried blood on his face. Then I became even more concerned. I remembered what the savior had said about Warrant when he was in his wolf form.

"Is he going to hurt me?"

"No, he's not."

My eyes darted from one to the other before I tried to climb the ravine. My feet slid in the dirt. I scrambled to get up the side, clutching onto the rocks, my feet seeking footing on the jagged terrain. The werewolf's head came up next to mine, Deputy Torrance sitting on his neck.

"Allow us to help you." He extended his hand to me. "It's much easier."

The wolf nudged my butt with his shoulder.

"What the hell? Get away from me." I tried to shoo him away, but I lost my balance. I toppled over backwards. The werewolf moved his shoulder to stop me from falling completely down the ravine. I peered back at Deputy Torrance, who sat nonchalantly on the wolf, acting as it was a normal thing for him.

"Really, just allow him to help you up the side." He smiled down at me, his elbows resting on his knees.

"No, thank you."

I attempted the side of the ravine again. The wolf crossed my path and continued up to the top.

"You are a stubborn woman."

"Yeah, well if you led the life I did, you'd understand."

I gripped onto the rocks and pulled myself up until my head was now above the ravine. Then my shoes slipped in the mud, throwing me back down. I slid. Rocks and branches scratched my face.

"Mother…" As I slid, the creature leapt to the ground below me.

My feet struck the side of his body, stopping me in my tracks. Deputy Torrance was no longer on his back. Instead, he cursed above me.

"Hey, asshole, you didn't have to drop me. Just give me a hint next time!" Deputy Torrance said.

The werewolf prodded me with his head. I hesitated. Then, I climbed upon him and allowed him to take me to the top. Deputy Torrance stood there, dirt and leaves all over his backside. I slid off of the wolf. In the distance, Jace and my savior battled it out. I peered back into the forest from where I had come.

"Who are those men to you?" the Deputy asked.

Unsure of what he wanted, I looked at him and said, "Nobody."

Deputy Torrance grunted in response to it.

"Why? What's it to you?" I asked.

He looked at me, and then back into the forest where the noises of the battle continued.

"It's nothing to me, but something to him." He motioned towards the werewolf.

I glanced back. Once again, the wolf seemed to be awestruck.

"What is his problem anyway? He keeps looking at me funny."

The Deputy chuckled, looking back at the wolf. "Maybe I should have him change into his human self. Maybe then, you might recognize him."

I turned to Torrance. "So, tell him to change. I want to see his face. I want to know who we're talking about. I know it's not Wayne."

A deep voice penetrated the air behind me. "Who's Wayne?"

I turned my head toward the location where the werewolf had been standing. A young man replaced the ghastly beast. He was almost six foot. He had dark hair with dark features similar to mine: big brown eyes and short nose. He was handsome. His naked body was lean and muscular, with wide shoulders. I could have easily mistaken him for a younger relative.

Then something triggered my memory.

*I lay on a hospital bed with my feet in stirrups, a blanket draped over my legs.*

*To my right, a man kissed me and then pressed his cheek against mine. "It's a boy, honey. It's a boy.*

*A baby cried. I turned toward the crying infant. The newborn, swaddled in blankets, was placed in my arms.*

My mouth dropped open. I stared at the naked man.

*"What's his name?" asked the doctor.*

*"Robert," Robert's father and I answered.*

*I smiled down at my baby boy. Tears of joy ran down my cheeks.*

*Robert nestled up against my chest, his cries quieting down.*

Was this man Robert?

At that brief second, with Warrant in healthy wolf form, my invisible friend latched on to me.

"No, wait!"

My savior didn't listen to me. Instead, we kept going.

I stared at the Deputy and the man. The nude man changed back into his wolf form. They vanished into the woods.

Another memory crept in.

*As we stared into the sunset, I pushed my six year old son on the swing.*

*"Mom?"*

*"Yes."*

*"Where did dad go?"*

*"I don't know, son."*

*As he swung back, I latched on to the chains. "It's getting late though. We should probably go home now."*

*His warm brown eyes stared up into mine. "I love you, Mom."*

*"I love you too, sweetie." I picked him up out of the seat and held him. He was my son.*

Yes, the nude man was Robert, my son. And, he was alive and well. My eyes welled over with tears.

As we disappeared into the night, the howls of nearby wolves in the distance escalated. Listening to them, I assumed Jace and David probably not only got their asses handed to them by Warrant and the invisible man, but had backed off due to the number of werewolves that appeared in the darkness. Warrant's backup had made their presence known to Jace.

Deputy Torrance's statement echoed in my ear, "*It's nothing to me, but something to him.*"

I found my son. I was sure of it.

I lay limp in my savior's arms, relying on him to take me back to the motel. I knew what my quest was for the next day while I lay against this cold hard body.

Also From
Cryptic Bones Publishing

# BAD ELEMENTS:
# BLOOD FOR BLOOD

THE SEQUEL TO THE DARK AND TWISTED BAD ELEMENTS
NOVEL, CRYSTAL DRAGON!

FOLLOW CRYSTAL ON HER SEARCH FOR HER SON AS THE
FAMILIAL TIES THAT ARE WOVEN BECOME STRAINED WHEN
JACE, A PRIOR CAPTOR, UNLEASHES HIS REVENGE ON HER,
FORCING CRYSTAL TO MAKE A DECISION THAT COULD KILL
HER AND HER FAMILY!

## COMING SOON

# ABOUT THE AUTHOR

LYNN MULLICAN was born and raised in Phoenix, Arizona, where she currently resides with her husband and three children. She has woven her fascination with the paranormal into written works including short stories, dramatic plays, poetry, and full length novels. In *Bad Elements: Crystal Dragon,* she incorporates years of knowledge in self defense and martial arts. Lynn began writing in her childhood, and to this day, her family has continued to support her dream.

www.ingramcontent.com/pod-product-compliance
Lightning Source LLC
Chambersburg PA
CBHW020600180626
46810CB00007B/2579